THE URBANA FREE LIBRARY
W9-BHK-473

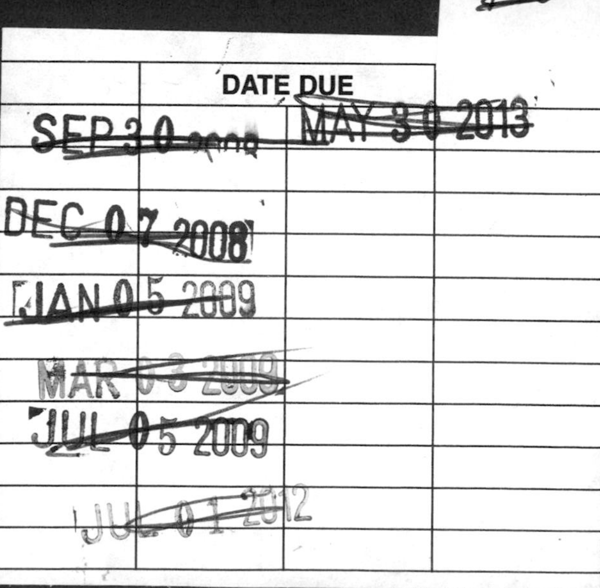
DATE DUE
SEP 3 0 2008
MAY 3 0 2013
DEC 0 7 2008
JAN 0 5 2009
MAR 0 3 2009
JUL 0 5 2009
JUL 0 1 2012

Will

By the same author

Peace Comes Dropping Slow
A Resurrection of a Kind
A Twelvemonth and a Day
Two Christmas Stories
Into the Ebb
Venus Peter
With Sharp Compassion (with John Shaw)
Where the Clock Stands Still (with Cliff Wilson)
Venus Peter Saves the Whale
Last Lesson of the Afternoon
To Travel Hopefully
Hellfire and Herring

Will

CHRISTOPHER RUSH

THE OVERLOOK PRESS
Woodstock & New York

In loving memory of my little brother John, who gave so much.

And in honour of Will's brilliant shadow, Ian McKellon.

A note on anachronism, accuracy and language

The Great Cham once said of Shakespeare that a pun was the fatal Cleopatra for which he lost the world. Not everyone would agree that things were quite that bad. What is indisputable is that the Bard's many anachronisms do not detract from his plays, which are, in the end, about people, and not about what they wore, whether knickers were invented or clocks ticked in the sixteenth century.

In writing this novel about Shakespeare's life I have followed the same principle and allowed the anachronism to boldly go wherever it led me. This relates to language. The Elizabethans did not think they were speaking 'Elizabethan', and so, while lacing the dialogue liberally with Shakespeare's own lines and with sixteenth century mannerisms, I have also tried to impart a modern feel to the language, allowing Will to speak directly to the third millenium reader, who will not, hopefully, come away from the book thinking, 'All very realistic, I'm sure – but why are they talking so funny?' It was a matter of balance and I hope I got it right.

Finally, on the question of accuracy, I have only very occasionally tweaked a date or a fact to suit the plot, apart from which I have stuck faithfully to the Shakespeare story in so far as it can ever be known.

First published in the United States in 2008 by
The Overlook Press, Peter Mayer Publishers, Inc.
Woodstock & New York

WOODSTOCK:
One Overlook Drive
Woodstock, NY 12498
www.overlookpress.com
[for individual orders, bulk and special sales, contact our Woodstock office]

NEW YORK:
141 Wooster Street
New York, NY 10012

Cataloging-in-Publication Data is available from the Library of Congress

Manufactured in the United States of America
FIRST EDITION
ISBN 978-1-59020-097-1
10 9 8 7 6 5 4 3 2 1

Prologue

Francis Collins came today. There's something about March that spurs lawyers on and whips them up afresh, following the long winter glooms, all eyes and ears and anxiousness again. Francis is no exception. I could hear him rubbing his fat palms together as he came up the path. I heard a knocking at the south entry. I was lying in bed but I could see him wiping off the money-smile before Mistress Anne answered the door. See him in my mind's eye, that is, making his fatal entrance. Strange how death's imminence sharpens the senses, enhances the fancy.

'Up today, is he?'

Bark bark, hack hack.

'Jesus, Will, that sounds bad. A churchyard cough. Better get this draft done and dusted.'

Before my own dust settles. I know. (Spoken aside).

Very well, I said – (spoken aloud) – let's draft all cares and business from our age.

He gave me that owl's look, going glassy and goggle-eyed as usual at the merest whiff of blank verse. Not strong on poetry, Francis Collins. Which makes him a good lawyer. And a dull human being. Who comes alive only when he eats and drinks.

'Cares and business, Will? Leave these to me, old friend.'

Gladly, Francis. And what else besides? That I unburdened may crawl towards death – and out of your whispering.

He smiled and shook his head, and I closed my eyes and thought of what's to come: a draft, a will, a death. And exit Will from the world's stage, his last words uninspired, dictated to a quillman, and quite undistinguished from his clerk's mentality. That made me protest a little, I must admit, roused up in me a moment of rebellious frenzy, unseemly to my years.

Is this it then, Francis? *I, William Shakespeare, do appoint...* Is this what it's really come to, in the end?

He put on his pious professional look.

'It's what it always comes to, Will. It's what it must come to.'

Golden lads and girls all must...

'There you are, you said it yourself.'

As chimney-sweepers come to dust.

'Exactly.'

More than exactly, Francis. Do you know what golden lads are – exactly?

'What do you mean?'

It's what we call dandelions in these parts, it's what I used to call them when I was little. Hence the dust idea, seeds, you know?

'I know. We used to call them pee-the-beds. It doesn't change the situation. You were the golden lad of the London theatre for twenty years. And now you're unwell, you're a husband and a father, making a will. And I'm here to assist you. So none of your posturing, master dramatist, and let's get down to it.'

What can you say? What can you do, when you're sick and tired, and your lawyer is pawing the floorboards like a little black bull? You get down to it, of course, just as he directs. Or rather you lie down to it and let him do the scribing – you've had enough of quillwork – and you grunt approval or denial every now and then. He knows your mind, you're surprised by how readily he reads it, telling you what you were going to say in any case. And before the bat has flown his cloistered flight your affairs are settled, your house is in order. As for the frail house of flesh, your tenancy is up, and it will soon be over with you now and forever.

But for you, my masters, my shadows, my audience, my charmed circle, for you it's different. Desire, not business, is your theme. Huddle up then, come close, forget Francis Collins, and tell me what you'd really like to hear. A speech of quality, no doubt, before this humdrum legalese? I can do you anything, gentle friends, any exit piece you care to name – tomorrow and tomorrow, never never never, ripeness is all, the rest is silence. The simplest words worked best, put into the mouths of doomed and dying mortals, words that made even the groundlings stop scratching, stand still and wet their cheeks, like trees bedashed with rain.

What do you say, then? Will you hear the will? – the words required by law, the skeleton text, the narrow facts, the miserly truth, the last anxious dictates of a spidery hand, the spindly paring down of language to one unquestionable unambiguous deed.

Or shall it be a soliloquy spoken from the shroud? If so, then I'm your man, an old actor, after all. Well, not old exactly, at fifty-one, yet that's not much, but frail and ailing in this mild March, gone suddenly cold, some forty plays and thirty years of theatre behind me, and nothing now between me and eternity but the elmwood coffin where my poor bones shall be thrown.

'That's enough of bones and shrouds from you, Master Shakespeare, it's a will I'm about to write out, not a death warrant!'

Francis brought the small table over to the bedside to save my voice and his ears, and started scratching out the opening formalities, ensuring my consent by saying each word out loud and clear, speaking slowly and emphatically as if to an old idiot.

'In the name of God, Amen. I, William Shakespeare, of Stratford upon Avon in the county of Warwick, gent., in perfect health and memory...'

Jesu, I thought, what, will this line stretch out until the crack of doom? I'll be dead before he finishes. But it's no matter. Let him scribble and drawl – that's what he's for, and how he's best contented. As for us, we have other talk on hand, and for that I'd be up and dressed, and out of this nightgown that really is beginning to feel like a shroud. How easy is it, then. Easy to close your eyes, rise like a wraith from your own carcass, don your best boots, your old outmoded apparel, snug enough weeds for Will, reach out across the desk, dip the quill for the last time into that pot of black gold, and with quivering wrist begin to write.

About death: the undiscovered country, the after-dinner sleep, the everlasting cold, the dread of kings, the poor man's friend. A subject on which I wrote with false authority. I became quietus' witness, a theatre expert, an illusionist, an imposture of the end. I killed off scores with quick stabs of the quill, made the parchment weep, made stone mouths bleed roses and Yorick's tongue take root. The words grew like flowers about the vanished lips, and a prince heard echoes of eternity in a silence that has no end. But the rest is never silence, sirs, it is loud with doubt, and eloquent with the unsaid. And as I sit here now and watch the slow dawns and sunsets set fire to Stratford, I ask myself for one last time, what is death? Somebody once said it has many mansions, and others say it's nothing: rottenness, silence, sleep. I don't know about the mansions. But I do know that death is not nothing. It is rather the sum of all it takes from us. By subtracting from us everything that we had, and reducing us to that much less than zero, to minus whatever we were, death turns out to be the opposite of nothing. It is, quite simply, everything. To know exactly what death is we must therefore know precisely what it is taking away. And so it is with me, in this my last performance. I must curl up once more and go to sleep in the womb. I must be born again. I have to go back to the beginning.

1

'Shall we make a start then, Will?'

They never go away, do they, those conveyancers, those raspers in your ear? Francis Collins poured himself a generous measure of my best burgundy, slugged back a gulletful, topped up the glass, and set it on the little table, next to the quill and ink, the near pristine parchment. I noticed how the bleak March sunlight leaked through the inverted red cone of wine and winked at me from the walls of my room, my death-chamber. Something of the old life stirred in me, something slipping away. But I can't get a grip on the quill. You see to it then, Francis, the penwork. Give me a cup of sack there.

'I know thee not, old man. Behave yourself. You'll have a small glass of what I'm having, and keep your head clear. Now where do you want to begin?'

That was a strange one – want to begin. You don't *want* to begin. The beginning is as out of your control as the end. Someone, something else decides. And where could it have begun but where it did?

In the county of Warwick.

'Yes, you've said that, Will. It's written down. *In the county of Warwick.*'

So come with me if you will. Follow the path of the rain. Jump on the back of an angel as it leaps like feathered Mercury from heaven's floor and descends upon a second heaven, this sceptred isle – and tell me what you see. The emerald heart of England. And winding its way across that fertile green zone, a silvery track, winking at the moon, silent, glittering, as though left there by some night-foundered snail.

Is that poetic enough, Francis? Does that outfox you? You've heard nothing yet. Nor have *you*, my shadows. Descend then, crowd about now, closer still. Descend. Come closer. That lozenge wedge is Warwickshire. The wake of the midnight snail makes a bright noise now in the morning air.

'The river Avon?'

Divider of fields and forests. Fielden to the south, Arden to the north, the Forest of Arden, the beautiful wild Norman country of Beaudesert. And of all these bounds, even from this line to this, with shadowy forests and with champains riched, with plenteous streams and wide-skirted meads, we make thee lady.

'That's a generous bequest, Will, but not to the purpose.'

That's what I call poetry. And that's what I said once to Anne Hathaway at the end of an afternoon's intimacy: a highly charged act in which I played the player king and made large promises, including loving her forever and knowing no other woman.

'Sounds familiar.'

I'm sure it does. But I'll come to all of that by and by.

By and by is easily said.

Like my name.

'I, William Shakespeare...'

Yes, thank you, Francis. I, William Shakespeare. It has a certain ring to it, you can't deny, no matter which way you say or spell it – and they weren't much fussy in Warwickshire in the good old sixties when I was busy learning to spell the names that God gave you. God had cloth ears. If the recording angel was anything like a Warwickshire scribe, your chances of being correctly identified in the Big Book on Judgement Day were less than one in ninety. This murdered sleep for a time. Supposing there were an orthographic error – and in the scribal confusion I ended up in hell? How have *you* spelt it, Francis? Let me see.

'Now there's really no need – '

Shakspear, Shokspere, Sakspere, Saxpere, Schakosper, Choxper, Shexper, Chacsper, Sadsper, Shagspear –

'Painful on the will.'

Shaxbee, Shaksbye, Sackspree, Sashpierre, Shakespert, Shakeschafte, Shakestaff – I can't make this out.

'God knows who you are, Will, and so does your lawyer. Never afflict yourself. What's in a name?'

Whole volumes in folio. Stories galore. Take Saxpere the foreign chronicler, Sodspar the bosun, Sucksperm the whaler, Sharpspoor the hunter, and old Señor Saspedro, the soldier of the family, who dreamed of cutting foreign throats, of healths five fathom deep, of breaches, ambuscadoes, Spanish blades. I fetch my life and being from men of royal siege.

'You're wandering, master Shakespeare. This is going to be a long day.'

A long line, though doubtless less dramatic than I invent. There was an Adam of Oldeditch once, my father told me. His son was royally rewarded for war service and he changed his name to Shakespeare to reflect his valour and the dauntless temper of his mind. And so there we were – heroes, self-named.

'Well, it's your descendants that matter now. And your survivors – not your ancestors.'

They were a motley lot, the Shakespeares. I'm talking about the real-life ones. But they were bound to the earth, from which I was determined to escape.

'We all go back to it, Will.'

Thank you for that. Most gladly would I have forgotten it.

'I'm here to remind you. And not only me, remember. Doctor and priest due in today.'

Out on you, owls! Nothing but songs of death. And no priest! What was I telling you about?

'Your ancestors.'

They swarmed out of the Plantagenet times and bred about the heart of the country, oh, two centuries ago. After Bosworth – so it ran from my father's tongue – Welsh Richmond, newly come to power as Henry Seven, and with his claim in his codpiece for all old England knew, making it none too big a claim at that, gave lands in Warwickshire to my great-grandfather.

'A curious lie of the land – and lucrative, if only you'd known where.'

And nobody ever did show me where exactly these lands were supposed to lie. Very likely they did lie, because if the story were true, wouldn't my grandfather have been called Henry, after the jumped-up jack-in-office, by the grateful receiver of the new king's bounty? Whereas my grandfather's name was none other than Richard, after the Tudor upstart's beaten enemy, the much maligned monster of the Yorkists, Crookback Dick. Anyway, they did their bit, the falcons of my folk-line, later to be handed a spear by the College of Heralds to shake and bristle, and so illustrate their name and valour, warlike then, the birds of my blood. And with phallic fancies too. Shake spear better than Fall staff, don't you think?

'Worthy of the name.'

I can tell you more.

'I can tell you're going to.'

Oh, but they were the strangest of folk, those ancestors. I could see them sometimes on summer nights, drifting in like milk-fog over the fields, anxious or angry in the late sunsets. Sometimes they were a cloud of gnats, human atomies dancing in the air; they were a rising steam, emanating from the early morning earth; a bubbling in the blood, a prickling in the marrow of the bones. I could hear them calling out to me, from out of the black belfries of all those ruined choirs –

'Where late the sweet birds sang.'

You steal my lines Francis. Stick to the numbers that become you! They turned over in their graves like beasts on a spit and made the earth's bedcover rumple and hiss. They fell like rain from a dank drizzling sky, all one long November's day, drowning me in their requiem for themselves. The whole world teemed with them and they rattled the shutters and trickled in at the slats.

'That's weird, Will.'

Weird is the word. I'm telling you how it was. I was fated, haunted. Anyway it was years ago. Now I lie here shivering in this freezing March –

'It's warm enough, Will.'

And what does it matter to me that I'm master of the best house in Stratford? The logs are piled high on the hearth. The blaze in my bones has gone out. Somebody's stone head lies white and heavy in my hands, laved by flames. I can barely feel them at all now, but I know that they died and that once they too must have lived, those Shakespeares of old.

'Old, Will? What's old?'

Old is poor and poor is starving, my mother used to say. My father's father was so old I never even saw him. He went under the Snitterfield snows, having come up there in old Henry the Eighth's time, and he'd pushed up four springloads of Snitterfield daisies before I arrived on the scene. He didn't starve, though. As tall a man as any in Warwickshire, he was a husbandman, our Richard, a yeoman with an ox-team and a hundred acres round about a peasant roof.

'He must have sweated, though.'

For duty, not for mead. You know how it goes. He tilled the leas, sowed his hops, white and red, bread-corn and drink-corn, wheat and rye, oats and barley, made his beer and cider, pastured his beasts, sheared and slaughtered – and kept his Catholic thoughts to himself.

'You took after him there, Will.'

In a world where even silence could attract an inquisition and send the executioner's hand reaching deep into your bowels to feed a Tyburn fire. That was Richard – and within the book and volume of my young brain that was old, for sure. By the time I was born, Richard Shakespeare had become landscape, that's all, something between the skyline and the mind's eye. He'd been young once, but now he'd become weather.

'Hard to picture that.'

Follow me, then. Stand on the whalebacks of the hills that swim blindly eastwards to Warwick – and you see what Richard Shakespeare saw before he left Budbroke, 1529 it was, to beget John, my father: continents of clouds, that's what, clouds like camels and weasels and whales, rolling endlessly over the earth's green quilt. Twitch it aside for a minute. It covers the hundreds of earlier Shakespeares, the unknowns, all those yeomen who'd made up that bed for generations, season after season, then turned in quietly and gone to sleep. Farming folk. The flocks cropped the grasses over their dead heads that had been wetted only yesterday in the stone fonts at Snitterfield and Rowington. Stone fonts, stone heads – everything petrifies. They lit up like dandelions and were blown out when I told the time, the Shakespeare heads, like moons that fade with morning, like spent stars, cosmic seeds, dust-worlds drifting into oblivion.

'That's poetical.'

It's natural.

'All that lives must die?'

He faded in his turn, passing through nature to eternity.

'You make it sound easy.'

Like most folk he worked his passage. Life doesn't come free, as God advised Adam at a moment of truth – and work is the curse. Richard farmed the land and rented the property of Robert Arden of Wilmcote: a man of some consequence.

For the record, Francis Collins yawned at this point. Hath he so long held out with me untired, and stops he now for breath? But he had an early start from Warwick, and will be missing his breakfast.

Very well then, permit Richard's brief star to twinkle till 1561. Follow him, linger your patience awhile, listen again. On your imaginary forces work. What do you hear? A thousand doves crooned in the great stone cot of the Ardens: providing meat for pies, feathers for mattresses, wings for letters, and cooing companions for the eight girls of Robert Arden, the youngest of whom was Mary. For decades the two men, Richard and Robert, lived and worked as tenant and owner, united and divided by the same farmland, little dreaming that the firstling and lastling of their respective loins would meet and mate and make them grandfathers in common. But that's how things can happen – the forked fates of divers folk fused by offspring into one family, for richer for poorer, for better for worse, often in sickness, sometimes in health, but unexpectedly, inextricably knit. What do you think?

'As a lawyer I've seen it happen.'

Richard Shakespeare changed his sky to Snitterfield, bright with lady-smocks and marigolds, where his sons were welcomed with holy water into a Catholic world and ushered out of it with bell and burial into the infant eternity of an unknown next. The turf heaves over them like the sea. No headstones, gentles, over bones as soft as buttercups. Shrouds, yes, sealed with a loving stitch. They didn't run to coffins then for shoals of small fry. The wind in the grass provides a plain enough song for much of the year. Rain is their requiem, no lack of it, the bluebell and the bee attendant angels in spring and summer.

'Very pretty, master poet. Very poignant.'

I do deaths, you see. And I can do the deaths of children. Their lips were four red roses on a stalk, which in their summer beauty kissed each other – that sort of thing. A few yards from where they lie, the parishioners of St James the Great file in, following the fashions of the liturgical year that ebb and flow by moon or monarch. The unending altered altar-going people. My father John and his brothers Henry and Thomas survived to join the queue. They were also spared the sterner stroke of schooling and never crept unwillingly like snail along Snitterfield High Street where Richard kept his house. There was no school there to dim their shining morning faces.

'Jesus, Will, don't remind me of school! God made buttocks for the sole purpose of impressing the Latin language on otherwise recalcitrant boys.'

School isn't forever. There are other rainclouds to dowse the fires of youth. A life yoked to the land doesn't suit everybody. It suited my Uncle Henry all right, limb of lion and soul of bull, and he farmed Snitterfield to the end of his days. It had suited Richard, who died worth forty pounds, not at all bad for a clodhopper. It didn't suit my father, though. Year by year the routine waves went over him: Snitterfield under the plough; Snitterfield pregnant with seed; Snitterfield green and gold; Snitterfield burnished, burnt-out, black; Snitterfield under snow. These waves break with painful slowness and an absence of music. They break over the land, they break over people, they break people, break hearts and backs, banish hopes, bow heads. Faces are forced into the dirt, and eyes lose the habit of the upward glance, even for the gentle rain. A man submits to what comes, whatever drops on his head. The grass keeps on growing and the earth never tires of swallowing. In time it swallows all aspiration. Life, the man concludes, doesn't go anywhere, it's just something that happens. With crushing monotony. And stops happening. With suddenness, time, unpredictability – and terrifying certainty. My father grew tired of seasons, grew tired of driving an eight-ox team under the Snitterfield skies. So he looked instead at the daughters of his employer, his father's old landlord, little lordly Robert Arden, and saw that they were fair. Fast married too, most of them – but not all. He looked hardest at the youngest of the clutch whom he'd known since her childhood, her father's favourite and ten years my father's junior at sweet seventeen.

'Sounds tempting – with respect to your mother, Will.'

There was something almost scriptural in what he saw. Eight offspring from the good old Catholic Arden loins and another four from Master Robert's second spouse, Agnes – making Mary the youngest of the twelve tribes of Israel and bearing the name of the ancient forest itself, mystical Arden. And though my old man was not the sort of stuff as dreams are made on, he must have *had* a dream at least once in his life.

'Even a wet one, eh? Saving his spirit.'

He ran on ambition, not imagination. Still, I'm going to credit him with a vision. Don't think for a moment that he told me anything of this, or even implied it. I'm doing his thinking for him – and his feeling. Not strong on feeling, my father. He looked at Mary and her prospects and saw land and love neatly yoked. The promised land was called Asbies and the milk and honey were in place, quite literally. So was everything else: malt in the quern, water in the pump, and bread baking in the ovens. Flagged floors, oak-beamed ceilings, a comfortable berth. Its leaded windows looked out across Asbies land, its fields bright with birdsong, where the bulls bugled and spurted and the cows crapped and called. The bells of St John the Baptist called too, from

Aston Cantlow, called on John Shakespeare to take the lady by the hand and sweep her off to church.

'You always did tell a great story.'

He must have weighed it up. Was he standing or sitting when he came to a decision? I have him standing – and alone. He looked over his shoulder four miles to the south-west across gorse-golden fields, where the setting sun drenched Stratford, and looked again at Mary, milking her father's ewes, not poor, but not exactly happy. She was aristocratic enough on the rustic scale and well used to work. The well-placed wench was unassailable to a mere creature of the clods, a bran bumpkin. He had that much wit. He looked at her strong working fingers, unringed as yet, her rosy cheek, unfurrowed by that old bastard, time. O, that I were a glove upon that hand, that I might touch that cheek!

'Ah, and there he had it!'

A glove, yes. A glove upon that hand could touch that heart.

And a glove that pointed to three owned houses in Stratford might touch the pride and purse of Robert Arden for a daughter and a dowry. A favourite daughter, a fancy dowry. He was no fool, my father. Don't kiss the feet of the lofty folk, he told me – kiss their hands instead, with fine white kid gloves. And go for the youngest girl, where a father's heart is fondest.

So he did what his father Richard had done before him, and changed his sky. To Stratford he turned, and to gloves.

'And he was so right!'

You would know, will-maker. When old Arden lay dying in the sere and yellow leaf of 1556, he bequeathed his soul to God and the Virgin Mary, a mere ten marks to his second spouse Agnes (and that not without conditions), and all his wealth in Wilmcote to the other Mary (also a virgin, I would warrant), the child of his age on whom he doted. Fifty or sixty acres were there and more in wait at Snitterfield, a hundred and fifty in all, if not more: the crop on the ground, tilled and sown as it was; houses and halls, hearts of oaks, barns and barley, bullocks and bees, bacon in the rafters, pewter on the dressers, painted cloths on the walls – not to leave out of the reckoning the beds and bedding, brass pots and ploughs, milk-churns and candlesticks, the pigs and the poultry, horses and cattle, corn in the bins, fruit on the bough and logs in the yard. Some billet, don't you think?

'A very tidy proposal, Will. He must have been tickled down to his balls.'

My mother was heiress to a substantial yeoman's nest-egg and sat on imminent brood. She was, you could say, something of a catch.

'You could say that – and you would not lie.'

Not on my death-bed. Old Arden went to bed forever then, who was too old and ill to last. A shroud was stitched up for him and a bride-bed made ready for Mary. The burial party filed down from the Wilmcote hilltop, trampling the grasses for the wedding party. Their destination was the same: green fields and a small stream. A good place for a wedding. A quiet resting place for a good Catholic soul. The funeral-baked meats furnished forth the marriage tables that day – but none too coldly. Joy and woe make a nice tight weave. A virgin makes a nice tight fit. Mary stepped lightly over her father's body in Aston Cantlow churchyard and stood at the church door with the new man from Stratford.

She was standing on his left, signifying Eve's godlike begetting from Adam's left side. *In nomine Patris, in nomine Filii, in nomine Spiritus Sancti, Amen.* And while this was being chanted, my father was placing a circle of gold on each finger in turn from the thumb to the fourth – to be left on that one because the vein from the fourth runs directly to the heart.

'I never knew that.'

I did. But I don't believe it. The fourth's just a good protected finger, that's all. Makes perfect practical sense to place it there. But the ring didn't go over bare fingers. There were gloves on her hands, white gloves, covering the smutches of work and weather. And when she walked through the big nailed doors there was that ring on her finger. And the sound of a mass in her ears.

'You don't want a mass, do you, Will?'

Would you have me die a papist? It was almost 1558. And another Mary had a mass in *her* ears. The namesake queen was about to die: that sad stubborn spinster who'd finally got laid to no avail and now lay with a whiff of syphilis in her pinched nostrils (so the wicked whisper went) – the gift of daddy of good and famous memory. Take a bow, Henry the Eighth – a murderous prick even from the grave. Oh, and a wolf in her womb. That much was true. Only cancer bred there, preparing a bed for the worms, in spite of her earnest supplications to her queen in heaven, whose fruitful womb was by contrast so blessed. Hail, Mary. Farewell, Bloody Mary.

'But Mary Arden – to return to the point.'

Mary Arden, now Mary Shakespeare, was ripe and ready to breed.

My mother was possessed of the usual urges and ambitions of her sex and class: hatching and houseminding. It's what women did, it's what they were for. Child-bearing beasts of burden, moveable chattels, items in the Warwickshire inventory, and in every other shire of England – as scratched out by those clerking Frenchies of old tight-arse himself, William of Normandy. Do you think women had come all that far since his day? They were the hand-luggage of the realm. Or they were receptacles for filth, as defined by those creepy old theologians who knew nothing of the subject beyond their dark imaginings and wet dreams. My mother was now ready as the repository of my father's sperm. One of which I account myself. Back we all go to the stinking drop. My mother was ripe for seeding. One of eight daughters from the same belly, she was ready to go the same procreative distance herself. And did. Eight, including me, and bore my father eight thousand nights on her romping belly.

'Jesus, not every night, surely?'

And she did it in Henley Street, Stratford, among the thousand windy elms that roared and bustled to the business, providing shady lanes for the younger lovers who coupled covertly out of doors. Had my father stayed in Snitterfield he'd have married some other woman and I'd never have been. Even if I had, I'd have died unlettered in Ingon or some such parish. Boggles the brain, doesn't it? That you could have been anyone, anywhere. Or no-one, nowhere. Never to have been at all. But eventually a man and a woman have to get down to it, and anywhere will do – any town, any street, or alley. A haycock will do. A bank where the wild thyme blows. A little patch of ground, two paces of the vilest earth – and wilderness is bliss, if the earth gives. We don't need much to spread out on, do we? We get buried in layers and we couple the same way, where there's still a choice as to who comes on top. As well a churchyard plot becomes a bed as half-acre tombs. And don't believe that it's not entirely random. The moonbeams on the sea are a golden bridge to nowhere. All flesh is Snitterfield grass. And bone of your bone is Stratford elm and nothing more, believe me. The grass withereth, the flower fadeth.

'And faileth.'

As I do now.

As did my first sisters, Joan and Margaret, heaven rest them now. Joan was born in the last months of bitter Mary's reign and lived for a brief space of days as an Elizabethan. Conceived when bleak December's bareness was on the Stratford elms. Born when they burned like torches through September mists. Suffered in the returning bareness, a winter infant, when the torches smiled and froze. Died in savage April, just as my glad mother was seeing if she could place her foot on nine daisies at once and sing that spring had come to save her baby, her firstborn. The daisies were sparse that year, she said, calling them days' eyes, according to her way. Not enough to make a daisy chain for the child in its coffin. Its first ever. Its last before the sudden frost. Its last ever. The baby girl never had time to find her feet and was soon under the spartan grass of that bitter spring – and her mother another Rachel, weeping for her child. There are many Rachels crying in that wilderness of infants.

'And always were.'

So nobody noticed when an old air started up from Henley Street: Mary Arden, down on her hunkers in the dust, bubbling and snivelling and singing her song. A wordless ballad that all mothers sing for a dead child. They know it by heart throughout the world, that raw crying. It's the coldest air in the universe. It never wakens the dead.

Never never never never never.

It was four years till my mother gave birth again. A new vicar tried his prentice hand at the new-fangled sacrament, a Protestant baptism. The new religion was starting to bite. The government called it true religion. Master John Bretchgirdle sprinkled the Holy Trinity font water, half frozen, over that second duckdown head. It was the second day of December in the year 1562. The following year, on the last day of April, he was scattering the first dry dust of the new season over her small corpse. My mother, childless again, put a daisy-chain about that slender neck. She wasn't five months old – and April was yet once more a cold month to the Shakespeares. It was not to be the last. The Lord giveth and the Lord taketh away. Seems pointless, doesn't it?

'I'm a lawyer, not a priest, Will.'

But you're meant to grovel in reverential dread and wonder at the sheer incomprehensibility of it and mutter *Blessed be the name of the Lord*, as if you're ready for any amount of this arbitrary insanity.

'A hard act to applaud.'

It's impossible. The pleasure of a night's coupling has produced that sudden miracle, the fruit of the womb – a little person. With tiny toes and fingers, organs, sensations, capabilities, the acorn brain, everything in place, but on a small and infinitely delicate scale. Wherever she plays and prattles, a dark corner of the house brightens. She is a pearl in your oyster morning, brought in by a special tide, not in the shipman's card. But all's too weak, too short. A bitter business, those brief mornings that slip through your fingers when pearls turn back to daisies in the grass: the long grasses of the churchyard where my sisters lie, anonymous among crowflowers and nettles in unmarked graves. Pearl-blossom and apple-flower fly from the bough like white smoke. Deadly heralds of early death in the annals of the Shakespeare blood. Where Aprils tolled like bells.

'Ah, the bells.'

Bells in the blood. Yes, I must have heard them soon after I was born, the bells of the Guild Chapel tolling for the plague dead, summoning me from infancy to eternity, to follow my sisters. I didn't answer the call, though my mother said the owl kept screeching in the elm just outside our house: the fatal bellman that gives the sternest goodnight. She panicked. She'd lost two pretty chickens already and the signs for the third were not good. I was born on a Sunday, you see, and should have been baptised by the Tuesday. But the 25th was an unlucky date in April, April again, St Mark the Evangelist's Day, when all the altars and crosses were hung with black.

'Scary stuff.'

Black Crosses, they called that day – and through the churchyards there glimmered the ghostly gatherings of those doomed to die in the coming year. Old Agnes Arden had seen the grisly sight up at Aston Cantlow. Call it a woman's story at a winter's fire, but strange truths sometimes quiver in these old birds' throats when their tongues catch fire. The graveyard had swarmed with ill-starred infants thronging the moonbeams. And the old folk too – they manifested themselves as mourners, their astral apparitions going a ghastly progress through the moon-mouldered tombs, while their bodies slept soundly in their beds, unaware of their own terrible fetches that crowded the watery beams.

'You're scaring the shit out of me. Stop it.'

'Don't baptise the boy on St Mark's Day,' Agnes entreated my parents, 'unless you want to lose him too. He'll join the girls, poor souls, you mark my word. Are you going to drop every fruit you bear straight into the grave? No, wait till the Wednesday and it'll be all right, you'll see.'

'And so they did?'

They waited the extra day. Bretchgirdle scooped a cold glimmer of God over my head and the parish clerk scratched in the register *Gulielmus filius Johannes Shakspere* –

'A poor Latinist. That should have been Johann*is*.'

The day being, in deference to the quaking Agnes, the twenty-sixth day of April. It was a Wednesday and the year was sixty-four, just on the cusp of challenge and change. The game was afoot. The fruit of Mary Arden's womb had dropped healthily into a sick and lethal world, the bloom of original sin had been washed by holy water clean from my skin. I was the apple of my mother's eye and the flag-bearer of my father's name. Adam's core was stuck in my throat but I had been inspected and approved by the church. Whatever happened to me now, I would not at least end up in limbo. Gift of God or accident of nature, I had made it.

'Phew!'

I know, I'm a miracle. But my mother trusted neither nature nor God. And when poor Oliver Gunne, my father's apprentice, departed this life she began to worry in earnest. He was buried on the very same day he died, the eleventh day of July, the reason for the haste being all too obvious to anyone looking over the parish clerk's shoulder that day as he scribbled again in the register, this time the chilling words, *Hic incepit pestis*. From the scratching of that sinister sentence until the close of the year there fell the time of horror, dreaded by those of all degree. Least of all by the poor, who had least to lose in losing life and most to gain in a recompensing eternity – but not even the poor man wanted to quit existence through that particular door. It was daubed with a bloody cross and opened onto unbelievable agonies, till death came as a friend. Such was the plague – carried to Stratford on this occasion by the soldiers of the Earl of Warwick coming home from the siege of Le Havre through the stricken streets of London.

'How you survived London...'

That's another miracle. But it didn't take long in '64 for a state of emergency to be called in sweltering Stratford. The almanac had been correct in predicting a hot summer – the plague's favourite habitat. Richard Symons, the town clerk, lost two sons and a daughter. In our own street the miller, Roger Green, buried four, same side of the street, just a few doors down. My father was a burgess then. He sat with the Council in the garden of the Guild Chapel, free among the fragrances of appleboughs and pears from the contagious confines of the Hall; and under the tall skies of August he and his fellow townsmen debated the question of relief for the stricken. They also formulated the only cure they could think of: fines for the keepers of muck-middens in which the plague bred with wicked swiftness right in front of folks' doors. Fine the fuckers! Fine them! The cry went up from the terrified townsmen.

They'll kill us all! My father had been fined himself a dozen years earlier for that very reason, in a Stratford which at that time had worried about the mere possibility of plague. He agreed that fines would be effective. He was wrong. The most frightening aspect of the plague, when it comes, is its complete unpredictability, the absence of all logic. That's what really terrifies.

While they talked my mother acted. I was stuffed into a small basket on a bed of rose-petals and lavendered linen, and in this aromatic ark I was stashed away like Moses, farmed out among the uncles and aunts and old folks of Ingon and Asbies: good tough sensible stock who didn't fall victim to plagues. I was kept in the country till the pestilence went off with the December cold. By that time it had visited two hundred Stratford souls and had ushered them into that eternity, Francis, that is the only known release from a disease so virulent and so unforgiving it is beyond any possible cure.

Of that interim evacuation to the farms I naturally recall nothing. I babbled and crapped among green fields, while Stratford, under attack, attacked its dungheaps and my father imposed fines. I was well versed later by Granny Arden, who lived till I was sixteen. And by Uncle Henry, that unkillable old ox – I'd written a dozen plays before he finally fell down. Henry was a crusty bugger and that was his charm.

'Fucking bad time of year anyway for you to poke your snout into the world,' he grumbled at me. 'April? I've shit better Aprils than you see them days. I've shit better primroses. Been no sun in the sky for fucking months, and your mother carrying you with a winter diet in her belly. Stupid time to pop your pod. What they go fucking one another in summer for? Ought to know April's the killing time for the Shakespeares. Then on top of that comes the fucking plague. Jesus. It killed Bretchgirdle quick enough, though.'

When was that, uncle?

'Can't you tell that? Any fool can tell that. Very year you were born, hard after he baptised you, gathered to his God right fucking fast. The plague don't hang about, you know. He should've drunk down some of that holy water went over your noodle. They say a bloody good draught of holy water keeps out the pest – right from the fucking font!'

Granny Arden says pigeons are best.

'She would. They're over their feet in pigeon shit down Asbies way. Fucking pigeons. Need fifty of the fuckers to fill a decent pie. One pig feeds an army. But they do say a pigeon can take away the poison sometimes if you clip its feathers behind and lay it right square on the sore, make your plague-boil kiss its arse – and then out goes your illness, up the bird's behind and you're saved from the plague-pit.'

Can you eat the pigeon after?

'How the fuck do I know? Old wives' tales, like their scripture. Bretchgirdle, Butcher, Heycroft – hang 'em, I've shit 'em all I tell you, I've shit 'em! I got my own God anyhow up here in Ingon, where you're a fucking sight closer to heaven. Just look at them clouds on Snitterfield – so close you could reach one down and blow your nose on it if you cared to. Or needed to – you're dribbling again, you little bugger. Come on, Will.'

'Will, Will...' Francis was bringing me back gently, sternly, as always.

He called me Will, my uncle, old Henry, who taught me how to swear and could swear Marlowe under the table if they met somewhere in the next world. Heaven seems unlikely for either, and hell's a fable. Call me Will, then, if it pleases you. Bretchgirdle called me William in God's hearing but my mother especially willed me to endure, to outlast angry April, to survive summer stenches and the plague-bitten butt-end of the year. I rode it all out. Time and the hour runs through the roughest day.

'And you were the first child to stay the course.'

And five followed after. Let me become a register then, a book of death, let me tell you the days, the names, the years.

'I'd rather you make some bequests.'

Joan and Margaret were tiny white sticks in the earth, known only unto God and the worms. Little Margaret lived out her few brief days in the year that brought *Gorboduc* to a still birth on the stage.

'*Gorboduc*! Jesus, I remember that – just.'

Not that you'd want to. I was born, baptised, and lived, Robert Dudley was made Earl of Leicester, and that brave new word – Puritanism – was born in folks' mouths.

'And came out of arseholes.'

It did not sound well.

'Not worth a fart!'

After me came Gilbert, named for Gilbert Bradley in our street.

'Was that the glover?'

A friend of my father's. And that was in the October of '66, when Essex and Ed Alleyn and the future King James all saw the light of day too.

'In perfect health and memory, did we say? Well, I grant you the memory, Will. You would have made a good lawyer.'

I nearly did. Gilbert died four years back – he was only forty-four. After him came the second Joan, in the middle of April; '69 as I recall.

'Greasy Joan.'

Doth keel the pot. Plenty of that from our sensible Joan. She married Hatter Hart, who lives still.

'Only just.'

While Joan looks set to outlast the pyramids.

'Fit to fell them first, I'd say.'

Greasy Joan. She used up all the family strength, it all went her way. Little Anne had no strength at all, poor lamb. She came in '72 when I was nearly eight and she lived on palely for a time. She was about to be eight herself when she left us. I remember the eight pennies my father paid for bell and pall. Eightpence. A penny for each of her years. Richard came after her in '74 and died the year after Gilbert, three years gone by. Anne died in April.

'April again.'

Murderous brutal bastard April. And Richard in freezing February, I remember that well enough. And it was even colder when Edmund died. Last day of the year, 1607, and him only twenty-seven and still unwed, same as Richard. Seems like yesterday I saw him interred in Mary Overy.

'Even such is time.'

Seems like yesterday I saw my father standing like a fool at the font and Edmund a babe in May.

'Seems like lots of yesterdays, doesn't it?'

Lighting fools the way to dusty death.

'As one of your old actors famously said.'

Aye, Burbage.

'Hamlet?'

Macbeth. Still, you spotted a line, old Francis. Not altogether ignorant, are you, though you profess to eschew art?'

'I like to keep an eye on my clients – and their affairs.'

And what do you think of the production?

'*Macbeth*?'

No, not that production – propagation, procreation, engendering, begetting.

'Ah! Well, not an impressive account, is it? I've seen worse, much worse, but it's not altogether wonderful, is it, the Shakespeare performance? Let's see if I've got this right. Eight offspring: four girls, four boys. Only one of the surviving females takes a spouse, and only one of the males. The boys do not beget sons that know the secrets of survival. One boy buries a bastard in the Cripplegate – am I correct? – and a legitimate son lies near your first two sisters in Holy Trinity's earth, here in Stratford. You're right, Will, the lifespans are dismal. But cheer up, man, you're not dead yet.'

My days are numbered. And only one left after me. When you look back along that line of cribs and coffins, you wonder what all the toil and trouble was for. We copulate in shrouds and give birth on biers. The umbilical dangles bloodily like the hangman's noose. We fat all creatures else to fat us –

'Jesus, he's off.'

And we fat ourselves for maggots, and that's the end, alas, alas. Easy to see it that way anyway.

'Look at it another way – it makes the will less complicated.'

Ah, pardon me my morbid memories. I'm chewing on gristle now.

'You're drinking too much perries.'

Black bile and melancholy. And an old man's mind clouds and sickens somewhat. But if you sit here just a little longer, the picture may improve, and after I'm gone you'll be left with something softer, a mellow haze, a nice memory imprinting the air. Who knows, it may outlive my life half a year.

'You're a good man, Will, but it's your present memory that's at fault. I'm here for your will, remember? And a will is not exclusively about death. There may be children, grandchildren. You've got to get the old grim reaper out of your skull and think further ahead – think not of death but of birth.'

2

Let's talk of worms.

'No, let's talk of wombs. You promised, remember?'

Did I?

'Yes, a solemn promise.'

That's a lie, then. I'd never have said that. There's no such thing as a solemn promise, there's just a promise. It means what it says. Words mean what they say.

'Well then, forget the worms.'

They're coming up with the plough out there. Look at those crows. A good feeding for them in March. And after March comes April. A cold month for the Shakespeares.

'So you've told me.'

It's the one door in the year my mother always dreaded passing through. April is the time of epitaphs, so she would say, the time of year for the Shakespeares to carve their names in stone.

And there's many a spring raindrop has ploughed through the smart new chiselled lettering of our slabs. That's how she put it. Fear it, Will, fear it. April's a marble month. She had a turn of phrase, my mother.

'Words in the blood, is it?'

She was a charmer, and could almost read the thoughts of people.

'Let's get back to the wombs.'

And yet I was born in April, born on a Sunday, born to the sounds of plague-bells and crows, calling fields and folk to a harsh re-birth.

'Over-poetical.'

Virgins and primroses died unmarried –

'Worse and worse.'

Of greensickness, gales, and unknown griefs.

'There's no stopping you, is there?'

I, William Shakespeare –

'At last!'

No, Francis, not yet. I, William Shakespeare, survived, my frail vessel escaping the cold tidal pull of April – just. My mother believed it was because I was born late in the month.

'She had some sense.'

If I'd been born betimes I'd never have hung on, so she said. As it was I had only a week to do battle with the killer of Shakespeares.

'Lucky Will.'

You speak true. And so I won. But still she hated April.

'An April baby. Look at you now.'

An April corpse. Call for the shroud, the pick-axe and the spade, to take me back to the womb.

'Here we go.'

Look, here's my mother, come to cradle me again. Fifty-two years, a blink ago, and I was born. She pushed me out from between her legs and into time, where the unstoppable clock started up, and the women wasted not a second.

'A good example. Let's follow it.'

These were the certainties. Wash off the blood, the muddle and the mire, swaddle me well from the cold, show my father what he has done, and bring me quickly back to the breast that bulges for me already. Lay me there like a leech, my lips to the nipple. Butter and honey first, laid on my tongue, and later the jellied brains of the hare.

'Ugh. Never fancied hare.'

Jug jug. Don't knock it. Something kept me going. Who's to say it wasn't hare's brains?

'Jellied down. Jesus. Can't stand the texture.'

On the Wednesday my father carried the fruit of his loins from Henley Street to the church, where they dipped me into the font water, gave me a name, and put a chrisom cloth on my head. If I'd died within the month it would have been my shroud.

'Thrift, thrift.'

Who said that? Horatio? Thrift's the word, a quick and convenient step from baptism to burial. But it never happened. It was third time lucky for John and Mary. And for me, little William the Conqueror they called me. I had beaten the odds and would live to die at a later date.

'For unto them a son was born.'

You said it, a lucky son. Lucky I didn't join my infant sisters, early conscripts in the ranks of death, under Holy Trinity's damp grasses. Or those poor brothers of mine, now so dead. Lucky? Lucky I didn't become a plague-bill number, cannon-fodder, chance casualty of some awful affray that sent brains and bones screaming to the sky and scarred the moon with splinters.

'You always had a way of putting things, Will.'

And my eyes, moist as they are, they might have been pearls by now, my bones to coral turned. Or I could have watched my tripes tumble bloodily through the Tyburn sky. Or a red hell scorch me to a Smithfield cinder.

'Nice way to go.'

There's only one entrance to the great stage of fools, unless untimely ripped, but there are a thousand early exits. I avoided all of them. I escaped, opened hell's trapdoor, and stepped out onto the London stage.

'To become the foremost playwright of your time.'

Known to queen and king, and known in the country too. A life well lived, you could say.

'You could. Let's wrap it up then, shall we?'

And usher me into eternity? Pause there awhile, give me breathing space, some shriving time allowed, you fat bastard.

'You starveling, you bull's pizzle, you've put on weight yourself, though.'

And lost it again. Don't be in such a hurry to close the gate. Offer me my infancy at least.

'Your infancy. What was it?'

It was a wasp, dizzy with drink, banqueting to abandonment in the black mortuary juice of the September plum, where it throbbed and blundered. It was the cat-opened carcass of a pigeon – a silent murdered metropolis, roaring with maggots. It was the dried skeleton of the heretic spider, strung out on the wheel of its web, dead in the corner of my room for decades of dawns, a ghostly medieval martyr with the daylight showing through. It was the knots in the floorboards, charting the kingdoms of my childhood with their own special geography of fear, knots that ran along the beams like tigers, roaming the roofs and rafters, changing to cannibals, swarming down the walls and up the legs of the bed – the Anthropophagi, and men whose heads do grow beneath their shoulders.

'That's a fantastic start to life.'

After that I remember the fields, turning over like the sea, like Uncle Henry and Aunt Margaret in their sleep, the Snitterfield sleep, and in the slow sleep of their lives, every day turning back to the earth they tilled, turning to dust – John Shakespeare's and Mary Arden's folk. How quickly and quietly they turned, though it seemed slow at the time, those fields of folk. And the folk themselves died without fuss, like beasts turning over in the fields. Only sometimes they turned like beasts on the spit, spitting and snarling in their juices, the red-faced fevered farmers of Snitterfield, roasting in their beds at nights, wallowing and swallowing and snorting, revolving over the snarling coals and the hissing logs, getting ready for hell. I could smell them cooking in their beds, baking in the ovens of an imminent eternity, filling the house with last supper whisperings.

'Not short on imagination. Born with it, I suppose?'

Everything seemed to be turning at that time – the Arden doves spinning in tight little circles as they died, headless and dizzy by the dozen. They whirled like dervishes, as if death were a dance. Then they took a bow and lay down, exhausted, their legs in the air. Not like the animals at the Rothermarket, down from our shop, where beasts struggled and slipped in the greasy shambles and the bluebottles went mad among the wet red yells, whizzing through the screaming and the stench. Death didn't come easy at the slaughter-house.

'You shouldn't have looked. I'd have looked away.'

It was my first experience of treachery. You give an animal a name, as if it were a sister, a brother, a Christian soul. You scratch its back and tickle its chin, babble your baby-talk to its silly snout, stick daisies and dogroses behind its ears. You feed it from your hand – and it comes running to the sound of your voice. It's one of the family. Then comes the day of the great betrayal.

And as the butcher takes away the calf, and binds the wretch and beats it when it strays, bearing it to the bloody slaughter-house; and as the dam runs lowing up and down, looking the way her harmless young one went, and can do nought but wail her darling's loss...

'Whoa! Whoa!'

Woe's the word.

And you see your father as you've never seen him before, stained with the purple butchery of his business, your loving father with his brandished steel, which smoked with bloody execution...

'All right, all right, you've made your point.'

It never left me, that farewell to infancy. And its emblem, one figure standing brutally above another, murder most foul. I see it in silhouette, and memory blurs the detail, but I know it's my father, the two-footed one with arm raised high, with axe in hand, over the four-footed one, the victim. Down comes the blade – and no, not now, not never, not even if he wanted to, can the executioner leave off his hacking and slicing, not till he unseams him from gullet to groin, releasing the terrible torrent. It hits the floor, steaming, the high-pitched screaming dies away and the silence that follows fills your ears like blood.

'That's horrible.'

O, horrible! O, horrible! Most horrible!

'I said that.'

My father, methinks I see my father.

'Let's change the subject.'

Even to this day I avoid Rother Street if I can. Or I find myself unawares, creeping past the shambles and starting like a guilty thing upon a fearful summons, just like I did when I was a boy.

'Buttoned it up, did you?'

If you want to know where my player's days really began, it was right there in the Rothermarket. I'd entered the theatre of blood, and the only defence was to whip on the visor, stop up the access and passage to remorse. False face must hide what the false heart doth know.

'Your own special room in hell, eh?'

Reserved for me alone. No-one else seemed to mind.

'Young Will. Well, well, well.'

As to the fireside fears, they were different, ensnaring the mind, not the senses, the stories told by the wind to the chimney when the storms over Snitterfield made the flames burn blue. Henry said it was just weather in the grate, that cold blue firelight. But Asbies Agnes said it was ghosts, come to populate your hearth and dreams.

'And give you a good night's sleep.'

Aye, revenants from a darkness almost unimaginable. Almost. But she made me imagine it, all the same. The spectres slipped like shadows from their graves, where the worm forked and fretted, and they swarmed across the sleeping town, just like the million eels Henry said he once saw migrating by moonlight across the fields, downhill all the way, down on Stratford, an eerie exodus.

'They was ghosts,' Agnes shrieked, 'they was spirits, you old disbeliever – they was white ladies!'

'I know a fucking lady when I sees one,' roared old Henry. 'They was fucking eels! And a million too, just like I said. I stood and counted them, I did. Every fucking one!'

Eels or spirits – it made no difference to the spirits that the darkness now unleashed upon Stratford, making straight for my bedchamber. I saw the wraiths, made white by the moon, sliding like fog against the closed shutters and gnashing whatever they had for teeth in their frustrated rage and envy of the fireside sitters and snug sleepers – while they, the souls of the dead, had no beds to return to but cold clay, no halls but the wet echoings of the eternity they inhabited, no amber-chaired companions of the chimneyside – only the slimy probing worm. And so they'd slither up the whispering eaves, over the anxious prickling thatch (just birds and rats in the roof, Henry said, but Agnes knew better), and so down the chimney, still shivering, to make the flames change colour, the stones of the grate go violent blue, and the lamps round the kitchen shrink and quiver like frightened hares. I sat there too, twitching and trembling, listening to the oldest terrors of the earth.

'Fucking bad weather coming, that's all,' growled Henry, 'storm in the chimbley. Severn Jacks coming up from Wales. Always from the south-west, those fucking clouds, and always bringing rain.'

But I didn't believe him. Agnes had spitted me on her tongue.

'The hour of the phantom. Never went there myself. Don't go there now. An evil hour.' Francis was giving me his reproachful look.

When spooks troop home from churchyards and ghosts break up their graves, moaning in the icy winds, scrabbling to be let in out of the streaming rain.

'History's full of ghosts.'

We didn't have classical ghosts in Stratford – not the text-book types from Julius Caesar's time, when graves stood tenantless and the sheeted dead did squeak and gibber in the Roman streets. These were schoolboy ghosts and appeared later. My childhood ghosts, country shadows, came out of the arms and hands and fingers of the trees, they came drifting out of the marshes and sweating out of clammy gravestones, out of damp flagged parlour floors. They coiled up round your knees and ankles like cats, hissing and sidling, and were sucked up into your nostrils to enter your blood and take hold of your soul. Old Agnes ladled them into me with broth and brew.

'Everybody's ideal aunt.'

The archetypal granny, crammed with comforts. She'd seen fairies in foxgloves, she'd seen Queen Mab and had been Mab-led herself, all the way to madness, and had met the man in the moon, come down with his lantern and his dog and his bundle of thorns. She'd seen devils too, she said, as well as ghosts, seen them in fields and forests – now as toads, sometimes as snakes. The wingpath of the crow to the rooky wood, the shard-borne beetle with his drowsy hums, the bat's cloistered passage through the thickening light – they took on a thousand different disguises. They even grew up out of the ground, materialising as mushrooms, delectable to the eye, but they turned men mad if they ate them, made them want to tear up trees and topple castles down. This was the insane root that takes the reason prisoner.

'She'd been around.'

And if you were a girl and stepped by accident into a ring of these demonic toadstools, they ripped themselves out of the forest floor, screaming like mandrakes, and whirled about you till you fell mesmerised among the ferns. Then they had you at their mercy and came roaring up your skirt for fun and fury – mob-raped by phallic fungi you were, but you never fell pregnant, not unless you told. After which you swelled up all in one day and went on swelling till you burst and died.

'For fuck's sake.'

And if you were a boy and ate one of them by mistake you'd wake up that night and find your willie turned into a toadstool.

'Holy Thomas!'

Then goats would come and find you and nibble it down to the root, and they'd go mad in the moon with pure lust, and roam the countryside looking for upland virgins to deflower – and for staid old wives, to make them flower again, good country rides that they once were, leaving their stunned spouses – sexless since seventy – foundered in their beds, de-masted and derelict like wrecked men-o'-war.

'Fancy filling your noodle with all that!'

That was how Agnes ran it. Uncle Henry told me a different story.

'Listen, Will,' he said, 'Agnes Arden brought old Arden's grey hairs down to the grave before his time – but not with sorrow, as the scriptures say, *O noni fucking no*, but many a time and oft on that good old truckle-bed of theirs. Never stayed at anchor long, that bed, bucking like a brig on the Bay of Fucking Biscay-O! – where O! was the only word. Oh yes, she quickened his end all right. No bugger can have his end away at that rate and hope to see out his three score years and ten. For the life of a wick depends on the dipping, don't it? And as scripture also tells us, there's a time to fuck and a time to refrain from fucking – and Agnes Arden needed a fucking clock!'

'A ninety-year-old itching for it!'

'As for her stories, pay no fucking attention to them, young Will, because I'm telling you straight, now that her well's dried up, she tickles herself by getting a young lad's fancy going with forest fairy stories, love-juice of flowers and all that crap, when all the world knows what kind of juice she ran on in her day, that's run out now. Shut your ears, my lad, or she'll pour her spirits in and charm you with her tongue. And fuck knows where that's been!'

'What a woman! What a man!' Francis as tickled as I was.

Crude old bastard, was Henry, and full of vigour and prickly common sense. But it was hard to banish old Agnes's demons. I could hear them booming like bitterns in the darkness of the far-off foggy fens. I could see them falling as rain. They hissed at my shutters on cloudburst days and stormy nights and I shut my eyes tight in my terror. I couldn't shut them out. She told me about witchcraft too, and long before I read Reginald Scot and Royal Jamie, long before I could even read, I was a graduate and an authority, petrified by my own knowledge. Agnes cracked it open for me, the secret hive, broke the earth's crust, and I saw straight into the sombre comb of horrors, hell's black honey, hot and ripe for mischief.

'Do I look like I want a lesson on witches, Will? Do my lips say so?'

They're purple with my wine. Pour me another glass, you gormandiser.

'And let's drown Agnes in it, I beg you.'

She taught me all the steps of the Satanic ball, from the first pact with the Dark Master to the last handful of ashes scattered to the four winds: the ghastly gatherings on blasted heaths when the west bled like a black pig and the wolfish wind came prowling over the Welcombe hill in thunder, lightning, and in rain. Crops rotted in the flood, cattle toppled and died, women's breasts gave gall, the milk of human kindness curdled, and the infant sickened and stiffened in the crib. A man's member melted between his legs, and as he lay supine beside his sleeping spouse the succubus slid in from the fog and filthy air, hovered over him, lingering on the ceiling. Waking him into stiffness. Descending wide-legged and purple with love's wound onto his unlawful erection – and the night was stabbed by the surrendering sperm, sucked up and shot out into that thing of darkness. Which flew off then, metamorphosed into male. Over the rooftops and down the chambered chimneys. To find out some sleeping female, a virgin or a nun, to thrust into her with a will, to complete the deep deed of diabolical cross-fertilisation, while bees and birds slept out their innocent sleep and the foul and ugly night limped tediously away.

'Angels and ministers of grace defend us!' Francis suiting the action to the word, melodramatic. Wine turned even this lawyer theatrical.

You might have made an actor, Francis.

'A small part, perhaps.'

For a large man.

'Well, goodnight to demons, and good morning, Stratford!'

Ah, but not until a world of horrors had been consummated before dawn: pig-killing, shipwrecking storms, direful thunders, drugs and drunkenness, fucking the devil, fucking the dead, tucking into the exhumed flesh of unbaptised infants, concoctions gathered by the midnight moon, stewed into brews that would make even hell's bones burn and tremble.

'Mine ache to think on't. Anything more?'

A filthy whore heaved in a ditch, open-legged, and strangled the infant even as it slipped from her belly. A sow gorged on its litter of nine, chopping and crunching, till every one was back inside her, bloodily. A murderer swung on the gibbet and the fat was melted from his bones by the same greasy finger that cut the liver from a Jew and sifted the stomach contents of a shark – plucked from the ocean by what terrible force? Slice the lips from a Tartar, tear out a tiger's entrails, snort a root of hemlock, cool it with a baboon's blood – and your dream is sealed.

'Some dream.'

Wicked dreams abuse the curtained sleep, witchcraft celebrates pale Hecate's offerings, and withered murder, alarmed by his sentinel, the wolf, whose howl's his watch, thus with his stealthy pace, with Tarquin's ravishing strides, towards his design moves like a ghost.

'Sounds like a good night.'

There was always worse to follow.

'Jesus, what could be worse?'

That's what I asked.

'And what was the answer?'

And what was it? – I asked Agnes – too terrified to know, yet having to.

The old woman's throat quavered in the firelight.

'I'll tell you,' she said. 'It was a deed. It was a deed – '

A deed without a name?

Too terrible to hear. So shocking a whole parish would be infected with fear. The hammering on the door at four in the morning, following the night's debate, the stripping and searching for the devil's mark, for the supernumerary nipples, cunningly camouflaged as warts and moles and callouses and scars. Or hidden with diabolical invisibility in ears and armpits, nostrils and hair. Under the eyelids, the tongue, the fingernails, and feet. Even far into the fundament and the secret clefts, as deep as the probes of pricker and inquisitor might breathlessly search. Investigation by question and needle and a fine excuse for peering into the pudenda – they had to be certain in their examination.

'So certain?'

That's why every hair had to be shaved clean from the body and the head left bald as a turnip, prior to the interrogation under torture. Think of it as method, procedure, system, due and necessary process of law: extraction of cuticles; application of thumbscrew and boot, with consequent dislocation and pulverisation of bones; application of rack, with teasing of joints, stretching of skin and sinew and consequent crippling.

'Christ Almighty.'

Ignore the nipples crisped and torn off with white-hot pincers. Ignore the tender tongue, sensitive as a snail, quivering in the vice, while the long needles go savagely to work, wedded in lust to a quest for truth that can have only one answer. Ignore the hammer-blows descending on the legs with excruciating and insistent zeal. Ignore the split skin and the burst bowels when the rackman goes too far. Ignore the fingers dangling like crushed radishes, the tangled red roots that were toes and the mangled meat that was legs. Ignore the screams.

Especially ignore the screams.

'Will, enough! I'm a lawyer. Do you think I need you to tell me what I already know only too well?'

But don't miss one syllable of what comes out of that sobbing mouth by way of confession. Because every word that you hear justifies the torture. The confession is essential for the salvation of the soul. And after all this, with not even an eyebrow left on her white egg head, what kind of thing do you suppose it was that they finally dragged on a hurdle to the stake that had been prepared for her?

'I've told you – you can spare me the details.'

A witch, of course. Not a woman, that's for sure, otherwise how could you look in your glass, knowing what you'd just done to another human being? No, it was easier to point to the thing with jellied legs and shaved noodle, the thing that couldn't even hold itself upright as it was chained to the stake – and to say that it was a witch and not a woman that was being smeared with pitch from the barrel beneath the broken feet. The bible said it clearly. *Thou shalt not suffer a witch to live.* You had God's own backing for it. And the biblical injunction was to be carried out with the utmost barbarity. Cite scripture and you can get away with anything.

'Even murder.'

The stake was piled high with faggots – the crowd seethed round it like the sea, hissing its hatred, its derision, spitting into that wild white face. A mob hungry to feed on the terror in the eyes. Anxious not to miss out on a single note of the screaming that would start up after the officials thrust their torches into the bundles, and the raging white-haired ministers of religion yelled at the unrepentant wretch: that the agonies in which she would presently expire were a mere foretaste of the red eternity that awaited her. Unless of course she elected to confess and save her soul. Confess, you whore! You fucking witch! Confess! Confess!

'Jesu.'

Oh yes, it was safer to libel it as a witch, that broken thing on the barrel, turning slowly to a shrieking blue blister behind the shooting curtains of sparks. Never a simple illiterate country girl who'd made extracts from herbs and flowers for eye-brighteners, breath-sweeteners, and reddening of the lips. Not surely some gossiping old grandmother with a squint in her eye and with nothing left in her life but to confide in the cat and tell lies to the spiders on the wall. That's the cunning of the creatures, to play the innocents. Country wenches? Country's the word, all right. Country cunts! No, burn the fuckers, burn the bitches to the bare bone – and damn their souls to hell!

'Hell on earth. It stayed with you, what your old gran described.'

On my imaginary forces worked. All the everyday horrors faded by comparison into thin air. The roaring thoroughfares of those carcasses, mad with maggots; the dead cats in the ditches, stuck to the frozen drift of leaves, frost-furred and open-eyed, stiff and snarling at the moon; the moon itself, that scowling cindered old skull in the sky, yellow with death. Even my shithouse terrors: the Old Men that lurked in the privies, long-lost forgotten gong-scourers with arms long enough to reach up through the shithole and drag me down deep into the black stench of their bowel-world, alive with excrement and flies – even all this was nothing to the terrors told round winter fires. From old remembering mouths. Into fresh ears too horrified to hear but unable to close the doors.

'Doors that never close, eh?'

Never. So the Bloody Mary burnings were endlessly rekindled in the heads of the old ones, they just couldn't let them die out, could they? And the slow old syllables were blown from their lips, lazily, like stray sparks, to land on me and set me suddenly on fire, to make me grip the sides of the stool till my knuckles were white to the bone. I couldn't stir. My feet were packed hard with faggots. Waiting for the flames. They fanned them with their failing breath, those pitiless old chroniclers of winter, till the blaze was roaring about my ears and I couldn't rise from the chair because of the chain round my middle. Soon it would be holding a blackened skeleton to a smoking stake. The charred memory of a person, collapsing into a black bundle of bones, to be blown to the winds. All I could do was to sit on, held in the shackles of the familiar sentences, waiting for the winter burnings to begin again.

'Childhood entertainment? Childhood abuse, more like. What was the worst story?'

Latimer and Ridley. One of the old ones up at Asbies, or maybe it was Snitterfield, told me how he'd walked all the way to Oxford to watch them burn, being a good Catholic subject, as we were on both sides, and loyal to both Marys on their thrones, down in London and up in heaven. Yes, he said, he wanted to see those bastards burn well – infamous spawn of Luther that they were, fine fuel for perdition and the fires that never die. He wanted to hear them howl in the flames, so that he would have some idea of their torments in hell.

And once I'd heard that story, I was part of it, and it of me. I re-enacted it a thousand thousand times, walking down to Oxford. I remembered the old man's voice:

'I arrived at the scene just in time to see the executioner pulling off their stockings and it struck me like a thunderbolt. I thought, Hold it right there, sir, don't you see it? These execrable heretics – they wear *stockings*! Like me, like you. The stockings will burn anyway, mere cobwebs in the greatness of the flame. Why bother to remove them? Will this ridiculous procedure somehow obliterate their spiritual error? Execute them the more effectively? And their trusses, shirts and shoes, such necessary items even for a brace of nefarious apostates and traitors – surely these homely weeds, innocent enough in themselves after all, could be permitted to remain? In any case they'll scarcely protect them from the unbelievable pain to follow, won't keep it from them for more than a moment. And if heresy is such a plague, wouldn't it be better if every last scrap of their clothing were to be burnt and perish along with them?

'Yet there they were, two old men standing barefoot in their shrouds, waiting to be burned. It was the middle of October, the first chill in the air, and I couldn't help noticing how Master Ridley's toes curled a little when he felt the first coldness of the ground beneath his now shoeless stockingless feet that would be the first parts of him to feel the fire. So his toes twitched blindly. For some reason it made me think of my fields up here, what with the first frosts coming on, and how I'd soon be bringing my beasts inside. Fuck me, you wouldn't even treat an animal the way these poor old buggers were now to be served. That's when it hit me that it was real and not just some theological game. These two old gentlemen, one of them shivering a bit, really were going to be burned alive. I'd been shouting along with the mindless mob, chucking in my Catholic groatsworth, but from that moment on I never uttered another word. The executioner stepped forward with his torch alight, ready to thrust it into the faggots, and at that point the crowd fell silent too, holding its breath.

'I watched amazed as Latimer stretched out his arm and laved his face in the first flame as if he were washing, and it was a relief to see how easily he expired, his open mouth filled with fire, quickly choking off the brief screams, so I began to think how efficiently after all the blaze ate away the enemies of the true religion. But it had a short life, that thought. Because Master Ridley's experience of the flames turned out to be very different – and here's how it happened.

'For a start some of the wood they were using was completely unseasoned, as any fool could see, unless that was deliberate. And it was no farmer who'd made up that fire, that was obvious, because the stupid bastards had heaped up the faggots much too close to the poor old bugger's face and chest. Fucking well-wishers, thinking to speed things up by piling on the fuel, when all they succeeded in doing was stopping the flames from really taking off. So that for what seemed like hours his lower parts went on burning till they were thoroughly consumed, and him screaming out to the people closest to the fire to stir up the sticks if they could, for pity's sake, and let the fire come to him above his middle, so that he could even begin to die. But what with the buzzing sparks and the hissing smoke, the crackling of green wood and the hellish din going on round about him – fiddlers and jugglers and drunkards, acrobats and balladeers – they got the wrong message altogether from the poor man's screams and they packed the wood all the tighter, over-stoking and slowing down the whole fucking business.

'It was awful – beyond anything imaginable. The flames just went on gnawing at his legs and roasting his lower portions with no effect whatever on the vital parts, so that he started leaping up and down in the blaze with a ghastly alacrity for an old man. Till the time came when he could leap no more because his legs were quite gone. How cruelly they'd botched the fire, those Oxford oafs who stood that day in front of Balliol, preaching at the man whose torments they'd so intensified and prolonged. Fucking inhuman bunglers! I wanted to tell them what should be done but I couldn't find my tongue in all that crowd and anyway I was nowhere near the front. I just stood there, gorgonised by what I saw.'

'I know, I know. What kind of fucking men were they?'

O! you are men of stones. Had I your tongues and eyes, I'd use them so that heaven's vault should crack.

'Meanwhile Ridley must have felt the bottom of the stake crumbling away to nothing and he was terrified he'd fall out of the fire only half burnt because he wailed out to the officers to pin him with their pikes to what was left of the stake. But they did fuck-all, the bastards.

"I can't burn!" he kept shrieking. "I can't burn! I can't burn!"

'At last somebody with half a brain in his head reached up with a pole and pulled the faggots away from the man's chest and a sudden tongue of flame shot upwards and a little to one side, and Ridley leaned himself as far to that side as he could stretch and into the flame, as though he were a starving man reaching after food. Not long after that a finger of flame touched the little cask of gunpowder that somebody – his brother-in-law, I think – had hung round his neck, and when that exploded in his face he stopped screaming and moved no more.

'It was just in time because less than a minute later the stake burnt right through and the upper half of Ridley fell out of the flames right down dead at Latimer's feet. Everybody could see that there was nothing there but charred black bone that separated itself from the upper half as soon as it fell. So a man had been burnt in half for his religion, who'd lit a candle in England that would never be put out, so Latimer had said. Latimer who'd laved himself in flame as though he were a lover taking a bath. Well, Ridley's candle still burns in this old head, I can tell you, though as to his religion I can say nothing. What I do say is that his killers were so God-inspired they couldn't even light a fucking fire. Another thing, when I walked back up here again it took me two days and I never spoke a single word to man or beast all the way.'

'God in heaven! How do you remember all that and stay sane?'

It was only a story. But I lived it, all right. And I reached out from where I was sitting and shielded my face from the fire for a moment. Reached out with my right hand to feel just a hundredth of the heat that had raged through Ridley's lower bones for uncountable agonies of time. Till he was roasted, marrow and all. Half a chestnut, blackened in the fire.

The very next year it was the turn of Cranmer who'd helped Henry in his big break with Rome but was forced to change his tune under Mary and recant. Cranmer too reached out with his right hand, only he plunged it right into the fire. As he stood among the faggots he held out the hand that had signed the recantation (before he'd regained his courage and recanted his recantation) and he kept the hand there in the flames till it was blistered and black, the hand that had signed and sinned, punishing it before the rest of his body, making it suffer first for its weakness and its fear. Then the queen's fire went on to punish all the other parts of Cranmer for his stubbornness in refusing to accept her Catholic credo. And as the torment took hold, that old familiar screaming started up again. Because no matter how right you are, or think you are, your rightness is in your mind, and it's not your mind they burn, it's your feet and legs and belly and bowels, and your heart and lungs and lips. And every last hair on your head. Till you're a charred and twisted cinder, a smoking ruin. It's your body that feels the pain of the fire, not your mind. Just keep your mind shuttered, that's all. The martyrs built themselves big wide windows in their souls and let the whole world see in. Honourable – and ill-advised. The martyrs have no voice in my plays. They did plenty screaming already. But silence – man, that's pure gold. Silence keeps a man alive. Keep your own counsel and you'll lie quiet in the earth one day and never know the flames.

3

'And get rid of those,' muttered Mistress Mine, bustling in and pointing to the chest in the corner. 'Are you needing stoked up, Master Francis? Apart from the wine, that is.'

Disapproval stood easily on her furrowed brow. Always did.

'Early in the day, I'll admit,' said Francis in his sweetest pudding voice, 'and all the more reason to take advantage of your kind offer. Wine and work do give an edge to appetite.'

'It's only the cold shoulder from yesterday, but maybe it will fire you up. What have you achieved?'

He spread his fat fingers.

'Well – Will's been reminiscing a bit.'

On came the frown, double helping of displeasure. And up came the beef, brought in by little Alison, nice little tits.

'Mustard?' Anne could always make an invitation sound like a reproach.

'Beef without mustard – '

Is like war without fire. The Henry Five plan of attack, to see old England through. Not a hunter's breakfast exactly but better than powdered beef, or horse food.

Anne ushered bewitching tits out of the room and out of my imagining, pointing again to the chest.

'Leave them to whoever you like but don't leave them here! I don't want them clogging up our life.'

Our life. Interesting expression. What life was that then? We never had a life together, not to speak of. Our life. After I'm gone is what she meant. How easily she dismissed me.

And out she went.

Francis fell on the meat like a maniac and filled up my glass in his good nature. I'll never eat meat again. Only after he'd gulped down a single forkful that would have stood my Sunday lunch did he burp, sit back a bit, and ask, 'What's in the chest?'

More than she thinks. My supply, stashed away. For a minute

there I thought we were in trouble.

I finished my glass, bent my elbow, and made more drinking motions, indicating the chest with a wink.

Down at the bottom.

'What's on top?'

The Arden hangings, that's all.

'What, painted cloths – in that wee box?'

In there.

'They'll be crushed to hell.'

Francis gobbled another gargantuan gobbet of beef, Harry Five dressing, washed it down with the best I'd got, and clumped over to the old oak chest to ferret for more.

Out came Dives and Lazarus.

'As I said, crushed to hell. What's she want rid of them for?'

You'll see. Spread it out a moment.

'Pretty crude, isn't it?'

Dives was the rich bastard. Not unlike you, Francis.

'Do me a favour, Will. I may have a paunch but he's got a pie-shop!'

Dives sits sumptuously in a waterfall of purple, and with a purple glass raised to his purple lips. The table groans before him, a longship of delicacies overloaded to sinking – whole beasts gone to the spit. His dogs crouch at his knee, snapping at the scraps as they fall.

'Crumbs? They're fucking tennis balls! What this man wasted would have fed a colony of lepers.'

And he didn't give a fart for the leprous beggar lying at his gates.

'So this was your introduction to art, Will.'

That was Lazarus.

'Hardly Holbein, is it?'

All the better for it. Cloths and woodcuts and Coventry capers – they did the business for a young boy. Close to comic, don't you think? That thin line dividing tragedy and travesty, laughter and horror.

'Made an impression on you.'

Still does. I always noticed how nobody pays any attention to him, he's just too ugly for words. Even the flunkeys avert their cold faces from the hailstorm of boils that have landed on him, striking him from head to foot as he lies there, flung in the gutter. Only the dogs come and lick his sores.

'Makes you want to yell into the ears of this rich idle bugger, doesn't it?'

Take physic, pomp! Expose thyself to feel what wretches feel, that thou may'st shake the superflux to them and show the heavens more just!

'But he just keeps on stuffing himself.'

Every bite damnation. You shouldn't wolf your food, Francis.

Even holding up the cloth he couldn't stay away from the trough.

'You should talk. You always wolfed it down. You always liked to pack it away.'

I had an excuse.

Francis tried to snort and choked instead.

Too busy scribbling. Never ate properly.

'Well, he got his come-uppins, I see.'

Yes, you can see God's justice plain in the picture, plain as that boozy Bardolph nose on your face. And you can see how clever God was to invent death, the great gateway and reverser. Because although this poor bugger could never get through the rich man's gates, death was his pathway to paradise, and the rich bastard's into hell.

'Very neat.'

Yes, there's Lazarus, cleansed of his sores, lying high in Abraham's bosom. And there's Dives lying now at the bottom of the picture, as Lazarus had done, just inside the gates.

'But now it's the gates of hell.'

As you say; a nice reversal. And a clever parallel too, because it shows you that Dives' house was really a kind of hell all along, like Macbeth's. All this time he's been damning himself.

'And now the flames are licking at his lower portions, the fat fucker.'

Like dogs eating him alive.

'Forever.'

That's the frightening thing, and that's why it scared me, the absolute fixity of it. A play breaks up – but a picture stays the same. It never goes away.

'So Dives burns in the flames.'

Burns on. For ever and ever. Just like Ridley.

The thought didn't stop Francis tucking in.

'Do you think hell's a fable, Will?'

Hell on earth isn't. But according to those papists, when that keg of powder went off in Ridley's face, it wasn't the finish for him, it was simply the signal for the lighting of the eternal flame. The poor bastard's sufferings weren't over, they were only just beginning. And they would never end, never. Hell is forever.

'Jesus, let's call up old Marlowe. I think we'll become necromancers – and atheists.'

They'll burn you for that too. No, the safest way forward is to provide for the poor. Ten pounds to the poor of Stratford, write it down.

'Ten pounds! There's no need to go mad!'

It's modest and you know it. Do as I say.

'Don't take it that much to heart, Will. It's only a picture, a story.'

It's more than that.

'It's not worth ten pounds. And ten pounds is not modest.'

Item, I give and bequeath unto the poor of Stratford aforesaid ten pounds.

'That'll come later on. We're going in circles here.'

No, we're getting somewhere. Make a note of it, go on, note it down. We'll get the order right anon. This is only a draft.

'Well, it did haunt you, didn't it?'

Like the moth to the arras, like the fly to the flame, hovering and enthralled, I kept coming back to it, sneaking into the room. Old Henry used to point to it and came out with the same line every time.

'Behold the rich fucker! Fallen in purple and shorn of his glory, eaten now by the flames, the glutton consumed!'

'Yes, that would have appealed to the old bugger.'

And yet, you know Francis, let me tell you something curious. Dives was the one I felt for, not poor Lazarus, licked by dogs.

'Well, you always saw the other side of things – too many sides, if you ask me.'

Ah, but look at Lazarus now, clothed in purple and ringed by the radiance of eternity, he'd become a mere abstraction to me, an indifference, the apotheosis of an ending.

'You're losing me. Why don't you eat something?'

It's simple, Francis. He'd been a ragged beggar all his life, he'd no distance left to fall, his only path lay upwards – and that was no spectacle. It's the downward path that impresses. The Hell trajectory.

The higher the man rises the harder he falls. And when he falls, he falls like Lucifer. Never to rise again. That's tragedy.

'Hell trajectory, tragedy! Are you going to eat what's on that plate or not, old man?'

Francis had done the rummaging and came up with a grunt from the bottom of the chest with one of the burgundies, clandestinely wrapped in another of the hangings. I always knew my hoard was safe in there. Anne hated those cloths and wouldn't go near them. They were Ardens for a start, and she had a thing about my mother, thinking that I had a thing about her too – a different thing. But as to the cloths themselves, it wasn't their crudity that offended her – she never had an eye for art anyway – it was their next-worldliness. Anne was always of this world – doesn't like to be reminded of what's to come. That's why she'll stay safely out of the way, till the will's made out. Whenever that may be, with Francis now making for trough number two, fork at the ready. They call him Francis the fork because of his fancy for that entirely unnecessary tool.

'Are you sure now?'

It'll only go to waste.

'You never kept dogs, did you, Will?'

They lick lepers' sores. And worse things.

'Well, if you're quite certain – '

Go on, get it into your belly, you roasted Manningtree ox –

'You elf-skin.'

You sheath.

'You tailor's yard.'

You dried neat's-tongue.

'You stock-fish.'

Bed-presser.

'Bow-case.'

Horseback-breaker.

'You always win. Hand it over anyway.'

Aren't you forgetting something? Glug glug. A fair exchange.

'What a man for Bacchus.'

And for Venus in my time.

'No more o' that, Master Shakespeare. We're respectable men now, doing the right thing, parcelling out your possessions. What's this one?'

Ah, that's the other Lazarus. Hold it up. I'll talk you through it.

'I thought you would.'

That's the Lazarus who died, and made Jesus cry, causing the angels to weep.

'Tears of heaven.'

Sublime. But Jesus was so crushed by grief, he did what each one of us would gladly do, we'd do it in a twinkling if only we could – he brought his dead friend back to life.

'Quite a crowd come to watch the show, I see.'

Wouldn't you, Francis? I wish I'd been there. I'd have given anything.

'Brrr! Not for me, thank you. Morbid stuff. A gathering of ghouls.'

Not a whit, Francis, don't you see? This man's been among the dead, he's been among worms and stars, he's known the secrets of the grave, the undiscovered country –

'From whose bourne no traveller returns.'

And now a traveller has returned. And he's come back trailing clouds of glory, the veils of an unknowable mystery.

'That's got nothing to do with it, it's sheer spectacle, that's all. That's why it appealed to you.'

You're not altogether wrong. It's the greatest show on earth, the loftiest spectacle of all time. The crowds have gathered in the place of tombs.

'Bit of a blur to me. Where's my spectacles?'

And yes look here, some of Lazarus's friends are remonstrating with Jesus. Master, we beg you, think what you're about to do. We know you can walk on water, change water into wine, still the restless wave, feed five thousand. But this isn't a case of deafness or lameness, leprosy, demonic possession, loss of sight, this is different. The man is gone, he's no more, he's dead and rotten, three days buried. And in these temperatures, even in the coolness of the tomb, his flesh will be putrid already. He'll be stinking.

'Pooh! They have a point.'

But Jesus presses right on through the graves till he comes to the doors of Lazarus's tomb. Just look at the audience reaction, even in this vulgar patch of daubery!

'Ah, the audience! Where would you be without them?'

Some are fanning themselves because of the heat, some holding their handkerchiefs to their noses, one or two averting their eyes.

'Exceedingly realistic.'

But most are straining to get a good view.

'Important for a spectator, especially if he's paid for a good seat.'

Standing room only, a groundling's gala.

'An on-the-ground event.'

Deeper than that. While from on high, sure enough, the angels rain down golden tears, because Jesus has wept.

'Jesus wept. Hear the pennies raining. Always kept an eye on your audience, didn't you, Will?'

Never mind about the audience. Look at these splendid sepulchral gates, stuck so absurdly in the middle of this desert.

'Out of place, you have to say.'

Should have been a rock, a boulder, not this blazing cathedral. But never mind.

'One door's as good as another.'

Up steps Jesus, strikes them hard, they swing open, and he shouts the famous words, 'Lazarus, come forth!'

Scrolling out of his mouth, look, in this lurid red paint, just like blood. You can feel the force of it, booming out, like a burst artery.

'Right up your bum!'

Shall we say groin?

'Fit to give you the shits.'

I always felt the thrill of it, though.

Lazarus, come forth!

Silence. Every eye riveted to that black hole in the rock, behind the yawning gates, a black mouth winding down into the gullet of the grave –

'Steady on, old man.'

That brutal gash in the earth's crust, into which we all go eventually, unwilling emigrants to the unknown region, where all identities disappear, all nations meet and merge. They're all staring into it now, expectant, unbelieving. They know very well that nothing ever comes back up out of that blackness.

Lazarus, come forth!

Nothing.

Nothing will come of nothing. Speak again.

But Jesus doesn't. The crowd has already relaxed a little, knowing it's unreal, facing the truth that we all have to face, following the first numbness, the shock of loss. And those wild ideas that the loved one is still in some sense around us, quite close by, next door, perched on the clouds perhaps, or deep in our hearts, keeping an eye on us.

'It's hard to let go.'

Hard? It's impossible. But there's no option, is there, when even Jesus can't raise the dead. Accept the obvious then. This is one miracle that isn't going to come off. Death really is the end. They're never coming back, are they? And at the end of all reflection maybe there is something almost soothing about this thought, and the absolute ordinariness of it. Dead men rise up never. And in an uncertain world we can even take comfort from that one certainty, death's complete finality.

'Not me. I'm for life and hope. Give me a bit more of that beef. That's what I call comfort.'

And then it happens, doesn't it? A white speck at the end of the long black tunnel. A trick of the eye? No, it's not one of those dancing specks bedevilling the brain, it's something steady in the eye, a faint muslin flimsiness in the distance, but getting bigger, coming closer.

Look, my lord, it comes!

'Angels and ministers of grace defend us!'

That line again, Francis? Twice in one morning.

'Oh, I can see him now.'

I remember when I first saw him.

A blind white figure, bound from head to foot. A blind bandaged figure, cocooned like a caterpillar, swathed like a mummy. Lazarus born again, wrapped in swaddling clothes, Lazarus in his birthday shroud, stepping out gingerly into the bright new sunshine, blinking in bewilderment when they unwrapped the bandages. Uncertain and awkward about his sudden guest appearance on this great stage of fools, this unexpected encore. And entirely without words for the occasion.

'God, what a script you could have given him, Will!'

Yes, and to my eternal disappointment there he was, speechless in time, rescued from eternity without a syllable to spend.

'I'd rather have syllabub.'

And why? Because everybody was so stunned by the event, nobody actually remembered to ask the most momentous question of all time. Not a soul took it into his head to put to this newly returned traveller to the next world the ultimate query, the riddle of existence, the enigma of the universe –

'I know what's coming.'

Lazarus, what was it like – being dead?

'Now why didn't I think of that?'

Returning travellers are usually more than happy to share their experiences, and the stay-at-homes always greedy to hear them. But on this great occasion nobody asked – and he never said.

'Maybe it didn't matter to him – the undiscovered country and all that.'

Maybe not, now that he'd come home again to the sights and shapes and sounds and scents of the dear old earth that we all know. I told you, he'd traded secrets with worms and stars, he'd heard the harmony of immortal souls. But now he was just glad to put it back on, the muddy vesture of decay, to be grossly closed in again, not to hear that impossibly perfect music.

'Maybe the next world is – well, boring.'

Happiness can be.

'But supposing – just supposing somebody did ask the big question that day.'

Thou comest in such a questionable shape that I will speak to thee. O! answer me: let me not burst in ignorance, but tell why thy canonized bones, hearsed in death, have burst their cerements, why the sepulchre, wherein we saw thee quietly inurned, hath oped his ponderous and marble jaws to cast thee up again? What may this mean, dead corpse?

'And maybe Lazarus was not allowed to answer.'

But that I am forbid to tell the secrets of my prison-house, I could a tale unfold whose lightest word would harrow up thy soul. But this eternal blazon must not be to ears of flesh and blood.

'Like state secrets.'

Like the music of the spheres, which we're too gross to hear. Like Bottom's dream, untranslatable to a fool. Or by an ass.

'Or it's even possible that scripture got it wrong, missed something out. I mean, the bible wasn't actually written by God, with pen and ink. Scribes did it. And if they were anything like the scribes in my office...'

Say no more, Francis. Suffice it to say, the moment was missed, the great opportunity neglected. It remained unexplored, that hidden space behind the stage, where the dead actors go to, once they've made their final exits, the unseen dimension of the great globe.

'Talking of actors, Will – '

The drama of Lazarus stayed frozen on the cloth. But I'll tell you something, Francis. Now, all these years later, as I approach the answer to the question myself, I know that if it had been chronicled that day, it would have spelled the death of all drama and the end of all art. I'd never have written a single line.

'How do you mean?'

Simple, Francis. There would have been nothing left to know.

'Well, I don't know about that. What good does it do you to know about death? I mean, what use is it?'

The ultimate subject. The only subject.

'Oh, come off it! Philosophy, medicine, astronomy – the law!'

Too service and illiberal for me.

'Oh God, I know what's coming next.'

This study fits a mercenary drudge –

'Who aims at nothing but external trash!' Francis pleased with his quotation.

'And speaking of trash, how many more of these monstrosities are there in the chest?'

Nine. There were eleven in all.

'Jesus Christ! Right, back they go! Any more burgundy in there? By the time we go through one wee chest, moth and rust will have corrupted your entire estate!'

Or you'll have eaten and drunk me out of house and home, you huge bombard of sack!

'You leek!'

You trunk of humours!

'You radish!'

You bolting-hutch of beastliness, you swollen parcel of dropsies, you stuffed cloak-bag of guts –

'All right, all right, I can't compete! But I congratulate you, Will. You never over-spice your meat.'

I had enough of that in London. You said something about actors a minute ago.

'Later. One thing at a time. Who are these cloths to go to? Decide, quick.'

No, you heard what she said. Don't mention them in particular. They can be lumped in with the rest of the domestic clutter.

'Which is going where? Be specific.'

Item, all the rest of my goods, chattels, leases, plate, jewels, and household stuff whatsoever, after my debts and legacies paid, and my funeral expenses discharged, I give, devise and bequeath to my son-in-law, John Hall, gent., and my daughter Susanna his wife.

'Hang on, this will's back to front and upside down. It's arse over tit!'

Never mind. And add on there, after John and Susanna – *whom I ordain and make executors of this my last will and testament.*

'Well, that's something settled. Now let's get back to the beginning.'

The beginning. Ah yes, of course. That's what I was telling you about.

4

'They got you going though, those cloths.'

They were silent theatre, the first step on the road to the real thing.

'A long long trail a-winding, friend.'

And yet, suddenly now, it seems short.

'That's life. Not short on example though, were you?'

I don't know why everybody doesn't become a playwright. All those images that were fed in from infancy: the biting on a forbidden fruit, a brother's brains bright on a sudden club –

'The dogs licking a leper's sores.' Francis put Lazarus to bed and brought out more burgundy.

They didn't lick Jezebel though.

'And the angels combing their golden hair and harps.'

And just beneath them, just under that lovely rain of tears, a man sitting naked in the ash-pit, scraping the boils from his skin with shards of broken pottery.

'Stop it, Will. Still, it taught you the patience of Job, I suppose.'

Had it pleased heaven to try me with affliction –

'Rained all kinds of sores and shames on your bare head?'

Well, I had my share of those.

'Where it doesn't show, I hope.'

Nor in the heart, nor in the head. Fancy's like the fires of Venus – bred elsewhere. And I didn't lack tutors. I must have been fed the complete works of God by the time I was three, narrated on the Snitterfield heights by a crusty old uncle. That was world history as far as I was concerned, starting with Adam – God's chronicles handed down like tablets, complete with Henry's catechisms.

'What were they?'

– What was the first corpse in the world?

Its blood bubbling up from the ground like a voice. Murderer! A brother's murder. What if this hand –

– Who were swifter than eagles and stronger than lions?

Bellona's bridegrooms, slain on the high places, struck full of spears, left on Mount Gilboa, unburied, too gorgeous for the grave.

– Who was the death-kisser?

Hanging from an elder tree, the kiss and the corpse, his blood-money lying scattered where it fell, thirty pieces of silver, strewn like Christ's tears to buy the potter's field. If it were done when 'tis done –

'Not exactly history without tears.'

Who'd be without tears? There are tears for things, Francis. And if there weren't, the actors would be out of a job.

'Let's talk about actors, Will – '

And somewhere on the other side of the Snitterfield clouds sat God, the owner of the great globe, apart from it all, transcending child-time, transcending all time, toasting his toes in front of the white flame of eternity. He was waiting for history to end, so that he could stop the play.

'Ah. And then what?'

The serious business. Away with days, weeks and months, the old rags of time, and in with God's great alternative –

'What's that?'

The alternative to time, the new scheme. Starting with resurrection.

'Do you believe in resurrection, Will? I mean – really, seriously, believe?'

That's a big question. And it filled my infancy with even bigger ones – the mind-bogglers, about how it was all to be achieved, in practical terms. I mean, difficult enough even if everybody died in one piece. But what was to happen to the leg you lost at Cadiz? to the head spiked on London Bridge, peeled clean of skin by the blistering air, whose birds had extracted the eyes like snails? Where were the bowels burnt by the Tyburn fire, the quartered criminals, the leg left in London, the arm sent to Wales, the gutted torso to Scotland, the discarded genitals chewed by some dog? Where was that hound now? And if you'd been drowned off the Azores and passed through the stomach of the ravined salt-sea shark – by what unimaginable feat would God re-assemble these fair sailors who'd ended their navy days as nothing more identifiable than fish excrement, a drift of shark-shit floating in the blind and listless sea? These were teasers that tore the brain in two.

'I note you haven't answered my question, though.'

What question was that, Francis?'

'The resurrection question.'

I believe I've answered it.

'Missed that somehow.'

In my plays.

'Oh, very clever. If you think I'm going to trail all the way to London – '

Some of them are in print.

'Indeed they are. And now, if we can return to the matter of your will, old friend, I'd like to get something in place in the first paragraph, if you don't mind, something about that resurrection you're so anxious to avoid.'

Anxious to avoid? *Au contraire*, Francis. I'm all for resurrection. It's death I'm anxious to avoid.

'Anxious to avoid committing yourself to the concept, is what I mean, as you well know, old fox. I just want to get the formalities sorted out. Can we say, for example, *First, I commend my soul into the hands of God my Creator, hoping and assuredly believing through the only merits of Jesus Christ my Saviour, to be made partaker of life everlasting.* How does that sound?'

Sounds fine to me, Francis, if that's what you want to say.

'It's what you want to say that matters.'

Does it? Well, I'll go along with it. And can you add in there – *and my body to the earth whereof it is made.*

'After *everlasting*?'

After *everlasting.* That's the one part I'm sure about, the earth bit – not the everlasting bit.

'Good. We've made a proper start. After all, there are rules, Will, there is convention.'

Long live convention.

'Amen. And speaking of convention, now that you've assured me of the place God occupied in your young life, how much do you propose to leave to the church, and in what form?'

By this time the fat man was mopping up the final drops of onion juice, and he put the last question to me with the remnants of a loaf poised at the open portals of his mouth.

The church, Francis. I'm glad you asked that question.

The portals widened into a smile of anticipation.

As for the church, well now, the church can have that last crust of bread – if you can spare it, that is.

The crust – it would have stuffed a goose – disappeared in a twinkling and the next words came out obscure and oniony.

'What's that you say? Nothing to the church?'

Not a penny. And don't speak with your mouth full. Or breathe on me like that.

'Oh, but you know, it's customary for a good man to leave even a small sum.'

Am I a good man?

'Your credit's good, as your old Shylock would say. Look here, Will, it's no skin off my nose – '

Redder than ever.

'But I think it would look good – '

In as much as ye have done it unto one of the least of these my brethren –

'Ye have done it unto me. Yes, I know. But *le bon Dieu* wasn't thinking of a will. It's quite traditional.'

Is it really?

'Yes.'

Traditional occasional or traditional common?

'Well – '

Ten pounds to the poor of Stratford, that takes care of it. Let the poor be my church – they're always there. Churches come and go. They change their principles. They change their politics. They've been known to kill.

'Are the poor so pure?'

Sheep and chickens, harmless on the whole. I've known better poor folk than prelates.

'So you're quite – '

Not a penny, not a penny.

'I'd better make a note of that – lest there be questions later.'

Note it down, Francis, if you will insist on wasting my ink and paper. But no mention of the church in the final deed, understood?

'I've got it. But I'm noting it down.'

Give Francis Collins a crust of bread and a stoup of wine and he'll make notes on anything from here to doomsday, and on doomsday too. He'd make a good recording angel – if he weren't too fat to fly.

5

My glass shall not persuade me I am old – so I once wrote, not believing a word of it. Now I can barely believe it's really me in there, looking back out at what's left of myself.

'I need to make a great pee,' said Francis, putting the quill into the pot.

No running brook, I'm afraid, under the house of easement, but I like to keep it sweet as my parlour. That's another thing I had enough of in London – houses not of easement but of excrement.

Francis went off to point his thing at the privy – to pluck a rose, as he politely put it in little Alison's hearing. Her mistress came in behind her to watch her take away the clutter, Falstaff having cleaned up both trenchers, and to watch me watching her – with sixty winters besieging the furrowed brow. The sight of those pert tits and pouting belly makes me regretful, not lustful, all the more conscious of this dreadful physical decline.

I got myself out of bed somehow and tottered over to the reflector, lifting the nightshirt to have another look at the poor bare forked animal. Off, off, you lendings! Jesus God, was that really me in there, trapped in that battered carcass? When you look at what confronts you, what you're made of now, the crow feet and hen's neck, the sagging sandbag belly with the sand running out, the shrunk shanks – yes, this is the sixth age all right, come too soon and almost over – then your ending is despair. And talking of endings, as Francis would say, behold that shrivelled radish, well past its use for the likes of Alison. And those hands, that tangle of blue roots dangling from corky arms, can you imagine them cupping her firm and pristine tits, as smooth as monumental alabaster – ?

'That's horrible!'

Francis came clumping back in and looked over my shoulder into the mirror.

'You're all the colours of the Pharaohs, my boy – a mummy gone rotten!'

Not a pretty sight, is it?

'Put your shirt down – you'll crack the glass and give us all seven years' bad luck!'

I haven't got seven *weeks*.

'And get back into bed – you won't get better by staring at your willie!'

Better? Who said anything about getting better? I'm like Percy here – dust, and food for worms.

Francis chimed in with me theatrically.

'For worms, brave Percy, for worms!'

You can't be around a playwright without picking up a line or two. Even if you're a lawyer, more into venison than verse.

Well, what am I but a corpse waiting to be washed?

'Here we go again. Call for cock-robin – '

Don't misquote.

'And the sexton.'

And don't mention that old bastard.

'What's wrong with him?'

Sextons in general, I mean.

'Somebody's got to shovel us into eternity.'

Yes, and some of them do it with relish. The one I knew really loved his job.

'Might as well be happy at your work.'

He gave me nightmares.

'A frightener of little boys?'

Terrifying. He laid it on. I can still see him, I can see him now among skulls and crosses, standing chest-high in some poor bugger's new-dug pit, munching his bread-and-bacon break –

'Oh, now that goes round my heart! A bit of bread and bacon would go down nicely!'

Stuffing it in with fingers ringed by worms, the wet sexton – he was always black and damp and smelly, as if he were made out of kirkyard mould. I didn't think he was made of flesh at all. A thing of earth.

'I bet you just couldn't stay away.'

How well you know me. Attracted by what appalled, creeping even slower than to school, sidling up that long avenue of limes, on either side of which lay the long dead, the fresh dead of Stratford, scared shitless I was, but too scared to stay away. And there it was.

'There what was?'

The sacred storehouse of my predecessors, Stratford's anonymous dead, and guardian of their bones.

'Eh?'

The charnel-house.

'Ah. Can't get that bacon out of my mind now.'

The grass was seamless, like human flesh. But two or three times a week – oftener in winter – the sexton came along and unseamed it, unceremoniously, with a grunt and a curse and a fart or two, ripping it up with rude pickaxe and wounding spade, breaking into the sombre honeycomb beneath, invading what had seemed inviolable green.

'Got new guests coming in,' he'd say, scarring the earth with a shrug and a song and a fart gratis, 'got new tenants for this here house, got to get rid of the old ones, see? Present incumbetents been in over long.'

'Sounds cheery enough.'

And the evicted bones he trundled over to the charnel-house and flung them onto the existing pile, just like a log-pile blown down in a gale. There must have been a few sextons before that old bugger, and a huge mound of bones had accumulated there, a cadaverous army, ready to rattle into action as soon as God gave the doomsday word. My feet drew me a thousand times to this awful edifice, protesting every step of the way, and my eye came up close to the rusty iron grille.

'Charming habits you had.'

Five years old, and all those black eye-sockets staring at you, like big black raisins in a cake, only they reeked of earth.

'Well, they would.'

Maybe that was it, the fact that death seemed so mundane, so deprived of metaphor.

'You've just said – raisins in a cake.'

You know what I mean. None of the softening euphemisms of art, transfiguring scripture. Death as a sleep is attractive enough, after all – balm of hurt minds, sore labour's bath, the sleeping and the dead are but as pictures. The undiscovered country carries the lure of exploration, the long journey –

'Sounds tiring. Balm and baths are all right.'

Even an everlasting cold feels bearable in its own way.

'Curable with an infinite supply of friar's balsam and plenty of tot, eh?'

But the charnel-house had none of that, Francis. It reduced the king of terrors to a heap of mortal rubble, whole generations jumbled in an impossible jigsaw. Impossible to believe that those yellowed shanks had once leapt astride stallions and spurred them into battle, had parted in bed to wrap themselves around a lover's thrusting buttocks, a slender waist –

'Hey, steady on!'

You couldn't even say what sex they'd been, or known. And now this boneyard – showing you what you really were.

'Frighten you to death.'

I died a thousand deaths at the charnel-house door, picturing myself on the other side of that grille, a bundle of bones, shut in there one day by the farting sexton, subject to his contempt.

'Not worth a fart now,' he'd say.

'Surprising choice of image.'

And he'd toss my skull aside as I'd seen him lob many another out of the ground and send it rolling over the turf – not worth a fart, my lord!

'Suiting the action to the word, no doubt. Letting it rip.'

The sexton himself would never die. He'd see me into the ground, all right. He was Death with spade and pickaxe, and bread and bacon for breakfast.

'Stop talking about bacon!'

He was too busy to die.

I remember once I stood there clasping the grille, my nose between the bars, my eyeballs out on threads, staring into those empty sockets, and he crept up behind me, the bastard, pinned me to the bars, thrust the rusty old key up my nostrils and threatened to turn it in the gate and lock me in for the night.

'How'd you fancy that, young sir, eh? Shut in there all night long with all that lot – them as has seen the secrets of the grave and are raging sore at having been torn up from their eternity, where they belong. Yes, I tell you, each one of them bones is filled with rage. Look at how they be all jammed up. There's a powerful pile of anger packed in there, I tell you. How d'you think you'd get on, all the hours from dark till dawn, with all them spirits screeching like mandrakes at you? My God, boy, I think you'd take up one of them big yellow shanks and dash your desperate brains out long afore light, that's what I think. If not I reckon you'd be white-haired by sunrise and a raving bedlamite to boot!'

'Nice man.'

And he laughed so much he let loose a whole string of farts and let me go, hugging his sides while I ran for the gates, terrified. Ran all the way to Asbies to ask old Agnes if what the gravedigger had said was true. Uncle Henry butted in.

'Don't you pay any heed to that old farter! Time turns us all to shit, boy, and that demented freak has spent so many hours shovelling it, his brains have turned already! Forget him – and eat up your mutton! Bones without marrow in them got no strength to harm you.'

'Marrow. Why do you always come back to food?'

But Agnes knew differently. She knew well enough what went on with the tormented souls of those who'd been denied a decent burial. Murderers and suicides and such like of the damned, buried at crossroads with stakes through their black hearts. Or rattling in chains on lonely gibbets. Or thrown to the winds and waves. Spirits like these wandered the earth forever, like Cain, with not a grave to call their own. It was an alternative hell. Worse perhaps – even hell is preferable to no place at all. You can get used to any place in time. But to have not even your own two paces of the vilest earth to lie down in. The old sexton was right. You could hear the yells of exiles like these on dark nights, wild on the winter wind, and it froze your blood to hear them. Seamen had heard them shrieking over the waves, howling like sea-wolves in the grey mists, making their ships shiver from topmast to keel, causing the helm to tremble and the rudder to turn to stone. 'Stay away from the charnel-house then,' said Agnes, 'be a good child, and make sure you earn a good burial. Safe from the spade of some rude knave in centuries unborn.'

'And did you?'

Stay away? What do you think? But when your bones lie defenceless in their grave, when you're prey to a posterity that knows nothing of you except your faded name and maybe not even that, when brazen tombs fall foul of cormorant devouring time, and brass eternal slave to mortal rage – what can you do to escape the fate of the exile and the ultimate indignity of the charnel-house? Good friend, for Jesus' sake forbear... What can a man do? What more can he do, Francis, than to curse the spade that stirs his dust? The hand that moves his bones.

'What are you getting at, Will?'

I'm saying I want provision made here and now for what happens to my bones.

'What sort of provision?'

I don't want to be dug up again – simple as that. I don't want to be knocked about the bonce with a dirty shovel. Keep those sextons and their spades away from me. Make a note of it.

'You can't put that in a will.'

Why not – if it's my will? Go on, note it down.

'Let's ask for a bit of bacon for lunch.'

Stop changing the subject. Write it down, what I asked you. I'm never to be disinterred.

'All right, but that's a separate arrangement. It has no part in the will.'

Then we'd better discuss the separate arrangement.

'Later. Let's get the will done first. We've a long way to go. You shouldn't have got onto all that scary stuff.'

Oh, it was just something else to give me the shits when the storms over Stratford made the flames burn blue and ghosts were sticky as Snitterfield snot on a frosty morning. Tangible, as a whore's tail, those stinking spooks, old Agnes swore. You could smell them, taste them, coming up out of the ground like worms from their beds in all weathers, the dead of Warwickshire that refused to lie down but burst their cerements like Lazarus –

'Not him again!'

And came at me and kept on coming and wouldn't let me be, revisiting the glimpses of the moon, making night hideous.

'Lie down? It's you that won't let the poor buggers sleep!'

Not that they'd open a chink a whisper wide to reveal an inkling of their immortality. Of what went on in the dark. Stones have been known to move and trees to speak, but the spirits of Stratford kept the secrets of the next world, the merest whiff of which, Agnes said, would freeze thy young blood – the old bird's very words – make thy two eyes, like stars, start from their spheres, thy knotted and combined locks to part, and each particular hair to stand on end, like quills upon the fretful porpentine. Lazarus kept his mouth shut.

'So they kept their mouths shut.'

So the occulted secrets of eternity stayed unkennelled. Not one word. Not even from my father, decades later, after his death, when I dreamt about him, dreaming I was a boy again, and he came to me in sleep – a spirit or a dream? – and for a second lifted up his head, as if he would speak, whisper a secret to me in the dark.

'Only a dream, I'd say.'

It was a figure like my father. These hands are not more like. But even then the morning cock crew loud and at the sound it shrunk in haste away and vanished from my sight.

'An apparition?'

Who knows? It faded on the crowing of the cock. Agnes said that on Christmas Eve the cock crows all night long. 'And then,' she said, 'no spirit can walk abroad, the nights are wholesome, then no planets strike, no fairy takes, nor witch hath power to charm, so hallowed and so gracious is the time.'

'Will, you're on another planet yourself. Come out of it, do you hear me?'

Do ghosts feel the cold, granny?

'Go to sleep, Will.'

6

Sleep? I'll sleep soon enough. And long enough.

But sometimes it was impossible to sleep in those days, for sheer fear and cold, when ghosts whooed me out of bed in the long nights and I had to run outside in the dark to see to the needs of nature. Picture me if you will, sweet Francis, should you feel sufficiently cruel –

'No problem.'

Snivelling in the winter shithouse up at Snitterfield at night, when there wasn't the sliver of a moon to light up my solitary stooling.

'Ooh, don't make me shiver!'

And the icicles glittered wickedly in the starlight, hanging from the privy roof.

'Good grief!'

Night after night they'd lengthened in the fast frosts and I had to duck under them in the end to get to the thunderbox, where I sat and shat at glacier speed, picturing the daggers getting longer by the turd, imprisoning me like a portcullis before I'd done.

'Castle Crap. Jesus.'

Spring would come around the corner like a green turnkey, blowing on the icicles with the breath of the bull, dissolving the freezing bars – but only my skeleton would be found in there, straddling the shithole, and the surprised flies would buzz out through the cage of bones like black sparks from a cold hell.

'The curse of fancy, Will. Why didn't you just finish your crap!'

Not all craps were as bad as that, though winter shits were dire.

'Suppose we change the subject.'

Let me take you briefly through what I would class as a good one, notwithstanding winter.

'I don't believe I'm hearing this!'

You are.

'Posterity at least will be spared – unless you want your craps itemized!'

A dim dawn over Snitterfield, an angry smudge of blood on the skyline, the stars still crackling in the sky, and me shivering on the throne, hidden behind the portcullis as usual, watching those icy teeth, catching the stars, the glint of day. A poetic moment, my masters.

'Nothing so poetic as a privy.'

Anyway I don't have the chance to commune with nature. Just as I screw up my eyes and draw in my clouded breath for the big one, there's a loud hurly-burly and a certain scene takes place, of a low bucolic nature.

'Which you will now describe.'

The screams that shattered the sanctity of the privy council and ruined my concentration issued from the right hefty lungs of no less a lass than Marian the milkmaid. Who was being chased as usual by Dick the shepherd, the randiest bastard in Snitterfield. She to her milch kine and he to his sheep each morning, but their beasts sometimes had to wait until the beast with two backs had been seen to first. Not this morning, though, it was too ball-freezing for bull-work, and they settled instead for this wild Arcadian cavort. Dick caught up with Marian right at the shithouse door, snapped off one of my prison bars – which made me blink but improved my view – and grabbing her round the waist, thrust the glittering icicle all the way up her skirt.

Scream? I doubt if a higher note were ever sounded on this planet, nor emitted even by the spheres. Or their driving angels.

'There you are, stick that one in your oven – and that'll be quicker than a sea-coal fire for a nice hot brew!'

Marian screamed again and jabbed at his groin with her knee.

'I'll melt *you* down in a minute, you fucker!'

But Dick had parried many a pass of that sort and took advantage of her one leg to tip her off balance and send her flying backward among last month's frozen leaves. Her skirt flew up, her legs spread wide and I caught my first ever sight of pussy. Scarcely an ideal or expected setting for this gratuitous glimpse of the gates of life, but young as I was, my prick tingled. And there was something else: I felt my whole will plume up, felt godlike, sat there like the Ancient of Days, unseen by Adam and Eve, and the man about to know the woman. A far cry from the voice in the garden taking the cool of the day. But I, Will Shakespeare, was their Lord God and I knew her already, better than Dick, because she didn't *know* that I'd seen her, seen that crushed fruit between her thighs, and that I'd hold it there forever, the apple of my eye, for memory's the warder of the brain, you know. Even now it thrills me, like the first shiver of the morning air, like a whore's hand clutching your balls.

Dick, following his name and nature, opted to go all the way after all. He threw himself on Marian, baring his backside, despite December, but she flapped her skirt back down and stabbed at his groin with the icicle.

'Fuck off, Prickdick! Come any closer and I'll trim your yard to a fucking inch! I'll give you a crook to shag your sheep with!'

Her laughter rose shivering to the stars and she ran off, glowing with the sunrise and her youth. I blew on my numb knees and rose stiffly into the stars. My prick was on fire with the frost and my balls were bound in brass for Marian alone. I stretched. Snitterfield was waking to its work, the same and only work it had known since the world began.

'Is that the end of that scene, Will?'

Yes.

'Pity. I was enjoying that.'

There's more background though.

'Very good. But warm it up.'

Ah, but it was a cold cold world in winter, cold enough to put out the fires of the robins, though their upturned breasts still embered in the snow, the last tired braziers of the year. Kettles froze overnight by the hearths, where the ash was turned to snow by morning. Cattle died on all fours, stopped dead in their tracks and traces, even the strongest – stalwart bulls gorgonized by winter. Fish were stilled in the iron streams, fish that glittered like Greek stars, ice-eyed, frozen in their courses. Huge oaks split with the overnight frost that was fleeter than lightning on its lethal feet – you could hear them going off, bursting like bombs in the night, echoing over the white tight rooftops, and the owl's inscrutable stare went wider in the moon.

A tough world, my masters.

But always it throbbed with life. I sat in the arctic chill, my lips two frozen roses, glued to my knees, my ears bitten to buggery. The frost shot up my behind like white fire and a brace of Russian gun-stones graced my groin. Even so it was a turning time for me. A time when the balls buzzed like a saw and the blood danced and sang, answering the angels. I had known Marian the milkmaid, known her like a god, better than Dick the shepherd, this bumpkin, this mere mortal, this man of mud. I had carnal knowledge of her. From the cool of the privy I, the Lord God, secret as a serpent, invisible as a voice, had known her through the keyhole. I had tingled to a billion tendrils, the universe reaching out to my tongue. And my tongue took root and sang. And the stars sang too.

'What was it they sang now?'

When icicles hang by the wall...

A fine song, a fair song, an old song of winter. I heard it in the breeze that blows from childhood. A song of icicles and logs and bitter winds. You know how it goes. The birds are pissed off, your feet and fingers frozen stiff, your robin reduced to a blue acorn, your nose is red raw, you're up to your knees in snow and sludge, can't hear a word the parson says for every other bugger coughing down the kirk. But there was a certain merriness in winter, outside the usual clutch of churchyard coughs and sudden graves. We kept red with labour and laughter, splitting our sides, splitting logs, hedging and ditching and dodging Uncle Henry. The hot poker sizzled in the jug of ale, Dick's sizzled in Marian and was dowsed – once too often – and by the time Plough Monday came in early January she hallooed his name to the reverberate hills, poor bugger, and the fields and forests rang with proclamations that Dick had done his ploughing early that year and for what wages – well, that would show soon enough. The wages of sin is death – and there's no death so hard as an unexpected marriage and a bellyful of bitter fruit. But that's the way the land lay. He'd tilled her and she'd cropped.

And a merry enough mating for a winter month that one was – followed by the sickly time, when Marian puked up with the lark and nightly pissed with the staring owl, and Dick's wick went down and burned as low as the sun's. But by Lady Day the sun had recovered from his winter sickness and everybody came out of doors to wish him well again. The men sowed their fields and the women their gardens, putting in lettuces and radishes, cucumbers and mustard, spinach, rosemary, sage and thyme, eyebright, bloodwort, liverwort, lavender – and loads of lovage too. It was the time of year when ladysmocks silvered the meadows and virgins' smocks lay bleached in the summer field. Marian bleached hers too – to brighten her ripening belly and to bewail her long forgotten virginity, if she'd ever had a virginity, who knows. And Dick, fast married, heard the cuckoo call for the first time with a difference. *Cuckoo, cuckoo. O, word of fear.* Unpleasing to a married ear.

Unpleasing to a prickdick perhaps. But nothing could compare with the pleasure of that first spring day when the starved cattle tasted the young grass. Or when the sheep took their first green mouthful of May. Summer's lease, my friend, hath all too short a date. Soon they went shorn and shivering into rainy July. Hay-making, harvest, the world a whirl of wheat and barley, and suddenly the cattle were dunging the stubble again and the butcher grinding his blade. Michaelmas gales stripped the acorns from the trees by quarterday, bringing the hogs gruntling round the trunks while we gathered in the berries.

So we yoked ourselves to the light, following it all the year round. We were the oxen of the sun. And I formed fellowships with flowers: daffodils that come before the swallow dares and take the winds of March with beauty; violets dim but sweeter than the lids of Juno's eyes or Cytherea's breath; pale primroses that die unmarried ere they can behold bright Phoebus in his strength, a malady most incident to maids; bold oxlips and the crown imperial; lilies of all kinds, the flower-de-luce being one; hot lavender, mints, marjoram, the marigold that goes to bed with the sun and with him rises weeping – I remember them all, remember them well, better than the sunless times, the flowerless times, when the gilded puddle lay on the land. That was the grisly time, the Martinmas, when the beasts were slaughtered for salting down and that old screaming and slithering started up all over again. Even the barrels of meat refused to keep quiet. They were packed hard with agony, a compression of sounds and struggles that never go away. No escape, no escape from the life of the land – you'd have to be invisible.

I tried it once. I was crying that day, I remember, sitting snivelling in the Snitterfield shithouse, don't ask me why, two days after Christmas it was, with the door shut fast on my bad temper, when uncle Henry put his eye to the chink and told me about the fernseed, to try to bring me out of my dumps.

'Can't see me, can you, young Will? But I can see you sitting there. How'd you like to have that power, then, eh? You can have it too if you search far and hard enough, today being St John's Day. If you can find fernseed today, you'll take on its powers and become invisible, you mark my words, lad, you'll see the whole world and stay unseen yourself, you'll be so secret you'll be able to hear folk think.

So I came out of the shithouse and combed the frozen fields

and forest flowers that day, sifting the snowdust with fingers that were flakes of fire and thumbs as numb as thunder, blue as devils they were, searching for green seeds under all that woven snow. Well done, old Henry – he got me out of the shitter, all right, and out of the house all day. And I stumbled home and fell asleep at once, and woke up not invisible but feeling a lot better, and wondering if you ever could be so invisible – able to hear men's thoughts, without them hearing you. No, you couldn't.

Or could you? Once I did achieve invisibility – of a kind. I was coming from the well one morning, earlier than anyone. A Snitterfield summer it was, the one that rounded Marian's belly, and only the blue larksong breaking the silence. That was the morning she came to wash herself, moving sleepily, as if in a pleasant dream, yawning and stretching, one hand rubbing her eyes, the other rumpling my hair as she passed me on her way to the water – 'Morning, young Will' – pulling off her smock as she went by, throwing it aside like a swimmer shaking off a wave. I turned and stared, taking in the naked Marian from the back as she bent over the well. The bucket came up with a clatter and a thump and she threw the water over her shoulders in a bright shawl of music. The droplets splashed my face and rang in my ears and I licked them up, each note sanctified by contact with the suddenly mysterious Marian. I'd never seen her like this before, never seen anyone so naked, and so I came round to the other side of the well for a frontal view. Marian saw only a child, little Will Shakespeare, not yet at school, not till after summer, the immunity of infancy sitting on me like a mantle, and she never minded me for a moment. 'What's the matter, young Will, never seen pussy at the well till now?' Silvery laugh, like the larks. And she took my hand and placed it pat on her belly, taut as a pod. I stood no higher than her waist, and placing both hands now on the big globe of her belly, I peered hard into her navel. More larksong.

'Ah, see something I can't, can you? Little friend for you coming out of there soon. Not out of that hole, though – lower down, where you mustn't look, you little bugger, not for another ten years. Oh yes, you can look up here, though, bless your little balls!'

I, the Lord God, beheld the two planets that hung in space above me. Her face and neck had caught all the sun that shone in Warwickshire that summer, her arms too, freckled and golden brown, but her breasts were blinding white worlds, as white as morning milk, and the shocked nipples stood up among the cold waterdrops like raspberries in the rain. I reached up with my two hands and she bent to let me feel their weight.

'Like them, do you, little bugger? Well, that's what your friend Dick's gone and done to me – filled me up with milk, just like my dairies, bloody bull among cows. And who's going to milk *me* then, eh Will? Off with you anyways, it's time for work.'

And she threw her smock over her, shrouding the moons, the huge Jupiter of her belly, the black burning bush between her thighs. She left me full of fernseed. I had known her all over. I, Will Shakespeare, was once again the Lord God of Snitterfield. And Marian was the fairest of the creation, with her great gravid belly filling the sky over my head and her cratered moon-tits dancing attendance. For weeks afterwards I walked around in a dream, not seeing what was in front of me, bumping into walls, breaking my head, stubbing my toes, stumbling into pot-holes and ruts, till everybody thought I was going blind. I wasn't, I was drifting through the geography of Marian's unclothed globes, the only Eden, and I its only god. And all I could hear was that line of hers, 'Never seen pussy at the well before?' The thrill of it filled my ears for reasons unknown. I heard nothing else. Apparently I was going deaf as well. At nights she descended on me from the ceiling. Belly first like a setting moon, the succubus of Snitterfield. She was still there at dawn, perched on my prick, taking advantage of my early erections. They couldn't get her off me, couldn't get me out of bed. Now I was a cripple too.

It didn't last. By the autumn I was in school and being beaten back into worldly awareness – and Marian's belly had gone down. Out of it had come a pink bawling blob that turned Dick's prick to a shithouse icicle and Marian's temper to sour milk. When I asked her one morning if I could see pussy at the well again, she made my ear sing a different song. The Snitterfield idyll was over. But while it lasted maid Marian was the wonder of the world.

'Will, you are the wonder of the world. Even a dunce like me sees other worlds – when your words are working their magic.'

7

Magic. Ah yes, magic. It was years till she was equalled – overtaken, and left far behind, courtesy of a passion for poetry, an imagination run wild, and a fabulous fortune in hard cash.

Not that the experience cost me a personal penny. It was all down to Robert Dudley, Earl of Leicester, bonny sweet Robin, once all the queen's joy. In those days if you wanted to get well in with Gloriana you were expected to throw a nine-days' wonder of a party. Leicester doubled it and added one more for luck. He didn't just want to get in *with* her, he wanted to get *in*. Into politics, into her petticoats and all the rest, the whole way. Hence a nineteen-day beanfeast at a thousand pounds a day. He never really recovered from it. And if it did get him past the Gloriana garters (and that's not entirely certain) it never got him much further. Leicester thought it brave to be a king and ride in triumph into Kenilworth and that's why he threw the most famous thrash in all England.

It passed into the folklore of the age and into its mouth and mind. If you tried to borrow too much money for someone's purse, the outraged creditor would start off with 'Neither a borrower nor a lender be' and hope you'd be impressed by sage economic advice. If you persisted and reduced the sum but he still considered it excessive, he'd say, 'What, lend you thus much moneys? Do you think I'm come from Kenilworth?' Another stock reply was: 'You're asking *me* for that much? You know what they call me, well enough – the name's not Leicester, you know!' Or again, with a touch of colour: 'That much? Tell you what, fish me a mermaid first – and I'll give you a thousand pounds for free!'

A mermaid. That's what I remember. Fireworks, feasting, jugglers and viols – that wasn't enough to impress a queen, not in Leicester's eyes, he wanted something more elaborate, so he had a hundred lackeys, lashed with sweat, dig him out a great lake in front of Kenilworth and whip it up with artificial waves, working in shifts. Into this instant water attraction went all sorts of marine marvels, including the monstrous mermaid, twenty feet of her, and Arion on a dolphin, who reeled off his speech to the queen without a stumble, but then, being the worse for wine, dispelled the magic by throwing off his mask and shouting, 'I'm none of Arion neither, but honest Harry Goldingham!' And Leicester doubtless had his arse for that. As for me, it didn't matter. Mermaids and dolphins survived Harry Goldingham's rough abjuration. My father set me down on a grassy mound to get a better view, and from this little eminence, under a universe of sulphur and stars, I watched the newest wonder of the world, a once-upon-a-time phenomenon, when once I sat upon a promontory and saw a mermaid on a dolphin's back, uttering such dulcet and harmonious breath, that the rude sea grew civil at her song, and certain stars shot madly from their spheres to hear the sea-maid's music.

Years later I recreated the Kenilworth magic at almost no cost at all, in words, though behind the beauty was another ass's head than Leicester's, and another honest artisan, a weaver who had had a most rare vision.

Such were the Leicester fireworks, shooting stars laid on. And a mermaid singing to a queen. Well done, Dudley, well conceived – even though *she* couldn't. Or wouldn't. A mermaid – and a monarch with a membrane: 'Two cuntless wonders of the thronèd west,' old Henry said. Not that I recall seeing the queen that day, but I remember the mermaid and her song, and all those other miracles, staged under the stars by the greatest star in England, his castle the grotto of the globe. Fresh fish plucked from the lake and sizzling on fires, all kinds of wines, full cups on the hour (and that was every hour of every day for all those nineteen days) with the gods themselves presiding, Neptune on the seafood, Bacchus at the bar, Vulcan and Jupiter firemasters extraordinary. And Venus flitting through the chambers, to the galloping of haunches, all night long.

For twenty miles around they say they heard the revelry, saw the lights in the sky, felt the deep-throated cannon roar the royal pledge. Boom! Elizabeth bent her virgin elbow, wetted her chaste lips, knocked back some more of Leicester's liquor, bleeding him dry, because every time she lifted her glass a thousand nodding nobles drank with her, their wrists on puppet strings. Boom boom! Hear that one? Dudley's at it even now, getting his money's worth out of the queen's private purse, high-reaching Leicester, reaching lower now, well beneath the girdle. Boom boom! Come again, Dudley – let the great cannon to the clouds tell all, and the queen's carouse the heavens shall bruit again, re-speaking earthly thunder.

Did they copulate? It's the universal question, isn't it? Everybody always wants to know if two together did the deed of darkness. But Leicester's courtship of the queen was politics and religion too. Of much greater moment than the friction of two members and an ejaculatory discharge. Well, if Dudley did discharge his part, doubtless he discharged it well. Her Majesty had been most royally entertained. Thousands had watched the most public courtship in the realm, including me. Not that I knew much at my tender age about what was really going on. Next day we went back home to Stratford.

It was the hottest July of all time. And Stratford lay quivering in front of us, violent in the waves of heat. I could hear them already as we drew near, the summer flies that quickened in the shambles, buzz buzz, and settled in clumps, black daisies bedecking the slaughter block. Yes, I could smell death in the air again, assaulting the sky with offal, making a mockery of the fields. A long way back now to inhabit Leicester's fabled world, where sea-maids sang to virgins, queens quaffed kisses left in the cup, and honest kersey Harry Goldingham was a poet on a dolphin for a day. A long way from home.

And suddenly I felt like an orphan without hopes. But it set up in me a longing to bring it all back to life again. Dudley's diablerie had given me such an unaccustomed dram that my blood was truly corrupted. And I knew I'd never rest until that ring was rung, that charmed circle drawn again and set in the sensible fields, the island of illusion I once called art. I had drunk the spider, spinner of dreams, and my knowledge was infected. Work, work, my medicine, the subtle poisoner said, the god of dreams. I was a client of Dr Thespius, my wit diseased. I told my father I was too hot, that was all. A fair excuse. The sun was thumping me on the nose as we finally came drifting back into Stratford, two long shadows on the road, the long nettles were flicking and teasing, and there was something infinitely pleasurable about that green drenching nettle-dust, powdering my nostrils, peppering the air with life.

8

By this time it was impossible to keep fat Francis from his flitch, which was duly brought up on a tray, much less tempting to me than the tits of little Alison that surmounted it, as she brought it to the table with that sly little smile of hers, secretive as the fauns among the ferns in the times before we were born, before Stratford was even heard of. I couldn't even smile back at her, as Mistress Mine, never one to rove, was frowning at her back, though I winked at the small beer that came with it, which I thought permissible. Anne thought otherwise.

'To wash it down, Master Collins – but not for the old and ailing, if you please. He's had enough of that to be going on with.'

Enough for a lifetime is what she meant.

'Oh, enough's never enough, Mistress Anne.'

Purse of the mouth, frown of the brow, twitch of the nose – and the twin temptations were escorted from my eyes, leaving only the ale. Bacon is beyond my capabilities now – thin gruel's my last diet – and so is Alison, though thought's free. In my mind's eye she dipped her nipples in the jug and bid me wet my lips.

'Care for a drop, old man?'

It was Francis, offering me my own hospitality.

Pour away, my friend, the usual two fingers' worth for me. And you can make free with the flitch.

'I intend to. And intend to make progress from where we stand, which is no further, other than some household stuff to the Halls – painted cloths unspecified – and ten pounds to the poor of Stratford.'

Ah yes, Stratford. And my father, the big man of the place. Had we been squirrels we might have leapt from bough to bough across the entire country, especially in wooded Warwickshire. Being man and boy, my father and I, we walked. Down through dubious Arden, where Guy of Warwick in days gone by became an old religious man after he'd finished frowning on Danes and splitting their skulls. That was achieved on a diet of roast beef of old England and buckets of beer

– which he gave up for river-cress, river-water, a life lived among lecturing trees and schoolmastering streams, and the serendipity that lets you find sermons in stones, books in the running brooks.

'Our local hero.'

Stratford. What was it anyway?

'What is any place?'

Faces at first. Wedgewood was the tailor. He was our neighbour in Henley Street, a peeled radish of a creature whom I rarely saw in his shop. He was forever skipping around the corner to Hornby's smithy just below the stream – usually with shears and measure in hands and the latest news hot on his lips. If you peered in through the heat haze you'd see him hopping excitedly about the giant Hornby on slippers that he'd thrust on the wrong feet in his hurry to purvey his piece of gossip. They'd be joined soon enough by the furious customer that Wedgewood had left rudely half-measured in Henley Street for doublet and hose, while Hornby stood clothed with smoke, listening gravely, oblivious to the flying sparks that bounced off his chest like baffled bees. One or two always lodged in the tangle of hair and beard and burned briefly there till Hornby brushed them away with a strange gentleness, while the iron cooled on the anvil and the huge mouth opened wider to swallow the thimbleful of rumour that Wedgewood could make outlast the shoeing of a hundred horse. You'd think the gaping Hornby would swallow Wedgewood too, for the mere fly that he was. But he was a busy little fly to boot, for the randy bastard was known to have two wives and had flown to Stratford to escape the first.

'And he wasn't the first to fly from a female.'

Not far from where Wedgewood buzzed like some inextinguishable spark about the labouring listening Hornby, stood a shop in the High Street that fairly drew me in.

'Like the charnel-house?'

Not far off it. Philip Rogers, apothecary, in tattered weeds with overwhelming brows – his looks were meagre, sharp misery had worn him to the bones, and in his needy shop a tortoise hung, an alligator stuffed, some other skins of ill-shaped fishes, and about his shelves a beggarly account of empty boxes, green earthen pots, bladders, and musty seeds, remnants of packthread and old cakes of roses, thinly scattered to make up something of a show. He could have been taken for one of his own exhibits, except that you might have detected more humanity in the alligator, more movement in the tortoise. He could barely be said to keep the shop – rather he hung about it, haunted it like something almost obsolete, an ancient haze, scarcely visible. Rogers was what was left over. He was part of the smell.

'Don't put me off my bacon.' Munch munch.

It wasn't all bad. Master Philip also sold sweet confections, liquorice, aniseed, sarsparilla, Hawkins's hellweed, the infamous tobacco, poppy, mandragora, and all the drowsy syrups of the east. But he sold poisons too – so mortal, they said, that if you dipped a knife in one of them, where it drew blood no cataplasm so rare, collected from all herbs that have virtue under the moon, could save the thing from death that received the merest scratch. If you had the strength of twenty men it would make you drop down dead on the spot.

'And so,' croaked Rogers – whispering so softly it could have been an exhalation in the air, an unstoppered phial, your own foul imaginings – 'And so, my friend, if you have a troublesome rat that comes about your chickens, or a two-legged one, let's say, that comes between your sheets and troubles your dearest chuck too sweetly for your taste, come to old Rogers and he'll rid you of the fear of them with one noxious drop.'

'A friend in need.'

Such was the gossip, drawn out of the eerie odours of the shop, spun from a glance, that was all – and it was enough. Famine was in those cheeks, need and oppression shining in the eyes, contempt and beggary hanging on his back.

'Who needs starve – when bacon's as plentiful as blackberries?'

Apparently it was all an illusion. Rogers had a cook who swore he ate like a horse and wouldn't throw a crumb to a sparrow, and the shop did a fair business. Roaring trade would be a metaphor inappropriate to the ambience but there was, let's say, a steady susurration. The scrapings and siftings, all the distillations of the world had made their way to London and up the hundred mile road to Stratford to sit like defecations of the devil on Rogers' shelves and draw out my mind through my nostrils, so intoxicating were they to the eye, these scourings of strange continents and shavings of unchartered parts. This was the crucible of forbidden dreams. I wanted desperately to suck the liquorice offered me once by the gimlet-eyed apothecary but was terrified by the thought of what else that claw hand had touched, in what powdered bowels the bony finger had raggled and groped, and what I might turn into if I tasted even the fumes of that liquorice on the air. Agnes assured me that the stuffed alligator suspended from the ceiling was once a Stratford boy who'd eaten too much liquorice and was metamorphosed as a warning to sweet-toothed juveniles who started with liquorice and went on from there, tempted to tinker wickedly with worse weeds.

'All balls,' swore Henry. 'She just don't want you shitting yourself, that's all, and don't want you going up in smoke neither.'

But I believed this story of the alligator well into my schooldays.

'Sure you don't fancy a rasher?'

They were mines of magic, these shops. Another trader called Baynton had sugar loaves and gunpowder on his shelves, and everybody said that when Baynton became too free among the winepots the night before, he put the gunpowder instead of the sugar into the bread, and the flour into the gunpowder, and so if you dared trade with Baynton your enemies would live to laugh at you, for your shot would fall like bad dough but he'd sell you a loaf and blow you at the moon. I carried home the bread from Baynton's like a bomb, in arms that were rigid, and I took the first bite with a face on me, they said, like one looking at a bare bodkin.

'So that was your Stratford, Will.'

A market town, a trading place, and all the trades shop-fronted by talking faces. They talked about wool, the weather, animals, and each other. The drapers Barnhurst and Badger, both of Sheep Street, sold you scripture first and cloth second. The cloth was the same – the scripture was of an entirely different weave. Arch enemies, they argued about God and split him down the middle, ripping the seamless garment of the gospel and making a rag of religion in the same street. Protestant Barnhurst wiped his arse, he said, against the Catholic fabric of his rival, and Badger, who wouldn't even piss on Protestant weave, swore he wasn't the only papist in town to sell good Catholic cloth. That was true enough, said Barnhurst, the whole town knowing from Wedgewood how alderman Whately kept more than bees in his garden. He had two brothers who were priests on the run – while Ralph Cawdrey had a sprog who was a Jesuit for certain.

'Tittle-tattle, eh?'

'And he'll see butchery enough,' says Wedgewood to Hornby, 'if young Cawdrey gets caught in a priest-hole one fine day. He'd be safer up the queen's cunt, for that's never searched, they say, (hee-hee) nothing gets up there, not even Leicester's lofty knob, for how can the Dudley dolphin penetrate a cleft-less mermaid eh, Master Hornby? Work that out if you can...'

And Hornby's grin grew wider and redder than the iron that he spread out on the anvil, but he kept on hammering all the same, while Wedgewood's clients raged for their late breeches and his second wife swore they'd be beggars in hell, what with her loose-mouthed husband's shit-stirring and that idle tailor's tongue of his tattling away nineteen to the dozen.

'Gossiping goshawks.'

'So what I say, Master Blacksmith, and wisely is it said,' Wedgewood stopped for no wife, first or second, 'that Cawdrey the younger will wish he'd stuck to butchery when his time comes to be the scaffold calf, as come it will, and be turned off at Tyburn, for there'll be butchery enough will stick to *him* when that day comes. And as for Whately's bees, I can tell you this much about them, they're taught to buzz abroad the Catholic creed, it's true, I've heard them, they fly into folk's gardens for the purpose and infect their flowers and their children that pick them. Put your ears to the foxgloves and you'll hear them, I tell you, bees buzzing in Latin. Man's a fucking wizard. And a traitor to boot. Trade with Whately and you die, it's that simple.'

'Yackety-yack.'

That's how it was – a treasury of talk in Stratford, where trades were tongues in faces, clacking about politics and God, you couldn't keep them apart. And besides the drapers there was another Protestant and Catholic battleground, again in the same street, occupied by the landlords of two inns. John Sadler, the miller, kept *The Bear* and was rival to Thomas Dixon Waterman, owner of *The Swan*. But there was a third Bridge Street inn, *The Angel*, which was reckoned to be the safest place to knock back your ale if you didn't want to be marked down as Rome or anti-Rome by the faceless tavern spies. For although she who sat on the throne was a notorious sitter on the fence, you never knew when the chair might suddenly be empty again, to be re-occupied by papist or Protestant, there was no certainty. In the meantime the workings of your soul were always a matter of interest to the tavern spies, who were as thirsty as the next man when ale was on tap. So in spite of its name a drink at *The Angel* was likely to keep you well away from the angelic host, so it was reckoned. A nice neutral hostelry. Through its doors came the High Street bakers Hamnet and Judith Sadler (for whom I named my twins), Quiney the vintner, Gilbert Bradley our neighbour (that my brother Gilbert was named for), and many friends of my father, trading in leather, wool and wine, bread and beer. And in words. Words, words, words. They grew on folks' lips slowly enough at times like wool on sheep's backs or like pears on the trees, but sometimes brightly like daisies in the fields. And they rang in my ears like uncracked gold clattering on the counter.

'Keeps life lively.'

Stratford was also women: milchers, churners, gardeners, cooks, nurses, midwives, makers of candles and fires, spreaders of beds and floors, tellers of stories and household accounts, spinsters, weavers, butchers, bakers, brewers and hewers and drawers of water, they grew herbs and stuffed rabbits and jugged hares, they ploughed and sowed, reaped and mowed, dressed salads and corpses, served men on their feet and knees by day and on their backs by night. Beasts of burden in the social scheme and brood mares in the old eye of heaven, they lay down for us from the very beginning and stood up straight when we were prostrated by love, illness or death. White brides, black widows, and wearers of all colours and callings in between, they were the mainstay and mystery of our lives. And that too was my Stratford.

'Anything else?'

Stratford was a twenty-minute walk encircling two hundred houses and fifteen hundred folk. Seven hundred of them poor folk, if you want to see it with a social squint, some of them lacking parents, spouses, jobs, legs, arms, eyes. Roger Asplyn had four motherless children who along with their father were all whipped for begging, including fourteen-year-old Cycely who was blind but had been driven out by the corporation. A blind and motherless child. That was Stratford.

'A nice picture.'

Or Stratford was ten hamlets making up a parish. Stratford if you care to play on the word, was streets. And a river. Chapel Lane, Sheep Street, Bridge Street, all coming up from the water, a half right turn at the top of Bridge Street taking you up Henley Street, on the north side of which I was born, with the fields sweeping in like the sea to my feet, along the Guild Pits and into our back gardens. Green fields like a green bible. And Stratford was houses. In the poorer ones the strewn rushes went untouched for years, woven with shit and spit, fishbones and puke, the leakages of dogs and the siftings of the human epidermis. Otherwise it was cracked flagged floors, Wilmcote limestone and limewashed thatches, houses like timbered ships drifting effortlessly through time, built to last the tug of centuries and tides of change. Old black beams with the curves of the forest in them, passing like waves along the white plastered walls, and penthouses pulled like hats over the beetle brows, shading the petty paces and ferret eyes of the sad little traders underneath, the ones who kept their souls in their pockets and would bring them out for a bargain.

Whereas, for those who wore their souls proudly like plumed hats and swords, Stratford was its church. And for the desperado legging it up that long avenue of limes, the heart of Stratford was the all-precious sanctuary knocker, one touch of which, before the arm of the law could reach him, meant despised life for another thirty-seven days at least, if sanctuary was to be observed. It wasn't always respected. The scene on the Guild Chapel walls, where Thomas à Becket's once unstoppable blood ran down, had reminded everybody before I was born that even a churchman in a church could be hacked down like a pig if the breath of kings dictated. But we were all Beckets, all liable for the chop, and the Puritans had stopped his blood with bucket and brush. On another of the Chapel walls, lurking under the whitewash, a devil shook an axe at a bunch of terrified sinners, hustled into hell for their eternity of pain. They were starting day one of a stretch that knew no end of days. 'They didn't look like thieves and murderers,' muttered old Henry, 'some of them were even children' – and that was the frightening thing for me. And that again was Stratford, as were the duckings of shrews to make them dulcet-tongued –

'A lovely thing in woman.'

The pillory, the stocks, the nailed ears, slit noses and the bloody backs of whipped whores, fucked by their whippers the night before. And your dulcet woman quickly develops a tongue with a tang.

'Nothing changes.'

It was fires and floods, spittle and stew on the rushes, beer stains and bones, the screeching of women and pigs, blood on the Rothermarket block, blood in the childbed and the deathbed, dripping nipples, and white stiff bundles of stillborn joy, hurried out of the house and under the daisy-decked bedcovers of the churchyard, safe away from limbo, with worms for chambermaids, and owls for wise uncles and the Avon crooning its cradle songs in their deaf ears, while the whole earth, a crib and a coffin, rocked imperceptibly among the stars.

'It's taking shape – unlike your will.'

Add the rotten diseases of the south, the guts-griping, ruptures, catarrhs, cold palsies, lethargies, gravel in the back, dirt-rotten livers, raw eyes, wheezing lungs, bladders with abscesses, sciaticas, lime-kilns in the palm, insufferable bone-ache, itches and vomitings and general leprosy. Add that and you almost have Stratford.

'I think we're there.'

No, wait, there's worse. Include the cures – the webs of spiders and fried mice, the viper's flesh, poultice of swallows' nests, dung and all, boiled in oil of chemomel and lilies, beaten with white dogs' turds, water of frog-spawn, powder of earthworms, shavings of ivory, fume of horse hoofs, and the white of old henshit stirred up in white wine.

'And that's just the tasty ones?'

Try hedgehog's testicles, powdered, for pissing the bed. Or if you're pissing brimstone, powdered crabs' eyes and the bone in a carp's head. Or if you can't piss at all, some choice big lice, introduced into the innermost hole of your prick.

'You're making me want to piss again.'

I'm sorry, Francis. Be an asthmatic instead – the lungs of a fox washed in herbs, liquorice and wine. Do you have the quinsy? Try powdered burnt swallow, feathers and all, or some of your own dung, also burnt, with a little honey, and a dry white wine.

'Always the wine. How else could you stomach it?'

As for the procedures – enforced vomitings, wild bleedings, sudden shittings and pints of heated wine hosed heartily up the arse to cure wind and colic, if you weren't bleeding or spewing before the cures you'd be spouting torrents afterwards from one end or the other and from orifices you didn't even know you had. Ill health was hell from the inside: torn-out teeth, pissing red-hot blades, vicious chatterings, bloody fluxes, wastings, and, for victims of violent accident, amputations, with spurting red stumps thrust into hot pitch, enough to cauterise the very soul from the body and stop the heart with shock. As it sometimes did.

'I've heard enough.'

You're too young to have heard a tithe of it. There was childbed fever, babies strangled before birth with the cords around their necks, swinging in the gallows-womb, babies strangled after birth, ditch-delivered by a drab – and bony young virgins with the greensickness paling daily into memories of themselves, fading out into nothing more than white anonymous daisies scattered on the green earth – remembered voices, soft on the low sad winds.

'Eternal rest grant them, O Lord.'

On it went. And the best way forward was simply to pray that neither the grim reaper nor the zealous doctor ever crossed your threshold; to keep out damps, draughts and evil company; to say your prayers, and to keep eating salt fish, salt meat, salt sweat for sauce, milk frozen in February and curdled in June. And cheeses – cheese as white as snow is, as endowed with eyes as Argus was, as old as Methusalem might have been, as rough as hairy Esau and as full of whey and weeping as Mary Magdalene and of scabs as spotted Lazarus. Banbury cheeses were best if you deigned to eat white meat, but the old Stratford folk wouldn't, not if they could eat beef or mutton and veal instead.

'Veal!'

Or even hares – that nourished melancholy and whose amputated ears brought the trout to the hook by country magic if you had the cunning and the skill. And if you wanted desperately to swim against the cold stream of death and keep your special child alive, you fed him with apricots and dewberries, with purple grapes, green figs and mulberries – unless of course you overfed him and he'd go down with the summer complaint and shit his way quickly into eternity.

'Death by shitting – sweet Jesus!'

As you say, *requiem aeternam*. That was the fruity end of the Stratford experience. Which also had its good side. Strawberries swimming in the cream was Stratford in summer, and schoolboys playing in the stream. But it was burnt bacon on black bread in winter, and if all was well some raisins in hot milk for supper.

'This bacon's the best – and to hell with raisins!'

Stratford, if you were a man of some substance, meant pewter on the table, a chimney for the fire and a fair skin for females – or it was skin cured like ham for all the family if you could afford only a hole in the roof and food picked from the board with filthy fingers. Stratford was either a bolster or pillow, or it was a good round log for the head that had sore need of sleep and resting – and dreams with hard shutters that banged shut in the morning. It was soft flock, feathers of down, or it was a sack of chaff, a pallet of pricking straw. As in any other place a Stratford sleep was a green sea flecked by the bright white horses of sweet dreams – or it heaved with nightmares, and sharks roamed the blanket of the dark as the brain lay trapped in the wallowing corpse.

'Only if you were a poet.'

But Stratford was also the relief of morning, with the river a glittering track through fields of light. It was fairs and fairies and festivals, pancakes and simnel cakes and maypoles. It was Shrovetides and Whitsuns and boars' heads at Christmas. More than anything it was a patchwork of sounds and scents and shapes: the shape of the poor dead hedgehog after the school bullies, those base football players, had finished their game; the shapes of strange crocodiles haunting the long slavering skylines, pretending to be clouds; the shapes of murderers hunched unforgiven in their graves, unsettling the turfs; or murderers still alive, lurking clumsily in the clouds when the west yet glimmered with some streaks of day. Stratford was water and wind in the trees, willow and ash and elm, it was bright birdsong by day, birds brave, unlimed and free, and owls from Athens in night-barns and branches, when the thatch came creepily alive over your head and your ears twitched with the nearness of talon and claw. And Stratford smelled to heaven. There was not rain enough in the sweet heaven to wash it white as snow. It had the primal eldest curse upon it, a rank offence to God, who'd put the carrion birds there, the hawks and kites and buzzards, to prey on garbage and be the cleaners of the world. And always, like antidotes to terror, the swans sailed the river, beautiful silver barges bearing death away.

'I'm all for birds that bear death away. Like your little Alison, for example.'

She's a darling. It kept on coming back, though – death – because Stratford was also God.

'Jesus, you say right.'

And God was a god of death, still invisibly strolling in the cool of the Reformation day, along the narrow corridors of the queen's compromise. All the same Stratford was obedience, it was having your name taken if you took mass, it was being on a list. It was attendance at the Church of England, fines of twelve pence a week for recusants, rising to a ruinous twenty pounds a month as the Catholic clouds came over the edge of the world and out of the sea, filling the sky – the Paris Massacre, Mary of Scots. And missionary priests that slipped into the country from Douai – the secret soldiers of the devil. An invisible army trained by foreign sovereigns to infiltrate the realm, to corrupt men's souls to Catholicism and overthrow the Bastard Queen, the Whore of Babylon. She could be killed on the streets by her subjects and the Pope would bless the bloody business. He had absolved them of all allegiance to her and dangled daggers and pardons before their eyes. Pardons in advance. Murder in this case would be a ticket to the Paradiso. And if you asked any of the queen's ministers for the definition of a Catholic, the answer you'd likely get would be: a traitor.

'Yet she refused to go on the witch-hunt, Will.'

Even after the scheming schismatics, who attended the accepted services but were known to be church papists, wolves in the fold, flaunting their white fleece. As for those who came out of the closet, proclaiming the dogmas of Rome like braying asses and refusing the Oath of Supremacy – well, even the liberal Elizabeth couldn't save them. It was impossible – and understandable. Jesuits were underneath your floorboards and behind your walls, quite literally, rats ordained to carry the spiritual plague. And the queen's rat-catchers went about their work with their hands tied by the very sovereign they were trying to protect. The truth of the matter was that she had some family sympathy for the Catholics, in spite of the frightful record of her dead sister Mary, the fanatic of the flame – and the rumour ran round even in sleepy Stratford that Elizabeth took Mass herself in secret. She was a chip off the old block, Rome ran in her blood, and on the back stairs one virgin whispered to the other, from earth to heaven. Anything's possible. The flies on the wall would know.

'And where did Stratford stand?'

Stratford for now was a place of compromise and commonsense, while remaining in the jaundiced eye of government a somewhat ungodly town, on the blind side of the bishop's diocese. I was put through all the proper motions: learning my Catechism before Evensong on Sundays and Holy Days; attending Matins and Evensong and Holy Communion three times a year; hearing and reading the word of God in the Old and New Testaments from cover to cover, Revelation excepted; singing the Psalms; accepting the exhortations of the Homilies; praying for my Queen against rebellion, civil war, foreign invasion, and all traitors who dared to threaten her and the God-ordained order of all things. Order was what really mattered, knowing your place, not breaking ranks, not stepping out of line. Do that if you dare, take but degree away, untune that string – and hark! What discord follows.

'Hark indeed. And did you?'

I'd no choice but to hearken, Sunday after homiletic Sunday. I breathed in that philosophy like air, accepted the ideas like stones and stars, that were simply there, put in place by God. Actually a somewhat dull dog in the end, the Lord God, who took his predictable Sunday constitutional, strolling sternly as ever in the easy afternoon, while the children skulked in the bushes, playing doctors and nurses, stealing apples, ignoring order. Don't touch that cursèd fruit! Do – and there'll be hell to pay. Literally. Follow my meaning? Follow the line, young Will – and don't go too near the river. Yes, master.

'Did you some good, though.'

You're left with an obsession for order, there's no escaping that. But you nurture something else as well – a wild admiration for those who break the rules. Who rattle the chain of being and cause chaos among statesmen and stars. These fellows have some soul – so your Satanic instincts whisper in your ear. What, after all, is a life impeccably and merely correct?

'So you cheered on the wicked.'

Adam and Cain and their kind, who stirred up trouble in the schoolroom, made life more interesting, provoked thought, passed the time, the apple and the axe, and provided the populace with play.

'Which God did not much like.'

Because God, as you know quite well by now, was also a Stratford schoolmaster, and a Catholic one at that, three in a row, Hunt and Jenkins and Cottam, all Romish, causing great government concern over the daily Catholic corruption sown by such teachers in the minds and souls of Elizabeth's little innocents.

9

'Talking of schools, Will – '

Aha!

'My pen is poised.'

I wish mine were.

'Leaving anything, by any chance, to the establishment that set you up so solidly?'

I won't dignify that question with an answer.

'I thought I'd ask. The King's School, after all. A scholarship? A deserving child?'

Not a penny.

'Not well paid, the school master.'

A corrupter of Protestants, wilfully hired by a Catholic corporation, held sway at the King's School behind the Guild Chapel, where I started Petty School at five years old, getting up at five in the morning to prepare for the five-minute walk to Church Street. It was a two-minute trot, but even for a snail an eternity wouldn't have been long enough to postpone the evil hour. I came in under the eagle eye of the usher, Higges, to learn my alphabet and the penitential psalms, to be initiated into the mysteries of reading and writing from the Primer and Catechism, and to learn how to count. My hornbook was looped about my neck – the cord was too loose and it banged my cold knees all the way. In summer the schoolroom was cool enough, blotting out the sun – and in the winters it was freezing cold.

'Jesu, I remember too.'

Blowing on our fingers, we hugged our empty stomachs for five frosty hours. Fifteen minutes allowed for mid-morning breakfast – which took fifteen seconds to swallow, after which there was another long wait for the awful meat and coarse black bread that we washed down with sour ale.

'Takes me back.'

We also swallowed mountains of intellectual grist. *Scriptum est: non in solo pane vivit homo* – ranted Higges. We'd gladly have lived on less knowledge and more bread – and just a little heat. Talk of hell and I think not of a lake of fire but of that King's School classroom, heated only by the bodies of small boys and the brief vapour of their breaths.

'Not brief enough for me.'

To begin with I sat between the master and his assistant, afraid to move the fishmonger slabs that were my feet.

'Keep them still, you useless little shuffler, it is vain for thee to kick against the pricks!' So Higges would say. Jesus, I couldn't have kicked if I'd tried, couldn't even feel my feet after the first hour, and in any case it was the pricks that did the kicking at King's. After lessons I used to run up and down the town for half an hour just to get a heat on my feet and save my toes from atrophy. I studied many disciplines in Church Street but mostly I studied endurance. By the age of ten I was already an antique Roman.

'You were a Dane in drinking.'

Once. But that came later. Our feet were in no real danger and neither were our arses – it was hardening of the brain that was the hazard. You came out of that school full of knowledge but with hardly a thought in your stuffed noodle. Information and authority were the fashion, a ready-made morality, and a pile of absolute certainties. And if you begin with certainties you will end in nakedness and doubts – and nakedness, Francis, wears out the moon. Under which belief turns pale and dies. A caster of shadows, the moon, that old glimmering spinner of distrust.

But no such moon shone in school, except the hard wolfish moons of winter dawns. What school gave me was matter and discipline, which I sifted and stored. Acquisitive, eclectic, open unto the universe, I learned under the steady barrage of instruction and booklore. History was turned into moral philosophy and political viewpoints were passed around like fossils, for observation, not for discussion. Very little was up for discussion in Church Street, where Higges was in charge. Small have continual plodders ever won save base authority from others' books. And Higges was a great plodder. He referred to the long afternoon as the posteriors of the day and kept himself warm by beating the posteriors of small hungry boys.

'A muttonhead.'

Who'd lived on the alms-basket of words and existed solely for sniffing out blunders and bogus Latin, and for flogging and repetition. Jesus, it must have been soothing to his absolute absence of intellect to listen to us all day and every day chanting the unchanging truths of all the worlds, natural, political, temporal, eternal, according to and beginning with Our Father.

Our Father, Our Queen, Son and Holy Ghost, make me to know mine end and the measure of my years, that I may know how frail I am, and make me to know mine *a b c*, my one two three, that I may count my blessings and my beatings all the days of my life, three score years and ten, January, February, and shun my sins, Pride, Envy, and know thy Word, Genesis, Exodus, and accept my strokes, one, two, one to six, one to seven, six graces, seven deadlies, six days of the week, seven penitentials, schooling forty-six weeks of the year, spring, summer, autumn, winter, what freezings have I felt, what dark days seen, December days of Latin and the lash, correctness and correction, with one solitary lapse intolerable to Higges, for that was a sure sign of the devil that was known to lurk in all boys and must be birched out at all costs just as soon as Satan betrays himself by a wrong answer, a moment's loss of concentration.

'For what is youth but an untamed beast,' said Higges, 'and what is the rod but a divine weapon against that beast and a sword against Satan? Therefore when I beat you I love you, for I drive out folly and let in wisdom and save your souls from hell, so to spare you is to hate you and to fail most miserably in my duty, for which I am paid four pounds a year, and by God's grace and the strength of my right arm I shall earn them every penny, so bend over now you little bastards, and we'll begin.'

'He was right, of course.'

Learning saved souls, everybody knew that, and boys who turned out as thieves and murderers, ending their damnable days on the gibbet, were the victims of bad schoolmastering, or none at all. In either case a plentiful lack of flogging. You're right about the theory. So the principal vocation of Higges was to flog us until we were seven, after which we passed out of his correction and care and into that of the schoolmaster, who advised us that if we wanted the flogging to cease we should address ourselves for the next seven years to the perfections of the Latin grammar, at the end of which period of plenty our minds would be crammed full like the granaries of Egypt in the time of Joseph. From now on therefore our lives were entirely latinized and we submitted every day to the grinding disciplines of Lily and his infernal accidence.

'But old Jenkins wasn't so bad, was he?'

By the time Thomas Jenkins arrived at the King's School in my twelfth year I was ready for the diet of literature he served up daily: Ovid and Virgil, Lucretius and Horace – with Ovid always first on the table, the main dish every day, sometimes garnished with Golding's fourteeners, but always Ovid, honey-tongued Ovid, the first and lasting taste in the mouth. Turn around the letters in the poet's name and you get VOID – which is what my schooling hugely was till Ovid came along and filled it like a god. 'Ah, Mantuan! Good old Mantuan! Old Mantuan! Who understandeth thee not loves thee not!' So crooned Jenkins. He melted so much at the touch of Ovid, it was almost possible to believe that our stern schoolmaster was, just like ourselves, the proud possessor of *hic penis*, and that if *hic vulva* had bloomed like a rose out of Ovid's pages he'd have thrown off his gown, cast his Lily to the winds and got stuck in.

10

'You stuck in at school, Will.'

And beyond.

'Your little Alison now – '

Talking of sticking in, you mean. Leave her out of it. She's not my little Alison. And she's a sweet child.

'You stuck in more than you should have done though, old man.'

Not at school.

'Jesus, I should hope not.'

That's not what I meant. The keyhole was about the only place at school you could stick into. And Ovid was the keyhole through which I peered excitedly into my teens. What I saw there, caught in the forbidden frames of those pagan metres, was a sex scene that changed my life – Venus and Adonis hard at it, *hic penis* and *hic vulva* coming together and making sense of things at last. Not that Ovid provided the details, but on the doorsill of adolescence it was enough. Out the window went Adam and Eve's furtive fucking in the bushes in the cool of the day, with God gloating knowingly on. Away too went sheep-shagging Dick and Marian with her bursting udders and bovine belly. No more o' that, sirs. Those bucolic lunges now disgusted me.

'Good old Mantuan had done it for you, eh?'

Transience, longing, change, the inevitability of it all. And he'd brought sex right out of the cupboard, (where the bible stood on the shelf), and away from the shithouse door. When I looked through the keyhole I saw the open countryside round Stratford, with gods and mortals making love there under the wide sky.

'Saw nothing but sheep myself. And sheep-shaggers.'

In that infinite blue emptiness there was no Jehovah to be seen and not a cloud in sight. There was no serpent under the flowers, no god lurking among leaves.

'A schoolboy's dream.'

I ran up to Snitterfield where the long hot grasses of June lashed and maddened me beyond reason. They were well flattened in one frequented spot where Venus had lain down there with her Adonis less than an hour ago. I put my nose to the ground like a hunter. Those grass blades quivered with the recent memory of breasts and thighs. In those green dents her fair elbows had rested fleetingly, imprinting the earth – in those deeper mounds her buttocks.

'Couple of copulating rustics. You disturbed them.'

She'd long ceased caring for her sea-shores, stopped going to sea-girt Paphos, to Cnidos, fecund with fishes, or Amathis with its mint of minerals. Olympus itself could hold her no more. She spent her days roaming the rocks and ridges, the woods and fields, her dress up to her knees, exposing her legs, heedless. She'd searched the globe for the one she wanted.

'And naturally she'd come all the way to Stratford and lain on the Snitterfield rise.'

Where else should she have come but here?

'It was Marian down on Dick.'

For here was her Adonis, right here in Stratford, just waiting for the goddess to come round a corner, rise up out of the grasses, and pin me to the earth. Yes, Francis, I was Adonis, all right, there was no doubt of that. I'd drunk that verse so deeply it had washed out of me anything that existed of the pre-Ovidian Will. He was a ghost. I looked down at my feet and they'd gone – I saw only grass. I'd disappeared. I was that wind-flower trembling in the breeze. Metamorphosis was mine. I was the anemone, Adonis, bloodstaining that hot compacted grass, where she'd lain and languished. And she wouldn't leave off, I knew it for certain, she'd be back on the hunt, flushed with lust, dripping and sweating, to find me in the fields before the start of school.

'I hope you got up early.'

Absurdly! In the summer dawns to meet her in the meadows and lie with her a full two hours before running back ravished into town to sit before Jenkins and translate. But little did he know and little did my classmates realise just who was in their midst, interpreting Ovid with the inward eye of one who knew. I myself was Ovid. Will Shakespeare was my oafish English alias, my Stratford disguise. Hot from the mould, I was a newly minted myth, drunk with experience, protean knowledge of the gods, and nobody had a clue just how rare and randy I was.

'Naturally you kept it to yourself, this information.'

Naturally. Then I'd get into school and find Jenkins in his harsh historical mood, ready for Livy, Tacitus, and Caesar, and my spirits would be dashed for a day. Unless of course he brought out North's Plutarch and a rougher magic worked its spell.

'Rough's the word.'

Not one to send me out into the fields to wait for gods. But Plutarch's stories filled these dry classical days with purple.

'Filled mine with boredom. Still, you need Latin for the law. Livy was even worse.'

Not even Jenkins languished over Livy. He gave us Plautus and Terence too, and some Seneca –

'Gleefully godless and shockingly horrible.'

Go on through the lofty spaces of high heaven and bear witness where you ride that there are no gods. It is the mind only that makes a king – the kingdom each man bestows upon himself. A lesson in tragedy. I never forgot it.

'So old Seneca left his mark.'

The drama was good. But in the morn and liquid dew of youth it was Ovid that bore the palm away. He was my man. He fell like dew on ignorance and nothing was left untransformed. Not that I was alone in knowing Ovidian delights. Others had been there before me, as I now realised, understanding now from my earliest days certain sounds from my mother's bed on certain nights.

'Oh God, yes. I knew what was happening, though. Didn't you?'

I wondered if she were in pain and I lay awake, listening, wanting to go through to her, to comfort her, asking myself why my father didn't wake and soothe her. Till it came to me that he was lying awake with her and making her moan, and that he was moaning too, making a fiercer music that I couldn't understand.

'Where ignorance was bliss.'

Not all bliss. The bed they lay in creaked like a ship in a storm and that combined moaning of theirs was the hurricane that howled about their vessel as it ploughed and dipped and bucked and rolled in the surge.

'Jesus, you took notes.'

And yet it was a sweet storm too, in which they seemed to want to go down and perish. I listened, amazed, to the crescendo and melody of their anguish, their sheer willingness to die, to expire together and leave me desolate in my bed, unwanted, ignored.

'You poor little fucker.'

It wasn't the first betrayal. The first happened long before then, when my mother banished me from their bed, where I'd burrowed into the soft nest of her belly and buried my blind pink face in her queen-bee honeybags.

'You don't remember that!'

Ample udders on my mother, I can assure you, memory's the warder of the brain, and I stayed longer than I should have done, longer than my father wanted, I shouldn't wonder. I was two years old when Gilbert came, and though I must have been cuckooed out of the nest well before then, I can still capture the Judas moment, the first evidence of female treachery.

'Frailty! thy name is woman.'

I was excluded from their private paradise. I was outside the gates. Adam was long dead but in my father's mansion he was alive again. And kicking. John Shakespeare *knew* his wife. Mary Arden was in Eden, and the two of them going at it bush to bush, thinking themselves unheard, little knowing that I heard everything and that I, the Lord their God, was a jealous god.

'Master John Shakespeare, Mary Arden, a well-left wench,' Agnes said. 'Whoever marries her shall have the chinks, that he shall. And your father did just that, he heard the chink of silver when he saw our Mary, and she's done well by him with her own sweet chink, done her duty has that lass. Well, Joan and Margaret are with God, but that's past matter. Mary Arden has given him the chink, over and over, and the chinks in plenty too. A good man. And a lucky man, your father, luckier than a king.'

The king my father. Master of the Mary, master of the chinks.

'A good man, Will?'

He was a man. Take him for all in all. His beard was grizzled. But he looked smilingly.

'Something wrong with that?'

One may smile and smile and be a villain, Francis.

11

'And was he – a villain?'

We are arrant knaves all. I can only tell you how he was. John Shakespeare: glover and whittawer, dresser of white leather; also fleece-dealer, wheeler and dealer, trader in timber, talker and smiler, house-owner, shop-runner, glove-shopman, wool-shopman, investor, landlord, and money-lender too – yes, usury, that's my word – a good man, a sound man, for twenty years a solid man, – since he climbed out of the shoe-sucking clay and came to Stratford in '53, where he quickly made his way. And there you have him: John Shakespeare, man of business, fee simple, an uncomplicated man.

'That it?'

I can do him for you another way, if you like. Tell you about the civic man. John Shakespeare: ale-taster, constable, affeeror, burgess, chamberlain, alderman, bailiff – and as such last, almoner, coroner, escheator, Clerk of the Market and Justice of the Peace, with mace-bearing sergeants conducting him to the Guild Hall through all the town streets, a matter of some pride to me when I was small in years and understanding, before I saw through furred gowns, yes indeed, sirs, a man of standing, a man of consequence. A front-pew man when he went to church – a thing he did less often as time went by.

'No more but so?'

I can also do you the spiritual man. Not a tedious business, I can give it to you in one word: Catholic. But if you ask me was he a good Catholic, I'd have to answer that's two words, and more than twice as difficult to determine. All the same I'd be bound to admit that good Catholics didn't always die in their beds and they sometimes lost their bowels before they died, and their balls before that. They were made of sterner stuff than my father. So by the highest standards of the day I'd have to say that he was like hundreds around him – believed one thing, did another, talked about neither, kept his tongue tight behind his teeth, a hypocrite survivor, nothing much wrong with that, and not so deeply religious as to die for a belief, still less for the family tradition of the old Catholic Shakespeares. Tradition? Belief? What do they count for compared with a comfortable living and a clean death, genitals intact? Easy for me to say, I know. I should be grateful. And am. My father had a wife and family to think about. He was looking out for them, not just for himself. He was taking care of me. A good man, then.

'And yet?'

And yet this same John Shakespeare, the king my father, once the top dog of Stratford, this Catholic cur, drove out the curate Roger Dyos with his vote – Catholic Dyos who only the year before had baptised his first child, my dead little sister, Joan. Yes, Catholic Dyos was expelled from Stratford by proscribing, pricking voices such as my father's. They kicked the scapegoat out into the wilderness to starve, the bastards, the survivors, the ruthless pragmatic men. And it was John Shakespeare and his fellow burgesses who obliterated the old Catholic art of Stratford, swept away pictures and monuments, dismissing them as the dust on antique time. Into the Guild Chapel they came with their brushes and buckets, the year before I was born, and whitewashed out a thousand years of culture, St George and the Dragon, Constantine's vision, Becket going down like a beast in the Canterbury shambles, and the whole old Vision of Judgement, complete with Catholic purgatory and red-hot chains cordoning off the damned.

'Call that culture? Maybe it hurt him, though.'

Knowing him, I doubt it. They saved the vestments, the stained glass, and as many of the paintings as they dared. And whitewash comes off again – should the times change. A practical man, my father, a realist untroubled by imagination or belief, a doer not a thinker. He swam with the stream. He kept his balance in a world grown slippery underfoot and succeeded in living on into his seventies and dying between clean sheets. Not a bad achievement for a man who once took me to Sir William Catesby's house to receive a personal copy of the Catholic Testament from the hands of Father Edmund Campion himself.

'You never told me that, Will.'

I never told anybody.

'Why now?'

Look at me. I'm inches from eternity. I reckon I'm safe. So is the book.

'I won't ask where. But when was this, if you don't mind the question?'

I don't mind, not now. It was during the Jesuit mission to Warwickshire in 1580. I was sixteen at the time so I remember Campion well. Eyes that burned with an unearthly fire.

'Unhealthy.'

A fire that only Tyburn could put out.

'Men with eyes like that seldom die in their beds. A man should keep his eyes down.'

I could read Tyburn in those eyes. Tyburn was his destiny. It was what he was born for. It was where he was headed – and he probably knew it – when he first stepped off the boat at Dover in a black hat and cloak, the greatest scholar of his day disguised as a gentleman but bent on his mission, fighting for freedom with the weapon of terror. The following year he was caught, interrogated, starved, thumbscrewed, fingernailed, compressed in the Scavenger's Daughter, and left for a week in the darkness of the Pit – all without a result.

'Strength from somewhere, god or devil.'

The queen herself even examined him at Leicester House. She would have saved him if she could. She'd heard him lecture at Oxford on the moon and the tides, when he was a young man. But he didn't say the right thing when she asked him The Bloody Question.

'Which was?'

'If the Pope invaded, which side would you fight on?'

He said: 'I should so as God should give me grace.'

'Equivocal.'

Unacceptable.

After that the warrants were issued to place him on the rack, where he stayed until his joints broke.

'It never fails, does it?'

Inevitably the names began to come out, between the screams, names shrieked out of him by his torturers. And the horsemen arrived at the houses.

'And the birds fled to the woods.'

If they had the chance. There were imprisonments, mysterious deaths. The Stratford schoolmaster left his post – unsurprising as his Jesuit brother was a member of the Campion mission and was tried along with him. At their trial Campion struck out. 'In condemning us you condemn all your ancestors, all the ancient bishops and kings, all that was once the glory of England.'

'Stirring stuff.'

If you're a Catholic. He was then taken to Tyburn where he parted company with his genitals, bowels, and heart.

'I like a bit of heart. Do we have to go into this?'

It was the first day of December, a chilly day for the solemn opening of the doors of your belly, when you feel the frost in your intestines. The snow goes gory for a moment and Campion's body heat rises hissing from the ground. Heaven? That's somewhere above the spectators' heads, so they say, but the smoke of bloody execution vanishes before it even reaches eye level, it's so cold. That's how easy it is to snuff out a fire in the guts, no matter how holy the fuel, how heavenly the vision.

'Out, out, brief candle – did somebody once say?'

I'll wager Campion didn't find it easy, though.

'And I'll wager nobody saw his soul as it rose up through the steam and made for paradise...'

Nobody saw my kinsman Edward Arden's either, not even those members of our family who went up to London in secret to be there for him, to give moral support from the crowd – though what support you give to a man minus half his innards is a curious question.

'Interesting family background, Will. And when was that one?'

That happened two years after Campion, courtesy of our local Puritan big cheese, Sir Thomas Lucy, under orders from Protestant Robert Dudley, now Elizabeth's number one earl. Lucy harassed my father. And I took more than rabbits from his warren to pay him back for that.

'Now Will, there are certain things a lawyer shouldn't know.'

The time's long gone by since that was actionable. I was young and high-spirited, and he made poaching a felony. But better a poacher than a Catholic, if Lucy was after your blood.

'Was he such a thorn in your flesh?'

It was Lucy who helped mastermind the raids on known Catholic houses in Warwickshire, including a strike against our kinsman. Arden was arrested on false charges of conspiracy to kill the queen. His only crime, if you can call it that, had been to refuse to wear Leicester's livery during the Kenilworth fireworks, preferring instead to refer to Dudley as an upstart adulterer. His real crime, of course, was that he was a Catholic, a member of the Old Religion and of the old gentry of Warwickshire, the enemies of the Elizabethan élite.

'Dangerous days.'

Days you might never live through safely – not if you were a Catholic and they were on your trail. So the Queen's agents rampaged through houses like wild leopards, pawing the panels, squinting wild-eyed and whiskered for secret chambers, sniffing the beds to see if they'd been slept in. Were there hairs on the pillows? Siftings of skin? Were the mattresses still warm? No, they weren't, because the women had turned them over and re-made the beds. That didn't persuade the Jesuit hunters. They had nostrils like the hounds of God that could sniff out papists even when they were standing ankle-deep in the effluence of the principal shitter, the *cloaca maxima*, that emptied into the moat.

'Your family must have been all the time on edge.'

It was families like my mother's that left the little local churches their best black damask gowns to be made into copes, and their two-year old heifers to help towards the maintenance of the church bells. And this was the extent of Arden's villainy, this affection for the old churches, the old saints, and the older version of world history, which in their long view went right back to Peter and to Jesus Christ.

'So they believed.'

A belief is enough. A belief can kill you. It was enough to put him in the picture – the Somerville-Throgmorton frame.

'What?'

Yet another plot against the life of Elizabeth. So Arden was hanged, drawn, and quartered at Smithfield and his head spiked on London Bridge five days before yuletide.'

'Gentle Jesus!'

Five years later, when I made my move to the capital, it was still there, the head. I couldn't recognise him. You wouldn't believe how a spell on London Bridge alters a man's features so that even his own family can't pick him out from the crowd. And there's quite a crowd of heads on good old London Bridge.

'I know, I've seen them.'

Just before I left for London my father took me up to the Henley Street loft and showed me something he'd hidden between the eaves and the joists when they'd searched our houses after Arden's execution. It was his own copy of the Catholic Testament, also the gift of Campion, whose tarred and eyeless head now gaped blackly over the Thames. He seemed to have forgotten about my copy, and I never troubled him with the thought of it.

'Look at it, Will,' he whispered, so softly that you'd have thought the earth-clad mole deep beneath us listened for every word.

'And read it, Will, read it aloud, quietly as you can.'

I knew it already, but I looked and read.

It was the same six-page book, each page handwritten and then signed in the name of John Shakespeare, who protested thereby that he was both willing and did infinitely desire that of this his last will and testament the glorious Virgin Mary might be chief Executresse, together with all the saints etcetera. And he begged and beseeched all his kinsfolk, in the bowels of his Saviour Jesus Christ, to sing masses for his soul after his death especially, he said, as I may be possibly cut off even in the blossoms of my sin.

'Jesus.'

Exactly. After I'd finished reading I felt the hand that killed the cattle tightening on mine.

'Pray for my soul in purgatory, Will.'

And pity me not. But lend thy serious hearing to what I shall unfold.

He then launched into the longest speech I ever heard from him. 'Keep your beliefs just like this' (that's how it went) 'hidden away up in the roof of your head. Don't let anybody look into the windows of your eyes. And above all let nothing slip out of the door.'

'Your gob?'

'Give every man thine ear but few thy voice.'

'Ah, old Polonius!'

'Be thou familiar but by no means vulgar, beware of entrance to a quarrel, take each man's censure but reserve thy judgement, costly thy habit as thy purse can buy, neither a borrower nor a lender be' – yes, that was my father, no philosopher.

'To thine own self be true?'

It would never even have occurred to him, not in a month of martyrs, quite the reverse, I can assure you. No, that was me, a humble line but 'twas mine own. My father didn't get where he was by being true to himself. Truth was hardly the currency of the age, was it?

'You say right.'

When he'd finished that longest speech of his life he asked me to kiss the little book that Campion had given to him, as he had to me with eyes on fire. It wouldn't necessarily save your soul, he said, but it could easily shorten your life. Let it stay where it is, then. And he tucked it away, wedged it back into its hiding place, wrapped up in blackness, but close to the blue air and the eyes of cherubim and birds.

I expect it's still there to this day.

'What, up in Henley Street? Jesus!'

A careful man, my father. It wasn't until Leicester died that he told me what he knew: that Protestant Leicester, who didn't like the Ardens in general and had fought with Edward Arden in particular, had made up his mind to crush the family, and that's why he had Edward arrested on those trumped up charges of treason. He was able to do it and to get away with it, the Puritan prick, though his own prick was far from pure. At that time he was dipping it on a regular basis well into a certain lady-in-waiting to the queen, while waiting his chance to fuck Her Majesty – in the very same house where he was busy screwing the gentlewoman.

'The things you've known, Will.'

I suppose you could admire the sheer nerve of the bastard. But how the queen, who didn't like Puritans, liked Leicester, remains something of an irony to me, though I've long ceased to puzzle over the power of a straight pizzle to bend the judgement of a pliable lady – whether she's in waiting or in power.

'So long as she's in bed.'

The rules of the bed-game change all the others – politics, religion, even plain old-fashioned commonsense. The curious thing is that even as I stood at Leicester's Fantasia in 1575 with my eyes popping out on stalks, the maestro himself was probably busy in the real world, plotting to crush the Ardens. Even at that time. And even at that time I knew that we were outsiders, keeping our outsides inside – discreetly hidden from the queen's thought-spies.

'It's little wonder you're old before your time – saving your presence.'

The following year the queen set up her Grand Commission to order, correct, reform, and punish any persons wilfully and obstinately absenting themselves from church and service. Civic officers such as my father now had to take the oath of allegiance to the queen – and their allegiance included religious allegiance to a monarch who was supreme head of the English Church.

'Shades of Henry the Eighth.'

No shades of Thomas More, though, not in my father. When he

said that he was not the stuff of which martyrs were made, he meant it. Nevertheless fines were levied against Catholics – which he refused to pay – and names were demanded.

'You were on the wrong end of a witch-hunt.'

That's putting it mildly. Some folk had even begun to laugh at witches. Nobody laughed at Catholics. And it wasn't long afterwards that my father's troubles started. He woke up one morning to find himself being prosecuted for shadowy dealings in usury and in wool – there were strict laws about brogging and shylocking – though I can tell you that the man who informed against him could hardly have been described as one of Warwickshire's most honest and industrious characters.

'Langrake?'

A rapist and an assassin. Also a small-fry spy, the kind of scum that those in power scoop up, dry out, and put in store for their purposes. Not that any of this mattered. My father, high on the wheel for twenty years and more, took the downward turn.

'Never to come up again.'

He left off attending his council meetings, mortgaged and lost properties, houses, lands in Wilmcote and Snitterfield, was fined for various legal indiscretions and circumstances with his neighbours, and was also penalised for non-attendance at church, which he shunned like the plague for fear of process for debt – a debtor was always a good target on a Sunday, in spite of the injunction to let trespasses be forgiven. It's true that there were some well-heeled Catholics who pretended to be bankrupt as an excuse for not attending the Anglican services, but my father wasn't one of them. His eyes twinkled in the good times – they never burned like Campion's. He never wore his Catholicism on his sleeve and he suffered the badge of the new compromise religion sensibly, going to church like a good child of the times.

'So it was really money troubles that kept him away in the end?'

But in the eyes of the true Catholics he was just another backslider, a time-server and a liar, his spiritual bankruptcy echoing his empty coffers. And the richly left Mary Arden saw all her substance swiftly eaten away around the financial failures of this Snitterfield nobody who'd risen fast and far but had overreached himself in the end. Do you know she had her own private seal? A galloping horse. She had energy and pride. Whether or not he was on one of the blacklists of church or state made no difference to my mother. She was a spirited woman and understood one thing – that whatever the reason for it, social decline went only one way and that was down the road of humiliation and disgrace.

'A big come-down.'

Especially as the drinking started then, and the vicious mole of nature came out in him. How could I blame him? He became funnier in a way – more human. Toby, Falstaff, Claudius, Cassio – human beings, Francis. But sweep away the fun, and what are you left with? Failure. Not that I didn't sympathize with failure, with a fallen man, a troubled king.

There was a bitter price for me too. I was told one morning that my time with Jenkins was over, and without warning I exchanged the golden world of Ovid for the blood and grease of the Rothermarket and the stench of the shambles. Jenkins had said I might go to university. Destiny now demanded that I should be a butcher, a dresser of leather and a maker of gloves. My father's fall changed everything.

'Things could hardly have gotten worse.'

They could have got a lot worse. And almost did. I was sent off to Lancashire for a while.

'That sink of popery.'

Well put, Francis. I was almost washed down with the best of them. That's when I saw Campion again, not long before he was caught, and the whole sticky web was spun around me – to change the metaphor. I don't like images of drowning.

'What was going on?'

What was going on? There was always something going on. It went on for years. My old schoolmaster, Simon Hunt, had defected to Douai, taking with him one of his pupils, Robert Debdale, not much older than me. He had family in Shottery. Then schoolmaster John Cottam's brother Thomas started off for Shottery with beads and crucifix and self-damning letter from Debdale. He never made it. He lay with the Scavenger's Daughter before he was hanged and disembowelled – as was Debdale. They all came to the scaffold in time.

'Did they try to involve you?'

What do you think? They were suicidal freaks, holy soldiers. I could have gone to Shottery under orders. As it was I went there on another mission – a mission of the heart – after I came back from Lancashire.

'What were you doing in Shottery?'

All in good time, Francis. This was a melancholy time in our lives, after my father's fall. And to further mark that melancholy time came three deaths that joined hands in triumvirate and sat on brood over an altered existence. The hatch and disclose would cast a blackness over the start of the eighties.

12

Francis had done rather well for a beefy lawyer, but at the mention of three deaths, he wilted and went off for another piss. When he returned he was revived, but not for chatter, or for legal work.

'Will, if we're to continue, can you order up some lunch?'

Yes, Francis, what's your fancy?

'Well, the subject of veal came up not so long ago. I don't suppose – '

I'll see what I can do.

Ding-dong bell.

It took some time and led to much small talk over much small beer that I'd managed to ask Alison to smuggle in. She's a good girl, and helps me out. When she appeared with the veal, however, she was attended by Anne, whose only service was a shadow's, casting that long look of reproach over the proceedings, as if the veal itself were in some measure accessory to a deathbed plot to outface the grim reaper with junket and jest. The beer was by that time under the bed, thanks to Francis's fat but nimble fingers, though she may have nosed it as she came in. I know every nerve in that face, and in the merest arch of an eyebrow I have learned to read passages of disparagement for a life ill-lived. Probably she thinks I'm dying of the pox. And possibly I am. Who but Hermes knows what hidden harms remain to plague me? Well, veal won't cure me, whatever ails me, and that's a surety.

Now good digestion wait on appetite.

'And health on both.'

And all at once Francis was ripping into it like the good trencherman he'll always be. Unless one day he drops stone-dead without the shadow of a question on his fat lips, I'll be praying for him in eternity anon, to mend his ways.

'Do you want the mustard Will?'

Not without mustard. Yes, that would be Francis's last likely query, facing eternity. Hell on toast – and don't forget the mustard.

But no, Francis, I'm not even having the veal, in case you

hadn't noticed.

'What a waste! Well, all the more for the law, eh?'

But you may pour me some beer.

'I'll have some wine with this, if it's all right with you.'

Make yourself at home, my friend, and reckon not the cost. It'll all be coming out of my estate, won't it?

A veal-hung pause.

'Your estate. Ah, now I'm glad you asked that question. You've got one remaining sister.'

A sister. Yes, I had a little sister and the shadows took her. Till then death had been an abstraction, a bible story, a pile of bones, a slack-arsed old sexton. People turned pale, turned to stone, they dwindled – or they disappeared at once and you never saw them again. With Anne it was different. It was my first experience of death in the family.

One day in 1579 it was, when she suddenly fell ill. A hard February cough at first to keep the house awake, to stop me from sleeping in the chilly hours before dawn. Followed by a March fever, with weird little noises coming out of her, to the accompaniment of the crows in the elms, the bare winds banging the shutters. There was a flush on her face, roses damp with death's first dew. Early herald of its endless day. As we went into rainy April the fever passed – but still Anne failed to find the strength to rise. An April wasting that was sadder than the dribbling plainsong of the rain, day-long, night-long, down on quiet windows that year. I was fifteen at the time. She was seven. And the house grew heavy with the knowledge that she was going to die. She stopped asking questions about herself, about anything. She stopped answering, stopped listening, stopped eating and sleeping, she neither smiled nor cried. Then one day she simply stopped.

They called me to the bedside.

'Come and see your sister, Will, before she goes away. Come and say goodbye.'

I dragged my angry awkward adolescent limbs heavily over to the sheeted statue lying on display in the best bed. She'd been moved there for the important occasion of her dying. Sick at heart, I remembered the day she'd first come to us out of nowhere, a little white seabird that had just flown in and was fluttering on my mother's breast, filling the shorelines of the sheets with alien sounds. A curiosity that gradually grew into a sister, my bright little bird, Anne. It had never occurred to me that she would one day stop singing. But that day had now come and had taken away all her sound and motion, even her shape – a white hump in the bed, dead seabird, a snowdrift in the silence of the room. Such a cold white silence. And that blind unseeing face. Blind eyes of the newly born, the newly dead. What had the seven years in between actually meant? What had they been *for*? I kissed the ice-cold cheek of my dead, marble sister. 'Go on, Will, say something to her, you'll never see her again, speak now.'

Alas, she's cold. Her blood is settled and her joints are stiff. Death lies on her like an untimely frost upon the sweetest flower of all the field. Cold, cold, my girl.

I went with Gilbert and Joan and our parents to bury her. It was the fourth day of April and the sky a sudden bright blue, the grass sparked with daisies. The gravedigger had made a black hole in the ground where he said that the tiny bones of Margaret and the first Joan lay, dead in infancy twenty years ago. Anne went in beside them. How small a hole it was that contained all three. The churlish priest said very little to lay her to rest. I said it for him, inside my head.

Lay her in the earth. And from her fair and unpolluted flesh may violets spring.

We came up to the grave's edge with our flowers. The rain started again, whipped up by the wind, a vicious little squall, and the shivering vicar grumbled at us to hurry.

I tell thee, churlish priest, a ministering angel shall my sister be when thou liest howling.

'Quickly, Will, quickly – sweets to the sweet. Make haste.'

So we threw in our primroses while our mother wept.

Sweets to the sweet, farewell. I thought thy bride-bed to have decked, sweet maid, and not have strewed thy grave.

The first plunging drops struck my sister's shroud like daggers tearing apart the delicate scattering of primroses. In a single moment the rain increased to a waterfall and the shroud clung to the wasted little body, showing its oblivious contours, heightening its blind face. The already damp soil of Holy Trinity, too close to the Avon, couldn't hold the sudden volume of water. The grave started to flood. A wind tore down the long line of limes. A few steps from where we stood, a procession of swans sailed stiffly past, like silver barges down the river, proud heads bowed slightly into the wind, white sails ruffled by the storm. Fare thee well at once. We left them hurriedly, three sisters dead in earth, divided by two decades, together in eternity. Goodnight ladies, goodnight, sweet ladies, goodnight, goodnight.

'A thousand times farewell.'

Francis gave his benediction, between mouthfuls of beer and veal.

Just after Christmas the following year Granny Arden died and went under a shroud of snow up at Aston Cantlow where her two long-shrouded spouses lay and waited for her – Robert Arden for twenty-four years and old Hill himself more than thirty years in the ground. But what did the number matter to those now hidden in death's dateless night?

'Hard ground up here' – that was more to the quick of the matter for the grumbling gravedigger, not quite ready for us – 'and fucking worse at this time of the year, let me tell you. What a time to die, eh? There's a time to be born and a time to die and right now I'd rather be a priest than a sexton. What a time to have a man digging graves! Fuck me! Whoever arranges dates up there doesn't handle a spade! Angel of fucking death, eh?'

Asbies Agnes would have given the surly old bugger one of her mouthfuls if her ears hadn't gone deaf. But they were past hearing – and the chattering mouth that had rippled with gossip and brimmed with stories and ladled so much lore into me was stopped in the snow. A single iron flake had landed on her lips and she had ceased to care. It was 1580.

That was also the year that Kate Hamlet, maddened in her mind, drowned herself in the Avon.

'*Felo de se,* was it?'

Yes, she committed suicide. But Henry Rogers, who conducted the inquest, found that she had met with an accident.

'*Per infortunium.* That was a humane conclusion, and typical of him. I partly knew the man.'

It was a Sunday morning and we were all at home when Wedgewood brought the news. He was hopping from house to house to be the first bearer of bad tidings and was eager to be on his way, to outrun the wildfire pace that a tragic word always achieves. But we held him back, made him sit down with us and drink some small beer, and he succumbed easily to be the cynosure to the gallery of round mouths and eyes and the sensation of being set on a black and muffled stage, speaking of something terrible.

'Who found her, Robert?'

'Ah well, I'd be the first, you see, to have come across her.'

This was later discovered to be a typical Wedgewood lie. It was Ruth Wedgewood, his second wife, who'd seen the body floating near the banks and she'd hurried home and told him where and when and all the circumstance.

There is a willow grows aslant a brook, that shows his hoar leaves in the glassy stream...

'She's drowned, Robert, really drowned?'

'Drowned, drowned.'

No mistake. The froth shining wetly on his lips. The knowledge of it shining in his Delphic eyes. We all stared into them, trying to see what he had seen, trying to imagine the unimaginable, a young girl whom we all knew, sixteen years old, my own age, her eyes and mouth filled with the Avon, dead to the watery world while Stratford woke up to its Sunday. The young man she had been in love with – we all knew him too, also my age – had let her down. Had he bolted out of the affair when she missed her first monthly? Had he left her in the belly lurch? Was there an infant lying drowned in her womb's watery tomb while she drifted quietly in the silvery graveyard of the Avon? Whatever the reason, accident was unlikely in the circumstances and a verdict of suicide would be reached. And as the Everlasting had fixed his canon against self-slaughter, she was not only drowned but damned, said Wedgewood. There would be no mercy in the next world for Kate Hamlet.

I ran down to the place that Wedgewood had identified for us. The grasses were trampled by the many curious feet that had gathered there. For folk to conjecture and to stare. I waited till everybody had gone home and stood alone on the tragic spot, stood and stared for a long time at that part of the river in which her body had been found, face up, floating free, lips slightly parted to let in the Avon, unseeing eyes reflecting the sky. There was the very willow, slanting the glassy stream – just there.

There with fantastic garlands did she come, of crow-flowers, nettles, daisies, and long purples that liberal shepherds give a grosser name, but our cold maids do dead men's fingers call them.

Was it a Wedgewood invention? No, his tailor's brain was too threadbare to have thought up such a scene. It made perfect sense to me. She'd been left naked in her youth, stripped of love, so she'd covered herself with the beauty of the world and come down to the Avon, decked for death.

Naturally it was a kindness on the part of certain gentle souls to picture it differently.

There on the pendent boughs her coronet weeds clambering to hang, an envious sliver broke, when down her weedy trophies and herself fell in the weeping brook.

But it didn't happen like that, did it? She'd walked down to this bank and shoal of time, had slipped into the river and had simply drawn it over herself like a bedcover, like a glassy shroud, comfortably, coolly, putting out the pain of the world. How strange, I thought, that the river remained unmarked, that it carried no imprint of her agony, only weeds and water, nothing to commemorate her sad pastoral. But I could see it all with desperate clarity, how her clothes filled up, spread wide.

And mermaid-like awhile they bore her up, which time she chanted snatches of old tunes, as one incapable of her own distress, or like a creature native and indued unto that element.

Such was her swan-song, while the swans themselves sailed by like kings and queens to the sound of her singing.

But long it could not be till that her garments, heavy with their drink, pulled the poor wretch from her melodious lay to muddy death.

And muddy death was to the point according to my old nightmare friend, the sexton, who was digging her grave – 'Mud up her crutch, poor bitch, and bream buggering her all the way from backside to kingdom come. She didn't go down the Avon like no swan. No bugger does.'

He was digging in the consecrated part of the graveyard, much to the displeasure of the priest who'd bury her. The family had pleaded the ambiguity of her end, beseeching the benefit of the doubt, and the town council had prevailed. Her death was doubtful, muttered the priest – and the doubt should have been sufficient to consign her to the crossroads.

And but that great command o'ersways the order, she should in ground unsanctified have lodged till the last trumpet. For charitable prayers, shards, flints and pebbles should be thrown on her. Yet here she is allowed her virgin crants, her maiden strewments, and the bringing home of bell and burial.

But that was all she got. Even though her brother, wild with grief, begged for melody for the sister that had loved to sing. 'Must there no more be done?'

No more be done! The church was outraged. 'We should profane the service of the dead to sing sage requiem and such rest to her as to peace-parted souls. Now pile the earth on, master sexton!' And he closed the ceremony. '*Nunc dimittis*. Go back home, all of you.' Fuck off.

Another churlish priest. Like the one who buried my sister. Yet once more then, say it again. Lay her in the earth. And from her fair and unpolluted flesh may violets spring.

But the gravedigger wasn't interested in violets. He was holding up one of the flowers Kate Hamlet had died clutching. It was a long purple. The leering old devil put his hand inside the arrow-shaped leaf that cupped the flower and stroked the purple phallus with a salacious chuckle. I was just waiting for him to fart.

'Fancy killing yourself for that, now! Look around, lad – there are hundreds of them to be had for the plucking. And it's the same with pricks – plenty on offer and never out of season either, and all because one of them let her down.'

And he threw the flower into the grave. It landed in Kate Hamlet's lap. A last long purple for a dubious virgin.

Long purples then. Lords-and-ladies, if you're calling them by their polite name, though it comes to the same thing. Dead men's fingers, in the mouths of our chaste maids.

'Are you a scholar of the species?'

A cuckoo-pint is the flower in question. On the lips of the older folk like Agnes, Asbies way, they were cows-and-calves, Jack-in-the-pulpit. The ancient name was starchwort. But liberal shepherds and coarse-tongued sextons were alike in their gross libelling of these hedgerow vulgarities, calling them also tongues-in-tails. Or, if you prefer it no holds barred and with a lecherous sneer, pricks-in-pussies.

13

'Talking about flowers now, are you?'

There she was, in the room, frowning over us, standing in the echoes, the tangible traces of our maleness, and the two glasses set there on the table, filled up in guilt.

'Er, yes, I'm drinking for him though,' said Francis, taking a generous swig from my glass, not without relish, and setting it down away from me, well out of my reach.

'But it was sisters we were talking about, wasn't it, Will?'

The frown relaxed a little.

'Ah, well, he has only one left. And what will she be getting, may I ask?'

Francis spread his arms.

'Well, we hadn't actually – '

'Then hadn't you better actually?'

'Quite right, actually, Mistress Anne. Will, shouldn't we actually settle this one now?'

Item, I give and bequeath unto my said sister Joan twenty pounds.

'And she can have all your clothes too.'

I thought Alison gave me a pitying look, for which I felt grateful.

And all my wearing apparel, to be paid and delivered within one year after my decease.

Alison started to snivel and her mistress punched her in the back, indicating the dirty dishes.

And I do will and devise the house with the appurtenances in Stratford wherein she dwelleth, free of charge for her natural life.

'Free of charge!'

She placed her hands on her hips in that way she had, and swivelled round on the scratching lawyer.

'Master Collins!'

Francis raised the quill and peered at me.

'Will?'

What's the point? I asked myself.

Change that, Francis, to – *under the yearly rent of twelve pence.*

The hands came off the hips and the arms were folded, indicating displeasure but not full opposition. Francis paused, glanced both ways, weighed up the situation, and noted it down.

And also add in there, Francis, the following.

Item, I give and bequeath unto her three sons, William Hart – what's the second one's name, Anne?

'Always the Ardens.'

Francis looked perplexed – diplomatically, I thought.

'They're Harts actually, Mistress Anne.'

She swept from the room, pushing little Alison before her.

'You'll have to help me here, Will. What's the name of this second Hart son?'

Can't remember right now. We'll come back to him. The third one is Michael. Always the middle one, isn't it?

'*And Michael Hart* – how much?'

Five pounds apiece.

'To be paid when?'

To be paid within one year after my decease.

'Done!'

Francis glugged off my glass and took up his own.

'Hey, we're getting on now, shall we tie up some more? How about Judith?'

Judith's complicated. We'll come to her anon.

'And Elizabeth Hall, your niece?'

Equally complicated.

'Why? What's so difficult about her?'

Nothing – in itself, that is. Explain later. But meanwhile put down Elizabeth for all my plate – except for the broad silver gilt bowl. That's to go to Judith.

'*Item, I give and bequeath unto the said Elizabeth Hall all my plate, except my broad silver and gilt bowl, that I now have, at the date of this will.* That do?'

Yes. And then, *I give and bequeath to my said daughter Judith my broad silver and gilt bowl.* She always liked it.

'It's taken care of.'

Are you sure?

'Am I your lawyer?'

You are.

'Then rest assured.'

Rest? How can you rest among all these women? Why have I no son?

'You have what you have, Will. What life gave you.'

What it left me with. A clutter of females, all of them illiterate, not one of them able to read a word I wrote. Jesus, you don't see it coming down to this when you're eighteen years of age and you think women the wonder of the world, do you?

'That was a long time ago, Will. You were young. You were in love.'

Was I? Ah yes, pricks-in-pussies. And there was one pussy that took in my own innocent prick and changed my life forever. An old claw-cat now, a kitten in her day.

'Will, I'm buggered. I'm going to pull out your old truckle-bed from underneath you and sleep it off. Give me half an hour will you, old man?'

Have all the time you need, Francis. I'm not going anywhere.

Snore snore.

Old friends, Francis, the Shakespeares and the Hathaways. Are you half hearing me? I'll pretend you are. According to my mother, Richard Hathaway and my father used to drink Stratford dry and when these two put their heads together they forgot to unbend their elbows. Then they'd wax metaphysical about beasts and angels – their work and their religion. 'Man delights not them,' she'd say, 'no, nor women neither.' (She too had a tongue with a tang.) 'What gets that pair going is bulls and barley, the quality of angels' fleece, what their wings are made of, and whether God wears gloves.'

And as they drain their draughts of Rhenish down, the kettle-drum and trumpet thus bray out the triumph of their pledge.

'In their drunken dreams. Talkers are no good doers, Will. And as for drinkers – just listen to them. And bear in mind.'

A sensible woman, my mother. And if there was a sharp edge on her commonsense it was put there by what she referred to as my father's fall, followed by his increasing inclination to alcohol. She took an even sharper view of the genial John's readiness to prop up his poorer neighbours with loans. He'd stood surety already for Richard Hathaway and on his account had put himself smilingly into debt. This heavy-headed revel – drinking east and west as she put it in her homely country way – was no way to recover the debt. And why should she stand by and watch him helping his neighbours to his hard-earned money and to her hard-brewed beer? Not to mention helping his off-spring out of their inheritance and his eldest out of a place at Oxford. 'You've seen everybody all right and yourself all wrong,' she stormed at him, making him wince by flinging his own philosophy in his face. 'Listen to him talk! Neither a borrower nor a lender be, he says – for loan oft loses both itself and friend. And borrowing dulls the edge of husbandry. A great pity the old fool didn't reck his own rede and learn a little from his own wisdom!'

He was wise enough to keep his head down – but all the same she didn't miss him and hit the wall. Still my father had a great talent for remaining on good terms with his friends, even though they sometimes let him down badly, betraying his better nature. Richard Hathaway was one of those whose debt was never recovered yet he and John Shakespeare stayed thick in their cups. By that time Hathaway's first wife was long in her grave and he had four sons and three daughters. Unlike my father before me I didn't go for the youngest. As things turned out she had eight years on me – and you'd be tempted to conclude that she just sucked me in and blew me out in bubbles. But you'd be wrong. There was more to our meeting than that old story and she wasn't exactly on the shelf, though things might have looked that way.

Let me come to her then as I did many a time and oft – are you listening, Francis? Are you in there – somewhere inside all that slumbering blubber?

Snort snort – and a grumbled answer of sorts, blown up in spouts. A whale on siesta, breaching the truckle-bed. Ah well, half a hearer is better than none.

Anne Hathaway.

I was eighteen when I set eyes on her, having seen her hundreds of times as a child without ever really looking at her. Saw her now – for the first time – as a woman.

1582 threw up sudden and strong reasons for this change in my perception. Since leaving the King's School the following alterations had occurred to my person: voice gone gravelly, armpits gritty, face turned to pigskin, legs gangling like a new-born calf's, and my moods swinging wildly from inspired to suicidal. I spoke only to the mirror, despised my parents, and half the time wanted to kill my siblings. At first I attributed these upheavals to the loss of Ovid, an ingredient essential to the diet of a growing boy. But when a forest-fire of hair suddenly broke out on my groin and raged around my balls, I began to realise that something more serious was afoot. I woke up one morning to find a cannon in my crutch, trained on the world, banishing my lightfoot laddishness forever. Nights were worse – the penis swayed like a poplar, lifting the sheets like clouds. I woke up from wet dreams of my mother to find myself sticky with guilt and horror. I was a freak, a prodigy, a monster. And that's when I first saw Anne Hathaway, in the fullness of the flesh as it were, and saw that she was fair.

It was on one of my father's visits to the twelve-roomed house at Hewlands on the edge of the forest of Arden. A brilliant spring morning, when birds do sing, hey ding-a-ding-ding. The two fathers sat down at a bare board, and at a shout from Richard Hathaway a girl in green appeared and set down pewter between them with a hard clatter, as if she disapproved of setting them up for this early morning swigging. She had tits like unripe crab apples and as she left the room I noticed her fresh young bum, equally unripe. There was a hardness and tightness about both buttocks and breasts that troubled my prick not one whit. A curious disappointment, this Richard Hathaway creation, courtesy of his second wife, so I supposed. He looked at me from over the white moustache of beer-froth he'd suddenly grown, licked his lips, and winked at my father.

'Dull stuff, Will, for a red-blooded boy, listening to two old buffers babbling about business – why don't you go down to the buttery instead and spend some time with my daughter? There's more matter there for a May morning and she'd be glad of a hand. You might even get some haunch for breakfast!'

They winked and grinned and I went off, balancing the relief of leaving them against the prospect of an uninvited and uninviting interview with Miss Tight-Tits down in the buttery. But when I finally got there at a constipated snail's pace and glared through the open doorway, I received a pleasant surprise followed by a violent hard-on. The female standing by the churn, also wearing green, was bending so low that her face was hidden by her long fair hair, but it was perfectly obvious that it wasn't Brick-Bum. Not that her rear was in evidence – she was facing the door – but the generous percentage of tit afforded by her bending décolletage made it instantly apparent that Tight-Arse and the buttery-girl were not one and the same. These, Francis, were tits to give an angel an erection and make all heaven wet. My eyeballs came right out on double-threaded beams and disappeared down her dress as far as they could go, scrabbling like mad for the *just* unseeable nipples. Double curses.

'What's the matter – can't you find the cherries on the cake?'

She'd barely flicked an eyelash at me and carried on working, sleeves rolled right up, splashed to the elbows with rich white cream. Her wit was lost on me – I was lost in the valley of the tits.

'Don't just stand there, Will Shakespeare, you're gaping wider than the door!'

How could she know my name?

'Come closer, why don't you? You'll see more of me, I reckon, from over here.'

It must have been obvious that I was staring all the way down her dell. My erection must have been equally obvious, I thought, as I accompanied it gingerly over the splashed flagstones to stand beside her. Just as I did so, she unbent, stretching, from the churn, arms uplifted, flung back her head and rubbed a nostril with the back of her hand, wriggling her nose vigorously. A single drop of cream fell from her fingers and landed on a tit.

And that was the moment.

When I fell too.

'Arse over tit.' Francis shook off Morpheus.

God save us, the man's alive and hearing – and you can always count on a lawyer to find the right phrase.

He soon fell away again, though, rumbling and grumbling through my tale.

Head over heels. Just as you say, sweet sleeper – let's clean it up a bit. But it wasn't the tit that did the damage – it was the nose. And what's in a nose? The way Anne Hathaway wriggled hers that morning won me to her in a twinkling, turned my knees to jelly and my prick to iron. All previous erections were now classed as dress rehearsals, if not dry-runs. My balls blew up like pumpkins. I could feel the seeds bursting. Jesu. Even so quickly may one catch the plague? Even so quickly, I assure you, but I wasn't just plague-stricken, I was dumbfounded, couldn't find my tongue, just stood there and gawped at her like a glazed fish. She laughed.

'Well, what do you think, Will? Is it not well done?'

Excellent well done, every inch of her – but I had to find a compliment subtler than that. I racked my dazed brain and Ovid came to the rescue.

'Tis beauty truly blent, whose red and white nature's own sweet and cunning hand laid on.

Had I said that? Or just thought it?

'Oh, now that *is* well done! Well said, anyway.'

Obviously I'd spoken. Thank God.

'Poetic – and accurate too, since God did all. It'll endure wind and weather, Will. But you're staring! Is it a list you'd like? Item, two eyes, item, two lips, item, two breasts. Shall I make you out an inventory?'

Make me a willow cabin at your gate and call upon my soul within the house. Write loyal cantons of contemned love and sing them loud even in the dead of night. (Look to your throne, Ovid.) Halloo your name to the reverberate hills and make the babbling gossip of the air cry out—

'Cry out? Ooh, my name. You don't remember me, do you, Will Shakespeare?'

I admitted she had me at a disadvantage.

'Anne Hathaway.'

I looked hard at her. She wasn't unlike my mother, who looked young for her age. And a voice came up out of the wilderness of the bible, whispering in my inner ear. *Can a man enter his mother's womb a second time*? What was that old serpent up to now, I wondered. Anne Hathaway's voice broke in on it, bringing me out of my strange and sudden lusts.

'So what do you think then, Will – shall I die a maid? Or shall I sleep naked on St Andrew's Eve and see my future husband in a dream?'

It was hard to know what lay beneath the laughter that played around her lips. A deep longing? a controlled sadness? frustration? pain? Naturally I concluded that whatever it was, she'd been waiting all her life for me to walk through the open door, throw her over my shoulder and stride off with her into the dawn – and now here I was.

'No,' I said, 'you won't die a maid. I don't think you'll *live* a maid either. Not for much longer anyway, if only you throw *hate away*, Anne Hathaway.'

'You're clever with your answers, young man. But I wonder – do poets make good lovers?'

'They make the best lovers – because only true lovers can make true poems.'

'But,' said Anne Hathaway, the laughter on her lips again, 'the trouble is that both poets and lovers are liars.'

'Sometimes they die for their lies.'

'Men have died from time to time and worms have eaten them – but not for love. Men were deceivers ever.'

'Then sigh not so, but let them go – and be you blithe and bonny.'

'A good case against you,' she said (glancing at my groin) 'though not against *me*. But if you think different, Will Shakespeare, why don't you come anon and tell me about it?'

A genuine smile. And sweet.

'There is one thing you can do for me, though, before you go. If you'd be so kind.'

'Anything.'

She came up so close I could feel the folds of the green dress brushing my quaking knees. She was still holding her arms in the air and she jiggled her fingers, flicking white droplets into my eyes.

'One of my sleeves has come unrolled – would you care to fix it for me?'

I did so, looking into her eyes. Which never left mine.

'Thank you. Now bring your hand to the buttery-bar and let it drink.'

My reward.

I was being granted a feel. I'd never been greatly intimate with any female, not since Marian's moon-tits had swum into my ken all those years ago. But that infantile experience didn't count. Dazed and dreaming I watched my right arm reach out slowly and slide down into the open dress to clasp an Anne Hathaway breast in five buzzing fingers. Jesu! How long did I stand there like that – two minutes? two seconds? – the strangely fluid flesh cool against the paddling palm? It didn't matter. What mattered was that there was I, Will Shakespeare, standing in the buttery with a pretty woman's tit in my hand and my groin on fire with desire, while her talk washed over me like Ovidian metre come true.

'You need practice, Will. A working girl like me knows just what to do with her fingers. I like to rise early to be up with the cock and put out my hand to work with him, just as he stretches his red comb to greet the sunrise. I milked those cows myself this morning. A sweet milk-press makes the milk taste all the sweeter, you know, and I can handle the hive too, so subtly that the bee thinks I'm his queen and works off his honeybags to please me. That makes the thickest stickiest honey, believe me, and the sweetest. But I suppose the best I can hope for this springtime is to die unmarried and get me a good store of flowers stuck on my winding sheet to bewail my virginity. What a waste, eh, Will? What do you think?'

I couldn't say what I thought. I was dumb as a door and frantic with lust. Was she really a virgin? She was decked out in innocent green, not in the spoils of the silkworm but had some worm been at her already? Had some clodhopping spotted Hewlands Dick buried his bone-head between those magnificent mammaries and got in his thick dick where mine feared to tread? Already I was mad with mistrust and jealous rage. I'd just walked through the door three minutes ago and she'd let me grope her. Invited me, for Venus' sake. Milkmaid? She could be the Great Cow of Shottery for all I knew.

'What are you thinking, Will?'

'I'm thinking I'll come to Shottery.'

I withdrew my hand as I spoke, sensing the incongruity, to say the least, of carrying on a polite conversation with my arm at an awkward angle and this tit stuck firmly in my sweaty mitt.

She smiled in reply.

'Yes,' I said, as if we were discussing the weather, 'I'll walk out this way one evening.'

Another smile.

'Then I'll look for your coming.'

And she bent back to her work.

And that was it.

Anne Hathaway, buttery-bar girl, Hewlands farm girl, unmarried maid of Shottery parish, Anne Hathaway, milkmaid, ripe for plucking, bewailing her virginity and as good as handed it to me on the spot. Jesus, I'd felt like fucking her on the flagstones right there and then and adding to the spilt milk. And yes, yes, Will was hopelessly, uselessly in love for the first time in his circumscribed little life. And the very thought of this sudden object of my adoration lying dead in her winding sheet (a fate most incident to maids) all for lack of a lover – it was too much for me and I was struck so to the soul that I proclaimed my guilty secret aloud to the stars that same night. I love her, I want her, I want to lie with her, in her, on her, under her, and by God I will marry her!

I can. I will.

So it was not the Virgin Mary that brought me to Shottery, but the Virgin Anne, if maid she was. Not the Scavenger's Daughter I longed to lie with, but Richard Hathaway's. And by the time I was deep in Anne, Campion and Cottam and Debdale were dead. But I was made of flesh, not soul, and my flesh was for loving with, not for being slit open on the scaffold, and torn apart. The martyrs were to be pitied. But so was Anne, so close to her virgin's shroud. And my trust was not in Campion but in Cupid.

14

Only it wasn't Anne Hathaway's shroud that got stuck with yew that year – it was her father's. My father said that Richard Hathaway hadn't been well for nearly a year and had dwelt on death quite blithely when they'd had their last little chinwag. That was the day I'd been sent down to the buttery to meet my marital destiny, sealed by a feel and by a single longing note that was the undercurrent to everything she'd said.

I often wondered what else the two fathers had yapped about that day. Had they mentioned his will – which Hathaway had made out the previous September, as it turned out? Doubtless they'd discussed unmarried Anne and how to see her set on her feet once the old man had turned up his toes. And certainly I'd been a pawn in their game. Or not so much a pawn as a prince, and one more than ready to serve his queen. And to be checked and mated.

Even so in later life that thought kept on recurring – and rankling too. Money-borrowing Richard Hathaway, non-deliverer of debts, begging his old indulgent friend for one last favour before he quit this earthly scene – ah, never to return, old lad, never to return! That's it, squeeze another tear out of maudlin John, the Stratford soak, then carry on. To the unpaid forty pounds – and what's that to a man trembling on the edge of eternity? – add your eldest son: only eighteen but a bachelor and a handsome stripling too, a fine match for the spirited and intelligent Anne, who may turn out to be something of a shrew in the end but that's no bad thing, is it? Something of a dreamer, after all, is our young Will, in need of a hard-nosed lass to keep his feet planted in the muck and pluck his skull out of the stars. And it's not as if our Anne doesn't offer certain compensating qualities, eh? Well, have another drink, old man! Indeed, quite a bedful there and never once been put to it, though in long standing need of it, women have needs as well as us, just look at her, you can feel it from her eyes, wet for a man, she is. And sure she'll let him have his end away but she'll have her will in the end, for Anne *hath a way*, as we say in this family, eh? Said I well, John? What do you say, old boon companion? Old drunken crony? Let's further think on't.

And so the plot was hatched.

Easy with his money, my father. Easy with his offspring. Easy with his old friends. Not that Anne would have seemed all that bad a catch for a young man's family, even though old Hathaway left her nothing special to take to a husband, just the usual ten marks to be paid out on her wedding day. Oh, and one other item believe it or not – a sheep! Lest the bride failed to satisfy, so the old joke ran – and they'd be spluttering it into their ale no doubt.

These tedious old fools.

Nothing else? Well, there was the house at Hewlands but Anne's eldest brother Bartholomew had been instructed to take charge of that – as of the Hathaway widow, once she was no longer a wife. So in the end old Hathaway had done the Shakespeares no great favours. And why should he? Considering that John Shakespeare was never the kind to shit in a ditch and find the turd gold-plated the following day. Life went the other way for him, that was the tendency, time turning his treasures to turds. On the other hand the Hathaways were a good family and from the Shakespeare viewpoint a potential prop to my father's ailing assets. I dare say it made sense enough at the time, especially with a sweetener of beer slipped under the skin. As for the Hathaways, they might have seen the Shakespeare name as a sound one in spite of our problems, and myself as a shapely enough lad, on the verge of inheriting a shop in Stratford and a business behind it that might well be recouped, with a strong woman running the show. And a youthful husband too, with a stack of years ahead of him for the maturing daughter who, if she hadn't ought to have been married by now, could scarcely afford to let too much more time go by before she did. Finally there was a certain sympathy in religion. No need for me to say any more on that score, at least none too loudly. I've said enough already. And pitchers have ears – eh, Francis?

Silence and sleep, the whale in the sea of time, floating free of care.

As for the gap between the ages, family friendship would more than fill the breach and make that up. Anyway, once between the sheets, who'd be counting? Certainly not Anne. You forget your arithmetic when the lamp goes out – even the date of her last flow. As many a poor bungler has discovered to his cost, and hers. And if the same should happen to Anne and Will, well, that has been the way of it since time began, and they'll not be the last. Green grow the acres. And so on and so forth. Went it not so?

To the self-same tune and words, but with more policy and less wit, I shouldn't wonder. At such a time I'll loose my daughter to him. Be you and I behind an arras then. Mark the encounter. If he love her not, let me be no assistant to your state but keep a farm and carters, Hewlands Farm, and carters to Shottery. And down goes the buttery boy.

Had Anne been primed? Was she Ophelia? Or did they simply set the plot in motion, leaving it to time, fate, and genitals to do the rest? It's a question I never asked Anne, as often as it troubled me. But I had no such cares, I have to confess, in the giddy spring and heady summer of '82. And why should I have worried at the time, in youth when I did love, did love? I knew nothing but bitter-sweet itches then. When I left Hewlands with my father that fateful day, I understood only one thing. A woman called Anne Hathaway had me like the hangman, by heart and balls, a double clutch. I couldn't break free. I didn't want to. I was eager for the game. I was on fire. And verses bubbled in the blood.

O spirit of love! How quick and fresh art thou, that notwithstanding thy capacity receiveth as the sea, nought enters there of what validity and pitch soe'er but falls into abatement and low price even in a minute.

I was staring into that infinite ocean. I was standing on the edge. History a wrinkle on a green sea. Nothing else mattered. She was the wonder of the world. And all I could think about now was Anne Hathaway. Was she standing or lying? waking or sleeping? laughing or sad? at home or abroad? O mistress mine where are you roaming? Was she dreaming of me? Dying for me? How could she brook one moment's delay? Life at best's a doubtful bubble. What's to come is still unsure.

And youth?

'Youth's a stuff will not endure.'

Francis surprising me again. Maybe lawyers never go completely to sleep. There's always a tendril untouched by Morpheus.

And I'll not endure it, I said. And I couldn't, it was true. Couldn't work, couldn't eat, couldn't sleep. Took to rising from bed each night as soon as I could hear the walls of Henley Street begin to whisper with the sounds of snores, the combined undulations of roomfuls of breasts sighing like the sea. And it gave me a weird pleasure to be stealing from the house at this hour – tread softly that the blind mole may not hear a footfall! – to roam the deserted listening streets, gliding like a ghost, a murderer, a wolf, towards some terrible design: the taking of a Troy, the raping of an innocent, the killing of a king. Now o'er the one half world nature seems dead and wicked dreams abuse the curtained sleep. Even the very stones seemed to hear my steps and shout to all the world that Will Shakespeare was awake and stalking Anne Hathaway all the way to Shottery. Ring the alarm bell, summon the night watch! And I crouched with shadows and heard the thudding of a heart on fire for Hathaway.

Down Henley Street I stole, past the shops and houses whose moonlit roofs and battened shutters let out not the ghost of a sigh from all those bosoms hushed and swelling like some dark and distant tide; past the shambles whose spilt black pools mirrored the moon, its red stenches drenching the air. O, horrible! But I sped down Rother Street till I came to the turning into the Shottery footpath. There I relaxed and lingered, stopped to face the setting stars pouring slowly down the sky, the Virgin and the Lion lying down to sleep, and Hydra westering, settling to rest along the dim misty skyline. Behind me surfaced the summer constellations, rising to make love to the spring as they always did, faithful old flames wooing the wet fields night after night as May slipped into June, the Milky Way dripped over the forest of Arden, over the blind humps of the Snitterfield hill, like a golden bough laden with glittering fruit, and I tasted stars on my tongue.

So I passed like a shadow along the mile of fields to Shottery, the footpath sometimes black as a bat, sometimes white with moon and lonely in the night, apart from me, its only friend. Only the cattle coughed and the foxes barked and the owls screeched out their supperless laments as I bore down on Shottery. Hawthorn and honeysuckle were singing in my head, pollen powdering my nose, my feet washed with grasses and my hair brushed and heavy with dew, with the secret drops of the night. I was the complete lover, eager for action, perfumed by passion and pasture, groomed by the horses of the night. Daylight and champain! I was higher than madness or the dreams of wine – my feet never felt the ground.

Down I came to the farmhouse, the palace in the wild where she slept her unmindful sleep, calm queen of the night, and I stood there and drank the air, sharing it with her, the divine Hathaway. I held my breath. I was starstruck, moonstruck, *Anne*struck. When I exhaled again after an infinity of held breath, it was to expel the entire soul. Magically, my spirit drifted across the silent gardens, passed through the walls and latticed windows of the rooms, like a night mist, a fragrance, seeking that slumbering form. And there it was – a secret glowing pinkness, shrouded by the shocking whiteness of sheets, chaste and cold as a corpse.

O! she doth teach the torches to burn bright! It is her breathing that perfumes the chamber thus. The taper's flame bends to her in salutation and in flickering silence laves her lids, washes those windows, white and azure-veined, those shutters laced with blue of heaven's own tinct...

And there, on her left breast – heaven and earth, must I remember? – a mole, cinque-spotted, like the crimson drops streaked in the bottom of a cowslip. On that very spot where some time past a single drop of cream had splashed, masking that beautiful blemish. It stood out now, blinding my mind – more private than the secretest part of her.

Time had stopped here. Somewhere beyond Hewlands meaningless events were taking place. Stars were burning to waste, acts of love and treachery committed, sharks slamming madly through the dark, sleepless kings holding council, sleepless worms probing corpses in the clod – corpses oblivious of the calm constellations that went slow and stately by, over the graveyards of the earth, while the cold oceans washed the globe, slurped and bulged to the moonpull, and the tides sighed in their shackles. All slaves. All of them. Even those kings were the slaves of history, the stars the slaves of God's thoughts, thought of life itself, and life – time's fool. Only here did freedom exist, here in Anne Hathaway's room, this box within a sphere, this abstruse cube. She was the *primum mobile*. Without her the morning would never come.

So I sighed away the last of April and all of May and June. Violets died like greensick girls, the elves evacuated the cowslips, the harebells' blue music was heard no more. But the Milky Way, always in blossom, dusted the huge skies, the stars dripped on the elder trees and the trees on the fields, showering them with the strong white scents of life. Unable to stand upright, to remain sane in this dizzy wilderness, I dived instead into the darkness of woods, where late bluebells and buttercups bunched in the shadows like stranded angels dropped from a lost heaven, where, hugging the tree trunks, the toadstools lurked and tittered, listening for tell-tale whispers, waiting for the fragrance of woman, the swish of a skirt in the dew.

Madness. Midsummer madness.

By midsummer I was indeed so mad with lust I'd become a blue thread of life buzzing low over the baked landscape, a dragonfly of desire, deadly hovering, never at heart's ease. Till night fell like a drunkard, reeling with stars, and I cooled down a little and sang to the greenwood that Greensleeves was all my joy and Anne Hathaway my heart's delight. But the raving and the prickthirst simply couldn't be slaked by a few lines from an old lyric. It was the hour of pure longing, too violet and violent to deny. My balls were barbarians, the prick a giant thistle, its purple head bristling with lethal seeds. When I went out walking I carried a book to hide it. The vicar had given me a Caesar to keep my Latin alive after my exit from school, and the Gallic Wars were fought against my groin. Darkness came – and I threw off the camouflage, giving in to concupiscence. I rampaged round the Shottery field, a bull gone berserk, fell like Jupiter on an imaginary Anne Hathaway, crushing her loins with lavender, scattering the night-tripping fairies, bruising the thyme, releasing wild aromas so that heaven sniffed the dawn and bees came blundering from their hives, booming through the blackness. That quietened me for a moment and I lay back in the dark and watched a glow-worm, heard it speak to the stars.

It was unbearable. I pulled out my prick and made it flower. My hot white sperm shot up with all the vigour of juicy youth, stinging the stars, making another Milky Way, beautiful but brief. My soul sprang up with it, invincible, and the stars threw down their swords in surrender. The sperm grew cold and I rose groggily to test the ice-brook's temper, wash my shrinking dick. Then I ran, whooping, towards Hewlands. I had offended the angels but I didn't care. Not one whit. I was brushed by bats as I plunged through the long grasses, leaping like a gazelle. And flights of night-moths conducted me there with such glittering excitement in their tiny wings but with such infinite gentleness too. They were nature's escorts, alternative angels. And I was a god. I roared, diving for cover as I woke the Hewlands household from its sleep. They'd no business dozing anyway, the snoring drones, when their hive accommodated such a queen! Up, up, my lords! The sun doth gild our armour! Shake off this downy sleep, death's counterfeit, and from your graves rise up and walk like sprites!

Jesus, what a time it was!

15

It had to end. And end it did.

One early July dawn.

There was a soft rain falling that morning. It had been falling all night and I was lying half awake, listening to the rain falling on the rye and wondering what it felt like to be an ear of corn, a single grain, sodden by the downpour, out in the drowned fields all night long. Open unto the sky. It had become a habit with me recently, to enter into any other entity I might imagine or encounter: the wet wheat, the blind worm, the snail hearing the apocalyptic thunder of the rain booming on his back, echoing in his shell. But my mind's travels were interrupted by a faint but frantic knocking on our downstairs shutters and a girl's voice fluttering in the grey dawn, asking for John Shakespeare. My father shouted to me to see what was up. Rubbing gummed-up eyes I stuck my head out between flung shutters and saw the white upturned face of Alison Hathaway, Miss Marble-Mammaries herself. But I didn't think about any of that right then. There was something else in the air. The small white face looking up at me in the half light of that early hour of the morning was like the face of somebody lying dead in the bottom of a tomb.

'It's my father. He's – '

Yes. Of course he is. That was what was in the air, the scent of death. His time had come, then. And the time for the wearing of black.

And it was in black that we made our way to Shottery two days later – dry-footed as it turned out, the rain having stopped and the sun suddenly pumping out a fierce heat for the funeral of my father's old friend. The grasses we trailed through were bloodied with poppies, broken by the blue-white horses of cornflowers and daisies, flecking the fields. Richard Hathaway was now poppies and stars. He was the insect voices in ears of wheat. He was the dead leather on our shoes that tramped the footpath to his home. And he was still the focus of that home, the centre of a circle of staring faces, blanked by death. He was a stiffness in its shroud. A thing of nothing. They would return him to the dust before returning to their lives. They would bury and remember. And then forget. We looked at the dead white face for the last time. At the shut eyelids that locked in everything he'd ever been, all the secrets he'd ever known, and those he now knew. If any. *For the dead know not anything,* a voice whispered to me out of scripture. We lined up to kiss the coldness that was Richard Hathaway, the marble cheek that was his no longer but the stony earth's. Then we got ready to shoulder him out of his home and into that waiting hole in the ground.

But where was she? The room where the corpse was laid out was thick with cloaks and gowns, the air filled with their uneasy anonymous rustling. There was no sign in this black sea of the woman I'd worshipped all through these last mind-boggling months of madness and moonlight. She was crushed with grief, too heavy with her loss perhaps to make an appearance. Some women didn't attend funerals. And now the time had come to bear the body. The sons came forward.

'Wait.'

All heads turned to the door.

'Wait for me – I'm coming.'

One final bitter moment, then. The last goodbye.

The girl I'd last seen in springtime green. Clothed now in black from crown to toe, her face hidden. A sudden rustling from the little bunch of mourners as it parted, murmuring, to let her through the ranks of death. She crossed to where the body lay, bent over the bier, kissed the corpse through the veils.

The last kiss.

It was a long walk to Temple Grafton churchyard where the first Mistress Hathaway lay waiting, but the four sons who bore their father insisted they would have neither horse nor hearse. He had been a good father. A man should be carried by his own people. On the last long walk to his long home. It's short enough – next to eternity, if you care to look at it like that.

So the black crocodile procession wound its way across the green fields, irksomely beset by bees, bullied by the blinding sun that beat down on swathed faces and bodies drenched in jet. The sweat trickled down backs and buttocks, ran down our brows and stung our eyes as we dragged our feet respectfully through the long hot grasses where the crickets chirped and jigged, fiddling stridently, riotously, without a shred of decorum. It was a twisting trail. But at last we reached a gaping wound in the grass where butterflies danced and quivered like the sun on water. It was the last frenetic reminder of the quickness Richard Hathaway left behind him as he went into the blackness from which he would never return, in spite of Lazarus on the painted cloth, in spite of the preacher's platitudes and assurances, the sounding brass and tinkling cymbals. All hollow, all lies, and we knew it for sure, beneath all the consoling stories, the fairy tales.

The priest reached out to the upturned mound beside the grave, cupped a few flakes of earth in his fist, and assured us all that Richard Hathaway would live again. Then he flung his fistful into the grave. The sunbaked soil flew like breadcrumbs from the white unringed fingers and pattered over the shrouded corpse. Earth to earth, ashes to ashes, dust to dust. In sure and certain hope. Etcetera and amen. The gravedigger started shovelling in the clods. Afterwards he'd fit the squares of turf back over the grave, and time and nature would see to the stitching. Then the stitches would dissolve and the sweet green sea would blow over the spot where Richard Hathaway now lay again with his first wife. Death was the end of all marriages.

The mourners broke up and started to move away, people of the world again, walking briskly back to Shottery. The orderly black file had broken up into animated little bunches of folk, busy clearing their throats and complaining loudly about the sun. They were glad to be leaving death, that embarrassing old bastard, well behind them in Temple Grafton and to be thinking instead about a nice slice of cold shoulder and an even colder beer.

And Anne Hathaway? I lingered on the fringes, watching her as she stepped back lightly through the fields with the rest of the party. If she'd seen me at all she seemed oblivious of the fact. Not once had she as much as even glanced in my direction. And the banter in the buttery? Well, that's all it amounted to, banter and fantasy. My youthful ignorance. A fashion and a toy in blood. I'd made a madness out of the summer season. I felt sick with shame and disgust and there was a tightness in my chest as we approached Shottery, and the dislocated file of folk, unruly now, made for Hewlands to cheer on old Dickie boy into eternity with beef and beer. I decided to leave them to it and to go back to Stratford.

It was just as I made to turn east that I saw her stop. The last of the funeral party flowed past her into Hewlands and she stood there and let them. And stood, and stood. Then abruptly she turned north and started walking. On the road to nowhere, between Wilmcote and Snitterfield, with only the forest of Arden in front of her. With never a backward glance.

There is a tide in the affairs of men which, taken at the flood – leads on to fortune. Omitted, all the voyage of their life is bound in shallows and in miseries. I didn't know exactly what I was about as I stood there watching Anne Hathaway disappear into distance but I knew that I had to follow her. For we must take the current when it serves. Or lose our venture.

She went ahead of me with brisk compulsion, as though she walked with a purpose. Trip no further, pretty sweeting. There was a song in my head. Journeys end in lovers meeting. My heart beginning to thud and hurt, I stepped after her as she strode over the fields, a strange figure, still clad in black mourning, the fluttering veils clouding her head. In the distance the black froth of the forest was a frown on the skyline. Behind us Stratford shivered like a memory. I remembered the day seven years ago I'd come down from Kenilworth with mermaids and dolphins in my brain. Where had he gone to, that eleven-year-old boy? Only this field existed now, in which these great oaks and chestnuts spread themselves out in time. What is love? 'Tis not hereafter. The song spread out in my head. Present mirth hath present laughter. The trees' shadows had shortened for noon and the sensible cattle had got up from vanished canopies and gone to the streams for comfort. There they stood cooling their hooves and gaping at me as I hurried by. Where my tongue had once been, a scorched lizard lay in my mouth. Bees bumbled into me and strongholds of nettles loomed threateningly – ancient with expectation, alert with some wordless understanding. What was it they knew?

Did Anne know I was trailing her? I felt not so much that I was following her as being hauled in her wake. The swooping swallows tried to cut me off, criss-crossing the route. Still the bees were booming overhead, dropping pollen on their drunken homeward flights, bombarding my path. A spider on a gooseberry bush watched me from its throne of threads. The larks on invisible strings laughed at me, singing their blue songs.

And she carried on walking under the insistent brazen sunglare, past the blue crenellations of thistles, through swarms of purple dragonflies, tangles of campion and columbines, blue vetch, rank fumitory and old man's beard, wagging with disapproval. And on I went after her. Till she stopped dead at the edge of the wood. Stopped and stood unmoving, as if waiting. I stopped too, instinctively, looked at the black statue still a hundred yards ahead of me. Then I started off again, more slowly this time, coming through the final field that lay between us. The earth was pulsing through the balls of my feet, my eyeballs throbbing in the sun, the birds gone mad, the insects shrieking in my ears. I came up close, swishing the grasses and stopped within an arm's length of her. For a few more maddening moments she stayed as she was – then sawed round almost savagely to face me, but still veiled, an effigy in ebony, set weirdly in the green field. She bore no resemblance to my memory of the girl in the buttery who had seemed clothed with the young year. Greensleeves.

'You took your time,' she said.

'I came,' was all I said, 'nearly every night I came, though you didn't know it.'

'I knew it.'

The night-moths knew it too – and every owl between Stratford and Shottery.

'And I've thought about nothing else,' I said, 'nothing but you.'

'What did you expect me to do? Throw open my windows, hang down from the balcony? Shout to all the world, "Where are you, Will? Come up and take me!" The normal thing would be to call.'

'Is love normal?' I said. 'Is love easy? I thought it was a madness. That's what it feels like.'

'So you love me.'

I'd said it. There was no going back.

'I loved my father, Will.'

Her voice was very low.

'But I've laid more than my father to rest today. My eldest brother will run the house now, and with a wife of his own. From today Hewlands has its mistress and my stepmother sits in state. My own mother is in that grave with my father. I'm twenty-six years old and single. They all have their lives back there, and their futures. I'm alone. Alone in the world.'

I took a deep breath. As men do when they get ready for the big speech. The one they make for the first time. But I couldn't find my tongue. So I reached out instead and lifted her veil, slowly as if she were a bride. A bride in black. There was a single teardrop glittering on her eyelash. I fingered it off gently and tasted her pain. Sweet. O, you should not rest between the elements of air and earth but you should pity me. I cupped her face in my hands, fed on her eyes, her forehead, her lips; drank deep from the imagined goblet of her mouth. Still we hadn't kissed. She looked straight back at me, whispering, barely even breathing the words.

'I know...'

I know a bank where the wild thyme blows, where oxlips and the nodding violet grows. Quite over-canopied with luscious woodbine. With sweet musk-roses. And with eglantine.

'Take me. Show me.'

A thousand honey secrets shalt thou know. Feed where thou wilt, graze on my lips, stray lower where the pleasant fountains lie, round rising hillocks, sweet bottom grass – and bush obscure and rough. These blue-veined violets whereon we lean never can blab, nor know not what we mean. Then be my deer, since I am such a park. No dog shall rouse thee, though a thousand bark.

I followed her to that thyme-blown bank and we stood and looked at one another – and she sighed and kissed me hard, as hard as if she plucked up kisses by the roots that grew upon my lips. They were end-of-the-world kisses, and they took the reason prisoner. I'd gone into the forest of Arden, into the wild wood, into her wild mouth. And I'd never be seen again.

16

Like a unicorn. Like a unicorn under a spell, I followed Anne Hathaway into these woods. The virgin had me by the horn and Venus was cupping the balls. As fresh as yesterday, that bank where the wild thyme blew, and the memory still be green. There she laid me down, took my head between her hands and swooped on me – like a falcon falling on some wild thing that fluttered on my mouth. Her frantic hands were busy tearing at both our clothes. Bodice and doublet, belt and girdle, boots and bonnet, shirt and gown, stomacher, stockings, shoes – a black cataract of garments cascading to the grass. Adam and Eve emerging at last out of death's linen chrysalis to embrace nakedness and guilt. While high over Snitterfield God came strolling in his coat of clouds, drawing close, peering and prying, eyebeams slanting like swords of sunlight through the chequered net of leaves.

Out bobbed those glorious boobs – like two kittens suddenly born and bewildered and eager for play. Pussy at the well was a mere memory now, no more, Marian's nipples lost among icicles and the sound of Dick roaring like the Snitterfield bull. Here at last was the awesome orb. And its terrible twin. And two wild strawberries perched with shocking availability on those excitingly white and shivering swinging things. I touched the right one with my left hand and felt it slide and glide through my fingers like some strange virgin substance newly created, foreign, fluid, firm. I marvelled at how quickly her nipples swelled and hardened, responsive to the touch of digits, teeth, and tongue. Ovid had not warned me about this. What else had he kept back? I took a big breath, sat up, and stared straight down at what lay in the grass before me.

A head thrown back with shuttered eyes and open mouth like a saint in ecstasy. A river of hair waving among dim violets and twisted eglantine. The dramatic curves of waist and hips (oh, those buttercup-crushing buttocks!) and the dark cave of the navel attracting and arresting my eye with maddening brevity as it sped on downwards to take in the long strong thighs and calves, lightly covered with down that glowed like golden fire. Up again then from those funny little toes and hardened heels all the way up the lovely ladder of her life's history, the cuts and scars of childhood, the sobs and bruises whose records would stay with her till death, ingrained in her flesh, all the long anatomical return to that most stirring of all sights.

O, glorious pubes! The ultimate triangle, whose angles delve to hell but point to paradise. Let me sing the black banner, the blackbird's wing, the chink, the cleft, the keyhole in the door. The fig, the fanny, the cranny, the quim – I'd come close to it now, this sudden blush, this ancient avenue, the end of all odysseys and epic aim of life, pulling at my prick now, pulling like a lodestone.

Anne Hathaway's cow-milking fingers, cradling my balls in her almond palm, now took pity on the poor anguished erection, and in the infinite agony of her desire, guided it to the quick of the wound. At the same time I searched wildly with the fingers of my left hand, groping blind as Cyclops, found the pulpy furred wetness, parted the old lips of time and slipped my middle finger into the *sancta sanctorum*. It welcomed me with soft sucking sounds, syllables older than language, solace lovelier than words. She pulled my hand away, positioned the prick, slid her buttocks deep into the grass, raised her thighs back high, crossed her legs behind my back, dug her heels into my spine and hauled at me savagely and hard. I *fell* into her.

It was exhilarating, to be bounded in a nutshell and count myself a king of infinite space. But Anne Hathaway was a cruel queen. Her calves crushed my ribs, her crossed heels digging in hard, drawing me in deeper. She responded with those cries that men long to hear, the sweet deep moaning sounds that echo the sigh of oceans, the ebb and flow of fields, the sough of stars. So we drank from one another, clung together on the ship we'd made of ourselves, breasting the irrelevance of time.

All around us nature joined in: the sky-spearing oaks, the dragonflies poised like purple pricks, raping the air, flies fucking on the wing, insects gendering on stones, on the currents of the tumbling streams, the birds lechering endlessly among the leaves – even the sperm-spurting thistles sending the milky froth sliding like spittle back down their long hairy stems. Only the cattle were quiet, out in the fields, though the bull ruminated rape.

Streamers of heat lashed my back and shoulders and far beneath me now the body of Anne Hathaway began to rage and founder in the rising foam as I clung like a mariner to her heaving haunches, the deep keel of her backbone dipping and lifting through July, through the green surge of growth, till at last the moment came when some colossal wave flung her up high, and I held on for my life, and she screamed loud and long. Then O! then O! then O! my true love said and I felt death go through her. Our vessel ran shuddering onto the rocks, a wave of wetness ran through us, the air was rent with screams and I became aware that the bank on which we lay drenched and grounded was journey's end, love's end, the very sea-mark of our utmost sail.

I woke to find myself lying stranded, beached on my back, my head to one side, looking straight into it, the breach in nature. The legs were wide apart, just as I'd left them when I'd slipped out and rolled over in the shallows. The cunt gaped like a wounded fruit and the seeds of being were pouring from the core and into the shaggy crack between the pollinated buttocks, as if wild flowers would now spring from her cleft, the keyhole to Canaan, oozing milk and honey.

But what was this sorrow stealing over me now? This strange sadness taking hold? Was this really the promised land, this inflamed wound leaking frog-spawn and snail-slime, turning ugly in my eyes?

'O, Will, what hast thou done? Will, Will...'

It was Anne's voice, not God's. And her hand in my hand. And her deflowered body bestriding mine. And her cock-caressing, ball-brushing fingers twisting wild flowers round my poor ruined prick, to make it wild once more, to make it flower again, Titania twisting woodbine through my pubes.

'Anne hath a way with her hands, I see.'

And yes, I had risen and she was straddling me again, her hair lost in the blaze of the sky, her face one with the sun. And after a brief brutal thrusting she made me come again and was heavy and fulfilled on me, her locks soaking wet and her loins still at last under my spread hands.

The sun ticked round the sky.

'Well, you've had your will of me.'

Her voice was sleepy and smiling in my shoulder.

'And you've had *your* Will.'

'Yes, I've had my Will in me. And will he not come again?'

'No, no, he is dead.'

For the rest of the day anyway.

'But where there's a will – '

'Anne hath a way.'

Anne Hathaway.

When she stood up to gather her clothes I noticed a head of honeysuckle sticking to her left flank. Held there by pressure and perspiration. I picked it off, kissed the cheek it had imprinted, sniffed the bloom and stowed it away in my jerkin. An emblem of our fuck among the flowers, balmy symbol of the fidelity we were about to swear. I have it still, long withered. Its fragrance gone. Like the love we knew that day. Like that day itself. That can never come again.

17

Thus began the long summer of '82. We pressed every flower of the season under the wet weight of our one flesh and they winked at our wooing, whispering their names to us as we lay long hours with our faces close to theirs – tickle-my-fancy, pink-of-my-John, purple-love's-wound, love-dew-in-milk. She sat on the prick of noon and we made the night-snail gallop, grow wings, and fly. We claimed kinship with crickets, were on nodding terms with nettles. We wore out the summer constellations, saw the Great Square of Pegasus soaring out of the fields, like a colossus, bestraddling September.

'Do you love me, Will?'

And yes, she was the wonder of the world. Yes, I loved her.

Yet even so.

'Will.'

'Yes, Anne?'

'Tell me again.'

'Tell you what?'

'What it is to love.'

'Why again?'

'You tell it so well.'

'It is to be all made of sighs and tears. It is to be all made of faith and service. It is to be all made of fantasy, all made of passion, and all made of wishes. And so am I for you.'

'And I for you.'

'Forever and a day.'

'Will you come and see me tomorrow, Will?'

'Tomorrow and tomorrow and tomorrow.'

But when September ended, the bloody banner did not unfurl between Anne's much opened legs. There was still no show by October. I began to wish it away, this little blind guest in her belly, blocking the door. Sunday after Sunday swept by, like a rush of wings, ever faster, ever darkening. Sunday the eleventh, Sunday the eighteenth, Sunday the twenty-fifth of November.

Finally Anne said, 'There can be no banns called from Advent to Epiphany. You have to do something before the second day of December.'

So on that Monday morning I told my father just before breakfast. He looked at me across the unlaid table.

'Well, well, so you're going to make a grandfather of me. About time, I reckon. Half a century is a long wait. And she's a good lass. Good family.'

I nodded. What did I care about her family? He gave one of his little laughs. There was no beer for him to chuckle into. Or Dick Hathaway to give the wink.

'We didn't think it was gloves you were making with her at Shottery.'

And that was all he said.

After he'd gone up to tell my mother she came out and stood on the stairs, looking down at me, unspeaking. I never knew what was in that look. No reproach. A certain sadness, but not directed at me. At life, perhaps. But my father was all practical prattle. That's what he was good at.

'St Andrew's Day is, let's see, the last day of the month. This is the twenty-sixth. Tomorrow we'll go to Worcester. We'll have you wed by the end of the month. Failing that, on the first day of the last month. Jesu, I wish old Dick were here!'

So on the twenty-seventh day of November a small party made for Worcester, to the diocesan court, to obtain from Bishop John Whitgift a special licence to marry. 'Special, yes, but not entirely unheard of,' my father said. Henry Heicroft, vicar of Stratford, had been married after only one declaration of the banns instead of the usual three, finding himself and his lady friend in sudden need of such a licence. The lady in question was well known in Stratford. She was called Emme Careless. Whether she was or wasn't, she became Mistress Heicroft. And became him well. Anne Hathaway was to become Mistress Shakespeare.

The party that went to Worcester consisted of myself and my father and two Shottery farmers, Fulk Sandell and John Richardson, friends of the late Richard Hathaway. They provided a bond for forty pounds, indemnifying the bishop against any proceedings that might conceivably arise from our hurried marriage. We never saw the recipient of those forty pounds, the bishop himself. The bond was accepted by the Chancellor, the Registrar, and by the clerk of the consistory court, who also asked for a written allegation containing the reasons that pressed us into this sudden notion of matrimony. And for a signed statement from my parents, swearing that there was no impediment to the marriage by way of consanguinity or any pre-contractual arrangement.

It was all a far cry from Ovid and a little embarrassing. I needn't have worried. The clerk of court was a tired old cipher who paid little attention to his scribble. But his scratching did the business. A licence was issued to allow the banns, which were called once, on the last day of November. I heard with a mixture of bewilderment, detachment, and disbelief that two parties, a certain William Shakespeare of Stratford and an Anne Hathaway of Shottery were to be married. Who were these people?

On the first day of December we took the old west road from Shottery and made for Temple Grafton church where John Frith was vicar. On the way there we met a shepherd from Red Hill.

'Wouldn't get wed there if I was you folks.'

'Why not?'

'Considered unsound in his religion, is old Frith. He's on the list, you know.'

'What list is that, then?'

'Government list. Runs an old-style church, you know.'

'Nice quiet church, though,' my father suggested. 'Nicely out of the way. Nice quiet ceremony. Nothing much wrong with that. Nothing much wrong with Frith either, if you ask me.'

'Careful, John,' grumbled old Henry. 'Walsingham could be shitting in a thicket for all you know. Wouldn't be blabbing your opinions on the open road.'

The shepherd persisted.

'Blind old bungler, friend Frith – take it from me, knows more about birds than bible. Some kind of hawk doctor.'

This impressed Henry the other way.

'Well now, God knows his birds, don't he? Scripture says there's a special providence in the fall of a sparrow.'

The shepherd shook his slow old head.

'Don't know anything about that. But I do know there's a good strong Protestant priest in Stratford, Heycroft's your man, and I know as I wouldn't get wed by John Frith. How could you even be sure you was married by the end of it?'

There was something in what the old fellow said. Frith mumbled and stumbled his way through the ceremony with a sort of cidery benevolence. He then assured us we were married – and might he toast us on the path of life with a glass of primrose wine? Under his simple roof.

'Uncommon good wine to be got out of the primroses here at Temple Grafton – and that wine is a miracle of Cana, let me tell you, for the curing of sick hawks. It's wasted on men.'

And he took my father off under my mother's cloudy frown, Uncle Henry too, cups in hand, to examine the kinds of birds he was wise in curing.

The women hovered like bees about the queenly Anne of the pouting belly. Left alone for a moment I wandered outside to stand at Frith's gable-end and look down the long view south-west to the Cotswolds. Wondering what lay ahead of me on the path, with or without its primroses, culled by virgins, quaffed by drunkards, sipped by fallen hawks.

And then we went home, into a tiny Henley Street bedroom that black December night and huddled together between freezing white sheets. There were no carousals to the conquest of Anne's assaulted maidenhead. Nobody undressed me and brought me legless to bed to bray the triumph of Priapus. No one sewed up our sheets to delay the moment of midnight nuptials. We lay sexlessly, craving the blank of sleep.

It was broken by brass voices.

If thou dost break her virgin knot before all sanctimonious ceremonies may with full and holy rites be ministered, no sweet aspersion shall the heavens let fall to make this contract grow, but barren hate, sour-eyed disdain and discord shall bestrew the union of your bed with weeds so loathly that you shall hate it both. Therefore take heed, as Hymen's lamps shall light you.

Hymen wasn't in attendance that night. He was where we'd left him – in the forest of Arden, with Anne's lost maidenhead. And we began the next stage of our copulative lives in Richard Hathaway's inherited double bed – elderly enough, but eminently suited to the galloping of four bare legs. It served its turn. When the New Year began to grow, so did Anne. Apace. We were parents to be – the lover and his lass is what we'd *been*. With a hey and a ho and a hey nonino. We'd passed through the green cornfield, we'd lain between the acres of the rye, we pretty cuntrie folks, we'd rung our pretty ring time and had had our hour. Hey ho.

And that – is the Anne Hathaway story.

18

'And quite a story it is too, Will.'

Francis was half sitting up, leaning on one arm, the recumbent whale now a bleary sea-lion.

'And I'm sorry it's over.'

It was over a long time ago, my friend. How long have you been awake?

'You said it yourself – lawyers seldom sleep, not entirely.'

Always scratching out a living –

'A meagre one.'

Even inside your skulls.

'Even in our dreams. Talking of scratching – '

I know.

'Your talk of Anne is timely. What are we going to do about her?'

There's nothing to be done about her – she is as she is.

'I mean what do *you* want to do about her? In the will. What provision?'

None.

'You don't mean that.'

She'll not be destitute.

'Look old friend, you have to do the right thing.'

What's right? What's wrong?

'The fact is that most wills leave some sort of provision for the wife. Any old blanket phrase will do – *the residue of my estate*, or something of that nature. As your lawyer I have to advise you – '

Francis, stop worrying. She'll be taken care of. I have a daughter.

'You have two daughters, old man.'

Two daughters and no son, that's right.

'Well?'

Well, it was late in May my little Susanna was born – in May, when there's that greenness in the leaves that they'll never know again.

'Oh, Will, don't wander off again. I thought we were going to sew this up.'

When green virgins make dancing rings on the fresh green grass. And when young men, their fancies lightly turning to thoughts of love, give rings to girls to put their virginity to bed.

'This calls for more wine – to dull the pain of living!'

Help yourself, Francis – and another cup for me.

'You should stay clear-headed.'

More so you, quillman. Anne's ring grew wider than I'd have thought possible, allowing egress to our first born. Heycroft hurried from a day-bed where he'd left his Emme lying careless, having doubtless first taken good care of *her* ring, and he baptized Susanna for us on the twenty-sixth.

'Of '83?'

You keep count. That's what you're here for. A year later Anne's magic ring rang again, like uncracked gold, and at the end of the January the next year –

''85 then.'

We were surprised by the twins, Hamnet and Judith, baptized on Candlemas by Richard Barnton, Heycroft having gotten himself a better benefice in Rowington.

'A ten-mile walk to work and back again.'

Well worth it to fall into the pretty ring of careless Emme. And in Henley Street out went the light of love and we were left darkling.

'Don't make it sound so gloomy.'

My mother wasn't unpleased in the end. It was a house of five Shakespeare males, with Edmund still an infant. Here was an Anne to replace the one she'd lost – no greensick girl but a seasoned housewife, chasing thirty by the time the twins were born.

'Joan was the only Shakespeare girl.'

And Anne had added two more. Here was house-help and the sounds and scents of women. Good happenings for Mary Arden.

'Not for you?'

Not for a thoughtful man. Other than myself and my wife at Henley Street – a woman I hardly knew, let's face it, except as Adam knew Eve and she conceived – there were my father and mother, three brothers, two of them children, a sister of sixteen, a daughter of my own, of only twenty months, and now a set of new-born twins, for

God's sake.

'Eleven of you.'

From fifty-five down to infancy, all living under the same roof. Thought was crowded out. The private life was over, such as it had been. Not that it had ever been much, in Stratford. Sometimes I looked at my wife and mother together and could see not much difference between them. The voices started up again, poisonous minerals of the mind. Then let thy love be younger than thyself –

'Oh, not that old song again!'

Or thy affection cannot hold the bent.

'We're off again! For women are as roses – '

Whose fair flower, being once displayed, doth fall that very hour.

'That very hour? Poetic hyperbole.'

Women change the day they give birth.

'Not a gate I've been through myself.'

And out comes the shrew.

'Thanks for the warning.'

Stay single, Francis.

'I'll bear it in mind. But you didn't.'

Alas, alas.

'And now you have a wife and children to make provision for. How are you going to leave them?'

In a coffin, I'd say.

'Be serious. How do you intend that they should be left? Richly or beggarly or what?'

Nobody will be a beggar. But there are conditions must be met.

'There are no particular conditions in the January draft.'

The what?

The fat man took a long slow draught and smacked his lips.

'You know what I said, Will.'

I know what I told you – that document was to be destroyed! Fill me up, you tub of lard, and explain yourself.

'Lawyers don't destroy documents, old friend, they hold them back – just in case.'

I don't want that one held anywhere. It's history.

'Even history is on record. You can revoke it as soon as we've seen to this.'

Then we'd better see to it, then. Never mind your glass, give your pen something to drink, man. It's been in dry dock all day.

'You can put a thirst on it, then. Let's go.'

Try to stop me. *Item, I give and bequeath unto my son-in-law one hundred and fifty pounds of lawful English money –*

'Now you're talking!' Scribble scribble. 'Which son-in-law?'

What do you mean, son-in-law?

'You've just said, son-in-law. Quiney or Hall?'

Neither, neither, that's not my meaning.

'You're confused, old man. Shall we do this tomorrow?'

It was a slip, that's all. Still living in the past. Cross out *son-in-law* and put *my daughter Judith. One hundred and fifty pounds of lawful English money to be paid unto her in the manner and form following –*

'Just a moment, just a moment, let me get this down. We can work from the old draft – it'll be quicker.'

No, no, new pages, and get rid of that thing, cancel and tear to pieces that great bond which keeps me pale, yes, yes.

'*In the manner and form following*, right.'

That is to say, one hundred pounds in discharge of her marriage portion within one year after my decease, with consideration after the rate of two shillings in the pound for so long time as the same shall be unpaid unto her after my decease –

'Wait a minute, I can't keep up!'

Shorthand it!

'I like to be neat.'

It's only a draft.

'I don't do shorthand, my clerk does that.'

Get him here.

'He's in Warwick, Will, waken up. What next?'

Next – *and the fifty pounds residue thereof upon her surrendering of or giving of such sufficient security as the overseers of this my will shall like of –*

'That's me. Slow down.'

And Thomas Russell. And then go on – *to surrender or grant, all her estate and right that shall descend or come unto her after my decease, or that she now hath, of, in, or to, one copy-hold tenement, with the appurtenances* – keep scratching, Francis.

'You're going too fast, hang on. *One copy-hold tenement –* '

With the appurtenances, lying and being in Stratford upon Avon aforesaid in the said county of Warwick –

'I'll fill that in later.'

No you won't, I know you, you never get round to fair copies.

'It's still legal.'

I don't care. No mistakes, no loopholes, every word down now, verbatim.

'Jesus. The man's gone mad. What next?'

In the said county of Warwick –

'I can abbreviate that, I take it?'

Not funny – *being parcel or holden of the manor of Rowington, unto my daughter Susanna Hall and her heirs forever.*

'Susanna? Just a minute, what's going on?'

Explanations later. *Item, I give and bequeath unto my said daughter Judith one hundred and fifty pounds more, if she or any issue of her body be living at the end of three years next ensuing the day of the date of this my will* – what's the date today, Francis?

'25th March. Hang on a second... Right.'

During which time my executors to pay her consideration from my decease according to the rate aforesaid.

'Slower, slower.'

And if she die within the said term without issue of her body, then my will is, and I do give and bequeath one hundred pounds thereof to my niece Elizabeth Hall –

'Isn't that your grand-daughter?'

Did I say niece? My wit's diseased, Francis, scratch it out!

'I'll get it later, I can't keep up as it is.'

And the fifty pounds to be set forth by my executors during the life of my sister Joan Hart, and the use and profit thereof coming shall be paid to my said sister Joan –

'*Use and profit thereof* – '

And after her decease the said fifty pounds shall remain amongst the children of my said sister –

'Equally?'

Equally to be divided amongst them.

'And if Judith lives?'

But if my said daughter Judith be living at the end of the said three years –

'Or any issue?'

Or any issue of her body, then my will is, and so I devise and bequeath the said hundred and fifty pounds to be set out by my executors and overseers for the best benefit of her and her issue –

'You're running ahead of me again.'

And the stock not to be paid unto her so long as she shall be married and covert baron.

'But – '

But my will is, that she shall have the consideration yearly paid unto her during her life –

'I see.'

That's a good boy. Always useful to have a lawyer with half a brain.

'Sneck up, will you?'

And, after her decease, the said stock and consideration to be paid to her children, if she have any.

'And if not?'

And if not to her executors or assigns, she living the said term after my decease.

'End of paragraph.'

No, not quite. *Provided that if such husband as she shall at the end of the said three years be married unto, or attain after –*

'Such husband? What are you talking about?'

Such husband do sufficiently assure unto her and the issue of her body lands answerable to the portion of this my will given up to her, and to be adjudged so by my executors and overseers – and you're my man, Francis, a big man for a big provision – *then my will is, that the said £150 shall be paid to such husband as shall make assurance, to his own use.* Let's pause there.

'Pause? Jesus, let's have a drink! You should have been a lawyer after all, Will.'

I should have been lots of things. But it's too late now.

'Not if your will's made out.'

Francis chuckled fatly and waved the parchment beneath my nose. I always loved the smell of fresh ink.

We're not there yet, Francis. But we're getting there.

'Maybe so, old man. But what was all that about?'

Later. I need a drink myself.

'And if I'm invited to stay for dinner, by any chance – '

I want this signed today. I'm not letting you go until it's sealed.

'Then do you know what I'd fancy? A nice big capon – and lashings of sack!'

Sack makes a man fat and foggy, Francis.

'But comforts the spirits marvellously.'

There's no denying it. What would you say to a stewed carp instead? I could almost stomach a bite of fish.

'Ah, but the pike is to be preferred to the carp.'

Why so, Francis?

'Because the pike will already contain the carp – he's a great eater.'

Of his own kind. Very true. With pike you get the best of both worlds.

'And with a nice high Dutch sauce it would be almost irresistible. But no, I'm thinking capon today.'

And how would you like it?

'With honey and herbs and spices – begging your pardon, Will – loads of cloves and nutmeg, ground almonds, raisins of Corinth, rosemary, cinnamon, mace – and garnished with barberries and prunes.'

Ah, you mustn't omit the prunes.

'Prunes for the privy, they pave the way sweetly.'

If you even reach it in time. I don't want you on the close-stool – not as close as you are now, saving your presence.

'And as a next course to the capon, a nice blancmange of his brains. That's a tart to give courage to any man.'

Most tarts do get a man's courage up.

'Quite so. And a good slap of Hippocras to end with and wash it all down, well spiced with ginger, long pepper, and grains of paradise!'

Paradise, eh? That's much on my mind too, while Francis drools over his food like a poet praising his lady's eyebrow. He's missed his calling for sure – what a man for his belly! Very well, mistress, let the next course come on! With all the trimmings you can muster, for poor starved Francis – one fair capon and no more, the which he lovèth passing well.

19

'One fair capon and no more? You should have one, Will. They say a little chicken is good for the ailing.'

'What rubbish are you talking now?'

Mistress Mine was muttering in the doorway, as soon as she came up.

'From where I'm standing you two look like you've got till doomsday. How long does it take the two of you to cover a couple of sheets with lawyer's cant. Just do the deed – and sign it, for God's sake, if you can still hold a pen!'

Francis tried a sweetener.

'I've been hearing all about your courting days, Mistress Anne.'

I could have advised him otherwise, but how can you advise your lawyer? She gave me that look, the love-withering one, the one that would make wormwood seem sweet, and left the room.

'Oops.'

Francis followed on after her for his fifteenth piss and I managed at least to advise him to find Alison and ask her to smuggle us up some sack on the quiet, otherwise we'd never sniff a drop. When he came back light-footed, smiling and scratching his crutch, I reminded him I'd have to sing for my supper and he'd have to take down the notes.

When a fat face falls it's all the sadder.

'Oh, Will, I'm as melancholy as a gib-cat, or a lugged bear.'

At the thought of toil, yes. I'll allow you the bear image – but let's go to work.

'Right then, old man, you've done one daughter, supposing we do the other – for the sake of symmetry.'

Ah, they're not symmetrical. But well read, my thoughts. Are you ready?

'Like greyhounds in the slips.'

That's one image that won't wash.

Item, I give, will, bequeath and devise unto my daughter Susanna Hall, for better enabling of her to perform this my will, and towards the perform-

ance thereof, all that capital messuage or tenement with the appurtenances, in Stratford aforesaid, called the New Place wherein I now dwell –

'And where we now await our sack and capon.'

And two messuages or tenements with the appurtenances, situate, lying and being in Henley Street, within the borough of Stratford aforesaid –

'Got it. Don't run off from me, though.'

And all my barns, stables, orchards, gardens, lands, tenements, and hereditaments whatsoever, situate, lying and being or to be had, received, perceived, or taken –

'I'd ask you to draft my will for me if I thought you'd be around.'

Do you think there's any chance of it? *Or taken – within the towns, hamlets, villages, fields and grounds of Stratford upon Avon, old Stratford, Bishopton, and Welcombe, or in any of them in the said county of Warwick.*

'That wraps that up – good.'

And also all that messuage or tenement, with the appurtenances, wherein one John Robinson dwelleth –

'Remind me – who the hell is he?'

Nobody. *Situate, lying, and being in the Blackfriars in London –*

'Specifically?'

Near the Wardrobe.

'Aha!'

And all my other lands, tenements and hereditaments whatsoever, to have and to hold all –

'Ah, to have, to hold, and then to part – '

Is the greatest sorrow of the human heart. Strange you always think that way – until you come to make your will.

'And then?'

Then you come to realise that what you've held, and hold, and are about to part company with, is trash.

'To a man in your position, yes. But to the young and healthy, to the living – '

Worth holding onto. And worth securing it for them. So let's make things secure.

To have and to hold all and singular the said premises, with their appurtenances, unto the said Susanna Hall –

'Any conditions?'

For and during the term of her natural life.

'No conditions.'

And after her decease, to the first son of her body lawfully issuing –

'Never a fear of bastards there, eh?'

Never say never. *And to the heirs males of the body of the first son lawfully issuing; and for default of such issue, to the second son of her body lawfully issuing.*

'Right, I see how this is going – let me just put dashes here, I'll fill the rest in later.'

No, no, no, no, no, no, no – seven times no.

'Seven times. All right, all right, I have it in my head.'

I don't want it in your head. I want it in good black ink. Do it now. Write it down and read it back to me.

'Take a few minutes.'

As you see, I'm prepared to wait.

'No option but to tarry. Very well.'

While I rested and Francis scratched, little Alison stuck her head round the door and came skipping up to the bed. Francis kept scribbling but one eye glinted at her over his quill.

'What, no sack?'

She bent down and reached up inside her own skirts. That stopped the lawyer dead-eyed in his drafting. He stared with sagging chin and widening eye as Alison stood up again, fumbling under her dress.

With practised hands she detached the bottle from the sling around her waist, bent again, and slipped it in beside me with a wink, letting me see all the way down to her two unsucked nipples. Then she stood up, smoothing her skirts.

'Well, I'll be damned!'

I hope not, Francis. I'd like to have a word with you in the next world – and I don't want to be going there.

'Anything else, master?'

Yes, child, but I'll keep it to myself.

She gave me her faun's flutter and left.

Thank you, Alison. Keep at it, Francis. Nice little trick, eh?

'Incredible. That's me done. Shall I read it back to you?'

Every syllable.

'I hope you're ready for this.'

I'm ready and ripe and almost rotten. Take it from *second son.*

'And to the heirs male of the body of the second son lawfully issuing; and for default of such heirs, to the third son of the body of the said Susanna lawfully

issuing, and of the heirs males of the body of the said third son lawfully issuing; and for default of such issue, the same so to be and remain to the fourth, fifth, sixth, and seventh sons of her body issuing one after another and the heirs males of the bodies of the said fourth, fifth, sixth and seventh sons lawfully issuing, in such manner as it is before limited to be and remain to the first, second and third sons of her body, and to their heirs males; and for default of such issue, the said premises to be and remain to my said niece Hall – '

We corrected that earlier. It's *grand-daughter.*

'Of course. I'll see to it. *And the heirs males of her body lawfully issuing; and for default of such issue, to my daughter Judith –* '

Well foreseen, Francis.

'*And the heirs males of her body lawfully issuing; and for default of such issue, to the right heirs of me the said William Shakespeare.*'

For ever.

'Why not? *For ever.* How's that?'

Amen. And well done. You've earned your cup of sack. And your capon.

'I can smell it.'

It's on its way up. Did we say Judith's to get the bowl, the silver and gilt one?

'Done that.'

But Elizabeth's to get the rest of the plate?

'Seen to. Stop worrying, have a drink. And now let me check I've got this right so far.'

You've just been through it all. It's perfect.

'Construction, Will, construction. I'm executor as well as lawyer. I want to be sure I'm interpreting your wishes correctly.'

You want to be sure I haven't lost my marbles.

'The point being, you're attaching strings now to the January draft.'

Which no longer exists.

'Which is no longer tenable.'

O, Justinian!

'One hundred pounds to go to Judith for a marriage portion, but for the other fifty she's got to give up claim to what I take to be the Chapel Lane cottage – correct?'

That's correct.

'And if she or such offspring as she may produce are here three years from today, there's another hundred and fifty on the table?'

Correct.

'But if she dies barren instead during those three years, your grand-daughter, Elizabeth Hall – '

Not my *niece*.

'*Not* your niece – will come in for a hundred, and the remaining fifty will go to your sister Joan and her sons?'

Right.

'But if Judith or children of hers *are* around in three years time, then I'm to see to it – assuming I'm around myself – that she's paid the annual interest earned by the hundred and fifty.'

But *not* the principal, so long as she stays married.

'And her husband can only get his hands on the money if he settles on her lands to the value of the hundred and fifty.'

Brilliant.

'And as for Susanna, she walks away with almost the lot – if I may put it thus bluntly.'

You may, you may. I see a degree in the law was not wasted on you.

'To the extent that I can hardly help noticing a certain disparity between the estates of the two daughters. You still haven't told me what's going on.'

Nor have I. But we'll get to that.

'And your wife is out in the cold.'

She's not out in the cold, she's in with the Halls.

'Is that decided?'

It's understood – and here comes your capon.

The dishes were deposited in all their glory, Anne in attendance, on the look-out for liquor. The women were swept out, Francis rubbed his fat palms, and I rubbed the bottle of sack, safe between my legs, where Mistress Mine has not been or looked for thirty years. We sank back and congratulated ourselves on our labours.

'Whacking progress, Will. That was some burst! And a whacking capon too! Why don't you try some? I can spare a little.'

I might just do that.

And I chewed a forkful of meat in preference to the standing-pool scum that had been set down for me, gruel poorer than piss. I then got out the sack, plucked from under the blankets like a torch of life.

20

What are you, Will?

'Talking to yourself, old man?'

That's what she used to say to me. And could I blame her altogether for the catalogue of complaints she came out with? the sounds and smells of that hellish Henley Street shop, the cabin we were cribbed and coffined in, the puking, mewling infants, the confinements of the communal dining room – a babble of many voices with my father's growing beerier by the day and my mother needing more and more help. Nothing, it seemed, but work. And what was my work, she wanted to know? What are you, Will? A glorified butcher?

'A cutting question.'

Neither glover nor scholar, it was true. My father had provided me with sufficient schooling to make it impossible for me to draw a cart or eat dried oats. But what were the alternatives? Shopkeeper, usurer, dealer in timber or wool? Inheritor of John Shakespeare's failed fortunes, a counter-caster, to debitor and creditor bound? A chip off that worn old block? That's when I began to scent the breeze. The wind that scatters young men through the world, to seek their fortunes other than at home, where small experience grows. Even the soldier's uncertain life seemed preferable to this, the bubble reputation infinitely more attractive than the wars of the hearth. No, war is no strife – to the dark house and the detested wife.

Time and discontent. Late in the year 1582 I looked in my glass and I saw a stranger. He looked young but he didn't look hopeful. He was a husband and a father of three, stuck in a Stratford rut. He was a country nobody.

A decade later the crow had become an eagle, the Stratford hare a London tiger. The nobody had become a somebody.

'Metamorphosis.'

Yes, Francis, the essence of the human drama. The Stratford clod becomes a London luminary. *Tempora mutantur, nos et mutamur in illis.*

'Never forgot your Ovid, did you?'

Daphne and Apollo, flesh becomes grass. Apollo the archer, quiver full of arrows and each one tipped with flame. Swifter than quicksilver she flees from him, the wind baring her limbs, ripping her clothes from her as she runs. And just as the lovesick god reaches out to feel his first fistful of female flesh, the great change occurs. Her toes are rooting already – where she strains to leave the ground her feet have gone sluggish. Her outstretched arms are branches, tendril fingers turning to leaves, staining the skies with the green death which is her new life. Her hair is forest fleece, her heart beating under bark, her swinging tits two time-hardened knots, and all that alluring amber flesh impenetrable. The frozen fleeing girl has become a tree. Women are always turning into something else.

'And that's what happened with Anne Hathaway?'

As I said, a tongue with a tang. And when an English rose turns out to be a cabbage, you catch on at last that you must have needed spectacles. The rose lost its bloom, the great seductress of Shottery began to vegetate, the buttery-bar girl became a bore.

'And she looked on you as something of a let-down in the end?'

From buttery to butchery, the young poet who'd buttered her up at Hewlands was now stuck in Henley Street with the chopper and the slab. We stopped hearing the chimes at midnight. The gods had gone from Snitterfield, the nymphs played no more in the forest of Arden.

'Such is marriage.'

In the months following ours I thought that time would never turn our pages. I was locked into a plot that was interminable. No action, no development, no spectacle, no poetry. The script was rotten and the characters were dull, me most of all. Towards the mid-eighties the hand of Hathaway had grown less busy about my balls and more heftily directed at shoving me out of Henley Street in search of better employment. I could have argued that the hand of little employment hath the daintier sense but she'd have given me to understand that more work and less wit would better become my new roles as husband and father.

'And so it was that you to Henry Rogers did make love?'

Well, figuratively speaking, and the law proved tedious enough, and that was no surprise. And so did the schoolroom.

'What! Master Shakespeare, Stratford schoolmaster?'

Beater of boys, but unenthusiastic. I was dismissed. My replacement was a thug called Wymote, who battered them black and blue.

'Private tutor, then?'

Not for the first time. When Cottom was schoolmaster here his family in Lancashire had a Catholic neighbour called Alexander Houghton of Lea Hall. He needed a tutor for his children and my father needed extra cash. Cottom recommended me, and Houghton took to me, I'm not sure why – I wasn't a strict keeper of his warren of children.

'Had Cottom given him the Catholic whisper about you?'

That's how it started. But in the end Houghton may have fancied me just because of the play-acting.

'At last – the play thing!'

Among his servants Houghton kept a number of players, of whom he was unusually fond, and he asked me at Christmas if I'd fill in for one of them who was sick. It was nothing to speak of – a line hammed out, a mumble of mumming, a tumble or two, a humble bow to a murmur of aristocratic applause. But old Houghton approved. I'd made a start. And it made a difference. So did his will.

'A will? Ah, tell me about it.'

Houghton died when I was seventeen, but before he did he willed his half-brother Thomas either to take me into his service or help me to some good master. The good master the dead Houghton's brother helped me to turned out to be his brother-in-law, Thomas Hesketh, only ten miles off, at Rufford, and I was glad to get back north again when the chill winds cooled our bedsheets. Except that now I wasn't even tutor to a rich man's children, but simply another rich man's player, a move which did not go down too well in Henley Street. Player indeed. With precious little left to piss against the wall, let alone send back to Stratford. What is he playing *at*, that's the question?

I think I knew even then what I was playing at – what all players play at, illusion and escape.

Hesketh sent us now and again to Knowsley to play for his friends, the Stanleys, the great Earls of Derby, who kept their own players, the company of Lord Ferdinando Strange, the fifth earl. I didn't know it at the time, but the core of that company was destined to become the Lord Chamberlain's Men, the flower of the London theatre. And it was at Knowsley that I first came close to actors from London and got my first whiff of the capital in their sweat and breath, felt its life and vigour in their lunging strides and seductive speeches – the mean murderous magical metropolis.

'It was magic, magic that had ravished you!'

They sowed words like corn with a single telling gesture and reaped an instant reaction from their audiences. You could see a hallful of people stir like barley under the breath of a single whispered syllable. Here was power, right here. In a fistful of air. In the echoes of a few spent words.

'You must have seen the acting troupes before.'

Essex's Men and Stafford's came up, and Leicester's, led by Burbage, and Worcester's with Ned Alleyn as their glittering star.

'And then the Queen's?'

And then in the late June of '87 came the Queen's Men with two clowns, Dick Tarleton and Will Kempe. Kempe was at the start of his career, Tarleton a man nearing the end – a decaying hulk with melancholy eyes, whose power to pull the queen out of the dumps was as faded as his legend. Poverty, royal displeasure, and death by drinking were all awaiting him the following year. If I'd looked close enough I'd have seen his fate already written into his fat face. But like most of the other Stratford spectators I didn't come so near. Instead I watched him face out his inevitable fall with a fool-born jest and an irresistible grin, mocking the grin that mocks us all: the skull beneath the skin.

He was such a famous name that the Stratford crowd broke the windows of the Guild Hall in their determination to see him. Any view would do. Nobody was going to be robbed of the chance to get a glimpse of the fat little wizard who could so enchant a queen. His quips and cranks put her into such a good mood that condemned men waiting for the chop were spared at the last minute. They owed their lives to poor Tarleton – who couldn't in the end save himself. But none among us either inside or outside the Guild Hall that day knew much of that. Or of what lay ahead for the comedian as we watched him romp his way through the Seven Deadly Sins and take the fire out of hell.

'Farewell to Tarleton. And Stratford adieu!'

When their wagon disappeared in its cloud of dust it left me with a strangely empty feeling. The echoes died away. Stratford itself felt suddenly empty.

I went up to the Welcombe hill and looked about me. I saw an endless circle of flat farmlands lying quietly under Warwickshire's slow skies, that restless armada of clouds. Clouds that looked so close, as Uncle Henry always said, you could jump aboard one of them at random and sail off over those farmlands to something new. To be what? That was the question. What *not* to be was no longer in doubt. Beyond the circumference lay all of England. And beyond that – blue emptiness. And the untravelled world. I stood on Welcombe for a very long time, turning slowly round and round, environed by this vast circle. Its edges were the nagging skylines that held things tight and finite and yet pushed out into the future, the unknown. How to break the circle? To catch that cloud and steer it off into the blue compass.

I threw myself down and lay on my back in the grass, stretched out my body across the fields. They accepted it like the rack, as the sky accepted my soul, spun like beaten gold over all the counties of England. Everything whirled and went wild in my head, the shopboy servitude, the butchery, the grey boredom, life leaking away, a shrew always eating into my ears. If I stayed here one week longer I'd never leave at all. For the rest of my days I'd submit to the turnings of this great green clockface of fields and the blind succession of seasons that had turned the Snitterfield farmers in their sleep. I'd go under those fields myself, joining my ancestors in their graves, never having known anything else.

'And you at the great age of twenty-three?'

The year was 1587. And the time had come to do what John Shakespeare had done. What Richard Shakespeare had done before him. And what I should now do after them. Change my sky. That we would do we should do when we would. Or lose our venture. The tide had come in yet again. Time to take it, then. And with a free will go on.

'Free will and midsummer madness?'

A muddled broth of eleven souls bubbled beneath the Henley Street rafters. My father avoided my mother's eyes, in which he saw her lost heritage. Bile flecked Anne's tongue and the wormwood dripped in my ear. The twins fretted and teethed. There was no answer here.

All around us June burst like a green bomb, a slow explosion of energy. Pigeons and crows made a bedlam of the woods, the pear blossoms pounded with the peppering of tits, bees blundered among snowstorms of butterflies, and thistle-seeds, dozens deep, drifted thickly by, while the nettledust and the dry white dust of the roads stung the nostrils and pricked the eyes. Ants whizzed across the baked earth like the balls of black spit that bounced along winter stoves from the old Snitterfield mouths. I ran out into the fields, threw off my clothes and lay back again, looking up from the bottom of the ocean of growth. Through the greenness all was blue: blue trailing tangles of cornflowers, blue towers of thistles, castling the sky, blue bullets of dragonflies and the blue flames of field-fires, glassing the sun. Beyond the field, somewhere, the sea – blue water and the four points. Beyond the sun, infinity. And through all of Warwickshire I could hear it – the cuckoo, broadcasting its merciless monotonous message, cuckoo, cuckoo. Mocking married men. Cuckoo.

At nights the wicked gold of the stars melted and ran into my sleepless eyes and the wild garlic came knifing up the nostrils, through the open windows of that suffocating little room in Henley Street, filling the lungs. The thatch crackled as if it were set to burst into flame. I rose like a madman with the moon, staring up at its crazy frustrated face as if into a glass. I was led by a star that I could not see, but in which I trusted. It was lighting me the way to exile, banishment from heart and home. Standing by the window, I looked back at Anne, asleep in bed, bathed in silver like a corpse. Beneath that fresh white calico breathed the same body that had driven me mad with lust and longing five years earlier. Where does it go to, Francis, all that love?

Dawn came. I heard the swans taking off from the Avon, their long necks streaking like comets into the distance they were making theirs. The river they had left would be gliding at its own sweet pleasure, steadily out of Stratford this morning, as it did every morning, every moment of every day – coolly, maddeningly free.

Like the Queen's Men, who had left Stratford too – five days ago now, in their cloud of white dust. In that diminishing white dustcloud went gods and men, angels and devils, kings and clowns, courtesans, courtly lovers, ladies dead and lovely knights, flown with the fabulous swans. Another world on four wheels. I pictured the cart trundling and trumpeting across an England whose greenness and growing meant nothing to the players it carried, not this summer nor any other summer. They needed neither oak nor owl to measure their hours, their seasons. They were their own men, the Queen's Men. They were of no landscape, no age. They belonged to all ages and to the era of dreams. They were the abstracts and brief chronicles of the time.

'And so the decision was reached.'

I walked out of a Henley Street that was a blizzard of tears and torn hair and rent garments and disbelief. Assuring everyone that there was method in my madness I turned my back on the turning clods and clowns of Warwickshire and headed for Clopton Bridge.

Eighteen great arches that led out of Stratford, proudly providing the only egress south – that was Clopton Bridge. It was built in sumptuous stone, courtesy of adventuring Hugh Clopton who'd left Stratford for London, become its Lord Mayor, and returned in triumph as *Sir* Hugh to build himself a new house, New Place, and also this bridge, in a spirit of concern for the lives of the local drunks. An old wooden structure used to span the river at this point – and many's the pisshead whose drowning mouth had closed on the Avon after smashing through its rickety sides in a drunken plunge. I now stood on the last arch to leave the town.

It was a stand I'd taken time and time over as a boy to watch the swirl of the water at that juncture as it flowed under the bridge, hit a particular curve in the bank, and eddied for some seconds before changing direction and flooding back beneath the very same arch from which it had just come. We used to throw in a branch or a handful of hay and watch it sail underneath that eighteenth arch and out of Stratford, only to alter course and be swept back again. A child's game. And this bridge was the crossing point between youth and everything else that was left to come. I turned round in search of a twig or a clump of moss – and saw the disconsolate group standing at the south end of Bridge Street, watching my exit from their lives: mother, father, brothers, sister, children, wife. When they saw me turn like that, as if to re-cross the bridge, my four-year-old Susanna broke from her mother's hands, started forward, then stopped. That was it. The big wave came thumping up suddenly from my feet, choking me, blinding me. I opened my mouth to howl and nothing came. I was leaving behind three little sisters, dead in the Stratford earth. How did I know that none of my own three might not join them there, before I'd had a chance to see them again? And Susanna, turned to stone, was a lost girl, Perdita.

I wrenched myself round and hurried away from the bridge without even a last wave. In the child's game the branch would never fail to return to the arch. No game, this. Cut is the branch. The thing had to be now – or it would never be. To stay on now, to work Warwickshire, to die Warwickshire, to *be* Warwickshire, to become its fields and weathers – this would be death. Clouds would pile over my head like clods, burying me alive, deeper every day, a slow engrossing death, clouds with a voice in them, speaking to me now. Why in that rawness left you wife and child – those precious motives, those strong knots of love? I threw one terrified glance behind me and could still see Susanna's tiny white hand fluttering like a handkerchief on the other side of the river. I half stumbled as I turned south again, my face blind and streaming, for London.

21

There were two possible roads to the capital: Oxford to the right, Banbury to the left, and the carriers argued about them with dogged and sometimes drunken dogmatism, swearing by Charles's Wain over the new chimney at four in the morning, gabbling in their carriers' code. The Oxford road was the shorter, though either way took you through ruts and gullies, with muddied floods in winter and dust-laden desert tracks in summer. Wars and enclosures had spewed out onto these roads a race of masterless men – angry aggressive beings looking for a rough revenge for their ruined families, their solitary broken lives. No shortage of them – or of the ne'er-do-wells who needed no excuse for crime: common robbers, landraking longstaff sixpenny strikers, cut-throats for a groat, the lice of the land even among roadsters. Or there were the high-reaching highwaymen who robbed with a flourish. They slit your purse and spared your neck, unlike the rough scum who were inclined to go for both. The authorities hanged the ones they could catch. Those were few enough. As for casual players, they travelled these roads at their peril and were liable to fall foul of the authorities themselves even if they survived the attentions of the criminal element. Officially they *were* criminals and their unliveried backs were stripped and lashed bloodily by the commonweal – to a common weal. A lone traveller like myself would have found it safer to beg a lift from one of the carriers, or to hire a horse, but for my money on that first journey it was impossible. A four-day footslog was the best I could hope to manage, with a penny a bed and sixpence a meal at the inns on the way up.

There was a saying in Stratford that if Adam and Eve had come out of Arden and not Eden, they'd have taken the Banbury road to London, not the Oxford one. Old Granny Arden added that they'd certainly taken one of the roads, from what she'd heard of London, obeying to the full the divine injunction to go forth, be fruitful and multiply. When I reached London and saw the crowds I was inclined to agree with her.

I have a saying of my own, though, that if He'd followed the first couple, to spy on them during one of his constitutionals (and London would have been a mere stroll to him), God would have been dismayed to see them opting for the Oxford road. All the good books were in Oxford and knowledge was as plentiful as blackberries for anyone who took that road. Maybe that was why it was the route I came to prefer over the years. It was the route I chose for that first journey of many.

Travelling directly south all day, I exchanged the Avon for the Stour, passing through Atherstone and Newbold, which gave me my first sight of human beings since leaving Stratford, apart from flashes in far-off fields as the sun hit a scythe-blade or the lark-strung air caught a whistle or a shout.

After Shipston my path took me up again into the Cotswolds, to Long Compton, where I made a glum detour to the west to see my mother's sister, Aunt Joan, and my Uncle Edmund Lambert, at Barton-on-the-Heath. Among the shrills and sobs in Henley Street that morning were my father's pitiful – and pitiless – entreaties for me to see his brother-in-law and beg back from him the house and fifty-six acres in Wilmcote, my mother's house, mortgaged to him all of nine years ago for forty pounds, and to promise that I'd make the forty pounds in London and pay him back. If there hadn't been this new opportunity and this last hope lying on my London route, the Henley Street crowd would have tied me to a stake rather than let me go. My father had been the only willing one among them.

Aunt Joan gaped at me incredulously when I said I was on my way to London. Edmund Lambert for his part just gaped, his boiled blue eyes boring through me unseeingly – he was a man clearly dying. A hopeful sign. But when I raised the matter of the mortgage and reinforced it with the lie that I was being forced up to London against my will to restore the family fortunes, he pointed a white trembling finger at a shifty youth, little more than a frown in the shadows, and Joan translated snippily that John Lambert, her husband's son – *and heir* – would have to see to all of that. After an age of arguing, mostly sullen headshakes on his side, the scowling youth, responding to pursings of his mother's fat lips and intensifications of his father's vacant blue stare, agreed to accept a further twenty pounds on top of the original mortgage: a promise which the slippery bastard denied in court in front of my father only three months later.

I'd done the talking for all four and would have been out of patience with the dismal trio if it hadn't been for the arrival of their two transient guests, Lambert's cousin, a Justice from Pebworth, and *his* cousin from Gloucestershire, out of whose silent mists he appeared to have not quite emerged. These two piping ancients professed to know everybody in Stratford from the cradle upwards, and so, milking me for information, pursued each subject of their inquiry all the way to the grave. Dead? Jesu, death is certain, as the Psalmist says, and life's a vapour.

My London-bound irruption into that joyless household rekindled the two cousins' gleeful recollections of their own youth and its wildness and depravity. To celebrate this further they insisted on seeing me to the next stage of my journey and to the nearest inn. No question of hospitality for me here at the Lamberts. The twosome were on horseback for the sake of their ancient shanks but were happy to double up for a mile or two. I was well content to fall in with them and leave the Lamberts to the smells of avarice and death that co-mingled sickeningly within their four walls.

I came down the next day through Chipping Norton, Enstone, Woodstock, and the Cherwell valley without stopping for breath till I arrived at Oxford, where I slept badly at the Crown Tavern in Cornmarket Street, within spitting distance of the very spot where Latimer had writhed in Bloody Mary's flames.

I was on the road again even earlier next morning, determined to reach Uxbridge before nightfall. It was a forced march: Headington Hill, Wheatley, Tetsworth, Stokenchurch, over the Chilterns and down into High Wycombe, heading ever more easterly after that, through Beaconsfield and Gerrard's Cross, reaching Uxbridge in the long midsummer twilight only to fall into the most villainous house for fleas on all the road to London. By morning I was stung like a tench and woke to the stench of old piss festering among the ashes in the fireplace and breeding bugs as busily as a loach. I could see I was now saying goodbye to all pleasant connections with the countryside and when I stepped out to Southall and Acton I saw ahead of me such a pall of smoke that my first thought was that London was burning and would be gone before I ever saw it. A lame soldier I overtook and asked about it laughed acridly and assured me that London burned every day. The smoke I saw was merely the halo of its daily hell.

'By the time you're in the city you won't notice it,' he told me, 'you'll just be adding to it. And you'll soon lose your country fragrance.'

Then he did me for the price of a drink.

Leaving him far behind I passed Shepherd's Bush and came at last to terrible Tyburn. I stood and stared at the notorious triple tree. Everywhere, I thought, has its shambles, and this was London's. Here the blood happened to be human, that was the difference. Animals die expressing sheer terror, absolute agony. There is a terrible purity about it. This place was fouled by the curses of its victims and the obscenities of its audiences. What kind of people came here? To witness the spectacle of human butchery as eagerly as I had once fed on Kenilworth's carnival.

But the grim gallows gave way to the pleasantest of meadows, over which rooks and cuckoos presided in a sweet dissonance, elegists and lyricists, assuring me all over again of that fine weave made by joy and woe. There was a church and a leper hospital and I saw some chained men sitting on the grass. I was coming into the village of St Giles-in-the-Fields. As I took the road towards Holborn I passed more men in chains, two by two, travelling in the direction I'd just come from.

'You're on the wrong road for the play, young sir!' one of the prisoners shouted. 'Aren't you coming to see us turned off?'

'And then turned inside out,' his companion grinned at me. 'Come and give us a last handclap.'

I stared after them. They were bound for Tyburn. They would drink Adam's ale at St Giles' Bowl, their last refreshing in this life. Then they'd join their fellow criminals for a final rest in the fields before climbing the gallows. Yet they'd gone west with a not unfriendly quip to a fellow creature, one coming into London just as they passed out of it. And out of life. Facing out fear and death with a jest. I shivered and quickened my step. Hurrying away from their doomed backs and bravado, I came along Holborn Street and across the Fleet River, over Holborn Bridge, then past the churches of St Andrew and St Sepulchre, and so to Newgate.

I had arrived.

22

'History and whores, my boy, it was all waiting for you, wasn't it?'

Thirty years ago, yes, everything awaited me in London. And it wasn't just the city I walked into that summer morning, it was the age, hot with whores and history.

'You said it, lad.'

In entering London I entered the age incarnate, and the hot hole of the great whore of England.

'A window into hell.'

And hell, like any other whore's hole, was busy, a busy world of business and desire, a universe in which you had to bustle in or you'd be left chewing your snot and scratching your balls, your prick and purse strings flapping idly in the breeze that blew through England at that time. The dog looked up from its gutter-fucking and sniffed at something new, an era almost tangible. Jesus, even the worm in the clod looked fatly, twitchingly busy, as if it sensed the shiver of excitement that went through the earth then, a thrill of eagerness, some sort of curiosity, belief.

'For now sits expectation in the air...'

I felt it in my flesh, sensed myself sudden witness to a great happening, the like of which might never come again, as old as England might grow.

'That's youth for you.'

The planet was polished and green as a young apple, able to brush off time and circumstance like straw. A lustrous and ingenuous – what can I call it? – youthfulness hung in the clouds, and even dire events were laced with the moondew of dreams, strung with the drops of endless possibilities – and time off the leash.

And what a time it was! It was the age of production: linens and laces, silken girdles and silken terms precise, taffeta doublets, taffeta phrases, codpieces, characters, three-piled hyperboles, figures pedantical – and minds tossing on the ocean, the argosies pregnant with sail, signiors and rich burghers on the flood.

'Rich buggers everywhere, eh?'

And poor folk underwater and underfoot, poor folk soonest pissed on by the peers, poor houseless indigents under the yellow drench, paying for their houses too, the rich buggers' houses. Hung with Tyrian tapestries, ivory coffers stuffed with crowns, and cypress chests of arras counterpoints, their spouses' chests well worth the unbuttoning, their Turkish cushions bossed with pearls, valance of Venice, the vines of Burgundy and milk of France, gold in needlework, pewter and brass, a hundred milch-kine to the pail per burgessman, a brace of bulls to boot, and six-score fat oxen standing in the stalls, shitting the richest crap in Christendom.

Wealth. Wealth on the walls and fatness in the fields.

'It tickled your balls, my boy.'

I'd no wish to be one of the poor, not in the age of the rich bugger. For the poor you have ever with you, ten a penny. Only the unnumbered poor worked all day long for their solitary shilling, sixpence for some. And in that unlikely span of three score year and ten, would the poor man see a lifetime total of as much as two hundred pounds pass through his hard and horny hands?

'He'd slip into his grave owning nothing but the skin he'd lived and died in.'

Not even that, Francis, for there were priests that would tear the bedsheet from a dying man, and if they could find nothing else in his four bare walls as tithe, they'd skin him alive, the fuckers, and use his grease as lamp-oil, and there'd be precious little of that on a poor man's bones, he earned the wrong kind of currency, that's all, for the age offered only two kinds of coin – there was rich money and there was poor money.

'And you hadn't come to London for poor money, had you, Will?'

That's for sure – unlike what's to come. Which is never sure.

What's to come. But what had I really come for? What did I crave more than money? One thing more than anything – space. Strange to have been surrounded all my days by the broad acres of Warwickshire, and yet to be hemmed in, to feel in that very openness an incarceration of a kind.

'A dangerous time.'

London was lethal, but in one sense it was safer than Stratford.

Here you were a speck surrounded by strangers. Here you could slip the bonds of identity, of a known past. You could become someone else. This was the lure of London, especially of the London stage, where king and clown shared the same space, exchanged the same body sweat, could even be the same person. It was more than levelling, it was life-changing, it was metamorphic, Ovidian.

'So different from Stratford?'

Stratford. Infinite emptiness, the blue beyond, the quilted fields rumpling as far as the eye could stretch, covering all my dung-turning, dung-turned forebears, and I to follow them before I'd had even an hour of life to myself? No, that was not for me. But to stand that morning on the edge of a crowded London was to feel the palpable play of openness and opportunity. You stuck out your tongue and it tingled like it did when you were a child, catching the rain and the snow in your open upturned mouth. Just to speak in the streets of London was to be free. You heard your words ring out, the syllables clattering off the tongue and chiming like gold coins at your feet. You knew you could pick up a quill and scribble things on the sky, poems, plays, anything in this glorious new amplitude – and each particular syllable would prick heaven like a star. London was a whore all right, but you could woo her with words and make love to her with your tongue, right inside the crack.

'Behave yourself, my boy. Remember your age.'

It was the age of compromise. Dead Edward's Protestant Prayer Book, talking to God in English, private arrangement, do it yourself, a plain Protestant queen, no windows in men's souls, but windows in their bellies or oaths on their lips. Believe what you like, or must – only conform, and escape the hangman's noose, and worse, his blade. And make your faces vizors to your hearts.

It was the age of outwardness. Of seeming. Add to that plots and massacres and seminary scholars, a Bull of Excommunication on a sovereign queen, infiltrators from Douai, Rheims, holes in houses, priests in privies grinning up to their necks in rich reeking papish turds, a land honeycombed with secret cells, sticky with slime and Spain – and you have every sleeper in the country wide awake. The Spaniard alone proved a night-owl. Spain had also murdered sleep – and the knife was under Mary's pillow.

It was the age of plots. Elizabeth had grown up among plots. She herself was the fruit of her royal father's most infamous plot and as soon as he was dead the fruit scattered its seeds. She sat like a bright fly at the trembling centre of a web of spiders – not all of them Spanish spiders by any means: there were plenty of English house-spiders hidden in the cracks. They were going to stab her, smother her, blow her at the moon, infect her food and drink, poison her stirrup, her shoe, her dress, her comb, destroy her by some other horrible Italian device. Deadly perfumes were under concoction, inflammable oils for drawing curtains of flames across bedchambers, around the royal bed itself, sending a sleeping queen shrieking into a swift and red eternity. Oh, most horrible, I promise you! Most bloody, most sudden, most terrible – and most true.

It was the age of Mary. Quick to wrath, our English queen was slow enough to send her Scottish cousin into the next world. She'd been sitting on it for twenty years and in the year I came to London the egg finally hatched. And yet even then, when the serpent's egg cracked open and the papist snakes came slithering into her skirts, still she agonised. For there's such divinity doth hedge a king, or queen...

It was the age of Babington. Yes, the plot that finally brought Mary to the block, exchanging feathery metaphors for a sharp axe and a sealed coffin. When I came up from Stratford four months later it was still the talk of London.

It began with Ballard the priest, but a man called Poley was in there too. Ballard corrupted Babington, who'd been a page of Mary's when she was at Sheffield. A cat may look at a king, and a page can come pretty close to poor puss, especially when puss is pretty, and when pussy cares to purr, which Mary knew how to do. And Babington came of rich old church stock. To a papist no pussy purrs like Catholic pussy. He was an impressionable pot-head – easily infiltrated. Mary to him was next to mother of God and he dreamed of celestial intercourse. His political dreams were simple. And dreadful. And so he drew in a dozen conspirators, six of whom were to kill the queen, with Mary's written consent. Walsingham knew every word of it – letters intercepted, decoded, sent on again, the conspirers given all the rope they needed to hang themselves – and the Walsingham net closed, and the spymaster's spiders pounced.

There were traitors enough to require a two-day diet of executions, seven at a time brought onto the scaffold, a scene so frightful first time round that the crowd spared the second batch from the full rigour of the torments prescribed by law although the queen had specially requested new techniques to ensure maximum suffering for all. Even the hardened hangers-on at Tyburn, the mob-dogs that cheered on the executioner and lapped up the spillages, even this hard core were shaken by the brutality of the dismemberings and disembowellings. Babington himself was not deprived of his rightful share of the agonies of execution. He and his companions poured out their lives in pain – what Topcliffe the torturer had cleverly *left* them of their lives – and it was said that their screams from the scaffold could be heard over six counties of England, carrying even further than Edward the Second's when that white-hot poker shot up his back passage and frizzled his innards to nothing, to a black hole, in one unbelievable second. As for Babington's cries, I never heard them in Stratford and if I had I might have stayed far from London, for he and his companions died slowly and loudly and their excruciating shrieks sent flocks of shocked seabirds winging their way darkly northward, echoing the shrieks as they flew. An old man looks up from his September stubble, a witch-woman from her Snitterfield shithouse, they hear the cries, see the dark shapes in the sky and mutter their spooky conclusions: 'Ah! there go the souls of Babington and his friends, and they'll be snatched by the devil before they get far, you mark my words.' And so perish all the queen's enemies.

It was the age of Elizabeth. She was the belle of the English ball, and she queened it on the English stage. She could make the melody that England longed to hear, the song that sends men melting mad with ecstasy. She knew how to pluck St Crispin's string, to find it in the hearts of Englishmen and strum it as hard as Robin's robin.

'Bonny sweet Robin? Did you hear the redbreast sing?'

Yes, I heard it then, though the age of Leicester was worn bare by '87 and Dudley himself but a year left to live. He'd sprung from a race of greedy upstart crooks, his treacherous grandfather had been executed by axeman Henry and his plotter father by Mary and the sons sent to the Tower. There Dudley had met Bess, also a prisoner at the time, and mutual incarceration added to the chemistry, forming a strong bond.

'That's putting it politely, perchance?'

Some of the courtiers sniggered that he wetted her fancy whenever he entered the room – you could hear her itch for him – and when she came to power she made him Master of the Horse.

'Or Master of the Mare.'

As he was quickly christened. She might even have married him, except for the small matter of his being married already, to Amy Robsart. So when Amy was found at home one Sunday noon, dead at the bottom of a flight of stairs with broken neck, there was ample scope for speculation. She had breast cancer, it was said, though she suspected poison – and a servant's evidence pointed to suicide, to escape the pain and the full prowl of the wolf.

'Or the cancer of an aimless existence.'

There are worse things than the wolf. On the day she died everyone in the house had gone to Abingdon Fair, apart from a brace of ladies, so an assassin could have slipped in like a shadow and earned easy money – a simple push, an accident. She was drowsy with drugs after all, had been drinking a lot to dull the pain, and by this time had brittle bones. And who knows if that was all there was to it, unless you saw the hand of God there, clearing the way for a queen of England to marry a man she loved, and he an Englishman to boot, and down to his boots.

'And yet but a subject.'

And she a sovereign. And his family tainted with treason. Though the coroner's verdict was death by misadventure, the people's verdict was murder and they were muddied, thick and unwholesome in their thoughts and whispers for little Amy's death.

'And the sea-winds caught the gossip.'

In France Mary Stuart had shown her claws and sneered that the English queen was about to marry her horse-keeper, and other nations joined the French in asking what sort of religion held sway in a country where a subject murdered his wife and not only got away with it but was rewarded with his sovereign's hand in marriage. Besides which, to marry Dudley would have been to remove herself from the chessboard of the European marriage market.

An impossible choice. She dammed up desire and tried to act like a prince. But at Whitehall she had his suite of rooms moved to the first floor next to her own, his own ground floor apartments suffering from the damp – too close to the river, it would seem. And he'd come into her bedchamber at dawn and hand her her shift. Oh, she knew how to keep the dog panting, and he couldn't contemplate a second marriage while he was the object of the queen's affection. Yet this was the game he was expected to play and if it didn't end in bed it earned him the condemnation of the court for the ambitious upstart that he was.

And so: exhausted by her virginity, he started to sleep with Lettice Knollys, voluptuously lovely, Lady Hereford and the queen's first cousin. He'd already slept with Lady Sheffield, made her pregnant, and undergone a ceremony of sorts, all in hugger-mugger. Then, when Lord Hereford died, he tried to persuade Lady Sheffield to keep pussy in the bag, the ceremony never having amounted to a wedding. And for five years she'd thought herself fast married. The queen had given him Kenilworth back in the early sixties and he'd spent a dozen years turning it from a fortress to a palace. But even when publicly fêting and privately fucking his queen during the famous housewarming perchance, he was privily in the petticoats of a countess. Or two.

Three years later Leicester married Lettice – secretly again, when she was well pregnant. Or not so well. The infant died and they had to wait till the end of the seventies, for a son that lived. He was so adored by his parents they nicknamed him The Noble Imp. But their joy was cut short. He died aged four – and Leicester himself had only four years left, having suffered the worst of sorrows and lived long enough to feel a queen's hot breath go cold.

That was the end of Lettice. The Queen never forgave her for taking away her lover. She'd never let Leicester bring her to court, and she kept the knife in even after he was dead. The widow was made to pay back every penny her late husband owed the crown. She snatched back the estates she'd given him, and forced the countess to sell fifty thousand pounds of jewellery to come into the clear. While Elizabeth still sported a whole treasury of jewels that were Leicester's presents.

'In the end, though, it's not the jewels we remember best, is it?'

In any love affair, or any human bond. They say that going through her things after she died, they came across a scrap of folded parchment in a cabinet by her bed. Across it she'd written the words *His last letter.* It was only a scribbled note, thanking her for the prescriptions she'd sent him. Even a queen's medicines don't keep an earl from death, once his time has come. But in spite of the feud she let his body lie in peace at Warwick, next to the Noble Imp.

'The stuff of drama, Will.'

Drama was the trumpet that summoned the world to London, to my very doorstep, and it was no provincial matter now. I'd left the Stratford Guild Hall far behind. The whole of London was a theatre. I couldn't have come at a better time. The playhouse sat in my hand like an oyster. The trick was to pop in a pearl and make them think it real. I'd arrived on cue, ready for the uncurtained age. History took me by the hand. Anything was possible in an age which had put a girdle round about the earth.

It was the age of Drake. He'd left London ten years earlier, ringed the globe in three, and come back to London with most of his men, fleecing Philip's treasure fleet en route and disgorging a fortune at the queen's feet.

Drake had made it into the age. It was the age of London.

And to come to London was to come of age.

23

Newgate was my way in.

Running with the sun along the city walls you came to Aldersgate, Cripplegate, Moorgate, Bishopsgate, Aldgate, Ludgate – and so back to Newgate. All roads led to Newgate.

It was through that particular breach in the blood-and-mortared city walls that I entered London on the twenty-sixth day of June 1587, an anonymous shadow from Stratford, noticed by nobody. I came in on that sunlit morning without fuss but with my eyes wide open.

'What did you see, lad?'

Once the city had sucked you in through the wall, you didn't so much see London as hear it. The Stratford silences, the wide skies of Warwickshire still filled my head. And so it was the London din that hit me on that first morning.

The gun foundries were busy preparing for Spain, and from the corner of Thames Street and Water Lane down near the river, and from beyond Houndsditch, it sounded as if the business with the dons had already begun. Vulcan's stithy was hard at it and the smoke hung out in columns and flags to boast the enterprise all the way to the Bay and beyond.

'The Bay of Biscay-O.'

Down in the streets – the fractured clattering of all the London songs: sweep chimney sweep, brooms new brooms green brooms, small coals sea coals, hot peas ripe cherries water from the wells – clear water fresh wells, whelks and mussels and cockles in their shells. A clangorous crying like the sea. And all through it and over it like the wail of gulls a keening of a different kind: bread and meat for the Lord's sake to the poor prisoners of Newgate – the pathetic jabberings of starving jailbirds, ravenous for scraps.

'When I swing by the string – '

You shall hear the bell ring.

'A raucous throng, the London rabble. Can you still hear it, Will?'

Hear it years later, over these crows, the elegies from the elms, hear it coming through again, the curses, the prayers, the laughter and anger, thundering of hooves and clattering of barrows, whistling and spitting of prentice-boys, trilling and skirling of wet wenches on heat, the oaths of the urchins, the calls from the wharves and the echoing docklands, the sailor's sea-salted, hoarse-throated shout, the scream of the back-lashed whore, the yells of the wherrymen, the blackguards, the bullies, the beggars – the general gender, the distracted multitude, the lifeblood of London.

'Your future audience, lad. Your public.'

They came to hear a periwig-pated fellow tear a passion to tatters, to split their ears, then they'd go out and tear a poet to pieces, split open his belly if it suited their spleen. By day they were a froth, a floating scum, seething on the city's filth. By night they lived in its spinning innards. In the mornings they came out and hatched and hotched like lice on the open sores of dawn, and they lived and died like maggots in its rotting bowels.

'A far cry from Stratford.'

London was an offence to eyes, ears, and nostrils. The brick kilns at Islington were belching their reek and a red sea of hell was pumping into the city, billowing among its churches.

'Stinking it to high heaven.'

Its offence was rank. There was one noisesome stench above the rest that hit me as soon as I came through Newgate. I was just inside the wall. After a minute I moved on, but with the faltering step of a frightened man approaching the block. It was only when I came to St Nicholas-within-Newgate that I knew at once what it was that I was remembering.

'You heard the screaming of cattle?'

Smelt their blood first. Close to the gate stood the slaughter-house, St Nicholas' shambles. Here the streets glittered and stank and ran with grease, and the birds fell on the scavengings like black rain. The same old shivers came on me again, a helpless witness to screaming sheep, the convolutions of bowels that strewed the roads, slithering over stones, stilled streamers of life turning loathsome and stagnant and black.

'Home sweet home, eh?'

A grisly welcome to the Stratford shadow as it stole in under the archway and sped like an arrow out of the sight and sound and smell of horror. I went like a ghost among the oyster-wenches and serving maids, turning southwards up Ludgate Hill, came down in suddenness on the church whose bulk had held my eye for miles all the way in.

'The great St Paul's.'

A sight worse than anything hell could offer. The middle aisle was awash – with human scum. Here lawyers and clients worried the bones of their business like dubious sharp-faced wolves. Here the horniest hag-shaggers in London proclaimed their appetites, the bulging red-painted codpieces thrust out like bunched haemorrhoids as they strutted up and down as hot as monkeys, as prime as goats, as salt as wolves in pride – all looking for a fuck with the first available floosie to spread her shanks for sixpence. And here the fieriest Tybalts in the land paraded their blades of Spain, itching to pick a fight with killers of similar kidney.

'A den of thieves.'

The work of worship went on unregarded in the choir. Red-faced delivery men threaded their way through the throng, carrying coals and corpses and shitloads of everything, fagged out and farting under their burdens, grunting and sweating. As I stood and gaped there was a general shout and the whole concourse parted down the middle and swept back like the Sea of Egypt, leaving a narrow passage all down the aisle.

'Moses come again?'

A pack of mules and horses came clattering up the centre aisle. The crowd hissed and roared and the air burned blue with curses – to treat the path to God like a common causeway! – and then they were gone again in a thunder of hooves and a whiff of shit as the Red Sea closed before the echoes had even died away.

'I understand they call it Duke Humphrey's Walk.'

Where God and Mammon fought it out, God losing all the way where whores and pimps and pickpockets plied their trade, where idlers came to stare vaguely at bills for employment posted on the pillars, and shun work like death. Here you could show off your tackle or your tailor, pick up some gossip, a servant or a whore. You could cadge a loan, a drink, a meal, steal a purse, boot a beggar, spit on a bankrupt, avoid a creditor, a Puritan, a punk, and all by the prick of noon. After that you could have lunch or hear a play. And any left behind –

'Dined with Duke Humphrey.'

A good phrase for an empty belly. And somewhere under all this sacrilege lay the fresh green bones of Sir Philip Sidney, laid to rest in February, just the week before they killed the Scottish queen, Sweet Sir Philip, gentleman of English poetry and bullet-honoured hero of the walls of Zutphen, defender of the Dutch and golden verse, gently decomposing underneath my feet. There was more sweetness in his melting flesh, not nine months into its rotting, than in this quintessence of corruption.

'There's hell – '

The stink of derelicts lying drunk asleep about the doors, everything within them left in yellow pools on the stones, their feet and hair sodden with shared vomit as they lay and snored, oblivious of the din. All this and the piles of dogshit too, the curs lifting their legs to piss on sleepers, imitated by packs of brats, who made a jest of openly pissing on floors, turning them into slipways for the unwary walker – yes, this was hell. Or so I thought.

'But it was only the prologue?'

Let me give you London straight and whole. I give you its poor men's cottages and princes' palaces. I give you its timbered tenements eked out with mud and plaster and blossoming with bed-bugs and beetles from the flowering graveyards on which they were built and into which they crept, the short-lived living nudging aside the dead for a while, butting into their eternal rest, trampling on their bones. I give you the houses of unlawful and disorderly resort, the habitations of beggars, the hovels of the jobless poor, dissolute, loose and insolent beings, and the stables, alehouses, shithouses, whorehouses, dicing-houses, taverns, inns, bowling alleys, into which they crawled and swarmed like flies. I give you the horses, cats, and dogs decomposing in the fields and streets, where the channels were choked by the eternal blend of shit and piss and putrefying blood, London's horrible broth. When the sun came out this soup of the streets gave off a ghastly glitter and when it rained it streamed everywhere, a blackish porridge laving the bare feet of the shoeless populace, bathing its purulent sores. I give you the vagrants, the sacked and soaked scullions, the cursing cast-offs, the unemployables, the indescribables, the useless, the shifty, and the savage, the worse than worms, the last dregs of a population which in sheer incivility, coarseness, boorishness, and barbarity of nature yielded to none in the world: a city of shitheads, hardheads, hotheads, knuckleheads, knobheads, pissheads, and –

'And heads?'

And yes, I give you the heads – the heads of London. On Bishopsgate, on London Bridge, on the Temple Bar – see the heads: stark symbols of the sheer savagery of the law. That black rain of birds I'd seen at Newgate swooped first on the severed heads, gorging on treason. A fresh head did not betray the appetite, beginning with the dripping eyeball, spitted on the beak – Out vile jelly! where is thy lustre now? – and so on down to the tongue, torn from the unprotesting mouth or ripped from the gaping neck.

'That's enough of heads.'

I shall return to the heads, by and by. But let me also give you the lacerated ape, the split dog, and the mauled bear whose howls die out in that red crater that was his throat. Let me give you the twitching heart in the hangman's bloodied fist – the entrails trailing like Medusa's hair from the hand plunged deep in the secrets of the Jesuit's belly. Much more to come, Francis, of this fair city, and the place is full of frights and noises, long before you reach the Isle of Dogs. Hurry along Cheapside and Cornhill then, come with me now, and into Gracious Street. Go south to the river, the bridge, cross to the south bank and see all.

'What do you see now?'

Looking north on London, I see it again, the Tower, perched opposite Olaf's like some dark four-headed bird, bloody with prehistory and myth, gloomy with human wreckage and remembrance. See the freewheeling crows drift like black souls tethered to the turrets, and see higher still, soaring, the free spirits of the gulls, brushing the feet of God. Look now, how one solitary bird breaks the circle, goes winging westwards in its slow descent, past Baynard's Castle and St Paul's, to Blackfriars and the Temple, still soaring high above the spires and belfries of a hundred churches, the tall chimneys and roofs of windowed palaces. The water swarms with boats and the wharves with workers, and plumes of smoke are feathering the air, putting scrolls on the blue parchment of the sky. Follow that bird then, that white flash of wings drifting, spiralling downwards now, to guide you to the Thames, the long flowing ribbon of the great river – and a city dancing on its banks.

'The great vein of London.'

It was a moving wood, a Birnam forest of masts east downriver past the marshes, Clink and Marshalsea, and thirty-five miles off – far from the filth and glitter of the world-touched capital – the sea pulled in its ships from Denmark, Sweden, the Netherlands, and France. Closer to home, the river ran with the shit that slid in from the common sewer: two hundred thousand turds a day, and double that if every soul shat twice – and that's some shoal to be rubbing shoulders with the schools of fish that swam among the leaping silver salmon. Three million shits a week, sweet Jesus, sufficient seasoning for your fish-dish, fit for beggar or queen, for your turd is a great leveller, there being nothing to say, when two float together in the Thames, whether one has issued privily from noble bowels, Tudor bowels, and the other from the beggarliest arse that ever opened in the filthiest open shithouse under the sun. Poison the fish, Francis? – we *drank* that water! And many's the morning I dreamt of cupping a cold glimmer of Stratford sunlight in my palm, scooped from a Shottery brook.

Sweet Thames run softly till I end my song.

The swans sang too, graciously avoiding the carcasses, like gentlemen on the field, keeping to windward of mortality. Dead dogs rolled unbarking on the tide, past the tall ships loading, unloading at the crowded quays their cargoes of wool and grain and leather and salt and silks and spices and barrels of tar and casks of wine; past the barges and boats bobbing like pilot-fish about the queen, out on the river; or in the Armada year, past barges hung with black for Leicester's death, a school of dumb blind whales, mourning the queen's sweet Robin. And so on down to Wapping Old Stairs, to Execution Dock, where the rats and sea-rovers rattled and rotted in their chains, hanged in their old familiar element, and drowned in the washing of ten tides, though one salt wash sufficed to end all breath, and three was law.

And at last to Deptford, to the rotting hulk of the Hind that had once put that golden girdle round about the earth – now gloomy monument to the faded glories of a man: all golden fire once and a burnt-out hulk behind.

Sweet Thames run softly till I end my song.

Come back up river, come with me now – you can't avoid the watermen, who wherried me many's the time from Puddle Dock and Blackfriars stairs to Paris Garden, Horseshoe Alley, and so down Park Street to the Globe, or whisked me up to Whitehall, Greenwich, Richmond: a cold progress to the palace and a cold shilling from the king, or the sixpenny queen, for a winter play, and that was my payment for the colder penny pressed into the ice-hard palm of the waterman, whose curse was the curse of the Thames.

Sweet Thames run softly till I end my song.

There was nothing soft about the song of the waterman. Listen and you'll hear him, as we steal up river, hard at it among the clash of the watermills clattering like the tongues of shrews. He's a worse babbler than a barber, a long-tongued scourge that sprays the chatter of his customers from one to another faster than pollen from the feet of a bee. A pothead too, though the playhouses make an afternoon man of him and keep him rowing sober. He'll row like a slave to outstrip his mates and get back first for the following fare. Nothing will make him leave the river if there's a solitary penny to be picked up north or south, and only a hard frost can teach him any decent manners. And if you care to hear the worst language in the world, bluer than any brothel, take a wherry for a penny and as you're skimming like a bird and he's happily cursing everything and everybody in the world since time began, just see what happens when you chance to mention good old London Bridge.

'Surely a wonder to behold!'

The piers that held up the high arches were encased by starlings – islands that impeded the flow of the river turning it to a mad mill-race. When the tide was flooding, folk chose to get out and walk, re-embarking on the other side of the bridge and so robbing the boatman of a fraction of his fare.

What bone-brains built that bridge is what I'd like to know? Who needs it? This is your waterman's refrain. Even the Thames itself, he says, roars like a thing demented when it strikes the bridge that has intruded into its bowels. That bastard bridge – he says – sucks the shit from my arse – thus he curses – for if it wasn't for that dry cunt of a crossing I'd bring in a thousand fares a day, enough to sink my boat with pennies by nightfall. I'd fuck the best whores in London and I wouldn't work on Christmas!

'He sings both loud and long.'

Your London boatman keeps time to his own imprecations with the pull on his oars, and keeps time to the oars with the flow of his oaths. I didn't much like the bridge myself, except it kept me from the boatman's cursing. Made of elmwood, they said – the worst wood in the world for the fire, burning slow like churchyard mould. A Snitterfield saying, that one. Doesn't so much burn as rot, they'd mutter, as they spat on a grumbling log, dousing it with one good Snitterfield gob. Good in water though, rotting slower than a whore in hell, old Henry said, adding that elmwood answered much the same to flame or wave. Well, the waterman's bane stood solidly on islands of this stubborn stuff that had been sunk deep into the river bed and it was hard to picture it cracking even on the crack of doom.

'A safe crossing.'

From Fish Street to Southwark the road vanished into these archways. They were like dungeons, the buildings gloomed over your head, shutting out the light, and at dark doorways and windows up and down the street, an army of money-hungry merchants scurried like ants, each one scratching for a grain of profit. Even the waterman's honest cursing bettered this suffocating ugliness. My way was the waterway.

'Nothing to do with the heads, Will?'

Spiked up there on Bridge Gate, they compelled you to look, reluctant eyes riveted to their blind stare. You stood on the Southwark side, raised your head to look at the spiry skyline, and saw it through this macabre crowd of crowns, dead men's noodles, swaying on javelins, some like big black juicy olives, onions on toothpicks, others long turned to skulls, like faded white moons haunting the sky.

'A charming sight, I'm sure.'

An old legless wreck who begged there at the Gate-House could tell you every one for a penny, so he said, and whose had come off and whose had gone on, all the way back to Jack Cade's time when his grandfather's grandfather had taken part in the insurrection. The Cade head was up there, he swore, pointing to one of the spent moons, and my Lord Such-a-one's and my Lord Such-another's, remarkably like Cade's for all their greatness. And there too were the Babington heads, recent arrivals, not yet peeled clean by the shitehawks or scoured by cormorant time. Grinning wasn't the last thing they'd done before they died but the grins were starting to show. The truth ultimately does come through, my masters – and when it does it takes the shape of a skull.

'A fine full penny's worth there, Will.'

A long slow penny, and I never stood through the telling of it, though I paid it out for charity. And as you went under the arch to make your way into the city you couldn't avoid this chilling reminder: that treason kills. It was a truth that tingled in your unbroken bowels and inviolate balls and the sharpness of it went in at your navel and out at your arse. I sweat to think of it.

'You had good reason, lad – and close to home.'

Edward Arden. His head still stared unseeing across the city, as it had done since '83 when first impaled there at the entrance to the bridge. He'd always wanted to see more of London – that was the grim family joke, for as the saying went, if you want a better view of the capital, try a little treason. Then, after the elevation of the scaffold, it's up aloft with you, sailor boy, where the blue breezes blow, far above the London mob, in the uncrowded sky. A highly select society communes up there among the soaring birds, an exalted circle reserved only for the infamous. You are one of the chosen few, the company of hard core traitors – and the view is forever.

'Never to come down in the world – a thought to conjure with.'

Not unless they took you down to make a drinking vessel of your skull, after it was heard said that quaffing from such cups could well prove curative for certain forms of illness. And the men who worked with metals in the Tower Mint, and were suffering the effects of poisonous fumes – they drank most avidly from these bony beakers that were thought to contain antidotes to death. If some found relief it was most probably from the wine they knocked back. Most of them quickly joined the owners of the skulls in the next world, well beyond drinking and disease and the noxious confines of the Tower. Not a place you'd want to be – on any day of the week, the Tower.

'The ante-room to eternity.'

Eternity, I can shut it out with a blink – and when I open up again it's the Tower I'll show you, if you care to stay in my head. Stand on the south bank now and gaze at the city. When I first did so, it was Paul's that caught my eye, but once I knew the city it was that four-headed reptile, that held me, stayed with me, that vault of so much human suffering, of sundered souls and bodies. There Gloucester's blade wept blood for the butchered Henry the Sixth, Clarence's murdered mouth drowned on malmsey, and the Yorkist princes died a dry but brutal death, their heads islanded on their pillows – but like their wine-logged uncle, they died for want of air.

'Frightful, frightful.'

Founded on tears and corpses, its stones cemented by human blood, and at night its corridors and stairways stalked by the ghosts of all who'd come to the Bloody Tower through Traitors' Gate. The young Princess came through this gate one pouring Palm Sunday, sat down on the drenched steps, and cried out in the downpour that she was the truest subject landed there. She knew that the headless body of her mother lay buried and bloodstained somewhere inside those awful walls, behind which was Tower Hill, darkened by the shadow of scaffold and gibbet. Many proud heads bent and fell on Tower Green, the lopped flowers of the nobles. The last of the Plantagenets bled horribly to death there. Margaret of Salisbury, stubborn old nob, refusing point blank to put her head on the block simply to let Tudor Henry's head rest easier under its crown, and the poor old bitch was pursued by the headsman, who hacked her to death like a beast in the shambles, like a bolted cow.

'The stuff of nightmares.'

Near the Green a little chapel, St Peter ad Vincula, received in chains the headless dead – or in Margaret's case the butchered remains. Maybe she got a benediction, who knows, from the ghost of fish-blooded Exeter, inventor of the rack, fit triumph for the cold brother of glorious Henry Five. Margaret had died gorily but fast compared with those who went the Exeter way, and they were blessed indeed who went straight to the block, the last great privilege of the high born. Anyone who'd spent an hour lying on Exeter's Daughter was glad to die. She knew how to fuck you up, all right, and even if you lived you were fucked for life. Every night of what remains of your life thereafter the bed becomes a rack, and instead of the glad blank of sleep, it's back you go to lie in restless ecstasy. Lie with Exeter's lass and it's not like bedding down with any passing whore. Poxes come and go, but what you catch on the rack stays with you like a wife, till death do you part. Those who were racked in the Tower never walked out straight, never did anything straight again, and wished they'd never come out at all.

'Better be with the dead...'

The black barge took them under Tower Wharf and through the gate, behind them the grating grille and the slow wet slap and sarabande of slime to ferry them like Charon to the Bloody Tower – an ugly exit from the world's stage with its concupiscence and cares, and so into eternity, by Tower Green. One last look at the enormous emptiness of sky – oh, what infinite blue waste! – and then the last caress of all, clasping the block for dear, dear life. That insect scuttling fifteen inches from your head, the poor harmless beetle that we tread upon, is the very last thing that you will ever see, unaware of your end, your life, the business and desire that once were you...until the creature is suddenly floundering and drowning in your blood.

'Too dark, my friend.'

A dying man plays with sheets and shadows. What more would you see? The playhouses, palaces, brothels? where princes stepped in city shit, beggar's or beast's, a close weave, sodden in winter and in summer a filthy crust, frantic with flies. The poor lived just atop of corpses, human bones flecked the earth floors, gnawed by dogs, little to separate living from dead, and those above ground were often rotten before they died, as the old sexton said, and scarce able to stand the laying in.

'But life, Will. Life!'

There were wild radishes along the Thames by the Savoy, sprouting from the joints of the stones like sweet cherry nipples. There was whitlow grass whistling softly in the wind in Chancery Lane and five-finger coming out of the wall in Liver Lane, though you had to *sing* willow in Pope Lane where the willows were long gone from St Anne-in-the-Willows and even the old remembered the willows no more. Yes, nature had her say – and in Stinking Lane, shanties sprang up in the city ditch and scumbags grew gardens out of shit. London's poor. They lived like worms in turds in the entrails of the city: Liver Lane, Arsehole Alley, St Spittle's in the Pissing Conduits, St Stoppage in the Bowels, Farting in the Fields, Fucking in the Halls, menses and afterbirth floating in the gutters. And the Fleet Ditch poured into the Thames its daily offerings of the city shit, well mixed with the grease and hair of measled hogs, the black slurp of the shambles, the entrails, hides, hooves, and heads of beasts. The Fleet River itself was navigable only by turds. Ships had given way to shit. Everything had given way to shit. London was an open artery of excrement.

'A little harsh, Will, to the fairest city in the world?'

London offered the Newgate slaughterslops, the Fleet turds, the Tyburn leavings, the blown bodies of Wapping, the boiled limbs of traitors, the ripe heads, the pools of piss – and a city of nearly half a million armpits and more than a million and a half orifices, breathing, pissing, shitting, sneezing and snorting and spitting and hacking into the fog and filthy air God knows what in the way of human corruption, putrefaction, and disease.

'Finished?'

I've come short, I think, on the stench of sperm, and the whore-juice from the stews, in the suburbs of London's good pleasure. The Master of the Rolls might well stop his nose with a flourish and the

Bishop of Winchester deplore all whores, but some swore that the stews of Clerkenwell were patronised by the devil himself, who envied their diabolical aromas and collected invisible harvests of them to take back with him and out-smell hell. Maugre its malodorous reputation Clerkenwell was popular with the gallants from the Inns of Court – brave lads indeed to brave the smells of Lucy Negro's place, Black Luce, the self-styled Abbess of Clerkenwell who had known better days as Luce Morgan, one of the queen's gentlewomen. And now Black Luce looked after the needs of certain gentlemen who couldn't always find certain gentlewomen to serve their turn. So she set up a fleshmonger's in St John Street and there traded in lust and gainful brothelry. In time it became famous. She claimed it was little different from the brothelries of the court, except that it was more open, like the legs of her whores, who were perhaps half a degree less fussy than the ladies of the court in the matter of washing. The stench was legendary.

'Stiff competition put up, though, lad?'

Stiffly indeed – by the Southwark whores that thronged St George's Fields and added the unmistakeable odour of sex to the evening air. It would have needed a titan's windmill to winnow that rank particular wind. But there was a mill of an entirely different sort in Paris Garden Lane, where Shallow and Falstaff lay all night long while the whores ground their pricks to the chimes of St George the Martyr near Lambeth, beating over the fields.

'So London seethed.'

A bubbling stew of corruption festered under the southside skirts of the city, a licensed stew for Venus's thrusting vestals.

'There's hell again – '

There was darkness, there the sulphurous pit, burning, scalding, stench, consumption – and here's the smell of the blood still.

They took you in, the whores, not telling you they had their monthly curse, and only when you pulled out your pizzle and dressed in the sticky darkness did you smell the blood, drowned out till then by the chorus of other stenches that filled the night: the bad breath, blackened teeth, onion armpits, uncleaned arses. Beneath was all the fiends'.

'And the gods?'

Little above the girdle, in London's case, for the whole city was a whore, with her reeking armpits in Shoreditch and Clerkenwell, leaky breasts in Bishopsgate and Cripplegate, and a bellyful of debauchery bubbling within the girdling wall. South of that streamed the stinking river and the filthy skirts of Southwark and Bankside draggling down to St George's and Lambeth and Newington Butts, dark dens for pimps and punks, adulterers and murderers, cutpurses and cut-throats, all crawling like lice in the seething, shit-sodden underclothes of the Great Whore. And still as I sink into sleep and that delicate butterfly, the soul, escapes the frame and flies south over the city, that's what I see from on high, what I saw then – London spread out below me in all her abomination and ugliness: her knees in the air, Aldgate and Lincoln's Inn, and her feet going down to Deptford, Westminster, and to hell. The bridge, that passage in and out of the inferno, was the huge cunt of the cursing waterman's imagination, and her uterus was the Fleet, pissing its filth into the Thames, that common sewer into which she also shat.

'Sweet Thames run softly?'

The whole city was a stinking whore.

'Babylon couldn't compare.'

It was a hydra, a many-headed monster. Here was the riotous rabble who'd tear you for your good verses or bad or for no verses at all when Satan led the ball. Scholars were hanged with quills and inkhorns round their necks, and players in their own stage garters when this turbulent tide swept over London. They were the arbitrary ocean overpeering of his lists, they were the wild and violent sea, changeable and cruel. They had one mind which was no mind. And when the mob's blood is up, then no matter who or what you are, make yourself invisible if you can, for mischief, thou art afoot, take thou what course thou wilt.

'Untameable.'

Christ's Hospital took them when they were infants, St Thomas's when they were old and infirm, St Bartholomew's when they were sick, and Bethlehem's when they were insane. When they were poor and thriftless they were put into Bridewell for training and correction. Walking from my north lodgings to the Blackfriars, or to find a waterman to wherry me to Southwark and the Globe, I'd pass by Bridewell, and could hear, as I drew near, the screams of those being lashed for harlotry – not inside but outside the prison, offering a public show for those panting, canting, lusting hypocrites who'd gladly have sinned with them, given a fraction of a chance. The mob set off after the cart, tied to the back of which walked the prostitute, with beadles whipping her bare and bloodied back.

Thou rascal beadle, hold thy bloody hand! Why dost thou lash that whore? Strip thine own back – thou hotly lusts to use her in that kind for which thou whipp'st her!

'But they flogged on, eh? No lack of backs.'

Oh, they were ripe and black for the plucking. Such were the low lives. They had nowhere to go but downwards, though many achieved the ultimate elevation, the only elevation they ever knew, the all too brief one of the gallows.

'You still go back to Tyburn...'

The road to it began with Topcliffe, Master Topcliffe, chief of secret police, controller of informers and spies, and bosom leopard of Walsingham. Topcliffe, keeper of prison keys, of instruments of torture, of secrets whispered under duress, confessor to racked priests, keeper of their souls and genitals, keeper and cupper also of the queen's breasts, the part he loved to brag of to his captives on the rack. He had the key to her bodice, so he said, with all the valour of his tongue, grinning into your ear, pouring in the poison. Better than that, he knew how to unlock her cold knees, her chaste thighs. He was keeper of the first quim in the country. The long arm of Richard Topcliffe stretched further than any man's, reaching deep into the queen and into your heart, closing on its stickiest secrets. Then he accompanied you to Tyburn where he assisted assiduously at your public butchery.

'Starting with your balls.'

Where a man feels the first tingling of desire – except now it's the shock of dismemberment, following the formality of that swift simple swing on the gibbet, that leaves him no more than a little dazed and entirely aware, ready to experience in full the agonies to follow, as he is required by law to be and as it is laid down – *seeing and alive.* The penis is chopped off and the testicles sliced away. And the first thing he sees, looking up, is his privities sprouting from the hangman's sudden clutch, the first thing he feels is the London air entering the red mouth that was his manhood, a mouth gobbing gouts of blood onto the upturned faces and sprinkling the stage on which he plays – and loses his part. The unkindest cut of all, so you might think, metamorphosed into woman, a red wound between the legs, where once you were a man. Unkind? The hangman has a long way to go until he has exhausted his art. This is but the first cut on the way to butchermeat.

'Another shambles.'

You're a screaming freak, applauded by the most appreciative audience in London, the Tyburn playgoers who have come to watch your performance in the theatre of death. This is your public – your last chance to admire the dentistry of the age in all its carious crudity as a thousand mouths howl their derision, spitting and jeering, urging the hangman to move on to the next act, the opening of the belly. Already your private parts have become the public prologue. A dog will be eating them soon. Your innards – how private were they? No one ever saw them, not even your mother, not even yourself. In the twinkling of a blade they too will be staining the London stage, God's handiwork exhibited as art. But is a man really just so much tripe? The executioner's trade is truly wonderful. In a moment, he can show you a mystery, and you shall be changed.

'Most horribly.'

Not unlike the act of love – so Topcliffe liked to say. Consider the first thrust. A man may shoot his sperm into the belly of a woman in a few short seconds. But he can lengthen out the work for half an hour – half a night, it depends on his skill in the old art of love. The executioner should also love his craft, as should the torturer, each employing his tool long and lovingly as he draws apart the seamless curtains of the skin to let daylight enter for the first time. The lover wishes to die slowly – *O lente, lente* – enjoying to the utmost that last ecstasy as he sinks expiring on his loved one's breast, but the victim longs for brevity and for an end. The point of death is a pinprick, nothing more, between being and non-being. The process is an eternity of hell.

But for lovers no eternity can be too long – and there are no lovers like theatre lovers, and no theatre to compare with the scaffold, on which the hangman woos the martyr.

'And yet you gave them no say.'

The martyrs? No. I told you, no, their mouths are stopped. I kept my own mouth closed, never told my thinkings, kept on the player's mask, the false face of no man, everyman, the squint of the butcher's boy from Stratford – taciturn, tactful, night-tripping Will, invisible, inaudible, *sweet* Master Shakespeare.

'Master chameleon.'

Keep yourself private if you don't want to become that most public spectacle of all, the leading man, the chief actor in the theatre of blood, London's favourite show, with the groundlings up front and God and his angels watching discreetly from heaven. No *deus ex machina* ever descended to that bloody stage – that's a fable, friend, and Tyburn was real, and really was the end.

'And so – '

And so I built my fortunes on London's other stage, where blood was not real and men were harmless shadows of themselves. Old Burbage had put up the Theatre at Shoreditch a decade before I arrived on the scene, but when I came up, the wooden O in Curtain Close was newly built and two hundred yards closer to the city walls on the other side of Holywell Lane.

'That was Lanham's stage.'

Built to beguile the anguish of the hour, when men need more than life itself affords. It brought the people streaming across the fields and brought the Puritans to the brink of madness. It also brought us much needed cash when we played it as Chamberlain's Men in the nineties. But long before then Jerome Savage had built another stage in Newington in Surrey. It might have been a mile south-west of the bridge by my legs, on the other side of St George's Fields where the whores aired their tails.

'The old archery butts were there.'

So we called it Newington Butts, with a glance at the arses of the whores, though Ben Jonson, never one to glance, never called it anything but Newington Fucks. Savage never even troubled to give it a name.

'What's in a name, as you've said, lad?'

Scarcely necessary *then*. You built a theatre and men would swarm as fast as they did to the drabs. Playgoing and whoring – each offered a relief and a release from the grubby world. The theatres were blossoming all over London. And then came the Swan and the Fortune and the Hope, opening like roses, like prostitutes, the name means the same.

'Ah, the Rose!'

The rose of all the world was the Rose itself, the Great Whore, built on the stews in the Clink liberty between the river and Maid Lane – by that great controller of stews himself –

'Henslowe.'

Whoremaster and usurer, in partnership with son-in-law Ned Alleyn. They were still building it when I came on the scene and what a start it had! Marlowe had just come up from Cambridge with a bomb in his pocket, the manuscript of a new play. He tossed it into the Rose and down went all before him. Marlowe was only twenty-three – and seven years off a dagger in the brain. But Tamburlaine had arrived and Alleyn was the man. And Henslowe was up to his balls in box clover. Yes, that was the Rose of London – till we built the great Globe itself.

'The road to ruin.'

If you wanted to go to hell really cheaply with the crowd, all you had to do in '88 was roll up to the Rose and walk straight in for a penny. That's why the Puritans hated plays so bitterly, even more than they hated pipes or cups or whores – anybody could pay for it, all could afford to go to hell every afternoon of the week, and all were punished. In some whores you could stand six at a time and still find room for more. But in this particular rose, the Henslowe Hole, the Rose of all the world, there was standing room six times cheaper than that offered by your average whore – forget Nell Farthing, who rose and fell night and day in her Maiden Lane just yards from The Rose itself. And if the Rose were really hell, it was a lot more humorous than heaven, so men reckoned, if heaven's joys were measured by a Puritan prick. Easier to put an erection on an icicle in a Dutchman's beard.

'That requires some imagination.'

Whores and actors are not so far apart – both faking it for cash, and both die and rise again. But the Puritans accepted the whores as they could never accept the actors. Whores descend from Eve, theology sound as Genesis. The prostitute was easy to understand and to embrace. She was recognizable – her feet go down to death, her steps take hold on hell, her cunt is a cauldron of unholy lusts, and there is no whore without Eve. No Eve, no sin; no sin, no damnation; no damnation, no redemption – no Christ, no Church, no Pope. And no Pope, no Reformation, no Puritan to oppose the Great Whore herself, Babylon the great. The whores of London, kept the Puritan in his post, gave him his living. The Puritan could not exist without the whore. Whoredom was as needful to his church as it was to fallen man, fornicating his life away in London.

'And the players?'

With the players it was the contrary. Actors descend from neither Adam nor Eve but from Satan, who came onto the world's stage disguised as a serpent. It was the first costume and the devil the original actor, and a good one too. His tongue dropped honey and Eve was taken in. She fell down and worshipped him and her suddenly naked navel became the entrance to the theatre. That's why Puritans and players could never live together. Our false idols lined the route to hell – Dick Tarleton, Ned Alleyn, Bill Kempe popular as primroses – and so the player was far more damnable than the whore.

'Mass magic.'

Your whore can take in only one man at a time. If a dozen a day go through her she's doing well by doing ill. But a single player, he could command an entire theatre-load of spectators in one speech. In one word.

'Why, they would hang on him – '

As if increase of appetite had grown by what it fed on. One word? I tell you even a word was not necessary. Windy suspiration of forcèd breath, a sweeping gesture, your fingers on your lips I pray, yes, even silence. Even the very thought of silence. To die: to sleep; no more.

'No more.'

And that's how it was done. Nailed them to the ground and galleries and kept them from the pulpits, lured them to the theatres instead, to applaud the actors to the very echo that should applaud again, to wait breathless in the London afternoon for the next word, for the very next syllable. Oh yes, the player could do all this, all this and more. He was the god of the groundlings, idol of the aristocrats. The Puritan, though he played the orator as well as Nestor, could never sermonise an audience into such submission. Even the silver-tongued friar who made the fields his pulpit – the audiences walked over his ghost, trampling him into daisies, and streamed straight into the theatres. Fear had been the weapon up till now. But now seduction was stronger than fear, and seduction was in the air – no, it *was* the air, the very air we breathed. And all the Puritan could do was rage.

'Conscience, morality, divine reason?'

It was the theatres that brought men's humanity out of chests and closets and whispering chambers and placed it up on stage, where a handful of poor players, with four or five most vile and ragged foils, right ill disposed in brawl ridiculous, blazoned it to the world. As for right reason, the fear of God, wisdom, understanding, the knowledge of the holy – ah, these are not the stuff as dreams are made on, these are but pale shadows of people beside the player's ability to be a walking mirror to everyman, to show virtue her own feature, scorn her own image, and the very age and body of the time his form and pressure, to make every spectator in that wooden circle see himself standing up there, standing up in the world for exactly what he is: man, tragical-comical, historical-pastoral, aspiring-despairing, delighted-deluded, in love, in hate, in heaven, in hell, a thing of darkness and of light, a lover, a tyrant, a madman, a poet, a dragon, a worm. So the poor player that struts and frets his hour upon the stage was rich in that one enormous regard, his ability to see himself and present himself in the round and inside out by a species of sorcery that left the Puritan gaping.

For the player was the man who showed you life as it is, not as it ought to be, who said what he felt, not what he ought to say.

'Truth's a dog must to kennel, I remember from somewhere.'

But a man's occulted guilt can itself unkennel in one speech, and guilty creatures sitting at a play are struck so to the soul that suddenly their spirits are off the leash and barking out the theatre, howling through the world. Did the spectator leave the theatre a purged and purer person? Or did he leave it corrupted? All a player can say is that he sent the theatre-goer out more human than he'd come in – which is the end of art and no bad boast: to make us more ourselves, not *less* ourselves, as the Puritans would have had it, by plucking us out of the murk and mire of humankind.

Whatever the truth, the Puritan feared the player. And he feared the play, which staged several players, and the playhouse, which put out many plays. Theatres were outposts of hell, Satan's garrisons. Hell was an occupying force in England and its legions were in London, where the traffic of the stage took two thousand to hell in two hours. A frightening figure. Worse – with half a dozen plays running on any given afternoon the theatres were capable of ushering the entire cast of London into hell in ten days flat – which ought to have pleased your Puritan. So many souls bound straight for hell, with damnèd speeches buzzing in their ears, surely all the greater space for the elect and élite of God in their silent white heaven. But that perhaps is what they feared most – being with themselves.

'So you hated them, Will.'

The very name's a lie. Puritan. To the Puritan all things were impure. They could find no good in man, nor any god in man, and they lashed man himself and his eternal companion and corrupter, woman, for all evils. Even the queen was not spared. And Puritan Stubbes, who pamphleteered against her, had his offending hand cut off. But in all their accusations they never accused themselves, though within their snow-broth blood there bubbled the same old cauldron of unholy appetites. Your Puritan wants to fuck the thing he fears and then to kill the thing he fucks – or, if he cannot have it, he must kill it to ease his fury. What was he really? At best he was a boil on the bum, spoiling your seat in the theatre: at worst a wild beast in the bowels. The ultimate revenge is to put him in the play, show him sick of self-love and laugh him to scorn – or stop the laughter and make the people hate him for what he is: ambassador of death, killer of laughter, a syphilis in the soul, a negation of all that is human and lovely and of good report.

'And graven images – ?'

Are what we want – and what the players give us. We long for imitation. We long to be happy. Only the gods are bored, And the Puritans wanted us to be as gods. So I gave them instead unregenerate man, incapable of their Jesus: the poor wild Bedlam who ate the old rat in the fury of his heart, and the darkness that was Caliban. I gave them not their strait and narrow gateway to God, but the broad primrose way, the playhouse way. For the theatre was the only place in London you could go to outside the ale-house to hear an honest comment on our lives, uncoloured by fear of God or the grave. Here the players were indeed the only men. Their theatres were islands of art rising out of the crude sea of corruption that surrounded them on all sides. They were the clear clean bright bells of London, beating loudly and sweetly over the sodden city.

24

'Will, Will, Will...'

Had I three ears I'd hear thee. What is it, Francis?

'The day is wearing late – and I stay for supper.'

Supper?

'While you were in London, my boy, little Alison came up – and there's talk of a great pie. Before we get to it I'd like to draw together the last remaining threads.'

Threads?

'Your will, old lad, remember?'

Not unlike a great pie – many an item to be got right and many to be fed from it. But why the pie, may I ask?

'Dr Hall's orders. He's sent word you're to be taken off that gruel – and for three days you're to be fed like a fighting cock.'

I feel better already. I remember a nice piece of pie in Wood Street once.

'Don't start that.'

A French pie too. Remember Henry Field, the tanner, and his family? Henry's long gone now, his tanned and battered carcass well into decomposition even for a man in his line of work. He used to say that a tanner would last you nine years in the earth before he rotted, his hide being so tanned with his trade that he'd keep out water a great while. 'Water's the bugger,' he'd mutter. 'Your water's a sore decayer of your whoreson dead body. Once that's in, you're buggered for sure. It's rainwater kills a corpse, not worms. You ask old Tom, the sexton, he'll tell you.'

Well, old Henry may well have kept out the rain for nine years for all I know. When he heard I was headed for the capital, he had asked me to take a letter to his son, asking for money and news.

'Richard Field?'

Three years ahead of me at school, left Stratford eight years before.

'A bright bony sort of boy?'

That's him. Always with an eye and a tongue on London – it was his dream. Didn't care for tanning and signed up for seven years with a London printer, George Bishop, who arranged for him to see out his first six years at another printing shop, run by Thomas Vautrollier at Blackfriars.

'Ah, the French pie.'

Not exactly. Not him. Field was still with Vautrollier when I arrived in London – lots of staying power, young Richard, and the patience of a cat. And so, carrying his father's letter, I re-crossed the bridge and made my way westwards to Blackfriars, looking for the sign of the Splayed Eagle on Wood Street. And it was in Wood Street, at the sign of the Splayed Eagle, that I fell under the spell – and between the splayed thighs –

'Of the French pie?'

Jacqueline Vautrollier.

'What about *our* pie?'

The first thing I saw through the open door of the Splayed Eagle was the gangling Richard Field standing at his master's press, a large inkstain on his right cheekbone and both hands smudged front and back. A freshly printed quarto sheet trembled between clean fingertips and those well-remembered blue eyes were boring into the page. It took some time for him to notice that I was standing there, a Stratford silhouette in a London doorway, and another second or two for him to switch his mind from printing to tanning, with all its home-based thoughts. Then it registered. Spreading his arms wide with a bony grin and lankily avoiding the edge of a workbench as he strode to the door, he embraced me vigorously but with great precision so as not to mark my clothes or crumple the precious page.

'Will!' he shouted. 'Will Shakespeare!'

I could feel his elbows dug sharp in my ribs. He smelled of the press, the fresh, suddenly exciting smell of new books. His shout produced a shuffling sound in the adjoining chamber and a short paunchy little man stared in at us with sad brown eyes. Some spikes of pepper and salt still sprouted from the side of his head but he'd gone almost bald on top – the crown looked greasy and garlicky. He was breathing heavily and something rattled in his chest.

'Monsieur?' he inquired of me politely, holding out his hand.

This was Thomas Vautrollier.

Richard Field exuded the hot odour of the press, the scent of dangerous metaphors and forbidden phrases. He smelled of the book, its promise and fascination. But here the trail went dead. With Monsieur Vautrollier the writer seemed suddenly extinct.

Maybe I'd like to dip into *De Beau Chesne*? (he said dopily) or perhaps into Baildon's *Book Containing Divers Sorts of Hands*? Failing which, there were many other accomplished productions stacked under the spreading wings of the Splayed Eagle, mind-improving folios. Clearly Vautrollier handled the heaviest of printing assignments and prided himself on doing justice to serious and large-scale works, real hectoring stuff. I didn't smell Ovid here, or the open air. And certainly there was not one whiff of woman.

Or so I thought.

'What do you do for sport?' I asked Field when his employer had shuffled off to find me a copy of the newest version of the *Mirror For Magistrates*.

'Wait till supper,' Field whispered.

I waited.

I had just taken my first gulp of Bordeaux when she entered the room. When I say my first I'm being exact – it was my first taste of Bordeaux. I was just downing my first mouthful of this French drench when she appeared. I suppose I must have caught my breath. I certainly had little reason to expect that the sad little printer, this French egghead whose shelves were heavy with legal and moral instruction, could have been the owner of such a shapely and elegant volume.

Francis, she was beyond the dreams of desire. I breathed in my gobful and doubled up on my stool, choking and spluttering, the tears standing blind in my eyes and the wine dribbling down my chin and spraying from mouth and nostrils. Monsieur rose puffily to give my back the heel of his hand, while toothy Field creased himself quietly, his face split from huge ear to even bigger ear (he was a little lop-sided). She knitted her forehead, pursed her lips and made sympathetic little clucking noises with her tongue, interspersed with a staccato commentary of concern in her own language. '*O, ma foi! le pauvre homme! O, quelle dommage, c'est tant pis, nous avons tué le pauvre garçon!*' I expect I must have seemed little more than a *garçon* to her. And yet she wasn't old enough to be my mother, though she looked half a generation out of step with the dozy printer.

'Jacqueline Vautrollier.'

The very name still sends shudders up the ancient seam of my scrotum. Jacqueline Vautrollier. She was dark but fair, for the suns of France had looked on her, but so had Venus. She was desirable beyond anything I'd ever seen or imagined – gone forever was the golden-skinned Anne Hathaway and the Marians of freckled Warwickshire. This woman was of another breed. She had come from the lions' dens and the mountains of the leopards and her armpits were dark with lust, her secret clefts barbaric with black wild hair. Somebody had given me the fatal draught and I wanted to drink from those lips, drink hard, drink long, drink well.

'Dreenk, Weel?'

Drink, Will? Jesu. *Oui, Madame*. Her dress rustled against my leg as she stood beside me and poured. Jug jug. Her husband and Field were discussing Tottel's *Miscellany*, published thirty years ago to the very day, so the master printer mused.

'I never 'ad no need of Tottel at zat time,' he sighed, 'even wen I was wooing my fair Jackleen.'

He wagged his bald dome into his wine, not looking up at his wife, preferring to remember a time when there was hair on his head, fire in his heart and brimstone in his liver, and his breath came not short on the gallop, night after night. Meanwhile I imagined Jacklin Vautrollier with naked foot stalking in my chamber, her loose gown from her shoulders falling as she caught me in her long dark arms, kissed me ever so sweetly, inserted her French tongue into my mouth, slipped her cool hand down my front, with fingers spread wide to take pity on the hot throbbing knob, and softly said, *Dear heart* –

''Ow like you thees?'

'I cry you mercy, madame?'

Madame was at my side again, this time with a large platter. Field was laughing and pointing.

'Look how our partner's rapt.'

I stared dumbly across the table.

'Give me your favour: my dull brain was wrought with things forgotten.'

'Fine, but how about things French?'

'What?'

'Angelot, at your service.'

'I beg your pardon?'

'*Fromage*, my friend, a nice little rich one from Normandy – never passed a pair of Stratford lips, I'll warrant. Are you going to let Madame wait on you all night? Go on, bite on experience, or go shake your ears!'

I bit. And Madame Vautrollier withdrew her dark-downed arm and offered the platter to Field. Her husband returned broodingly to the subject of Richard Tottel, the Temple Bar printer.

'Thirty years, *ma foi! quand j'étais un jeune homme.*'

Vautrollier claimed to have been born along with English blank verse in 1540 (though he looked even older) and had helped Tottel in his teens at the Hand and Star, bringing out Surrey's *Aeneid* in the same year as the *Songes and Sonnettes*. He laboured himself out of his seat again and returned breathing heavily like the sea with a thickish octavo volume which he plumped down beside my cheese rinds. It was the second edition of the *Miscellany* dated 31st July.

'Monsieur Tottel was editing from April to August that year, '57, *mais*, zee second edition 'ere, eet was done in under sixty days. *C'est formidable, n'est-ce-pas*?'

To please the printer I feigned interest and leafed through the popular pages. They contained over three hundred love lyrics, smelling of a stilted generation, the failures of Wyatt, and the insecurities of a court living in constant fear of being farted on by Henry the Eighth.

'And I'd give forty shillings a song if I could only 'ave back again one single night of wot I was then.'

Madame Vautrollier caught my eye and the flush deepened under her dark throat.

'Now I 'ave no need of love songs, *mon Dieu*, zere are other lines in zere to send me on my way.'

Too right there were. The printer wasn't giving up. I caught sight of Lord Vaux's sombre numbers and started to recite an apt quatrain.

My lusts they do me leave,
My fancies all be fled.

Monsieur finished the stanza for me with grim relish, his tongue tolling like a bell.

And tracts of time begin to weave
Gray 'airs upon my 'ead.

His wife rose suddenly and left the table. He looked after her sadly. I looked after her too – observing the swing of her hips. It wasn't hard to imagine what lay beneath that French silk. It was hard, on the other hand, to picture baldie Vautrollier as a youthful lover with sexy Jacklin's legs round the nape of his neck and her hand cupping his swinging testicles. Long time ago. In youth when they did love, did love. When Wood Street heaved like a ship, and splayed legs under the Splayed Eagle tilted ceilingwards and soared like masts going mad beneath the stars.

But age, with his stealing steps,
Hath clawed me in his clutch,
And hath shipped me intil the land
As if I had never been such.

Vautrollier spoke like a gravedigger who'd never got used to his trade. Field just sat and grinned into his glass. His elbows and knees seemed to be everywhere at once. Nothing seemed to affect him much, not even wine or woman. So we sat on among the spluttering candles drinking and chattering and old Vautrollier regretting his shagging days and the vigour of his youth, while the tide of wine rose and fell and rose and fell and the blue chinks in the shutters darkened into night. Madame had not returned. She'd be through in the shop writing up the day's accounts. A wonderful woman, her husband assured me, groaning as he said it, as though a blessing were synonymous with a curse. I nodded boozily and was mightily relieved when the printer finally got up to snuff out the drowning wicks bidding goodnight to all as if this were time's last midnight. To bed, to bed, to bed.

An honoured guest, I was shown into the best room in the house. And was sitting there on the edge of the bed, nursing the monster in my groin and pondering how to kill it without crackling Jacklin's nice clean sheets, when in she walked without as much as a knock-knock.

She was carrying a basin of water. I made to accept it and noticed that her arms were entirely bare from the shoulders down. The bodice of her gown was missing and some white sleeveless item stood out white in the candlelight, out of which the two arms stretched like swans' necks, offering the water. Our four hands were on it and it flickered in the candleflame but I couldn't take it, just stood there, gaping into her armpits, transfixed by the hair that sprouted in thick rich tufts, beaded with pearls of sweat. And I thought of the midnight grass down below, of the apex of that inverted arrowhead and what it pointed to: the private territory of a sepulchral little French printer. How could she go back and undress before the bulging eyes of the bald little frog that had once been her French prince?

'Weel! You are speeling zee water!'

My hands were shaking, sloshing lumps of silvery water over the edge of the basin that still brimmed between us. I steadied my grip and it reverted to a trembling net of light and shadow. We stared into it as if it were a magic circle in which we could read our future. Jacqueline Vautrollier glimmered like a ghost in the candlelight.

'Jacklin,' I said, 'I am an English moth drawn to your French flame. I would be glad to die in you – '

'Weel!'

'And if it were now to die, 'twere now to be most happy.'

'O, Weel, you must not tell me zees sings.'

So we stood like two continents divided by a splash of sea, France and England facing one another, and expectation sitting once more in the air. A bird sang in her mouth.

'Weel, set down zee basin, *s'il te plait*, set it down, ah beg of you.'

'Jacklin, O sweet Jacklin, speak to me again in broken music – for your English is broken and your voice is music.'

She smiled with white teeth. I recalled old Vautrollier's garlicky gob, his few remaining monuments, like standing stones, broken and black, and his dog breath.

'*O, bon Dieu! les langues des hommes sont pleines des tromperies*!'

Oui, sweet Jacqueline, *oui oui*, you say right well, and yes, de tongs of de mans be full of deceits. And yet I love you, Jacklin, I love you true, and I am on fire with desire. Wilt thou then leave me so unsatisfied?

The dark eyes flashed.

'Wot satisfaction canst thou 'ave tonight?'

Slowly, as though we were cradling the oceans of the globe, we bent down together and placed the basin on the floor. Then we stood up, stared wildly – there was nothing between us now – and fell on one another like mad dogs.

Little Thomas Vautrollier had long passed his horizontal dancing days and the beast with two backs was a measure he clearly hadn't trod for many a moist moon. And under the watery stars, month by slow month, year by year, the utterly adorable Jacqueline had lain down unfurled and unfucked and had studied the knots in the ceiling, dark as Dian's pools. And when summer nights died on her and a crowd of shadows gave way to winter's raven wing, she closed her eyes on darkness and let her hand slide silently down her childless belly, while the sad fat little Frenchman snored and gurgled at her side, his leaden carcass rehearsing nightly for stiffening and nullity.

He was nearly there. The question that really intrigued me was why my fellow Stratfordian had failed to oblige a lady who stood in such obvious need of an ancient service. But Dickon was a canny lad and might have been biding his time. The time, my masters, had been mine – I'd made it so – and it was not the first time in London that a William came before a Richard.

Came. Yes, I'd come in grand style but now it was time I came out. I did so – and a little murmur of abandonment escaped the lips of fair Jacklin, followed by a pretty bark of desolation from my forlorn little French fox: the vixen with the bush so black and the wound so scarlet and her parted shanks now so be-rivered with the long strong stream of my Stratford seeds. She put her hand over the wound – O, such an admirable hand, such carved excellence of knuckles! – scooped up the blown spume and smeared it smilingly in slow circles into the hairs of my chest.

'Thank you, Weel, for your meelk.'

'I never gave it so gladly, lady.'

'Ah, you are kind, I sink.'

'It's the milk of human kindness, Jacqueline.'

'We should share it, zen.'

And so we did.

'Love me again, Weel!'

And I did.

'And were proud of yourself?' Francis was wearing his admonitory face.

Yes – and no. When I saw how Thomas Vautrollier looked at me next morning, I knew that he would not be anxious for me to spend one more night under the Splayed Eagle. From the splayed thighs of Jacklin he must have caught more than a whiff of hot Stratford sperm – and to speak true, the sight of that grey face with its rheumy reproachful eyes was more than I could bear. It was the Judas punishment and the old Adam was to blame. I had betrayed the host and fucked the hostess and tears would drown the wind. Therefore to horse – and let us not be dainty of leave-taking. In the chill dawn Jacklin would be Madame Vautrollier again, a bruised fruit. Besides I couldn't bear to look at her over cold shoulder and small beer. Instead I hugged the night's doings hard and hot between my thighs, and as I turned east into Cheapside, past the already buzzing stalls, and north up Gracious Street towards the Wall, heading across Moorfields for distant Shoreditch, my head was filled with her dark glories, dark lady with hair as black as goats, winding down the olive slopes of her shoulders, breath sweet as honey and quim like quince... And as I made my way up Bishopsgate and into Hog Lane, I pitied from the pits of my testicles all men who'd never had her and never would.

25

I made my way well beyond the city wall and Stinking Lane, where poppies blazed like whores' lips in gangrenous gardens and settlements of shit, and I came through Moorfields to Shoreditch. Here flitted the theatrical shadows to which Richard Field had reluctantly directed me. Here certain actors lurked, he said, living out their brief barely respectable lives before the final bow – Beeston in Hog Lane, Burbage and Cowley in Holywell Street, and Dick Tarleton too, the king of comedy, the god of laughter.

A crippled beggar did me for a penny and directed me to a Hog Lane tenement that looked and smelled like a shithouse. I knocked several times, and after an age of listening to a rattling cough dragging itself like shackles to the door, found myself looking into the sad fat face of a derelict.

Tarleton the Great. Tarleton who was so famous, old Henry said, they used his picture as an alehouse sign and even stuck it on privies, inside and out, to help the constipated. You could lose control laughing. Better than senna, rhubarb, or purgative drug. If you heard helpless shrieks from within and uninhibited volleys of farts and splashes, you knew it was a Tarleton lav, and that somebody was emptying his all on the other side. They came out from the crapper weak and shaking.

Such were old Henry's memories, and that was all right for the privy, he said. Not so funny when people pissed themselves in the playhouse, or shat themselves offstage, or even *on* the stage – the players were right in the firing line. Rehearsing with the fat bastard was no guarantee against fart-producing laughter, with potential for much worse. No one was iron-bowelled enough for sure, and a play with Tarleton in it rarely went off without a song and an accident. People used to laugh before he even came on stage. They came into the theatre grinning, paid their pennies smilingly, laughed just *knowing* he was about to come on. Then all the old joker had to do was peep from behind the curtain – and when they saw that fat face with the broad nose and squint, the mop of curls, the mischievous moustache and the twinkling eyes, they roared the place down and he hadn't said a word. It was said that Tarleton could make an angel fart and that even the Virgin Mary listened in.

Most of what he came out with concerned either cuckoldry or excrement and he had an unmatched ability to extemporise upon these grand themes and to feed the appetites of audiences for quips about privies and pricks, with endless variations on farts and fannies, his particular favourites. Apart from the jigs and jests he had a few routines that everybody looked forward to and he brought these out on stage no matter what the play or part. Had he lived, I'd have seen Hamlet done up differently. *My masters, the incredible antics of Mr Richard Tarleton and his dog, with many bawdy jests and jigs, including an appearance by Richard Burbage as the Prince of Denmark.* Yes, the groundlings would have lapped that up, like Tarleton's little pooch. He taught it to gobble what looked like its own turds. Maybe they were.

Once he staged a mock fight with the queen's little dog, Perrico de Faldas, complete with longsword and staff, screaming blue murder and begging her gracious Majesty to take away her hound. Right in the spirit of the thing, her majesty bawled back in turn for her ushers to take away the knave, he was making her laugh so much she was pissing her petticoats. What could you really expect from a queen who cackled at such drolleries? If you're a player you don't expect a fortune, that's for sure, from a queen who laughs at such a knave. But she didn't look after her knave either. Poor Tarleton. Gasping his life out on his deathbed, he scratched a letter to Walsingham, imploring him for protection for his little son only six years old, as if you could have sucked an ounce of compassion from the flinty bones of old Walsher, that spyer-out of thoughts. Thou canst not say I did it! Thy bones are marrowless, thy blood is cold! Cold, cold, my dear. Tarleton's death killed the Queen's Men's hearts and chaos came again.

When I looked into the face of the Hog Lane humorist that morning I knew at once I was looking at ruins. He had outlived himself. The pursy cheeks were so bloated, the eyes so black and swollen, it seemed impossible he could actually see out of that wreckage of a face. The chopped lips quivered and tried to part but stayed well stuck. Again he tried to say something, coughed horribly instead and a wave of sour small beer hit me, well garnished with onions and leeks. The breath smelled as old as the jokes. So this was what comic genius looked like at close quarters. I wanted the earth to gape but felt obliged to give him some garbage about the magic of the stage, and walking all the way from Stratford to answer the call of the theatre – that sort of speech. He too thought it was garbage. He would have winced if he could. Somewhere inside the folds of the soggy pastry that had been his face the memory of a muscle twitched, the two small eyes puckered like currants and the mouth started to form the uncertain outlines of an excuse. Bone weary, my boy, blinder of a head on me, a night with Bacchus, not so well these days I'm sad to say, shadow of my former, too early, friend, anyway, come back some other day, some sober October, afternoons preferred.

Much relieved, I was already on my way. But then the man's innate good nature got the better of him and he turned round to ask me where was that again I'd said I'd come from? Bloody Jesus, I can barely slog to the bog these days. I reminded him and he shook his faded curls and showed me his back again. Then the fat head swivelled and two spent candles flickered somewhere inside the ruin. 'Stratford?' The cracked lips fluttered. 'Stratford, did you say? Stratford? Jesus, yes, and oft upon the Avon, yes, I was there earlier this month, you say true. Tell me, young friend, did you ever see – ?'

'*The Seven Deadly Sins*? I saw it, all right, Master Tarleton. Who hasn't seen it! What did I think of it? Well to speak truth... What, you *wrote* it? Saw you in it, of course, but to think you're the author! Nay, do not think I flatter.'

For what advancement may I hope from thee, that nothing hast but thy good spirits to feed and clothe thee?

An ageing actor craves an audience even of one, straining for the applause of a single pair of hands – nothing in the world sadder than an old player without a script. Minutes later I was swallowing his stale ale and listening to tales of how he'd played The Curtain and The Bell, and doubled clown and judge in *The Famous Victories* at the Bull in Bishopsgate. And out from the chest came the famous suit of russet, the buttoned cap and tabor, the sword and staff – accompanied by the inevitable chest of jokes, a bottomless wardrobe of words, not one of them without a beard. By this time the armpit of a room had filled up with a crowd of elderly actors, the leavings of the Queen's Men, rising beerily from pallets and drifting through the open door, all of them egging on the fat shattered comedian to acrobatics inappropriate to his age and condition, all endlessly repeating their eminently forgettable one-line appearances. Forgettable? They'd never heard of each *other*! It was a sorry spectacle. But they were all busy scratching one another's backs and bidding a long farewell to all their greatness and all their imagined glories.

As morning wore into afternoon another barrel was brought up and broached, I wondered who was paying for all this beer and I felt a stab of panic when it struck me that perhaps I was. But it passed. And so did the beer, through half a dozen bladders. Meanwhile Tarleton was doing more falling down than getting up. Eventually he gave up on the getting up, his songs became slurred, his jokes jaded, and soon the curtains of sleep shut him off for a while. By evening, however, the company, having slumbered individually and severally, a much refreshed Dick held sway again over the tankards and trenchers and found fine and witty vein. A clever quipster, after all, it seemed to me, and well conceited, as I floated off again on a tide of ale, the distracted globe of my brain buzzing with the cries of players and my head roaring with Shoreditch.

I came to with the dawn light leaking in through broken shutters, revealing the various pools and spillages along the floor, on a level with my leaden head, some of them suspiciously yellow and green. For a minute – or an hour – I lay listening to the dawn chorus of grunts and snores, punctuated by the occasional anonymous fart. Then I noticed for the first time that Tarleton had had his dingy ceiling decorated with slapdash stars – suns and moons and planets painted roughly in between the beams. Even this dive was a stage, not unlike the world.

Levering myself painfully into a sitting position, I looked around.

There lay Tarleton, laced with his vomit, the sunken wreck of the Queen's, a man at the very end of his trade – no, well past even that. Alas, poor Dick. How ill white hairs become a fool and jester. Not that the queen took time to remember the laughs when he lay poor and dying in this Hog Lane hovel not long afterwards, old Shoreditch Dick, nursed only by Em Ball, a local tart of terrible reputation. One that would do the deed with a hundred an hour though the hundred eyes of Argus were upon her, but who had more care, in the autumn of '88, than all the court and its increasingly unsmiling queen.

Alas, for poor Tarleton, dead and buried in Shoreditch on the third day of September the year after I came up. The gravedigger who slung him in (a Dane called George) couldn't stop laughing, I remember, in spite of the rain, as he shovelled back the soil on the fat comedian who'd made the queen of England wet herself – and he tossed aside a stray skull that he'd unearthed and forgotten to return to the grave beside the shrouded jester. It lay upside down and began to collect rainwater. I wondered how long the untanned Tarleton would keep out the wet. Not long, according to Danish George, who knew a pox-eaten corpse when he saw one – and this was another one that had scarce held the laying in. He dissolved in giggles.

'Did you know him, sir? Did you ever see him on stage? I saw him many a time – at the Bull, it was. Laugh? He made us sore with laughing. I was right up at the front once, see? And he leaned over the stage and poured a flagon of ale all over my noodle. That made them laugh, all right. Jesus, what a mad bugger he was. Got away with blue murder, that he did, murder and buggery. But he'll be like this same skull, sir, in a year from now, and which of us could tell them apart? To what base uses we may return, that's my philosophy. And they say he shagged Em Ball till he grew too fat to fuck and his balls blew up with the dropsy, big as the bells of Shoreditch. And now my Lord Worm's in the cold ground, never to prick no more. Farewell to you then, Tarleton, you fat fucker. They say he made a good end.'

But I'd said my farewells to Tarleton long before he died. When I woke up from that second night in London I'd already made my decision – the Queen's Men were not for me. I smelled worse than wine and old leeks coming from poor old Dick, much worse than armpit and arse. I smelled the end of the Queen's. Tarleton had jigged and jested his way through his career with a flourish that made him the dog's bollocks, the nonpareil, but you can stand on one toe only so long before they want to see you go down and stay down.

The third morning in London, I left Hog Lane, well named, and its roomful of snorting old bores, went north over Finsbury, past Holywell, and came to the Theatre.

26

Ah, the Theatre! A place for viewing; a locus of life; a venue for all the multiplying miracles and villainies of nature that swarm upon this great stage of fools – with a seat reserved for the nobs, and farting room only for the groundlings. Well done, old Burbage, you took the drama off the streets and wagons, away from the piss-soaked cobbles and horseshit of innyards, out of the candied pomp of courts and halls, where we were but arse-licking grooms, out of the arenas of insolent Greece and haughty Rome – and set us up in our own solemn temple, where – he said – ye shall be as gods.

And so we were. And Burbage was the *primum mobile*. Burbage took the idea from his brother-in-law, John Brayne, a failed grocer who'd built a playhouse just outside Aldgate, at White Chapel, near the Red Lion, back in '67. Brayne then became a failed playhouse owner. But nine years later he teamed up with James (Snug) Burbage, a failed joiner. Undeterred by failure, he used to say that 'God himself was a joiner, and left the trade when he found better things to do. Nobody ever said Jesus was a bad carpenter but it wasn't his tables and chairs that made him famous. And in a world where joiners get themselves resurrected,' quipped Snuggie B., 'anything can happen.' Even the miracle of turning actors into idols. Into gods.

And Burbage did just that, and like God himself, split time, changed the calendar, in dramatic terms: before Burbage, after Burbage. Before Burbage the play took place on a borrowed stage and so became a borrowed thing in itself.

Burbage changed all that. The theatre now hung in space, resplendent, like a new planet in the morning. And the crowds flocked to it.

It was a grand scheme and needed hard cash. Burbage was out for profit, not for art. So Brayne put up the money, the joiner-grocer enterprise flourished and became the Holywell Theatre in St Leonard's parish, where a Benedictine priory once stood, and where Snug himself turned out to be something of an actor, as rude mechanicals do. It took some vision. The site was just a patch of waste ground, rampant with weeds and strewn with dog-merds and bones. 'To pay five ducats, five! I wouldn't farm it – wouldn't even fart on it,' yelped Brayne, lifting his leg in derision, suiting the action to the word, and refusing at first to part with a penny.

But Burbage was stubborn and devious – he hadn't got Leicester's patronage for nothing. He not only extracted the cash out of the grocer but soon had him and his wife Margaret slaving away on the site and working their tails off without two groats to rub together for their pains. Meanwhile brother-in-law Burbage helped himself generously during construction. He also helped himself to more than his fair share of the takings when things were up and running, filching cash from the box by the use of a secret key, and sticking coins in his mouth and chest and even up his arse, to diddle his partner. An incorrigible crook, our Snug. There was a joke went round the companies, when the coins were being counted, if one happened to slip through your fingers and roll away under the table: *You can have that one free, my friend – it's just dropped out of Snuggie's arse.* Wags who wanted to wind him up would make a great show of sniffing the takings during counting, and with sleight of hand or with a little shuffling, produce coins miraculously from their various orifices, and this would sometimes lead to violence. Snug was a man with a temper.

At last the pot boiled over. Brayne found out about the thieving, Burbage punched him and called his wife a whoring bitch who diddled her pimps and stuffed her customers' coins up her cunt. 'And *that* holds a fucking sight more than the box!' he roared. This produced a riot. Burbage junior (Richard of famous name) beat up one of Brayne's henchmen with a staff, and the grocer's party fled the field, old Burbage yelling after them that if he saw as much as their backs again his boys would throw down their staves, take up pistols and pepper their legs with powder and hempseed. Then they'd paunch them and turn them into tripe. That was a famous fight. It took place on the Theatre stage itself, where Brayne ended up unconscious in the hell-hole, with old man Burbage having to be restrained from pissing in on him. 'Better than Agincourt at the Globe,' he cackled much later.

Brayne died but his widow kept up the feuding and led other skirmishes, only to be routed again by young Richard and a broomstick. Meanwhile Burbage grew to fair round belly with good capon lined, and bucketsful of beer. He'd made it. He got the better of the rival groups, Pembroke's, Strange's, the Lord Admiral's, and worked it cunningly so that the Theatre never became the exclusive home to any one company. But Snuggie B. threatened to commit murder when a gentleman of means, Henry Lanman, opened up the Curtain at Moorfields, only two hundred yards to the south, in Curtain Close. 'Lanman? Lanman? I'll make him *Lame*man! I'll change his fucking name for him!' He needn't have worried. Lanman never did as well as Burbage. He was a nob, no more, and neither actor nor tradesman. In time he had the sense to go in with Burbage, letting his Curtain operate as something of an easer to the Theatre. They sorely needed an easer – for the crowds.

Across the Finsbury footpath they came, in swarms and droves, to the great house of dreams, to see the stage drowned in blood and tears and watch them cleave the general ear with horrid speech, make mad the guilty and appal the free.

The crowds came on in a gathering wave, a fieldful of folk, summoned at two o'clock in the afternoon by a triple blast on the trumpet – all that was needed to send a thousand souls northwards to Satan's chapel while hardly a handful of the faithful stuck it out at Paul's Cross, though the bell had clappered for a full hour, beseeching those impious wretches to stay and save their souls. But why listen to a long-faced sermon on the Vices when you could see and hear them instead, watch them brought to life on stage, comic or tragic, according to Burbage's bill for the day? So for two hours the play dulled the pain of living, by giving living some kind of sparkle, shape, and substance. Aimless, opaque, impalpable life, each day it slips through your fingers like the sea and you stand mystified on the shore. And night after night it sloshes round like wine in your tired brain. The play changed all that. The play was the ultimate flight from ordinariness and from the chaos of life. And for that hour or two of illusion they came running over the fields.

They wanted the magic, they needed the hell and heroics, God and Satan appearing in person, hoof and halo, and horns for cuckolds; to see the soul torn by questions and the body by devils. They wanted tears and laughter, big bold speeches, battles and blood. And the blood was sweated out of the spirit in bitter black verse: a great shedding of words.

The blood, the stage stuff, came from sheep and calves, as the spectators well knew – the blood of an ox or a cow was too thick – but if they wanted to see real blood these same playgoers would go down to the bearpit and watch the torn beast howl. For the bear had no words to melt their hearts, no power of speech to put honey in their heads. Howling was all there was. It's what the bear did best. You'd think such howls would melt hearts. But not the hearts of the bearpit crowd. They heard heroes die with brave, beautiful words in their mouths, but they knew the pain was acted, unlike the bear's that would have rent the heart of London – if London had a heart. But they were men of stones and their city was a beast without a heart, a city of cruelties, the whipping of blind bears, the lopping of hands and slitting of stomachs, the burning of bowels with the owner still alive, sites of pain, sites of pleasure, none better than the stage for the London crowd.

And so, getting a glass in their heads, they came and thundered at the playhouse, fought for bitten and bitter apples hurled down from the galleries with high scorn, belched out their herring and garlic breath, threw up their sweaty nightcaps, and roared out their displeasure if the play was too lofty or too tame.

It was the springtime of playing and the playhouses came out like primroses: the Bell and the Cross Keys in Gracechurch Street, the Bull in Bishopsgate Street, the Boar's Head near the Red Lion in Whitechapel, and the Bel Savage on Ludgate Hill. When I came to London they were already putting up the Rose. By any other name it would smell as sweet, but as the moon shines with a borrowed light, so the Rose of London stole its scent from one name only, and it was the only one worthy to stand with the Burbage Theatre.

27

Let us now praise Philip Henslowe: dock-owner, rent-collector, money-lender, slum landlord, pub landlord, pawnbroker and brothel-broker extraordinaire. Across the river, in Paris Garden country, among the bearpits and brothels stringing the riverbank, and on the shittiest of sites which had once smelled sweet with the scent of English roses, Philip Henslowe, working with a fat-fisted grocer – it was always a grocer – John Cholmley, built the first of the Bankside theatres and called it, not surprisingly, the Rose, erected on the site of a former brothel, and taking its name from the street term for a whore, appropriate enough for brothel-running Henslowe. It flourished over the existing shit and the air blew sweet again with the fragrance of English plays. The Rose grew to be the prime plot of drama, the hotbed of theatrical enterprise, Henslowe was the cunning gardener – and Christopher Marlowe was the migrant bird with strange seeds spilling from his beak. In the early nineties Strange's Men and the Admiral's Men married, like the incestuous buggers they were, and made the Rose their home. That was when the great Ned Alleyn came into his own. He divorced Burbage, who was up to his old hedgehog tricks again of milking the box in the night, threw in with Henslowe, lay with his daughter, married the young step-miss, and so became the dramatic darling of the southside. A smart card. But he couldn't have done it without father-in-law Philip.

Turn up the lamp again upon this wondrous necessary man.

Henslowe from Hounslow, hirer of props and plays, dyer turned theatre-owner who became the power behind the London stage and the last refuge of scoundrels, including down-and-out playwrights begging for work – hackwork, patchwork, advances, loans, commissions, crumbs from the table, anything at all that kept body and soul from the long divorce. Henslowe ignored nothing that meant money, no job too small, no plea too poor, though it was well known that he was more particular about his prostitutes than his players. He even interviewed his whores and found some to be unsuitable if they smelled too sweet. 'Aroint thee, punk! The customers will think you're trying to wash off the pox. No need to sweeten your cunt. Men want the stink of sin.' A Henslowe whore had to be horny. She could even be a man. But she had to stink.

When he renovated the Rose in '92 he got twenty-four turned balusters for tuppence farthing apiece and the next two dozen at a farthing discount each. A flint-fingered financier was old Phil. But he didn't stint on style. A new flagpole went up and a banner with a rose fluttering in the breeze. It had cost him twelve shillings, a tidy sum. He'd try anything, do anything, just for one brass farthing, and he liked to have writers under his thumb.

One thing, he would never see you stuck, always saw you round a hard corner. Drove you to regret it later, but without him there might never have been a later. He stood between some poor swine and suicide or the wolf at the door, and when times were hard in London I knew I could always go to Henslowe. He knew what he could wring out of me in return. 'Your pen is mine, Will. Write me a bright speech, finish me that dull play and make it sparkle, conclude that Act. I have a scene here needs re-working for tomorrow and there's no pen that speeds like your pen. Harry the Sixth? Harry the Sixth can wait. Harry the Sixth comes after Henslowe the First, Philip the Foremost.' (Philip the Foreskin to his debtors). 'Rank and file, Will – get them right and live well. Now how much did you say you needed? My purse is yours.' He sang a new song, naturally, when my Harry hit the stage – but till that time came I had good reason to be glad of Philip Henslowe.

But Henslowe's Rose was not then in season and when I walked from Hog Lane on that third morning and stood in Holywell, staring at the Theatre, I was looking then at the choicest London plum of its day, Burbage's castle in the air. Little did I think when I stared at the bones and turds and the muddied puddles of yesterday's crowds, that this would be the principal staging place for my plays for the next ten years. Little did I know I'd even *write* such plays. I watched a rat creep slyly out of the eyehole of a skull. The rat shot off, pursued by a dog, and from the other side of the playhouse I heard a sudden terrible scream. It went through me like a known knife. And even before edging around the building, I knew with dreadful certainty what I was going to see. Yes, there it was – the shambles. There stood the butcher with the knife, there the steaming pile of tripe under the buckling legs, the screaming ending in a terrified whimper. Jesus! Was this what I came for? Was there never to be an escape from it, the smell of the blood still? I'd lacked the courage to enter the Theatre but the sight and sound of the slaughterhouse lent me a courage built on cowardice. I fled – and went straight inside to look for James Burbage.

He was not to be found. Burbage was away, they said. No, they didn't know where, or when he would be likely to return, and no, they couldn't offer me any work at the Theatre, only Burbage himself could do that.

And that's why I found myself back in the shambles. Back again among the tumbling intestines and the terrified eyes of cattle. I tried to sleep in the nearby cesspit I'd rented. But the blackness was alive with eyes, eyes alive and seeing, eyes white and rolling and red with dread. I screwed mine up as tight as I could, to shut them out and the screams ran like blood down the inside walls of my head. I was trapped there till morning, just like a beast, howling in my sleep, waiting for day.

Dawn bled through.

From Stratford to Shoreditch I'd come, from shambles to shambles, and I spent the next three weeks there, steeped in gore. The animals shat themselves as a rule, as soon as they smelled the blood, so there was always a vile concoction over your feet. It didn't matter how carefully you stepped, you walked in filthy witness, and you could smell the fear from the beasts just as surely as they smelled death from you when they saw you approach with axe and knife and rope, Tyburn style. This was my world, the block and blade, and all that distinguished me from the hangman was that my victims were incapable of evil and incapable of protesting their innocence. They'd known no sin but they had no tongue. They were God's lambs. I was the sinner, and I betrayed the innocent blood. I played Judas in Shoreditch, just as I'd done in Stratford.

And play was the word. For I too wore a mask at my bloody work like the Tyburn man, a mask to keep Will from Will. Who else could it be, standing there, dyed in the Shoreditch blood and hauling on that rope? Hauling at lowered head and the helpless, dug-in hoofs, hoofs backing in vain, hoofs slithering through slime, away from the brandished steel, which smoked with bloody execution. Who else put in the knife and let out the life in that roaring torrent of red? Who was it who felt that huge shudder run through the bulk beneath his murdering hands? And from a creature whose most violent act was to chew meadowsweet and grass and trample daisies underfoot, the poor beast of the field, come to the block, where I waited with cruel knife, wore the mask and played the part. How else to get through the day?

My first job, then, as a London actor was not at the Theatre, it was next door. Will Shakespeare, slaughterer, trained in Stratford, practising in Shoreditch, and staying sane. Only the mad have stopped acting. It never troubled my father, though, the butchery. The apple-cheeked buffer I put into the ground fifteen years ago was a hard bugger in the back shop. He could stroke a lamb on the head while the other hand was slyly placing the knife at the point of insertion. What did it mean, after all, that treacherous caress? Calm down, old friend, I'm only going to butcher you. And if the beast turned stubborn he never troubled with the fondling, just grew angry and smashed the axe down on the protesting head. Hold still, you brute! I'll split your skull for you!

So frowned he once when in an angry parle he smote the sledded Polacks on the ice.

That was my father, a hero with the chopper, and not a man for talk. A man for action, not acting. A down-the-line man, an axe-and-slab man, made for alderman, but not for failure. An untheatrical man. Strange that he's a king.

My father. Methinks I see my father...

28

'Where, Will?'

Where what, Francis?

'Where do you see him?'

See? Whom?

'Your father. In your mind's eye again?'

Why no, look you there! Look how it steals away, my father in his habit as he lived. Look! where he goes, even now, out at the portal...

'Perhaps he came to chide you, to whet your almost blunted purpose.'

What purpose is that, Francis?

'The will.'

Do not forget... I *had* forgot.

'You need a good slice of great pie – when it comes.'

But thou wouldst not think how ill all's here about my heart...

'You need *two* slices of pie, a double helping. That'll cure your heartache.'

He got what he wanted.

'Who?'

My father.

'What was that?'

His coat of arms.

'Ah yes, he failed the first time, didn't he?'

Unsuccessful. Apply again. And it cost me a groaning to take off his edge, to slake his ambition.

'Recovered greatness?'

Something like that. What are sons for?

'But why the groaning? You had the time of your life in London. You were the belle of the ball.'

Did I? Was I? I spent the first three weeks of July in the steaming heat of the Shoreditch shambles – until one day Burbage suddenly appeared, a big-nosed bugger on horseback, clattering past the slaughteryard. I pumped the blood and grease from my hands and ran after him, feeding him an ancient concoction of turds about seeing him when I was nine years old back in Stratford and how I'd lived in the glow ever since and now I wanted to work for him.

He gave me a withering stare.

'Stratford? Fucking Stratford? Jesus, I remember that. Stratford wasn't too hearty when it laughed, I remember that much. And you won't get rich here either, shit-shifter, if *that's* your trade,' (waving the edge of his cloak theatrically at my blood-boltered clothes), 'not that you're ever likely to make much as an actor, by the looks of you. You'll more than likely starve.'

He dismounted and looked hard at me, sizing me up, and shook his head. Clearly I didn't improve under scrutiny.

'I can tell a great actor at a glance,' he said. 'You're not one.'

I turned away.

'I'll tell you what, though,' he said, 'I'll be needing some of that blood of yours next week for a new play – a damned good play.'

I asked him what it was called.

'Marvellous stuff. By a mad young bugger – and I mean *bugger.* Keep your arse to the post if you ever act with *him.*'

I asked him who'd written it. Burbage was the kind of man who always had to hold something back, even his excrement, such was his nature.

'See *Tamburlaine* and die, Stratford man!' he roared. 'And remember – buckets of blood. In the meantime, hold my horse – and don't fucking move!'

I held his horse and didn't move – for the rest of the day. The horse and I had pissed once together and twice alternately before Burbage finally came back. And the horse had shat once but convincingly, decorating my shoes. They were not up to much by this time in any case, sodden with excrement and urine and the innards of the animals I'd killed. As I stood there I started to dream about a pair of boots. Burbage had on a beautiful pair. It was what had struck me most of all as I'd watched him stride off into the Theatre to tell his actors about this exciting new play. I thought about that too – how brave it would be to be able to march into that building in a new pair of boots and waving in your fist the manuscript of a bold new drama, one that would make the crowd go wild.

Burbage gave me my first job in the theatre, holding the horses for the booted gentlemen and for the idlers who couldn't be arsed to cross Moorfields and Finsbury on foot, especially in the muddy weather and the ball-freezing frosts of early spring. Jesu. But country boy Will was a wizard with horses – I've always had a way with them. And I didn't just hold them, I groomed them as well and filled their twitching ears with words, for the Stratford shit-kicker was a wizard with words too. I crooned sonnets into those listening manes. I leaped into the saddle and became a prince, a king of England. I saw young Harry with his beaver on, rise from the ground like feathered Mercury. Cantering about the cobbles that rang beneath the prancing hooves, sawing at the reins, I urged on my troops, the English army in front of Harfleur. Once more unto the breach, dear friends, once more! I heard the shouts and drank in the applause of an audience enchanted by the horseman's words. The owners came out of the Theatre well satisfied to find their steeds in such fine fettle. They paid me handsomely. I hired beggar boys to handle more. A boy can be got for a groat and a groatsworth of wit in business is all you need to spin a shilling out of a penny and a pound out of a shilling. I rented decent lodgings, bought a horse of my own, and, at last – a decent pair of boots.

It didn't stop there. Burbage gave me more work. I carried for him – costumes, bread and beer, apples and oranges, cheeses, nuts. By this time I was inside the Theatre. In empty moments with nobody about I'd take the stage and I'd work on the imaginary forces of imaginary audiences. I was up there one day giving all I'd got when Burbage made an unexpected entrance.

O! for a Muse of fire, that would ascend
The brightest heaven of invention!

He stared at me, open-mouthed.

'What the fuck's that from?'

'Just something I heard,' I mumbled.

'Well, *I* haven't fucking heard it. You've got a good ear, friend. Let me hear more.'

I was a fair declaimer, he decided, not being much of an orator himself. From then on I assisted the prompter, marshalled the actors, kept them on cue, made up for sickness and slackness, hangovers and the pox, took on small parts, swept the shit from the stage, even looked after the box for Burbage and didn't let any other bugger near it. Lord

Burbage trusted me up to my ears and down to my balls. In short I too became a wondrous necessary man. Within fifteen months I had become an actor.

A Burbage man.

'And don't tell me it wasn't worth it, Will.'

It was without doubt the shittiest slog imaginable: the summer dust and sunburn of the provinces, to travel on the hard hoof from village to village for cheese and buttermilk and a shilling or two in cold cash, back to rainy London in cold October; then the cramped winter inns with their drunks and bugs, their thick smoke and thin rabble of yawning audiences; a brief chilly spring in the public theatres and out again on tour, through thistles and cowshit and itch, back to the bumpkins I'd come from.

And a hard grind it was rehearsing in the early mornings, performing every afternoon except Sundays, knocking up a different play every other day of the working week, fifteen shows a month and half of them new, taking on scores of piss-poor parts and storing them away in the ledgers of the brain, a feat performable only by the memorising freaks of the grammar schools. Weary with toil I haste me to my bed. By the end of my first season I'd stuffed out my player's hide with a hundred different parts. I barely knew myself. And I was only one of the pale fruitless moons. A star of the stage kept five thousand lines a week in his skull.

No, the stage was a far cry from the broad and pleasant path the Puritans spat and ranted of. Primrose path? Primrose pudding. As far as paths go, I recall only a cold and muddy one, trudging out of London behind the wet wagon and through the yelling sleet, with a hey-ho, the wind and the rain. Wind and rain – an actor's guaranteed audience, co-mates and brothers in exile. Counsellors that feelingly persuade me what I am. Here we go again, lads, out on the pissing road. Where, let me repeat, there were precious few primroses. Pimps and prostitutes, yes, and an army of beggars and such-like scum, but if acting was the beflowered route to the everlasting bonfire, I must have taken a wrong turning somewhere along the way. Dalliance my arse. What I knew about was frozen feet and fingers, polecap knees, peeled carrot nose, dripping nostrils, brass balls bitten to buggery, head down, shoulders hunched, hearing the grinding of the cartwheels over the ruts and rubble, the dead rats and frozen turds, and some fool singing in the rain that bloody song again, the useless chump.

But when I came to man's estate,
With hey, ho, the wind and the rain,
'Gainst knaves and thieves men shut their gates
For the rain it raineth every day.

Every fucking day. Once the damp creeps up your behind, you're never dry again – not till the spring, when the March winds invade your looped and windowed raggedness and blow up your bum, turning your bowels blue. That's when you catch a fiery chill and start shitting crocodiles.

And as to knaves and thieves, well, that's what we were to the good and godlies of church and council – no better than drifters, derelicts, drunkards, drabs, and devils in disguise. And there were times I'd have agreed with their surly definitions. What were we, after all, but a cry of clowns putting on dumb shows and jumps, cracking jokes for stinkards and yokels, scratching the itching humours of scabby minds with execrable oaths, obscene speeches, lascivious actions, and jests and jigs that reeked of excrement and sperm, Tarleton style? Many's the time we arrived at a town, they shook the whip and the rope in our faces and turned us from their gates. 'Go on, you fuckers, on your filthy way! We want none of your sort here!'

Fuck off was always the word, familiar as the frigging rain. I tell you, after a year I was fucking sick of it, the homelessness, the hard beds, the hard words, the hatred. I looked in my glass and what did I see? An ungodly, improvident, and obscene arsehole, dishonest and diseased: at worst a filthy pederast, at best a common beggar; a dazzling fraud on stage, offstage reckless and repellent, a source of unrest, infection, irresponsibility, of weird fantasies, wild feelings, fanaticism, and insurrection. Worse: a magnet of divine ire and an open invitation to God to bring down his scourge on the people in that worst of all forms, the plague. For the cause of plagues is sin and the cause of sin is plays, therefore the cause of plague is plays – so ran the argument.

Such were the fruits and purposes of playing. In addition to which (and lest I forget) there were the following: to corrupt innocence, teach falsehood, hypocrisy, scorn; to play the vice, to deflower honest wives, to murder, flay, kill, pick and steal, rob and riot, rebel against princes, commit treason, consume treasures, sing of sex and venereal disease, mock and scoff, flout and flatter, play the whoremaster, the glutton, the drunkard, the blasphemer – and above all to engage in public and private deception, to self-delude and lead others astray. For what was playing, after all, but mass foolery and fraud, a grand illusion? And what was a player but a nasty charlatan? I was a trickster, a sham, jetting in silks on stage and the next minute back with the scum on the streets: from king to beggar in one quick change of skin. I was the enemy of apprentices, discouraging them from their trades, and planting sedition in their heads. I was a drawer of crowds, leading to stealing and whoring and damage to property, not to mention insurrection, anarchy, and fray. And I was thoroughly detested for putting on plays on the Sabbath, creating false idols, spouting scurrility and smut, wearing women's clothes, keeping young boys as catamites and ill-minded ingles, and having the impudence to profit from a profession that was not even a legal occupation or decent calling at all, but a sheer blasphemy against God and man.

And if I lacked the power to articulate or remember all of that, John Fucking Stubbes had beat it out on a drum and spelt it out for all to read or hear in his right righteous and savagely indignant *Anatomy of Abuses*. Do they not maintain bawdry, insinuate foolery, and renew remembrance of heathen idolatry? Do they not induce whoredoms and uncleanness? Nay, are they not rather plain devourers of maidenly virginity and chastity? For proof whereof mark but the flocking and running to Theatres and Curtains, where such wanton gestures, such bawdy speeches, such laughing and leering, such clipping and culling, such winking and glancing of wanton eyes, and the like is used, as is wonderful to behold.

And the like. If only the half of it had been true. If all of it was, it was only some of the time, and all of it goes on at one time or another, whether or not the players are in town. When were fucking and filching and groping and gambling not in fashion? As for wonderful to behold, there was precious little wonderful about it, though it might have looked that way from under a Puritan's gown, where the balls burned in anguish, decades of sperm dammed up behind floodgates of fear and frustration. None but the lonely prick shall know mine anguish. It had seemed so in Stratford as I'd watched the Queen's Men clanking southward, trailing dust and dreams. Closer up it was different by a long john and a far cry from the vision that did the damage when I was eleven years old and sat upon that promontory and saw that mermaid on the dolphin's back, uttering her dulcet and harmonious breath. For all of the above simply substitute being breathed on at close quarters by a ranting old actor in whose filthy bowels and breath a plague of pickled herring has just come horribly to life. And that was the theatre. So a pox on that dolphin and fuck that fucking mermaid and all who sail on her!

But why in particular blame Leicester's mermaid? It was one of a great storm of seeds sown in my soul and now I was merely reaping the whirlwind. I'd seen the Slaughter of the Innocents and had staged it time and time over in the theatre of my mind. A boy in Stratford, king of the cornfields, I'd shouted to an audience of a million listening ears. I'd warned cities of grain of what would follow if they failed to surrender, and the sickle in my hand burned like a tartar's bow, the crescent moon I'd plucked down from the sky. Surrender, dogs, or see your naked infants spitted upon pikes, while the mad mothers with their howls confused do break the clouds, as did the wives of Jewry at Herod's bloody-hunting slaughtermen! Jesus. And the ranting six-year-old king made them swear on their swords a binding oath. A terrifying consent to death, to mass infanticide, offence's reddest seal, murder most foul. But we have sworn, my lord, already. Indeed, upon my sword, indeed, swear, swear by my sword.

And so the thing began. All roads lead to London – and I was led by time and fate to my own acting days in and out of Shoreditch: *King John*, *Henry Five*, *The True Chronicle of King Leir and His Three Daughters*, and such like dire dramas. In which I often lent my hand, touching up the parts, stiffening up the play, enlarging the action, making it flow. That was a bonus for Burbage, and for me it was relief at least. Sometimes though the only relief that's left is to discharge your part in private – and I did that to no applause but the twang of my own balls. Many a time and oft.

How I stuck it Christ knows. Days uncounted I nearly left the road and went straight back to Stratford. Once I remember – it was my turn for walking – I just stopped in my tracks and watched the wagon clanking on into nowhere in particular till it turned into a tiny cloud on the skyline, and of no more consequence, so it seemed than any of the other spots and specks on landscape and skyscape. Nothing of it had anything to do with me – I could have gone like an arrow into Warwickshire. Then, suddenly, I heard the clown Kempe's voice coming out of the cloud, a thin little birdsong on the wind.

When that I was and a little tiny boy
With hey, ho, the wind and the rain;
A foolish thing was but a toy,
For the rain it raineth every day.

Those were *my lines* Kempe was singing. I remembered he'd asked me for a song to help fill out a poor part and I'd dashed it off. When I heard it now wafting across the melancholy fields, made poignant by distance, it affected me strangely. The words transformed the landscape, turned it into a vast stage, while the landscape itself gave something back to the song: a context and a setting that made it echo and linger in the mind. It struck me as sadly pleasing. At the same time I thought the song a little too good for friend Kempe, a touch subtle for such an ordinary clown, though he was a cut or two above Tarleton. Even so, I thought, this song could grace another play. Or twinkle on the lips of a wiser fool than Kempe. Who knows? Cheered a little, I trudged on again after the wagon, in the wake of my own words about the wind and the rain, and through the wind and the rain themselves, somehow become a theatre, part of a vast setting, and the faceless actors in some impersonal universal play.

'So it was a near thing?'

There were many more hairline moments to come when I would have willingly given it all up and gone safely back to Stratford, back to the dungy comforts of obscurity. And might well have done so. Had it not been for Tamburlaine. The Scythian shepherd is as dead now as the dead shepherd of Canterbury, but in '87 he was the living legend of London. Tamburlaine the Great.

'Tell me more.'

Tell you about the man who made him, you mean, and in so doing made himself into the star of the English stage and the golden idol of yours truly, right worshipful Will. Oh yes, I hated the bastard. He was my god.

29

Christopher Marlowe. I even hated the sound of the name: the crisply decisive dactyl, and the surname introduced by that emphatic nasal. Christopher Marlowe sounded named for success. He was even born in front of me, beating me by two months. A man can write a play in two months and in two hours that play can change the world, putting all London at his feet. Marlowe came up to London on foot just like me, by a different road, and he saw his London with a difference. He had big cat's eyes, Kit Marlowe – Cat Marlowe to his rivals, and to his nancy boys with their claws out, rat-catcher Chris. His eyes burned wide and bright when he first saw the city stretched out in front of him.

Like Elysium to a new-come soul.

There was irony in these words, a mad Marlowe irony, because London turned out to be Marlowe's exit to eternity. The house in Deptford was waiting for him, and three men already sitting there in God's long look. They'd been waiting there since Genesis, three men spiked on the eyebeam of a cherub, an unholy trio who'd come by special arrangement to separate his soul from his body. Not quite a new-come soul – it was six years since he'd come through the gates of his imagined Elysium – but it was a lot sooner than even he could have conjectured, even with his feel for sudden tragic falls and his mind on fire with fate.

I remember the first time I saw him. It was in a den in Deptford and I heard him even before he came in. You always heard Marlowe before you saw him. Beer and Burbage were my only thoughts at that moment – it wasn't long after I'd acquired my new boots – when a gaggle of Ganymedes strutted in, demanding drink, and above their quack and chatter one voice stood out higher and more melodious than the rest, fluting like an oboe, and in Latin too, '*Quod me nutrit me destruit*,' adding the gloss, 'What feeds me kills me, lads – and I'm not referring to the sack you're about to buy me!'

Trills of dutiful laughter, over which the voice continued to preside. 'Every woman feeds and kills you – and the Muse is a woman, more's the pity!'

More laughter.

But it wasn't the words that distinguished the speaker, it was the drawling delivery, shrill yet strong, lilting, lazy, languorous – and controlling. He was clearly in charge of the throng of queers that surrounded him. They parted to sit down, awarding me my first sight of Christopher Marlowe, and he of me, or so I thought.

He saw a simple man in a drab jerkin but with glossy new boots. I saw a figure like Phoebus, framed by the open doorway. The sun was at his back, streaming through the windows, and his own corona seemed to grow from him. He fixed his wide eyes on me, taking in everything, a searching, fearless gaze that was almost insolent. The mouth was slightly pursed and impatient, as if he'd accept no lip from any man, unless a loving pair to match his own sensuous lower one; and this strong pout was accentuated by the close careful moustache and beard, also underlining the firm yet effeminate jaw. A face of contradictions. And not a face to forget, surrounded as it was by that shock of hair swept back over a high forehead.

If you could have forgotten the face you would not forget the attire, the amply slashed black velvet doublet studded with gold buttons, and the gashes revealing gold beneath – dozens of dagger-slashes exuding golden blood. This was no poor playwright. And yet a simple cobweb lawn collar instead of lace. His boots were not as new as mine – the whole costume was well worn – but he stood in them nobly and made me feel suddenly more fitted for a return to the shambles. There was a scarcely subdued combativeness in his stare, tacitly taunting. He looked arrogant and unpredictable.

'And what feeds *you*, Stratford man, apart from small beer?'

He was sitting down opposite me and staring at me with that open mocking half ironic smile that I came to know so well – but not too well.

'What feeds me is need,' I answered him truthfully.

'And beyond that?'

'Beyond that, ambition. How did you know I was a Stratford man?'

He smiled – very sweetly – commanded sack to be brought between us, swept my small beer aside, and relaxed.

'I know everything,' he said, glittering-eyed. 'I make it my business. You're Will Shakespeare, of good old Catholic stock, and you have a kinsman's head on London bridge.'

I resolved never to befriend this man. Religion was a forbidden subject with me, especially in taverns. He saw the sudden alarm in my face and laid his hand on mine. I noticed the other hand slide to his dagger, in case I misinterpreted the gesture. If I did, I didn't show it.

'Rest easy, friend, I'm no fleering tell-tale. Kit Marlowe at your service. And now, to set your mind more at ease, I'll tell you all about myself, all you want to know, and more than you need to learn.'

Of course he told me less than I might have needed to learn, and a lot more than I wanted to know. But when the sack was in him, Marlowe never stopped talking, and every line of his talk sounded like blank verse. He'd come to London at twenty-three, just like me, but with his heels in hell and his finger-ends scorched by stars – that was how he spoke – such was his blaze, such was his reach. 'Ours is a world,' he said, 'in which bricklayers and butchers and grocers refuse to follow their callings, answering instead to a certain buzzing in their brains, a beating in the blood.'

He could have beaten leather instead, son of a Canterbury cobbler and a dubious mother, and after seven years as a king's Scholar at Cambridge, could have taken holy orders.

'Father Marlowe – just imagine!' he laughed with those cold eyes, blessing the sack with two rood-making fingers and bidding me drink.

As things turned out, he said, his gifts were not for God. His leanings and bendings – and they were many – tended elsewhere: demonology, cosmography, politics, espionage, murder, oh yes, and the snares of Ovid. Quite a curriculum vitae. And that was leaving aside the hidden curriculum – the charms of boys and the addictions of alcohol, atheism and tobacco: a heady mixture.

What was he, this vibrant vision of a man, sitting across the table from me in a Deptford den and quaffing sack? A Catholic unbeliever who spied on Catholics abroad, a bar-brawler and street-fighter, keeper of company with poets, publishers, and filthy intellectuals – not all bad, then. But a heavy reckoning in a little room was only six years on, and the meteoric display was brief but intense. If the stars in their courses fought against Marlowe, they added to the blaze that surrounded him, burnishing the sun. In my first London years he was the brightest luminary on the bill, stunning the punters by the sheer arrogance of his poetic reach, his cosmic contempt for authority, society and ordinary human bonds. To hell with that, he cried – literally, to hell. Family, loyalty, humility, kindness, order, degree, tolerance, belief – all were but toys to Marlowe. He was the great sceptic, and when he hit London the sparks flew and it looked as if nobody could come near him. Untouchable as the sun, dubious as a comet, he opened his lips and his tongue took fire, scorching the gods.

'I have made a covenant with death,' he said, 'and with hell am I in agreement!'

I nodded. This sort of language landed you in jail, especially the way he said it, and this was the way it always was with Marlowe, man and dramatist inseparable, jostling for the stage, stealing each other's lines.

But he was the prince of playwrights and he made the theatres blaze with his blank verse. I'd never heard anything like it. The pentameters of the past were like trundling carts beside his golden carriages, they were fustian, they were dust beside this glorious stuff. Even Kyd sounded now like a clanking old ghost: Hamlet, revenge! *The Spanish Tragedy,* that had been the rage of the Rose, died in an afternoon. Burbage had been right about this new man when he spoke to me outside the Theatre that day about Marlowe, phrase-making, breathtaking, outrageous Marlowe, drunk wordsmith and master of a thousand monstrosities. Where else could you find poisoned convents, massacres in monasteries, boiling oil, infants swimming in their parents' blood, headless carcasses piled in heaps, virgins impaled on rings of pikes, and old men sprawled in the dust with swords stuck through their sides, their brains gushing out under the iron rain of blows? Where else does the seaman see the Hyades gather an army of Cimmerian clouds? Where else do you hear of Cubar where the negroes dwell, and the wide, the vast, the Euxine sea?

Nowhere in London. And its crowd went wild when they heard him. He knew how to make them roar, Master Marlowe, master of the mighty line and brave translunary things. And to my death-bed shame, confessing to deadly pride, I wanted to bring down his swaggering Scythian show-off hero, pull him off his pedestal and sweep him from the stage.

That looked to be impossible in '88, when *Tamburlaine* first exploded in the Rose and wooed the crowds to ecstasy. I remember the first moment, like yesterday. Ned Alleyn came in on the trumpet call, all decked out in copper-laced coat over crimson velvet breeches. He was singing of his mistress, doomed to die, and the language was like liquor. All who heard it got drunk on it. Words were a net he threw over the world, making it his own, whatever the experience. Listen.

Is it not passing brave to be a king and ride in triumph through Persepolis?

Hearing lines like that and then going home to look at the knots in the beams, the spiders on the walls, to watch the Shoreditch shadows gathering wordlessly – no, it was impossible to sit still after hearing it. The quill twitched in my fingers. I ranged round the room like a caged lion, calling on angels to walk the walls of heaven, to entertain divine Zenocrate, telling the men of Memphis to wake to the clang of trumpets, hear the Scythian basilisks that, roaring, shake Damascus' turrets down. And still it wasn't enough to get it out of my system. I was high as a whore's hem-line and hungry for more. Day after day I made a beeline for the Rose, got sucked in at Shoreditch, wherever it was playing.

Tamburlaine the Great, the wonder of the stage, the scourge of God and god of the split-eared groundlings for a whole year. Ned Alleyn of course, who could tear a cat upon the stage and strike spectators dead. A Scythian shepherd strides on stage (in russet mantle clad), looks about him, throws off his country cloak – a single arrogant gesture – sails from pastoral to heroic in one fell swoop and conquers all Asia in an hour. The sweep is breathtaking, the groundlings open-mouthed. London disappears around them. Only Tamburlaine exists. He slaughters the maids of Damascus, makes a footstool out of Turkey, fires the city in which his paramour has died, murders his own sons for milksops, drowns the whole of Babylon, and – most famously – forces two harnessed kings down on all fours, and with bitted mouths they draw him in his chariot till they drop. You pampered jades of Asia! What, can you draw but twenty miles a day? Pull or die.

But what was this Tamburlaine, after all, but a glorified butcher? The doubtful hero of a dubious drama that piles hyperbole on superlative till you feel it ought to pall. It never does, and that's the trick of it. Yet Tamburlaine is stricken with a terrible emptiness. And why? Because, like his creator, he cares nothing for people. He lacks the common touch. It came to me in a flash, the vital ingredient, the one that Tamburlaine lacked.

The Crowd.

And along with it the language the crowd knows and uses, the real vernacular of ordinary louts and yobs, not this blazing blank verse uttered by a strutting king clown. Marlowe himself was locked in his own language and like a whore unpacked his heart with words. He was bound upon a wheel of words. The wheel thunders on by, a chariot of fire; impressive to the ear and eye, except that it goes nowhere, only round and round, like the whirling sword in Genesis, sterile as a curse. Words, words, words. When you die you run out of words and the rest is silence. Words are not enough.

And nor is power. He rides in triumph through Persepolis but never stops to govern it. A hanger-on in his own play, a blind ranting mouth. Power as an end in itself is a blind alley, leading to death. Tamburlaine's days were numbered, I muttered, biding my time, my thoughts on brood. Hamlet and Henry Five were waiting to come on. I could hear them in the tiring-room, clearing their throats.

But in 1588 Marlowe was your only man. That was his glory hour. That was his year.

A year in which you didn't have time to take a breath. Mary Stuart to the block and Cadiz to the torch. The Rose sprang up and Marlowe showered it with his magic. Holinshed's *Chronicles* came out in a second, enlarged, edition and stood like a plum-tree heavy with history, rich and thick for stripping. But Holinshed's England was about to be shaken by a fiery wind from Spain so that history fell ripe and plump into the present and people picked up the fruit and bit into the core. I too tasted it, like the Genesis apple, and the knowledge altered everything. When the blast of war rang in our ears it had the sound of a sudden answer from the Muse.

War.

War was my way forward. The answer to Marlowe was almost upon us, and was about to erupt.

The Armada was on the move.

30

'So is that pie, I trust.'

What's that, Francis?

'The pie. On the move. I'm growing hungry again.'

Old Francis still. Always with an eye on his belly.

'Hard not to, with a paunch like mine.'

And I'm trying hard to equate a great pie and a great enterprise.

'What great enterprise?'

The Armada.

'Oh, no! Not history, I beg you!'

It's not about history, not as such. It's about how history was the answer to the present.

'You've lost me.'

How the Armada was the answer to Marlowe.

'You've lost me even more – deeper than ever.'

Elizabeth herself built the Armada. She struck the first blow to the first keel on the day Philip first realised she was never going to marry him. All the other slights and hostilities followed naturally: helping the Dutch rebels, raiding the Spanish ships, treating his ambassadors like excrement. Most monstrously of all, murdering a Catholic queen. Sixtus Five was a wily old bird as Popes go. He never had much belief in Philip's plan to beat us at sea. Philip, after squeezing Sixtus for cash without much return, squeezed his Italian bankers instead. Certain of support from twenty thousand English Catholics and appointing himself as the murdered Mary's heir, he finally screwed up his own courage and decided on a plan, a good old Spanish plan.

'I'd rather have a good old Spanish onion.'

This is how it went.

Parma would land from Flanders to liberate England from its ecclesiastical midnight. And to ensure his success a fantastic fleet of warships would control the crossing. The mighty Armada. This was the famous Enterprise of England, to which Sixtus gave his blessing but not his purse. The conjunctions told against him, though, so the astrologers murmured, shaking their heads at the stars, but Philip had had enough of Bitter Bess, the English heretic and cocktease of the century. Even after she had unleashed Drake and his dogs of war on Lisbon and Cadiz; even after the architect of the Armada, the Marquis of Santa Cruz had died, and was replaced by Medina Sidonia, a man with neither experience nor self-belief; even after the mocking weather dispersed his vessels, sending them back to Spain to reassemble; even after the storms cuffed and scattered his ships like acorn cups between Lisbon and Corunna; even after this complete programme of portents, still Philip wouldn't give up on his English Enterprise. The Pope waved the cross over the entire army, and every soldier and sailor went out onto the waves with the blood and body of God in his mouth. It was the twelfth of July and many of these mouths were soon to be filled with the sea and the Catholic God washed out – a bitter aftertaste to the blessed sacrament.

The floating army entered the Channel. A weird formation, it was like a magnificent crescent moon, seemingly impregnable even to the icy eye of Admiral Howard. England and France stood on either side like spectators at a ball while the two fleets did a stately sarabande up the Channel, a Spanish measure, suiting the girth of the galleons, the English treading water, curtseying to their hellbent guests. Drake came out of Plymouth like a hawk and began to pluck the Spanish feathers. Viciously ripped and stabbed at, the dons fluttered into the Calais Roads. But El Draco sent in his fireships, double-shotted and packed with tar, floating accidents, and the frantic Spaniards were compelled to cut loose and head for the open water, only to be battered off Gravelines. Even then many a man might have got a glimpse of Spain again before he died but for the god-sent gales that drove shoals of ships onto the sandbanks of the Netherlands to die there like stranded fish, while the tattered rags of the once proud Armada were driven north and north and north all round Scotland and Ireland to be smashed to splinters on their bleak island shores.

The riven ships disgorged their human cargoes into the sea's white throat. Most went straight to the cold bowels below. Some were torn on the grinding teeth of reefs and rocks. Others whose flailing feet found shore ran into a fury worse than the sea's. The Calibans of these islands stripped them bare of every shred of clothing they wore, butchering them without a shred of mercy. They were hanged, stabbed, pole-axed, cut into collops, or driven away stark naked to scratch for roots, gnaw at barks, suck limpets and seaweeds, nibble bitter berries, like starved spectral birds, till they retched and puked up everything from arsehole to Aragon and eked out an utterly miserable existence until they died. The looting Dutch and the tigerish Irish didn't exactly welcome them either as beings from a brave new world. Spanish bastards – say good-bye to your balls, if you have any! *Adios, amigos.*

The days went by and the bloated bodies came rolling in on the tides, dead heads lolling like blind seaweeds, hundreds of them belonging to beardless boys, the long imagined terror of the high sea, their genitals hacked off and stuffed into their gaping mouths by the frenzied females of these inhospitable regions, the witches of the Western Isles. Misery has many varieties. Apart from the sea, the rocks, starvation, and the barbarities inflicted by these savages, there was typhus and scurvy, dysentery and delirium, the ever-open doors through which hundreds more were ushered into a wide choice of graves. Not many made it back to Spain.

'Poor buggers.'

There were Englishmen who fared little better. While the services and celebrations were under way and painters and goldsmiths were getting rich on the harvest of God's great gale, the army that had cheered the queen at Tilbury was broken up to avoid the inconvenient little matter of wages. What, give you thus much moneys? Fuck you, friends, the war's over, or didn't you notice? English seamen dying of typhus were as useless as Spanish corpses to their paymasters. So these men died without two pennies to be laid on their staring eyes. Their wives were cheated of their wages and their children cried for hunger. Meanwhile long live England and hurrah for the Protestant wind!

The queen took little account of her gangrened sailors. The war was won. And Elizabeth grieved for only one man, a casualty of time, not war. Bonny sweet Robin had sung his last song and the brazier in his breast was extinct. All her joy for thirty years and her fury too, often enough, but still the star in her sky, snuffed out now – he died at Rycote in spite of the medicines she sent there to succour him. And as the barges went in black down the Thames, the muffled oars dripping quiet pearl in lucent drops, the great Leicester was laid low. Even his horses, it was said, drank with a deathly decorum. As for Elizabeth, she locked herself in her room till the doors had to be broken down and she had no rage left to storm at the courtiers who crowded in to console her and rescue her from her memories. She had fifteen years left to get over it.

She never did. Not even in that time. Another fifteen years till King Death finally seduced the Virgin Queen. But every year's a busy year for the King of Terrors, and '88 was exceptionally crowded. The sea rolled over the Spaniards, the autumn leaves flickered on the grave of Tarleton – and the crows picked out the unseeing eyes of Father William Hartley.

'Vile jellies again, where is thy lustre now?'

Where indeed? His October agony was over by then. That was the first time I saw with my own eyes on stalks just how the hangman carried out his trade. Hartley had been accused of carrying out exorcisms and that was more than enough to bring him to the scaffold. He was put to death at Shoreditch, quite close to the Theatre, in the melancholy vale, place of death and sorry execution, behind the ditches of the abbey.

It was a cold October morning. A string of geese came blaring overhead just as Hartley stepped out onto the scaffold, staggering a little. I remember how he looked up as he heard them calling, over the heads of the suddenly quietened crowd. How free they must have seemed to him. Sailing south. Soon to be crossing the river and the fields, then over the white cliffs and out into the unfenced blue immensities of sea and sky. Perhaps the priest saw them as symbols of his own soul, about to join them in their unfettered existence. I only recall the way the white-bearded chin jutted upwards for a moment and his eye caught the huge arrowhead flying by and everybody heard the wild trumpets and looked up too. Then the hangman pulled up Hartley's gown over his head in one sudden movement and the old man found himself standing stark naked in front of the crowd, who exploded into uproarious approval, and the geese were drowned out. When I glanced up again they were already a faint scribble on the sky over the Thames.

I looked back at the naked Hartley. He was murmuring something. 'Oh, it's cold, it's cold!' It reminded me of the story of Latimer and Ridley standing stockingless in Oxford, waiting to be burned.

The noose went round his neck. He gave a little shiver and the crowd grinned and rubbed its hands in mocking imitation. Then the hangman shoved his victim off the scaffold and as he swung there the crowd caught its breath.

In that moment of sudden dramatic silence Hartley seemed to

swing ever so slowly, twisting and turning, like a man floundering, drowning. It was as he swung back to the platform that the hangman's hand reached out with what looked like infinite slowness and clutched him by the genitals. The other hand came down simultaneously, a blade flashed in the cold October sunlight, and the old man was suddenly back on stage, prickless now and spouting blood from the gash at his groin. 'Oh, it stings! It stings!'

Like something a child might have cried out if he'd just cut his finger. The old man's severed cock and balls were actually in the executioner's fist and the poor old bugger was staggering about spouting blood but so far looking little more than dazed by his experience – the hangman had been careful not to swing him for more than a few seconds. The brief suspension and the genitals job – these were just the beginnings of the bloody business.

The executioner took hold of Hartley without warning, threw him down on his back, knelt over him with a big blade and slit him open – easy as unsealing a letter. Unseamed him from the nave to the chops. The crowd took in its breath again and the moment of silence was rent by one long loud shriek of pure pain. It tore the air as the knife had torn open the man's body. It seemed to use up all his ability to express his agony because he stayed strangely quiet and unmoving as the hangman's hand came out of the open doors of his belly, holding the bowels, trailing intestines like the locks of the Medusa. In he went for more, pulling it out in red fistfuls. No reaction. Somebody shouted that he must be dead already and the cry was taken up indignantly. He'd botched the job and cut short the fun.

Then as the executioner was reaching up into Hartley's chest to extract his dead heart, the body bucked suddenly as if it had been struck by a thunderbolt. He half sat up and both his arms shot out and grabbed the hangman by the throat. It gave him quite a shock. He fell back and tried to free himself. But Hartley seemed to have summoned up a preternatural energy in his last moments and the hangman had to shout for his assistant to come and tear the priest's hands away from his throat and hold him down while he went back to finish his grisly work. Bind fast his corky arms! They were like two wave-worn and sea-bleached sticks such as your boots might kick at on a dry old beach, sending them flying, sapless and light as air among the buzzing seaweeds and debris of the shore. Hartley had been apparently dead, yet he fought like a man of iron against his executioner, who now reached up again into the chest and took hold of the heart. And Hartley started to sit up a second time and the hangman put a knee on his chest and shouted again to the assistant executioner. He was kneeling behind the old man's head and he pulled back on both arms as hard as he could, to restrain him.

'Oh, stop, my friend, stop! You're hurting me!'

His privates had been sliced off, a red well was still pumping out blood from his groin, his innards stood in a steaming heap beside him on the scaffold, which was awash with blood – yet who would have thought the old man to have had so much blood in him? – and the hangman had his hand inside his chest, clutching his heart, ready to tear it out and put an end to life. All this – and the old man was wailing to the bastard behind him that he was twisting his arms! Somebody was hurting his arms. It would come all right if only he would stop. Do you mind, friend? That hurts, don't you see? Yet this old man, so gruesomely mangled, was just seconds from being a corpse.

Everybody could see from the executioner's face that he had the heart entirely in his grasp. He gave a huge wrench. As he did so Hartley came up again for the third and final time, like a spent swimmer taking his last lungful, so that still the heart didn't quite come out of the chest cavity, but you could hear the sound of the two ancient arms snapping like sticks. The assistant stood up at that point, grabbing him by his long white hair and pulling him back down flat on the scaffold. At the same time he placed his boot right across Hartley's throat and now the executioner's arm came back and shot high and straight in the air. Dripping and twitching at the end of it was what looked like a bag of jellied eels – the tiger heart of old Hartley, from whom there now issued one last long throaty sigh. After which he neither spoke nor moved again. His earthly struggles were over.

A great roar and a last cheer. Hartley had put on a fine show for a frail old priest. Ah, but these Catholics were full of the devil, naturally, and drew on darkness for their strength, Hartley being one of the most obdurate. That afternoon the crowd that had watched him die was still seething around Shoreditch, roaring drunk. They'd stayed on to wait for the Theatre to open.

31

I didn't go to the Theatre myself. I went home instead, sat down among the morning's breadcrumbs and bits of bacon and stared at the wall, two feet from my face. I closed my eyes. I could still see Hartley's insides slopped out on the scaffold beside him, steaming like puddings in a pile. I could see his heart still twitching in the hangman's raised fist. His privities had been thrown off the stage after being plucked from his dead gaping mouth. The dogs devoured them. Then out came the big choppers. They were going to quarter the corpse. Soon it would be a gutted torso, two arms, two legs, a severed head, for distribution, moral exhortation, political instruction, and dire threat.

Right then a huge roar went up from the nearby Theatre. Alleyn had come onstage as Tamburlaine. He was Burbage's for the day – that would change when he married Miss Henslowe. But for the next two hours the Theatre belonged to the scourge of God. Put but money in thy purse, Will, a voice in my head advised me. Any company that puts on your play is a good company, the gob of the groundlings in Finsbury Fields, and the spit turning to silver in Southwark. Put but money in thy purse. Another roar, and a rabble rolled past my window, singing hoarsely. By the sound of them they'd been too drunk even to make it into the performance and were out on the rampage instead. Somebody shouted 'Fuck Tamburlaine!' And somebody else 'Fuck the Papists!' Then the tune changed to 'Fuck the Spaniards!' and the chant was taken up.

The cries grew fainter. I shut my eyes again. It all went round in my head: Tarleton, Hartley, Jackie Vautrollier, Marlowe, Tamburlaine, the Armada, the drunken crowd, fuck the Pope, fuck Parma, long live the Queen! I swept aside the breadcrumbs with my sleeve, dipped a quill into the inkpot and held it over the paper. It didn't drip and I knew this would be a good pen and one without blots. Excellent, i'faith! I knew precisely what I was going to write. The Muse had flashed her garter at me and the urge had struck, sudden and sweet as Marlowe's Elysium, hot as Marlowe's hell. I could feel it like lust. That crowd down there in the street, full of blind energy and leonine pride – it was loose in London and it had no theatre for its will. It needed a stage. It needed to see *itself* up there. It needed a glass and a chronicler of the time. The future was *out there.*

Look out of the window, Will, and what do you see? A kingdom for a stage, princes to act, and monarchs to behold the swelling scene. Look in the streets and write. Look in Holinshed. Read and hear. Fuck Tamburlaine! Fuck the Spaniards! Fuck France! Long live England! England forever. You said it, sirs. The answer to Marlowe was ringing in my ears. It was the noise of the national theatre. It was good old Harry the Sixth, carnage and catastrophe and the country gone to the dogs, led by a crowd of bunglers and butchers, with thousands of brave Englishmen cut down like cattle and gone to their graves like beds. They were still lying out there, under the skies of France, embedded in English clay, just a few generations away. And on this boneyard I would build my big scene.

I scratched out most of *Harry* the following year, when the Spaniards, crushed and incensed by the Armada shambles, were planning another invasion, this time from Brittany. Things couldn't have suited me better. Who was this Tamburlaine anyway? A one-time warlord from Scythia. But what was Scythia compared to English national pride? I saw it in Holinshed and Hall, I heard it in the streets and it unfurled in my head in a flash. I had it in the palm of my closed fist, a hot secret, and I didn't want to miss the moment, the chance to reply to Marlowe, the new-come conjurer from Canterbury, the wizard of the Rose.

I drew the direful pageant of *Harry the Sixth*, a set of pictures to dazzle and entertain, a gallery for the illiterate, and my star went up over London. I'd resurrected the dead, they said. I'd made brave Talbot bleed again. Even Nashe came out on my side, his bitter ink turning to milk and honey. Talbot himself, he said, would have been happy to think that his dry old bones would be embalmed all over again with the patriotic tears of ten thousand cheering spectators.

It was my first taste of praise. It was also the hour of the crowd, time to let it have its say on stage. When Harry Six struck them, the groundlings stared open-mouthed – because what they saw up there on stage was none other than themselves. They were looking into a talking mirror, they heard their own voices echoing on the London air, the cadences of Jack Cade and his tribe. It was the sound of piss-heads in the streets and it was music to their ears.

And that was my first move against the mighty Marlowe, coming out as *The First Part of the Contention betwixt the Two Famous Houses of York and Lancaster.* It struck an unaccustomed hour in the life of the theatre and opened to huge crowds at the Rose on the Bankside, where the takings poured in like golden rain. The late winter of '92 was not a winter of discontent for Philip Henslowe.

But Robert Greene saw *Harry* at the Theatre, which gave him a winter in his spleen. There was more than one winter tale's worth in this, and Greene had an even bigger problem than his spleen. His liver and kidneys had rotted by this time and the rest of his body had followed suit. Greene's been dead and rotten these two dozen years. Be gracious then to a fallen enemy, Will, let him re-live his brief hour of fame, so at last his bitter ghost may quit the stage and leave yours free to speak.

32

Robert Greene, late deceased – and much diseased – in beggary. Six years older than me and dead at thirty-four. A legend in his lifetime and now a dead letter in the alphabet of literary England. More's the pity – he had vim and vigour in his pen, if too much Rhenish in his liver. A sad talent was that of Robert Greene: hell-raiser, hallelujah man, romancer, dramatist, pamphleteer, scholar, wit. Son of a saddler from Norwich, his beginnings were no better than mine, except that he went on to cover himself with degrees from both Oxford and Cambridge and never let himself or the world forget that he was Robert Greene, Master of Arseholes, with honours hung.

After that the rot set in. He began to follow the frettings of his own desires, as early pricks the tree that will prove a thorn. And prick is now the word. Fancied himself as a young Faust figure did Greene, doing a tour of Europe as the devil incarnate. He went off the rails in Italy and in Spain but came back home to hear the so-called Apostle of Norwich, John More, preach so blood-curdlingly about God's Judgement and how the flames of hell would frizzle his wicked willie to a white-hot worm, that he got down on his knees at once and became a new man. That was in St Andrew's church, Norwich. The new man rose to his feet, walked out of its doors, took yet one more degree from Clare Hall just to make certain, and married the virtuous Dorothea, whose patience was above Job's and her price above rubies – her biblical price, that is, not the price of her tail. Not for sale was this Dorothea – no hot whore for the once lascivious Faustus.

Ah, but it wasn't long before the old Adam got back under the skin of the new. He put dear Doll in the pudding club, left her in the lurch in Lincolnshire to beg or starve, and buggered off back to London to look up his old cronies of the bars and brothels, falling again, as he himself put it in that endearingly second-hand way he had of expressing himself, 'with the dog to his old vomit'. Incorrigible? Ah yes, incorrigible and as nasty and intractable as hell makes them. Hear Marlowe on Greene. 'Hang him up by that weird beard of his and he'd turn into the wind of any man's fart to get himself a groat. He'd crawl up the closest arsehole, truffling for excrements. He was a time-pleaser, an anus-appraiser, a rectum-rodder. Low-life was his middle name. Greene? He didn't deserve the name. It speaks of the fields and of the fraternity of the flesh, which is grass.' Thank you, Marlowe. On the other hand it speaks of the green-eyed monster, which is jealousy, that mocks the meat it feeds on. And that is apt to the purpose – because what happened next was that Master of Arts Greene aspired to be a writer.

Aspired indeed, aimed high as ever, but sold his soul too oft for the quick shilling, seldom rising above the shoulders of the greasy grubbing hacks, rubbed by Greene on a daily basis. So to cover the smell of his chosen company he kept a pocketful of posies, a bouquet of real-life cheap morality to season his ridiculous romances. Who did he think he was fooling? He couldn't even gull the groundlings, gormless as they were. They saw through his garbage. He was a seedy Bohemian, ready to waste his time in guttersniping and streetfighting. A churner-out of chapbooks and admonitory addresses, pamphlets about the cony-catchers and whores among whom he lived out his brief dissolute life – and from whom he purported to wish to save the young, the innocent, and the unwary. Excrement. Greene should have stripped his own back. He was a hair-raiser and a hypocrite, determined to wallow in the life-style he pretended to abhor.

And he achieved a fatal fluency, dodging deadlines, dashing off articles to cover the cost of the next quart of ale or bottle of German beer. A freelancer, making free with words on a free scale for a full belly of booze. A piece-worker and a hack, keeping the wolf from the door with increasing lack of success – till one day he felt the fangs clamp shut, fast on his balls. And it was goodbye Greene. But in the meantime give him a pin and he'd write about angels. There was something cheaply but impregnably professional about him, as there is about whores. Blowing the froth of a pint of yours (unreturned, naturally), he'd moralise about the Fall of Man as if he'd invented the whole concept.

But even he had his brief hour. And he dressed for the part. Like a scholar gentleman he swanned around London, cloaking his necessities and bitter existence under a gown with sleeves of a grave goose-turd green. Green? Yes, that was my word, green as goose-turd, though his hair, as long as Absalom's for vanity, was also as red as

Judas's in the Mysteries, emblem of his evil. And he had that beard to match. A famous sight in the city, the beard – a long tapering affair like the inverted spire of a steeple. You could hang a jewel from the extreme tip of it, like a drop of bright piss trembling at the end of a phallus. A vaporous drop, but unprofound. Got up in this fashion, Greene embarked on his writing career.

It began – and ended – with imitation. He did a fair attempt at imitating John Lyly in a stack of prose romances. (Later I quarried his *Pandosto* for *The Winter's Tale.)* He went on to set himself up as a playwright, imitating Marlowe, and achieved a travesty of Tamburlaine – *Alphonsus, King of Aragon*. He then re-wrote *Orlando Furioso* as a play, shamelessly selling it first to the Queen's Men and then to Strange's as soon as the Queen's had left town. A complete swindler too, well qualified to write about the London con-trade. But he captured the capital with *Friar Bacon and Friar Bungay,* bringing in more than twenty shillings a day for Henslowe. That was his hour. Except of course that it belonged as much to Nashe as to Greene, and I've heard it said that when they were collaborating on this one it was Nashe who held the pen while Greene did more of holding the bottle – and holding forth, as was his way, singing encouragement. Nashe said that in one day he pissed as much against the wall as nine men put together could have produced in the same space of time. Still it came out under both their names and gave Greene his long-hungered and half-borrowed moment of triumph.

After that came the waves of repentance pamphlets: *Greenes mourning garment*, *Greenes never too late*, *The Repentance of Robert Greene, Master of Arts*. The titles make you cringe. 'He'd have printed his name and letters on each and every one of his turds if he'd had the art' – Marlowe again – 'and would have counted such ordure sacred to God and Man.' By this time he had much need of repentance, having slid into unrestrained debauchery on a scale well beyond his licentious Italian Englishman period. His plays began to pall and he puked up sour grapes, professing contempt for such an unscholarly arena as the theatre, where his immortal words were made, as he put it, to jet upon the stage in tragical buskins, every word filling the mouth like the faburden of Bow Bell, daring God out of heaven with that atheist Tamburlaine. Where can such genius go but downhill?

So, he pawned his doublet and sword, drifted and shifted among the lowest lodgings and stews of the city, and rioted madly in pubs, known, as they said, in the revelry of taverns and the stink of brothels, becoming a fast favourite with the hostess of *The Red Lattice* in Turnbull Street, and finally taking up with that rotten old tart, Em Ball (once the regular whore of dead Tarleton) who bore him a bastard inaptly named Fortunatus, and whose brother, Cutting Ball, was, as the nickname implies, a notorious thief, destined for death on the Tyburn gibbet. This cutpurse was a cunt of the first class – so Jonson said in his blunt manner, even blunter than Marlowe – but attended Greene as faithfully as the lice that never left him in his last miserable and godforsaken days. He became a sort of bodyguard to him and creditors were scared to come too close for fear of the knife, preferring to serve writs instead. In time even the writ-servers lost their nerve. Greene forced one of them to eat the entire writ, complete with wax seal, while Cutting Ball held his dagger at the man's throat, wishing him *bon appetit* and threatening to slit his gizzard if he left a single scrap.

'Why waste time on such a turd in the teeth?'

Ah, Greene was one of the Wits, the quintessence of Oxford scum, the life-form out of which he grew, the roaring boys of the '80s, drunken, dangerous and wild. Nashe spoke for them. 'We scoff and are jocund' – he said – 'when the sword is ready to go through us. On our wine-benches we bid a Fico for ten thousand plagues.' But it was other plagues that killed them, mostly drink and the pox. Meanwhile they were poets and pamphleteers and they also wrote dramas, lowering themselves to provide for the theatre and sell their arses to Henslowe. How to be a Wit, was the question, and the answer was not hard. Requisites were: a degree from Oxford or Cambridge, a rare degree of envy, a taste for licentious living and early death, and arrant arrogance, with unfeigned contempt for commoners such as Will Shakespeare, especially if they had the temerity to take the bread out of your mouth by writing plays. More of which anon. The best of them apart from Marlowe (too talented to be a Wit) were Nashe and Lodge and Peele.

Nashe was well named, forever grinding his teeth on the emptiness of an unfulfilled talent. It was the same with Peele, George Peele, the English Ovid as some called him, when they weren't calling him frivolous, shiftless, sensual, drunken, dissipated and depraved. Dangerously like Greene again, the product of the London streets and gutters, not forgetting two degrees from Oxford. Filthy complexion, a squinting eye, the voice of a goat, the legs of a tortoise, a swart and stumpy lump of a man, but with lyrics singing in his head. Dead of the pox, poor Peele, picked up in the Clerkenwell stews, dead at forty and buried in Clerkenwell one old autumn afternoon, dead and rotten these twenty years, George Peele. Went whining to Burghley for a back-hander in his last illness, I remember: ten shillings, for the love of Christ, ten shillings to stupefy the *timor mortis* with a stoup of wine and a warm fire. The thick-skinned skinflint Lord Treasurer didn't even send back an answer. Peele died unsuccoured, while Burghley kept on pickling his liver, knocking back the next bottle of Bordeaux. Thinking of Peele now, I recall that poem of his about the old knight, turned from citadels to psalms. His helmet now shall make a hive for bees... In which particular part of this low thing of the gutters were poems spawned? The soul – a beautiful songbird, no matter in what vile nest it may fleetingly lodge.

No pun intended, for once, but speaking of Lodge – well, there was little enough talent lodged there. But little wits sometimes turn out books like *Rosalind*: a neat little story that set me thinking. Out of such sufficiently successful mush sometimes come plays – I scooped from it *As You Like It*. Thanks be to Lodge, then. Another Oxford man, he gave up the law for literature, at which he tried his hand at every conceivable style and strain, with a notable lack of success. To say truth he wasn't that much of a success as a Wit either: he lacked one serious qualification – the ability to die young, unlike Peele and Greene and Nashe and Marlowe. So he gave up being a Wit, tried medicine instead – and it worked. He lives still.

Panic ye not, Master Lodge. Living is not so much of a burden, even if it gets you kicked out of the Wit Club. I didn't belong myself. Never had the class, the charisma, the doctorate. Couldn't compete with all sorts of oddballs living on the fringes or in God's red-hot forge: mad Jack Donne, iconoclast Marlowe, duelling Jonson, or all those threadbare geniuses with their heads in the spires, in the Cambridge clouds, and for whom Oxford ordure was holy ground. Well-lettered down-and-outers. I was not of their element, keeping my head down, avoiding invitations, inventing excuses, and digesting my food sensibly, staying sensible and sane, refusing to kill myself with them, just as I'd refused to join the militant martyrs in their glorious deaths. Could have gone the way of Campion, could have gone the way of the Wits. But I had a revenge task to perform, to wrest back from fate what my father had lost. So I kept my eyes on the malleable mob with its shifting but eternal needs. I accepted their ready pennies, the gift of their praise. I was the man of their hour. I did not fear the Greeks.

The Wits hated men like me. Gossips and snobs, they were wolves in their academic sheepskin, which they wore like livery, though their Oxford and Cambridge degrees did them little good in the end. Nashe called me an excrementory dishlicker of learning, a Turkish target for the spit of the crowd in Finsbury Fields, in exchange for their vile trash. I was a shit-shifter, a base player, a vassal actor, a butcher and tradester, a Warwickshire clown. All that abuse. And this was the sullen brew on the floating scum of which Robert Greene was the bitterest bubble. Nobody hated me like Greene.

33

Greene's hatred had little to do with me – it was just part of the man and his bad-luck venture with life.

A born failure, such men as he be never at heart's ease whiles they behold a greater than themselves, and therefore are they very dangerous.

And in Greene's case he beheld every clerk with a quill in London as better than himself. But he fastened on me as the final victim on whom he would now empty all the concocted vials of his wrath. I say concocted because he had put it about among all those who cared to listen, that he, Robert Greene M.A., was the co-author of *Harry the Sixth* and that he'd been bought off to the tune of a few paltry pence, earning the quintessence of nothing from the huge takings that had so far been raked in. He'd been used and dumped – what else would you expect from a country con-man whose father was an usurer? That was his story and he may even have made himself believe it.

The truth was that he did have a hand in it – and he wasn't the only one. But if he did half a scene's worth of passable scripting, it ended there. Greene's writing hand was oftener busy on some rival project of his own, while the other was always in your pocket, scrabbling for an advance. He was an insult to trees and geese, even Winchester geese. I paid him off and re-drafted his scenes. He had no complaints at the time. Then when *Harry* became a hit, faring much better than his own plays at the Rose, Greene was all of a sudden a dropped co-author, unpaid collaborator, chronicler of genius, victim of my quill-filled envy, my fear of his fearful talent. That was the story that went the rounds of the taverns and was even dramatised extempore in Eastcheap. Nobody paid it much notice – they'd heard it all before. But Greene himself gave it his undivided attention and worked himself up into a jealous fury. On top of all of which, it cut deep with him that until quite recently he'd been principal writer for the Queen's and now they'd been seen off the stage by Strange's men whom I was with at the time. Fate was arsing him up again, using every arsehole from Stratford or wherever. Who'd be Robert Greene? Alas.

So he got roaring drunk on Rhenish wine with Nashe and gorged himself on pickled herring. That was his last big fling. His rotting, marinated carcass started to swell up with the dropsy as a hot dry summer hit the filthy city, and all the players just fucked off (as he put it) and stranded him among the turds and muck-middens they'd sweetly left behind. That was their gratitude for his genius. They'd lined their pockets with the money they'd made on his plays and now they'd gone off to fleece the rustics and rude mechanicals of the provinces, wringing what vile trash they could from their hard hands, while he stared starvation in the face. It was monstrous.

A couple of poor fools took him in. There was a shoemaker called Isam who had a shop in the Dowgate and he and his wife opened their hearts and their doors not only to the dying genius but to the genius's decayed whore, their bastard brawling brat, Fortunatus, so cruelly named, and also to the decayed whore's ruffian brother, Cutting Ball himself. Quite a happy family. And there, festering above the Dowgate, among fleas and vermin, the genius composed his shrill, self-pitying swansong. It was called – are you ready for this? – *A Groatsworth of Wit, bought with a million of Repentance. Describing the folly of youth, the falsehood of makeshift flatterers, the misery of the negligent, and mischiefs of deceiving Courtesans. Written before his death and published at his dying request.* These are the full works, Greene-style, known familiarly as *Greenes Groatsworth.*

It concerns – whom do you think, Francis? – one Roberto, the son of a greedy usurer. A picaro and a prodigal, a bookish lad who is left a solitary coin with which to buy himself a groatsworth of wit. He gets his rich brother tangled up with a whore and is kicked out to starve. Woe is he. Lamenting his lot, he comes across – wait for it, Will! – a common player from the country, a bumpkin with a thick provincial accent. The subtlety astonished me. But Roberto was also astonished – that such a clodhopper should be so successful on stage, and so Roberto decides to tread the boards himself and makes quite a thing of it, becoming gruesomely rich. But in the end money's not everything (an interesting philosophy, coming from Greene), it's a lackey's life and Roberto resolves that he should be above it. He throws it all up, falls in with a lewd crowd, and loses the lot, his whole fortune, except for this one solitary groat. How are the mighty fallen!

How indeed. Roberto, poet and dramatist of genius, despised

and neglected of authors, most misunderstood of men, down on his luck and supine in gutterland. He looks up and sees the stars scattered about the sky like silver groats, a million of them. Roberto has only one in his pocket. But a poet with a star in his pocket – why man, what can he not achieve? Not an inapt argument from Roberto's creator, who never had any golden words to spend, but this silver one will serve wherewith to purchase his million of repentance, Greene who swanned about the city eavesdropping on his own authorship, and had a lonely listening too.

And now comes his moment, the one he can't resist. The author stands up and cries out from the page, casting off the cloak, confessing with sudden loudness – and no surprise! – that his own life has been just like Roberto's, in much more than name, and he seizes this opportunity to warn his old cronies, Nashe and Marlowe and Peele, fellow *scholars* about this city, against the hated race of players, who pay talented playwrights a mere pittance and grow fat on their genius, one of them in particular even having the nerve to imitate his betters by writing his own plays. And a great pity it is that men of rare wits should be subject to the pleasure of such rude grooms.

'Trust them not,' (he says), 'for there is an upstart crow, beautified with our feathers' – 'beautified' is a vile phrase – 'that with his tiger's heart wrapped in a player's hide, supposes he is as well able to bombast out a blank verse as the best of you: and being an absolute *Johannes factotum*, is in his own conceit the only Shakescene in a country. O that I might entreat your rare wits to be employed in more profitable courses: and let those Apes imitate your past excellence, and never more acquaint them with your admired inventions. I know the best husband of you will never prove an Usurer...'

'Your first public notice, Will.'

Very pointed, you may say – glad you're still listening, Francis – and the point envenomed too. A grammar school upstart, a parvenu with thick provincial speech and ungainly country manners, like the crows in Macrobius and Martial and old Aesop, conceited and vain. Or like the one in Horace, a plagiarist and a thief. A commoner, a tradesman, Jack of all and master of none – and not a Master of Arts for sure. An opportunist with ideas above his station, an actor-turned-dramatist, too big for his buskins. Able to scribble plays for the companies he's working for, and killing literature by killing the Wits – the poor abused Wits who depend for their commissions on such scum of players. And those amount to something short of nothing.

'Is it really you, Will?'

Yes, it's me and my kind. My acting cronies and myself, pinch-fists and muckworms that we are, pay these literary giants their miserable pittance, and while they starve, we rude grooms (is that the phrase?) catch all the credit for mouthing the fine lines that emanate from their inspired minds. To crown it all, an ignorant oaf, a thick privy seat such as myself has not only had the effrontery to compete as a dramatist with his academic betters but seems to be better at it to boot. This above all: I'm a cruel and ungrateful colleague, a vicious rascal masquerading as a harmless country boy and humble player. The truth is, I'm the very devil got up on stage. I'm a tiger in disguise.

'Ah, he stabbed you with your own line!'

Harry was not even in print when Greene wrote this, but all three parts had been staged and you may suppose that Greene had a good ear and remembered well when he parodied the line about the tiger's heart. Well, you would suppose wrong, Francis. He didn't. It was one of the few lines Greene actually wrote himself in his capacity as so-called co-author, and one of that even rarer scattering of lines, the favoured few that I let remain in the script. No wonder he remembered it and flung it back in my face, together with the veiled hint that I'd refused him financial help. But lest you miss the point of the allusion, Francis, he went on from there to make sure of it, with a concluding allegory about a grasshopper and an ant.

'A tale within a tale.'

A poor starving grasshopper (think now who that might be) asks a busy ant for assistance as winter begins to bite, and the ant answers him that he should find his own food, 'for toiling labour hates an idle guest.' And now Greene *did* remember well exactly what I'd said to him when he last came to beg. Go to the ant, thou sluggard, and be wise, I told him. He had gone to the ant – and the ant had refused him out of the cruelty of its nature, possessing the spirit of a 'waspish little worm'.

A waspish little worm, that was me. The ant, prudent and thrifty rather than inspired, seems to be gloating over the grasshopper's plight. Yet it's the dying grasshopper that is the real genius. Leaping geniuses, you see, take no account of the coming winter – their thoughts are far above the fields and the loamy affairs of anthood. Ants may live longer, plodders as they are, but they will never see what has been seen on his higher flights by grasshopping Greene, who now takes his last farewell of his public and of his life.

'A good hatchet job – it must have made him feel better.'

Perhaps not. You spit poison and the taste stays in the mouth – bitterness at the thought that all those Oxford degrees and the graces and favours had failed to win the groundlings, while a social cipher didn't even have to learn to speak their language. Greene's trouble was not the lack of genius, he too lacked the common touch. And to rub salt in his wounds he was dying in the most awful squalor. His end was shitty – which unwiped lay upon his deathbed sheets, quipped the callous Marlowe, cackling falsetto – and his death was equally excremental.

'I wouldn't have cared to see either of them.'

Return you nonetheless to that lice-laden shoemaker's house in the Dowgate, where he lay abandoned by every one of his friends, attended only by an entourage of insects. His body, growing grosser by the hour, was crawling with them, and death was less than a month away, so he scratched furiously – not just at his rotting flesh but at his *Groatsworth*. It was all he had left. Even his stockings had been sold, together with the cloak and sword. His enemies sneered and cheered in their drinking circles and some of the sneers found their way into print.

A rakehell, a makeshift, a scribbling fool,
A famous bayard in city and school,
Now sick as a dog and ever brainsick,
Where such a raving and desperate Dick?

There were prayers, confessions, tears, scribbled letters, a world of sighs. And another of pain. All precursors to the much-feared next world, an uncertain venture for such a scapegrace. After the *Groatsworth* was completed he scribbled off his last letter – to his long-suffering, long-abandoned wife Dorothea (she whose price was above rubies) begging for her forgiveness. Oh – and tapping her for ten pounds, by the way, to pay his hosts, the Isams. 'For if they had not succoured me I had died in the streets.'

'Just couldn't help his nature, could he?'

Even on his death bed. Of your charity, dear Doll, and remembering all our former love, send the money for the love of God.

After that he cried out for a penny-pot of malmsey wine, so the story went about, starting from his tear-blubbered hostess. He may even have babbled of green fields for all I know. Then he went as cold as any stone, and the grasshopper out in the fields fell silent. Only the letters were left after his name. His hostess, following his pathetic last request, crowned the dead head with a garland of laurels, a tributary funeral wreath for a would-be poet. So the stricken scribbler lay for a day in death, lay in state above a vile shoemaker's shop – Marlowe laughed at that – wearing the laurels that life, the bitch, had denied him, and which only an illiterate idiot could have awarded him: the cherished bays he grudged to see decorating any other brows than his own. A sham king wearing his paper crown. Death had come at last and bored through his castle walls. A pin was all it took. And that long red flame of a beard frozen and gone out.

It was the third day of September, '92. They took him out and buried him in Moorfields, close to the madhouse, the Bethlehem Hospital – to its hellish requiem become a clod.

As soon as the bloated body began to stiffen and grow cold, the vultures gathered: Burby and Chettle and Wright. Chettle, the bastard, smelling scandal, was first out with the *Groatsworth*. Greene hadn't even been three weeks gone when it arrived on the bookstalls and everyone got the point, or so they thought. The genius was in his grave, the usual place for genius, all too familiar. The upstart crow was puffing up his ugly feathers and coining it in, courtesy of *Harry*, a play touched by the talent of the swindled Wit himself. And Henslowe wanted another Shakescene out of it for the *Rose* later in the year. The following month Ned Alleyn married Henslowe's daughter and there was yet another common player feathering his nest while genuine genius lay low. Meanwhile Tiger Will hadn't even had the common charity, had he, to save a fellow writer (and a greater writer) from starvation and the grave? A lousy lubber and a skinflint too. Whereas if truth were known, I'd slipped Greene a groat too many, till I then grew wise to him, in our brief partnership.

Not brief enough. I went straight to Chettle and protested, menacing him with a powerful friend and the feel of a fist round his genitals. These were damaging accusations. Greene had been a sick man – let's be charitable – when he penned them and Chettle ought to have taken account of this when he went to press. The grasshopper himself might even have toned down his chirping had he lived to see his last piece go through. Might even have refrained from publication in the end, who knows? And he was well known for his literary chicanery and playing the neglected genius. Speak ill of the dead, but what was he after all but an attitudinizing ass? And an arsehole to boot – added the powerful friend.

Chettle took the point, smiled wincingly when the pressure came off his own, and printed a handsome apology. Greene's rantings had been largely libellous and ought to have been edited. The upstart crow was in fact a good citizen and a talented and genuine writer: upright in his actions, honest in his dealings, civil in his demeanour, urbane in his art – and with a ball-crushing grip.

'I scarcely recognized you.'

I didn't recognise myself. Is that really me? Only the angels see that far into a man.

Still, all this was more than good enough at the time, though a memorial volume for Greene, published the following year, wrote of those who eclipsed his fame and purloined his plumes. And if the familiar feathers image wasn't a dark enough hint, a passing play of that same year satirised a certain Stratford sparrow, a lecherous bird of Venus and a cock of the game who had left his wife in the lurch.

But that came later. In '92 it was reputation saved and hurt pride salved. Henslowe put on *Harry* in December in front of the biggest crowds ever to keep coming back howling for more. The takings burst the box. Alleyn was ecstatic. By that time Robert Greene was busy fertilising Moorfields. If his dead ears had been capable of hearing they'd have caught the huge roars and rounds of applause rising up from the Rose and wafting over the Thames all the way to Moorfields and the Bedlam, making him writhe in his grave, drowning out the screams of the criminally insane.

34

'Do you know what goes into a great pie, Will?'

I feel you're going to tell me.

'Why not foretaste the pleasure, eh? It can't be that much longer now.'

Never took much interest in food myself, never really had the time, always eating on the hoof, never noticing what it was I was bolting down.

'You'd have noticed a great pie all right.'

Francis lay back down on the truckle-bed, closed his eyes, folded his fat fingers together across his vast paunch, and smiled dreamily.

'Let me whet your appetite.'

I have none.

'Apparently I'm to work on you. Doctor's orders. Now here goes. Into a great pie goes a piece of fair young beef and the suet of a nice fat one, though mutton will do just as well, and for my money it's even nicer. It'll be all minced up with onions and salt and pepper and prunes and dates, and put into an enormous pastry coffin.'

They'll need a big coffin when your time comes, Francis, but I'd rather you change that subject.

'Ah, of course. Well, that's only the start. After the coffin – saving your presence – heaven's the limit. You can take capons, mallards, woodcocks – I don't like pork myself, not in a great pie – and add all manner of spices, cinnamon, saffron, thyme and cloves, and more fruits too, currants and raisins and plums. Just picture all that in layers, piled a good foot high, and then the lid placed on the coffin – '

Francis.

'I cry you mercy. Cover the whole thing with good thick slitted pastry, glazed with eggs – and there's a feast fit for a king.'

But not for a dying man.

'The Halls are coming later. And so is Tom Russell. And there is Mistress Anne, of course, though she eats like a mouse.'

More like a shrew.

'And then there's me.'

Ah, say no more.

'Will you get up for it, Will?'

I'll see – when it comes.

Francis worked his mouth – a surprisingly small gateway to gluttony, for such a massive moon-faced man – and behind shut smiling eyes he said, 'I see swans gliding gracefully on pastry seas, all ready for roasting. Roast swan – to give it that indefinably noble touch.'

You're fantasising again, Francis. It'll be chicken and beef at the most – and a stray sparrow if you're lucky.

'Even a sparrow is welcome fare – with just a touch of saffron, boiled in wine.'

They say it keeps the moths away – and keeps your pistol's cock up too.

'Well, they say all sorts of things.'

Leeks and onions added, Francis, to provoke your procreative powers, though that's a fantasy, I'm sure, sprung from their shape.

'What's that?'

A leek and two onions – cock and balls.

'I'm as manly as the next man, Will, but I don't mix my pleasures, if you'll be so kind. When I see leeks and onions it's my belly I mind, not my softer parts.'

Yes indeed, softer parts, hard to say goodbye. It's strange, though, isn't it? I'm islanded in bed, a dying man, a month to go, less or more, it's no great matter. The floors are seas I can't cross, the walls are borders, the rooms beyond – other continents. I used to know them well but they've become strange lands I never visit, not any more. And drifting in and out of my island port are folk like Francis, from the everyday world that now seems strange. I yearn to wear their clothes, so tangibly simple, as I inhabit my shroud, laid out as I am on my winding-sheet. And this incessant talk of food. With Francis, of course, it's a passion. But they're all worrying and chattering about it, the daily bread of existence that I'm slowly leaving behind, letting it go.

'Well at least he didn't actually starve to death,' Francis suddenly said.

Starve? Who?

'Greene.'

Oh, Greene. No he didn't starve. And it could have been a lot worse than it was, with the pest well on the go. Plague was the roaring requiem and backdrop to Greene's exit from the world's stage, and the bell that tolled for Greene in the autumn of '92 tolled for ten thousand more between the next two Christmases: a vast mass of London flesh just plucked into the dark.

Yes, it was back. After decades of lurking in the dark, it returned with catastrophically ironic timing, on Midsummer's Day, at the height of human happiness.

'Inconsiderate.'

Unpredictable, Francis, like falling in love. Yes, even so quickly. You could be administering the sacrament, committing a murder, doing the very deed of darkness. And you could be ill before your prick was dry and the sweat grown cold on your balls. *Voilà*. One moment you're living your life, minding your own business, your hand in your purse or crutch, or someone else's, the next your world is smashed sideways by a force you can't even begin to understand. That's the two things about the plague that struck folk, apart from the pain: its speed and its complete absence of logic. It couldn't be rationalised or even imagined, except as God's ultimate arrow: accurate, afflictive, agonising, deadly – and, of course, divine: nippy as an angel on the wing, the angel of bloody death. Bloody is the word, Francis. You're just a slip of Warwick, too young to know. Do you want the symptoms?

'I want you to shut up. And I want my pie.'

It started innocuously enough. A-tishoo. Dear me, I must be coming down with something. Better wrap up... Three days later (four if you were unlucky) you'd be dead. But not before you'd been placed on a rack worse than anything even snow-blooded Exeter could have invented. Because, standing at the head of this particular bed of prostration, there was no rackmaster, nobody you could turn to and ask to lessen the pain, just a little, for a few minutes' respite, please, no kindly torturer, no-one, just that awful invisible adversary. You never saw who was actually turning the screws.

After the sneeze you could go one of two ways: the way of ice or the way of fire. If you experienced a sharp and sudden drop in temperature then you knew which route you were taking. On the way your lungs would fill up with bloody fluids which would find their exits when you coughed and sneezed or even talked, bloody syllables bubbling on your lips as you lay and shivered in thrilling regions of thick-ribbed ice: the road chosen for you by God. If you tried to rise and walk about to get warm, your limbs refused to obey your brain, behaving crazily, till eventually you fell into a chill stillness, out of which you never came.

'Never?'

Never.

If on the other hand the fever took you, then you were burned alive – convulsions, dizziness, delirium, stupefaction, shivering sweats – and vomiting blood from a carcass racked with agony from the hard and suppurating buboes, swellings the size of eggs and apples that lodged anywhere in the body but especially in armpits and groin – soft cradles for such rough and biting babies. When these buboes sweated and burst, the evil pus that spouted from them smelled worse than hell.

Sometimes the routes ran parallel and if your plague symptoms combined the two then you knew that you really were one of the chosen few, twice favoured by God. Because the plague, was actually seen by some as a blessing, not a curse: an affliction that placed you, like a leper, in a special relationship to the Almighty. You'd been smitten, singled out. The divine stroke had landed on *you*. That was something you could at least think about as you lay and suffered your double symptoms: the seas of sweat, the seas of ice, engulfing the agonized anatomy, the throat a desert, the lungs like icebergs, melting in hot blood, all your smooth skin a vile and loathsome crust, most lazarlike, the buboes blowing up under your arms, rivalling your balls in sensitivity and size, hammers in the head, skewers in the back, dreams and delirium in the fevered brain, floundering, drowning, raving, rotting – and all ending one way, from that first innocent sneeze to the final hectic welter of blood and puke or the dark door of the coma. Of the thousand natural shocks that flesh is heir to, Francis, none was more terrible than the plague. Could anything be worse?

'I'd have to answer no.'

You'd have to answer yes, much worse. The symptoms themselves were superficial, physical pain, nothing more – the ultimate horrors went deeper still, to the core of a humanity gone unbelievably rotten. People simply abandoned one another, terrified out of their minds by the fear of contagion.

The virulence was a fact, fabled from the fireside. The Stratford outbreak in the year I was born had revived the inherited memories of Granny Arden, who passed them on to me with grim relish, the stories of how the Black Death had first appeared.

'It was in the October of 1347 that a convoy of twelve Genoese galleys from the Crimea came limping into the straits of Messina, steered by dying men...'

She was off. And with such particularity and precision that the thing unrolled in front of me like one of the painted cloths.

'These sailors carried in their bones a disease so deadly that anyone who only spoke to them was seized by the terrible illness and couldn't escape death. Even those who merely looked at them were doomed...'

So spoke the chroniclers. So quavered Granny Arden.

Oh yes, I knew the stories all right. And when the plague attacked London in '92 I saw for myself that they were true.

Human beings were deserted by those closest to them, and the bonds of blood and the knots of the heart were snapped and unravelled. Wife left husband, brother left sister, parent left child. A mother ran from the cries of her own babies. Corpses piled up on the streets, shops were unkept, doors stood open, shutters swinging in the wind, criminals afraid to rob the dead and dying, though all they had to do was walk in and help themselves. Gravediggers grew rich quick – and sometimes died faster. Worse, priests walked out on their parishioners, overcome by mortal terror in spite of their immortal calling, refusing to attend deathbeds and administer the last rites to solace stricken souls. They went instead with the Levites. So the dying were ditched by friends and loved ones, and even by God – a terrible spectacle. And a frightening thing it was to die alone, utterly bereft of some word of comfort, some little touch of humanity in the night, a cup of water, a gentle tear, the squeeze of a hand, the last longing lingering look of farewell. There were stories of people sewing themselves up in their shrouds at the least sign of a shiver or a sneeze, accepting the inevitable. Or they rushed to the graveyards, screaming mad with pain, scooped out rough graves and, to the astonishment of the gravediggers, heaped the earth over themselves with dying hands – anything to avoid the ignominy of burial in unconsecrated ground and the fear of the eternal flame. Did such things really happen, Francis, in the last decade of the queen's reign? You only had to hear it to believe it. You saw plenty else with your own horrified eyes.

All the other refugees on the road, for example – it wasn't just the actors who fucked off to the provinces, to stamp around on boards and barrel-heads to the tune of an old cracked trumpet. People left London like rats from a house on fire, people shouldering sacks, struggling with chests, carrying purses bulging with money – bribes for their lives. You could hear their saddlebags chiming as they galloped past. If there had been any monasteries left they'd have thrown the bags over the walls – and the monks would have lobbed them back again, caring neither for the lucre nor for the filthy sinners who wanted shot of its contagion. In '92 the fear of infection was the beginning of wisdom. *Radix malorum est cupiditas.* And so, leaving behind Greene and a disintegrating city, the well-heeled passed us on the roads, making for the villages.

They might have saved themselves the trouble. Nobody wanted them for all their wealth, not even in their barns and hovels, for fear of the visitation. One poor rich bugger, begging for shelter, stood outside a pigsty all night, asking to be allowed at least to lie down with the occupants. He quoted scripture. 'Even the Prodigal Son,' he pleaded, 'lay down with the swine and ate their leavings, and God saved him in the end.' But the yokels kept the rich nob at pitchforks' length and, considering the wind of him, resorted to stones. 'The Prodigal Son wasn't carrying the fucking plague in his bowels, friend! We don't want our pigs infected, to pass it on to us! So you can take your prodigal arse out of here and back to fucking London!'

There are few times in the history of the world when money loses its power to persuade and to corrupt, and to blind men to the fear of death. This was one of them. So some rich buggers died on the skirts of villages where every single door stood shut and barred against them, and their corpses lay rotting in the sun, laden with maggots and silver. They might as well have been dead dogs in ditches, spurned by the very rats. Some of the bodies were wind-picked bones before anybody ventured near enough to take the trash from their pockets. But there were others who wouldn't even pick out the gold pieces that winked and glittered among the ribs, glinting in the sun. They believed the disease to be malignant enough to remain alive even in bleached bones and barren metal. And besides, the money was blood-money of a kind, and the place where it lay a potter's field.

Back in London, four days after Greene died, the City Council issued its first plague order for years. On account of the pestilence all performances were forbidden until further notice. Back on the road! Keep your players' hides hidden—and at least seven miles from the city.

Well, Francis, I wasn't going to stay away and let *Greenes Groatsworth* ruin my reputation, plague or no plague. The time was out of joint and I made sure I would set it right. That's when I came *back* to London, aiming for Chettle's testicles, and saw the city sights for myself.

'You went back, you asshead! I never cast you as a death-wisher.'

Apocalypse on show everywhere and admission free for anyone that had the brainlessness or the balls to attend. And so the powerful play went on, with real live actors, and plenty of dead ones too, jostling for the parts. Who needed theatres?

It was still raining when I arrived, God's great arrows raining down hard. I'd travelled all day and it was dark by the time I came through Newgate. All the way along Cheapside and Lombard Street and up Gracious Street to Bishopsgate and Shoreditch the burial parties were out with their torches and barrows. They scarcely needed the torches. There were fires everywhere and tar barrels burning at every corner, purging the air of pestilence – so they said, though the stench was like hell on a bad day, with the bloodshot columns of smoke blotting out the stars. 'Bring out your dead,' they bellowed, stopping their barrows at the doors daubed with red crosses and inscribed with the desperate words slashed in scarlet, *Lord have mercy upon us*! The bodies were put out for collection, some naked, still barely cold, and in some cases horribly disfigured, as though the buboes had crashed on them like black bombs, spattering the flesh from crown to toe, like old Job in the ash-pit. 'No more stews for you, friend, your days are numbered! And you in there – bring out your dead! Bring out your dead!' Cries that were accompanied by the dreadful tolling of bells.

But there were plenty who didn't bring out their dead, and watchers were employed to identify those suspected of infection or of harbouring an infected family. It was understandable. People didn't want their goods destroyed, they didn't want their houses shut up, didn't want to be quarantined, incarcerated, to be sealed in like the living dead. They didn't want their dearly beloved departed consigned to the ignominy of mass burial – a mother, a sister, a baby, humiliated along with hundreds of others, hurled into the pits to land horribly spread-eagled on a mountain of anonymous corpses, many of them naked and unwound. And so they tried to smuggle out the deceased by night and negligence, to bury their own dead, to corrupt the lurking watchers with huge sums to look the other way. The plague had become a kind of crime, the worst in the book. Thieves and murderers were small fry now.

Some of the sufferers, anxious to spare their families these horrors, took their own lives, ran to the river and hurled themselves cursing to their deaths. Some made little fuss over it. They walked up to the water, slipped softly in at the edge, just like Kate Hamlet, pulled the cool Thames quietly over their festering bodies, and said goodnight, quenching the fires of plague while fearing the fires of hell that now awaited them, suicides as they were. The flames of the disease raged through a man's body for three or four days at most – nothing compared to the lake of fire that burns forever. And yet such was the unbearable torment that people put an end to it there and then, unable to exist an hour longer on the miserable island that life had become for them, this bitter little bank and shoal. The fires of damnation had suddenly become preferable to those of the plague. Would Master Ridley have agreed, I wonder, burning in his fire outside Balliol? Or what would Dives have thought, watching from hell as they tore the clothes from their pain-racked frames and rushed to the riverbanks to die by flood, allowing their howling mouths to drown in silence on the cool and comfort of the river bed, down in the beautiful darkness, away from the shrieking, festering city? What would Dives have given for one drop of that precious water? Sweet Thames run softly.

Others were far less selfless. Sickening and dying, they leaned out of their windows and breathed into the faces of innocent pedestrians, spitting into the streets in the fury of their hearts. Or they threw their plague-plasters into the windows of healthy and wealthy homes. 'Here you are, you fuckers! Try these on for size! Why should you be spared? Have a gobful of bloody sputum! You can come to hell with us for company!' And the rich ran screaming from the sight of the cast linens splattered on their floors and festering in the streets, larded with suppurations and burst blood.

'Fucking hell!'

Oh, come on Francis, you can see why some were driven to it. It's human nature to seek out companions in misery, especially the rich and favoured ones – to want to ram the silver spoons right up their pampered arses. But there was something else too: the feeling that God had let them down, in spite of Lazarus, so-called levelling death preferring to huddle down not in princes' palaces but in poor men's cottages and the rat-infested slums. That's where the buboes bred best, there and in the bear-pits and brothels of Clerkenwell and Southwark and Shoreditch, the sinfully polluted suburbs.

And in the theatres, of course, death held court and pitched his tents, taking off the poor rather than the rich, in terrifying numbers. Worst of all was the lot of the prisoners, starving in the jails. Jack Donne's brother Henry ran into King Death in Newgate, where he was waiting to be tried on a charge of harbouring a priest. The plague took him apart, saving Tyburn the trouble. Hangmen grumbled that they were losing out on fees while the gravediggers were laughing all the way to the Rialto – those who didn't handle one plague-batch too many, that is.

There were few perks of the plague, and they were gruesome enough wages at that. Nurses robbed the dying of their last blankets and proved to be cunning murderers if a fat-pursed patient showed any alarming signs of recovery. Masons paid nothing for hair to mix their lime, nor glovers to stuff their balls with, not a penny, for they had it for nothing, it simply dropped off men's heads and beards faster than an army of barber-surgeons could have shaved it. The ground was adrift and it lay like snow. If hair breeches had been in fashion, they said, what a world it would have been for tailors. My father would have made a fortune. But few thought along these lines. Preserving life at all costs was more precious than the usual pursuits of money and power.

Charlatans flourished. The streets were leprous with them. And their purses hung from their belts like bulls' balls, though any of them seriously trying to combat the plague were pissing into the wind. But the drowning man will clutch at the straw, and a man drowning in his own blood in a city paralysed by fear will grab whatever comes his way even if the most clapped-out quack in Christendom slaps it down on the table as a cure for the incurable.

'How do you cure the incurable?'

Rosemary and onions, wormwood and lemons, vinegar and cloves, arsenic and mercury, held to the buboes to draw away the poison; tobacco and dried toads, smoked together; the inevitable white wine and henshit; sherry and gunpowder and salad oil concocted; aristolochia longa and celandine boiled together and strained through a cloth with a dram of the best mithridate and the same of ivory finely powdered, together with six spoonfuls of dragon-water, to be drunk each morning; the dried root of angelica, chewed or sniffed on the dried end of a ship-rope; plasters of egg yolk, honey, and herb-of-grace chopped small; hot bricks laid to the soles of the feet; even a live pullet held squawking against the sores and swellings till the venom entered the sacrificial bird and it died. Some doctors sliced the bird in two and clapped the bleeding sections, still twitching, to the suppurations.

'Horrible – and your son-in-law a physician too!'

And the ultimate cure, on which the swindling knaves grew fat: the horn of the unicorn grated and boiled in wine to hot-rinse the mouth. Or ground to a powder so fine it would cause a violent sweat and expel the plague poison at fever pitch. Where did the unicorns come from? The quacks were busy grating their own toenails, it was said, and passing it off as the sacred powder. All that was ever expelled by these bastards was the tortured life of the victim, poured out in a torrent of vomit and blood.

'Not a Dr Hall cure, that one?'

There was no *cure* for the plague. Catch the pestilence and thou art slain. No medicine in the world will do thee good. Not poppy, nor mandragora, nor all the drowsy syrups of the world shall ever medicine thee to that sweet sleep which thou hadst yesterday. And the dreams you endured instead burned like the mines of sulphur.

'Sweet dreams for me in Warwick – a nice safe neck of the woods.'

Nor was there explanation. What was the mysterious cause and purpose of it? Find out that and you could perhaps discover the ultimate prevention. Was it in the stars or in the air? Was it bred in dunghills or in brothels? Harboured by cats and dogs and pigs? Spread by the harlots? By the barbers who let blood in the streets, or by the pudding-wives and sellers of tripe who slurped their slops into the gutters meant for cleansing? Or by the slaughterers who let their bloody shambles run everywhere? All were culpable. The Corporation ordered them to contain their crap and carry it in tubs to the Thames, where it could safely be poured in – so that we could then drink it! Every day of our shortened lives!

'I'll never visit London again!'

Or it was the theatres to blame, the cause of plague being plays. It was always possible. The playhouses closed like daisies in the dark. And we poor fools melted into the wind. Nothing briefer than the breath of actors. Pembroke's Men had to pawn their costumes. The once proud Queen's Men degenerated into a tag-rag gaggle of broken down bumpkins, touring the sticks. Only ourselves and the Admiral's survived.

Ned Alleyn travelled to Newcastle, begging his new wife still in London to take what precautions she could for their family against the invisible enemy at the gates – on the walls, up the alleys, in the thatch, wherever it lay. But he wanted Joan to be a busy little mouse while he was in the country, throwing water before her door every night and having in her windows good store of rue and herb of grace. He also asked that the September parsley bed be sown with spinach. 'And I pray you, Jug, let my orange-tawny stockings of woollen be dyed a very good black against I come home, to wear in the winter.' That's what he wrote. She showed me the letter, since he wrote to a wife who could not read. Life goes on, in other words. Or at least you try to pretend that it does. Henslowe saw to the spinach. And I noticed the black stockings standing out against the snow that winter. It was the only black he needed. They all survived.

Robert Browne's family didn't. One time of Worcester's Men, he trod the boards at Frankfurt in the summer of '93 leaving them in the long slow malignant heat of Shoreditch. When he came back home not one of them remained. Wife, children, servants, all that could be found – the plague had raged through the whole household like a summer fire, executing every one, to a girl, to a boy, to a babe. Browne was inconsolable. I was in the Boar's Head with Dick Burbage and Austin Philips when he came through the door, white-faced and breathless from the empty house he'd just visited and not even a neighbour left to say him a single word of them.

What, all my pretty chickens and their dam at one fell swoop? Did you say all? O hell-kite, all? Did heaven look on and would not take their part? And I must be from thence...

And he pulled his hat over his brows after that and couldn't speak. I never saw such pain in a face and was glad when he hid it. But his silence was even worse.

Give sorrow words, we urged him. The grief that will not speak whispers the o'er-fraught heart and bids it break.

Browne did speak again, though. In time he asked another lady to marry him and she did, and he fathered another brood of chickens, all of them pretty. As I said, Francis, life goes on. Through the pain, life goes on. Not in plays perhaps, where a man has to take the classic stance, make the grand tragic gesture.

Life, if I lose thee, I lose a thing that none but fools would keep.

Here breasts are for beating, not feeling, clothes are for rending, not taking off, and hair is made of ash. If the maidens sit with gold combs in their locks, their lovers are sure to be drowned. In the world of the play a man weeps for Hecuba whom he never even knew. Did she ever even exist? Maybe not, but her tears do, and she weeps like Niobe. But in the real world life goes on, because we all have to die and we all want to live while we're waiting.

'It's natural.'

It's inevitable, like the plague itself. As it tore on through '93 and into '94 our world fell apart. Life had proved stronger than art after all. We were scattered like sheep before the wolf. You can picture me on the Italian waterways Francis. Or you can find me in Bath, up to my neck in salubrity. Or in Stratford for that matter, up to my balls in Anne Hathaway. You'd be wrong on that score. No more children from that coupling, though it hadn't been for want of trying again. And again. Eventually we stopped trying – and in time there seemed no reason left to couple at all.

'Better than life in a plague town.'

Though for all its horrors London was the place I'd rather be. The very danger made you feel more intensely alive. There was the thrill of simply taking your chances. I even went to see some of the open plague-pits in Finsbury and Moorfields, pulled there to the very brink by that morbid curiosity that makes us all want to stare. Not that they were easy to avoid, those open sores. They reeked with the stench of emptied bellies and intestinal tracts. We hovered on the edge of Gehenna and peered in at the horrors, unable to tear our eyes away from the vision of what was to come. Hell held no surprises for us now. The city graveyards could not contain the dead, were not tomb enough and continent to hide the slain, and so they opened up these huge black holes in the green fields and poured the bodies in.

They were a gruesome spectacle. Among the mounds of corpses that flickered palely in that ghastly torchlight I caught here and there an eye that blinked and held my horrified stare. I started forward, ready to point and protest. 'Hold off the earth awhile! There are people moving in there, not yet dead!' Then I hesitated – and stopped. Who in his right mind was going to wade into that massive tangle of human remains and pluck out a stray survivor? Was I going to see to it myself? Plunge into the very maelstrom of contagion and come out carrying the plague in my arms? I checked myself, stood there and watched as the gravediggers, ignoring the groans and twitchings, went berserk, spading on the earth, hurling it over the pale hundreds, hiding the vague stirrings, soaking up the groans.

And on the roofs of these very plague-pits, as soon as the earth was put back, drunken dancers went wild and the beast with two backs was rampant. It was said that women climaxed more ecstatically on the plague graves than anywhere else, even the perfumed chambers of the great, such was the savage will to survive, to feel alive, to feel anything at all, to proclaim the life-force in death's despite. And it was also said that the bastards born of these ghoulish couplings had the tempers of tigers and the appetites of sharks, conceived as they had been out of a diabolical and insane thrusting on. Meanwhile the whore-shops shook their timbers like ships in a storm. The whores of Clerkenwell complained that men came with madness in their eyes and brimstone in their pricks and that they pounded all night long and buggered them senseless in the morning. After that they buggered one another. They'd have buggered the devil himself if he'd bared his arse in Clerkenwell.

'And so, still London seethed.'

Its stews bubbled over. Worse than ever. The whorehouses of Southwark proclaimed they'd never done such a roaring trade – though the nearby Rose stood dark and empty, where not so long ago the groundlings had given it all they'd got for Talbot fallen in France, and Marlowe's mighty line had brought the house down in a thunder of applause. They were waiting for the Marlowe magic to return. But in the middle of all this, when the plague was at its height, something happened that changed the theatrical scene forever.

'What was that?'

You know what it was, Francis. The Marlowe magic was never going to come back. Not ever. Because before the end of May, Year of Our Lord 1593, Master Marlowe lay dead in Deptford with a dagger in his brain.

35

'I'll hear about that – and then the pie!'

Then lend thy serious hearing to what I shall unfold.

Christopher Marlowe came to Eleanor Bull's house on Deptford Strand at ten in the morning and was joined by three men: Ingram Frizer, Nicholas Skeres, and Robin Poley. They talked, ate, smoked, strolled in the garden, all rather civilised and subdued – an uncharacteristically muted Marlowe, you may say. Then they went in again around six for their evening meal, during which drink was taken. Quite a skinful. They supped some stuff. After dinner Marlowe left the table and flung himself down on an adjacent bed. The other three stayed where they were, Frizer sitting in the middle of the trio with his back to Marlowe. There wasn't a lot of room. Frizer especially, flanked by Skeres and Poley, was in what you might call a tight corner – Snug the joiner couldn't have fitted him up better. You'd have thought he was the one for the chop, not Marlowe. And there they were – all four from the seamy underbelly of the body politic, and not one of them a man you'd be wise to be sitting with in a Deptford drinker, particularly if you were wedged in...

The talk turned to the reckoning – who was to settle with Mistress Bull and how much the day's hospitality had cost them. That's when the fracas flared up, like lightning, and the prince of Cats came out with his claws as he was very apt to do, sudden and quick in quarrel. Only this time, oddly enough, he didn't rely on his own claws. Instead he snatched Frizer's dagger from its sheath at his back and wounded him twice in the head. Frizer, boxed in by his two associates, had little chance to defend himself against the murderous Marlowe, a formidable foe when in the violent vein. Yet somehow Frizer managed to turn it around (himself included) and fight back – and in the rammy retrieved his dagger and rammed it into Marlowe's forehead, just above the right eye. The mighty-liner screamed like a stuck pig and swore like a trooper (so they recalled). Then he fell down. And fell silent.

'Into the blind cave of eternal night.'

Well quoted, Francis. The author of *Faustus* and *Tamburlaine* and all those brave translunary things was no more. Like his dramatic raptures he was now air and fire. And earth. And not far from the water, as it happened. Dead over the merest trifle: a tavern tiff and who was to pick up the bill. Had the size of it tipped the balance? A great reckoning in a little room. It was 1593, seven o'clock in the evening, on the penultimate day of May, and rough winds had just shaken one of its darling buds, the Muses' darling. He was twenty-nine years old.

That at least was the official version, somewhat dramatised by me in the telling, mind you, Francis, for your better entertainment. And that roughly is how it was recorded two days later by the Royal Coroner, Sir William Danby, after the inquest, which was heard by a jury of sixteen men good and true, if you want to believe the adjectives – the number's accurate anyway. A sordid little case of manslaughter arising out of a banal little brawl, and occasioned by the ignoble question of who was to pay the bill or how it was to be apportioned. After all, when four men are dining one of them may drink more than his fair share. Sound all right to you, Francis? Smell sweet as a great pie, does it, in your expert nostrils? You're a lawyer, after all.

'It stinks and rings – hollow.'

As to the real version, the date is correct and so is the setting and the names of the cast. You can probably forget the rest. Unless you'd care to slip back with me thirteen years from the date of his death and hear something a little closer to the truth.

'How quickly can it be told, Will?'

In motion of no less celerity than that of thought. This is how it happened. When Marlowe went to Cambridge he was an unlikely enough undergraduate, more interested in politics and Ovid than in becoming a churchman. Still, he'd have been under plenty of persuasion. Campion and Parsons, along with a hundred other Jesuits, were busy targeting England in obedience to the Pope's command and fanatical call to arms. They were peaceful men, Campion especially, but there was nothing secret about the ultimate papal objective: the killing of the queen, the Jezebel whose version of religion was killing the country through the souls of its people. The political mission was therefore to kill *her.* Take with you the armour of God, the breastplate of righteousness, the shield of faith, the helmet of salvation, and the sword of the spirit which is the word of God (as interpreted in Rome). Together with whatever poisons and wicked little knives you can smuggle through. Naturally your feet will be shod with the gospel of peace.

To the self-same tune again. And you well know how even the devil can cite scripture for his purpose.

'Especially the devil.'

The Pope donned his horns and gave it the full Beelzebub treatment. We were marked men. England was under attack. Not that Campion ever saw it that way.

'We travelled only for souls?'

Something like that. 'We touched neither state nor policy. Assassination? Regicide? We had no such commission.' And even a triple measure of stretching and other procedures failed to move Campion from that idealistic angle of his, the one he was always coming from, the one I had seen in his eyes, the impossibly pious squint, burning there like a vision. Topcliffe tried hard enough to shift it, to straighten him out on the rack. 'Look, Edmund, let me put it to you this way. It's not just the hand that actually holds the dagger that's the guilty one, you know. Your hand, my dear, is as red as any man's. You don't agree? Oh, I'm sorry, perhaps I didn't hurt you enough. Let's try it again – but this time a different way.'

'A darling man, Topcliffe.'

But even when Campion lay like a dislocated elephant, unable to rise, and ate his bread like an ape, between cupped and crippled hands, still he refused to see it the government way, the Topcliffe way. And, to do them justice, the Privy Council were greatly impressed by the piety and purity of this gentle scholar. Even the queen, gave him a hearing, anxious to offer him an exit strategy.

'So you told me.'

So I did.

She put the questions herself. One word was all he needed to say. The way out was wide open for him. But he wouldn't take it. So they took him out and hanged him.

'His choice.'

No, God's – or the Pope's.

That was in July '81, only six months into Marlowe's student days. In his second year at Corpus Christi either the Catholics got to him or the Secret Service got there first and asked him to feign Catholicism, pass himself off as a Catholic student at Rheims and spy on the true Catholics, in other words on the traitors to the state and enemies of the queen. Marlowe the mole was doing intelligence work for the Cabinet long before he'd graduated. That was his first and only job, apart from writing, and all he ever gave away on that front was that even a dramatist earned more than a spy.

By the time he'd got his first degree, droves of Catholics had been slaughtered at Tyburn. Including Francis Throckmorton. Two sessions on the rack and one on the strappado had made him sing a different song from Campion. To wit: Spain would invade, Mary Stuart would be sprung from jail and crowned Queen of England, and the country would be under Catholic occupation until it settled down again to its natural state and true faith, the old religion.

'And Queen Elizabeth?'

Well, clearly there would be one place and one place only for her to lay her uneasy head, made easier by the removal of the crown.

Christopher Marlowe B.A. had graduated into a world of prejudice, terror, political paranoia, and intrigue.

'A mad world, my masters.'

A mad world Francis.

If a wild wave of Catholicism was sweeping the decade the response of the authorities was nothing less than hysterical. The hundred seminary priests sent across the Channel from the training camps at Douai, Rheims, and Rome were easily outnumbered by the vast army of agents employed by Secret Police Chief Francis Walsingham to track them down, root out their converts and protectors, and sniff out conspiracies, often while themselves posing as Catholics or sympathisers with Rome. They ranged from common cut-throats and scullions and flunkeys to intelligencers, double agents, *agents provocateurs*. Robin Poley, who fetched up at Eleanor Bull's house at the end of May, was a Catholic who betrayed Catholics and used sodomy in his honey traps.

'All nice people underneath!'

Marlowe was in much the same mould. Very shortly after he'd enrolled at Cambridge he started missing classes. In Walsingham's pay he went first to Paris and then to Rheims (the Jesuit training camp had moved from Douai in '78) to spy on the English ambassador there, a known crook. Skeres was an agent too at this time, while Poley strung Babington along, sweet as a harp, stroking his genitals as was his wont, knowing that the Babington genitals were numbered. They came off the year before Marlowe became a Master of Arts. After that Poley did two years in the Tower – part of his insurance cover plan – following the government round-up of the old suspects, though he lived the high life there, they say, well supplied with wine and whores.

'They look after their own.'

Only till their own become inconvenient. Both Poley and Marlowe later turned up in the Low Countries, where English spies were active. There were murmurs about English money being counterfeited, and Marlowe was ordered home. He retired from espionage and left for London, where he became an instant success and famous overnight, the toast of the town.

One of his closest cronies in London was Thomas Watson, scholar, soak, and sonneteer, much obsessed by time, classicism, and the pastoral.

'Never heard of him.'

Not surprising. Just another of the host of doomed poets who never made it out of the nineties – or out of their thirties, if you prefer to look at it that way. He too went down in '92. Marlowe shared lodgings with Watson in Norton Folgate. They drank and smoked at the Nag's Head in Cheapside, where they were roaring boys with Greene and Peele and Nashe. He also drank a lot with Thomas Kyd, with whom he had shared rooms in Shoreditch in '91.

'Roaring boys and nancy boys.'

Marlowe being Marlowe, he never went up Smock Alley or Petticoat Lane but preferred certain other passages – here he became a free and familiar spirit, haunting Damnation Dyke and the Devil's Gap. He also got into fights, most famously the Hog Lane fight in '89 when he fought with William Bradley, an innkeeper's son and a working villain who had an ongoing feud with Marlowe's friend Watson. He didn't exactly keep his head down in London.

And in no time at all he was a member of the notorious School of Night.

'They kept themselves dark – never heard of them either.'

Founded by Ralegh – a gathering of geographers, mathematicians, astronomers, alchemists, globemakers, poets. It was attacked by the shocked Jesuits as a school of atheism. They'd been seen to tear pages out of a bible to dry tobacco on – and that's the least of it. Others saw it at worst as a circle of wizards, at best as a respectable debating group, trying to reconcile religion with science and philosophy. In any case the members of this particular night school led dubious lives and embraced unsavoury ends – pun intended, I'm afraid. Ferdinando Stanley, Lord Strange (Lord Queer to some): poisoned gruesomely and died in agony. Henry Percy, ninth Earl of Northumberland, the scholar knight with the stutter and the long melancholy face: slung in jail by James. Henry Brooke, ninth Baron Cobham: jailed by the king for life. Richard Baines: agent, informer, assassin. Even Dr Dee, the notorious necromancer, had been asked along.

'Hardly the choice and master spirits of the age.'

And Chairman Ralegh. Brooke was actually on the block, seconds from headlessness, when he picked out Ralegh in a plot to kill the king. It was cutting it fine but his last minute fingering saved Brooke and dropped Ralegh straight into the shit, where he rots to this day, a turd among turds, festering in the Tower.

'Ah.'

Yes, you see what I mean? And then there was Marlowe. One by one the sceptics and scholars had a tendency to disappear from the scene, their inquiries cut short, invariably by a head. Wrapped up in their graves with their clever jaws clamped shut and their ears bandaged with a clout – deaf to any doubt. If they were lucky they did time. Suddenly stone walls and iron bars became the best possible place to be.

But when the plague struck London all the goldfinches flew to the woods. Anybody with any money to spare, that is, they just lost their nerve and fled. Plague brings panic, and panic prejudice, and prejudice all sorts of atrocities, including lies and libels. Marlowe took off to Canterbury, and an anti-Flemish poem appeared at the beginning of May, pasted up on the boundary wall of the Dutch churchyard in Broad Street. It expressed anti-Jewish sentiments too and threatened throat-cutting on a Parisian if not Scythian scale. Even in his drunkest dreams and at his most tobacco-happy Marlowe could never have written it. But in case anyone doubted that, it was signed Tamburlaine. Not that that fooled anybody, least of all the government, who offered a reward of a hundred crowns for information leading to the true author of this outrage. The following day a number of arrests were made – and there, trawled up in the shoal of unwilling witnesses, was Thomas Kyd.

'How fishy was he?'

Kyd had gone on from the glories of *The Spanish Tragedy* to co-script *Sir Thomas More* – which just happened to contain an unfortunate inflammatory element, unfortunate enough to make Kyd an easy suspect. He was handed over to Topcliffe in Bridewell, where he sang out against Marlowe. He came off the rack a broken man at thirty-four with less than a year left to live, ruined in spirit and flesh, right down to the last finger.

'Broken fingers – not good for a writer.'

A severe disqualification. They invented apt punishments. And what *had* he been writing recently? His rooms were ransacked and heretical papers discovered. Kyd promptly swore blind and blue that the papers must have been Marlowe's, inadvertently shuffled together with his own when they were sharing rooms in Shoreditch.

'A likely story.'

An untidy arsehole to doss down with, Marlowe, swore Kyd, and as for the sentiments, they got worse by the page, light as pipe-smoke and heard in every tavern in the town, Marlowe-talk, no question about it. Much coloured by Kyd's blood, mind you, Kyd's blood staining the rack –he proved marvellously inventive, surpassing even Topcliffe's relentless encouragement. It gave the Privy Council plenty to go on and an order went out for Marlowe's arrest.

'The stuff of drama, Will. You should have written about it.'

Haven't you learned anything, Francis? He was staying in Chislehurst at the time, at Scadbury, the house of his patron, Thomas Walsingham, cousin of Francis, his now extinct employer. When the Queen's messenger entered the room Marlowe was sitting writing, penning a reasonably respectable erotic poem about Hero and Leander, the first pages of which had already been in circulation for some years. Henry Maunder showed him the warrant and brought him out of his text and into the real world: the dangerous world of politics and the law. He was brought straight into the presence of the Privy Council in Whitehall and ordered to report to them daily until further notice. And that is what he did. He had little choice in the matter.

Nine days later the Privy Council found themselves looking at a document written by double agent Richard Baines of the School of Night – a note of no fewer than nineteen accusations made against Marlowe and quite a damning catalogue of his pernicious practices and opinions. The usual blasphemies, with several interesting extras: Moses was a juggler, Christ a bastard, his mother Mary a fornicator, Gabriel a pimp, and the Holy Ghost a client. Barabas was a better man than Jesus, Mary Magdalene a whore, the same as her sister Martha, both fucked by Christ – who also buggered St John the Sodomite Evangelist. Added to this, hell was a fable and the whole of religion invented for one purpose only: to hold men in awe and keep them in their place. As for the blessed sacrament, Christ would have done better to have instituted it in a tobacco-pipe and had a smoke instead.

To continue: Marlowe himself smoked like a winter chimney and was a practising homo and guilty a thousand times over of the capital offence, the cynosure of bumboys and pole-star of London's buggers. All deadly data, though much of it may have been a smoke-screen to divert attention from his real preoccupation – intelligence – while the Council, privy to his Secret Service work, had let him alone. But the Baines note went on: 'The said Marlowe not only believes all this but he persuades others to believe likewise and has in fact shared his opinions with certain great and powerful men, who shall in due course be named. All Christian men ought to see to it, therefore, that the mouth of such a dangerous man be stopped.'

Baines had written out Marlowe's death warrant. He had only three days left to live. On 30th May he reported early to the Council, then he went straight to Eleanor Bull's house on Deptford Strand to meet his destiny – two inches worth of dagger, itself worth twelve pence according to the coroner's report. Death from a one-shilling dagger, driven into the brain just above the right eye.

'Jesus, what an end!'

It was quick. Danby accepted the depositions of Poley, Skeres, and Frizer, the three men left of the four who had been in the room. The fact that they were three shits to a man was legally immaterial (even shits may speak true). But what they asked Danby to believe is that Frizer, pinned in on both sides by his two fellow turds and with his back to Marlowe, managed to reverse the situation – including his own trammelled carcass – and kill the Prince of Cats, thereby saving his own skin. Meanwhile, Agents Skeres and Poley sat there – so they swore – and gaped like codfish, these operators from the most dangerous occupation in Europe, while the fight went on inches from their ears. That was the scene so happily swallowed by the Royal Coroner – but mocked in every pub from Eastcheap to Norton Folgate and Drury Lane.

Marlowe was a pawn and a patsy who came between the pass and fell incensèd points of mighty opposites, Ralegh in one corner and in the other Poley's employer, the Earl of Essex. Or: Poley was a nancy boy and the killing was sexual, according to what turns queers on – and off. Or: Marlowe was sleeping not with Poley but with altogether bigger buggers (watch out, O womanly Walsingham, cousin of dead Francis!) and was about to blow the whistle. After all, queerness was a capital crime in the England of our Virgin Queen, where old buggers got to bend over the block if they got caught. Or perhaps this: Marlowe knew too much about certain other men in high places – powerful men whose weaknesses lay not in their pricks but in their consciences. He knew the secrets of their souls, knew their opinions on dangerous subjects – religion, for example, none more perilous. He knew who had enrolled in the School of Night and exactly what answers they had given to the eternal questions. And nobody knew just whom he might have slept with or what they might have said. The pillows may have been deaf but Marlowe wasn't – not to pillow talk. And the Privy Council began to lose sleep.

'Get him to Deptford,' says one of them (let's fashion it thus) – 'I have a cousin has a house there, close to the water. We could have a watery death, could we not? But no, wait, let's think. Tell him he can take the tide tomorrow, lie low in the Low Countries. It will be a night tide too. Tell him to wait there all day. Tell him what the fuck you like. Wine him and dine him – grand style and gratis. Hold hard there, though – on second thoughts don't say it's on the house, he'll smell a rat if the food and booze come free and he'll hear the fatted calf sizzling a mile away. Soft, let me see... I have it! Fill him with drink, all day long, wine sufficient to convince, and let him ply his music – then present him with a monstrous bill, one he's sure to quarrel with. A quarrelsome man is Agent Marlowe and a short-tempered guest at parties – a fiery cat. Go to it, then. Find out how much he knows before you eliminate him. Pump him and see what spills, and don't miss a drop – or you'll be for the short drop yourselves. Very well then. After that bring him down. And make sure he doesn't get up again.'

So Skeres the swindler, Frizer the shadow, and Poley the knife (perjurer and double agent to boot) go into action. An unholy trinity and each one a Judas, they spend the day with Marlowe and help him to eat his last supper, Dr Faustus fashion. Betrayal is the name of the game. The demi-god is about to go under, the star of the stage, farewell.

Come, thick night and pall thee in the dunnest smoke of hell, that my keen knife see not the wound it makes, nor heaven peep through the blanket of the dark to cry 'Hold! Hold!'

Afterwards Frizer exhibited his hurt head, a brace of grazes. As if the Cat's claws wouldn't have produced a lot worse if they'd really been out that day. But 'twill serve, sir, 'tis enough – the script continues. Danby slaps on the whitewash, pockets his backhander, Frizer gets his Queen's pardon and goes straight back into the service of Walsingham, Poley and Skeres slip off into the shadows, their natural element, shadows that they are, Eleanor Bull (for the record) says sweet nothing, nor any of her servants (all gone deaf and blind that day apparently) – only the three hit-men have their say. And Marlowe's body is taken into the churchyard of St Nicholas on the first day of June and deposited in an unmarked grave. Laid to rest.

But the rest is not silence. Destiny never defames herself, said Nashe, but when she lets an excellent poet die. His pen was like a poniard. Each page he wrote on was like a burning glass to set all his readers on fire. He was the wittiest knave that ever God made – and in comparison with the tongue's impunity he held his life in utter contempt. Goodnight then, sweet Prince of Cats, come short on angels, I suspect, to sing thee to thy rest.

'And that was it, Will?'

A casualty not of the plague, but of the plague of politics, that leaves none of us untouched. In Marlowe's case the touch was mortal. Once more, then, farewell the mighty line. Hard to imagine that the Rose would never ring out with new words, phrases fresh minted from the Marlowe mind, now he lay dead, dead shepherd, fresh dead in Deptford. The theatres too stood dead after that, as if in mourning.

'Hard to imagine all of that, stopped.'

But imagine it all the same, Francis, come with me once more through the empty streets, past the idle unshuttered shops, past the vast black scabs of earth, scarring the green fields, those ugly anonymous monuments to the dead in their mass graves. Come with me through the silent watches of the nights, when being in London was like being locked in a charnel-house, when the cobbles rang to the rumbling tumbrils as the corpse-gatherers made their grisly rounds, gleaning God's frightful harvest during the terrible flame-lit night.

These are the images that lit up Marlowe's death, Francis, pictures that stay with you for the rest of your life. Nashe made a poem out of them.

'Or the plague made a poet out of Nashe?'

Not the greatest versifier, you may be right, but the pestilence may have pulled out of him this one poem I often wish I'd written.

'Really? How does it go?'

Stick it up your nostrils, Francis, this Nashe nosegay, and remember London in 1593, In Time of Pestilence. Sample the scent of death.

Adieu, farewell earth's bliss,
This world uncertain is;
Fond are life's lustful joys,
Death proves them all but toys,
None from his dart can fly.
I am sick, I must die.
Lord have mercy on us!

Rich men, trust not in wealth,
Gold cannot buy you health:
Physic himself must fade,
All things to end are made.
The plague full swift goes by.
I am sick, I must die.
Lord have mercy on us!

Beauty is but a flower
Which wrinkles will devour;
Brightness falls from the air,
Queens have died young and fair,
Dust hath closed Helen's eye,
I am sick, I must die.
Lord have mercy on us!

'He rather caught the mood, didn't he?'

He made hell sound almost heavenly. And that's a poet's job. He saw it as Summer's Last Will and Testament.

'Ah, Last Will and Testament! Now there's a phrase!'

We're nearly there, Francis. Enjoy your pie first. It wasn't Nashe's last will anyway. A decade was left in him. He survived, in spite of his poetic farewell, but still died young at thirty-three, and left us this lyrical picture of a city in crisis. Peele had gone before him, and Kyd before Peele, and Greene before Kyd, and Marlowe before Greene, all in their twenties and thirties. It's as I told you. London was lethal but youthful. Nobody lived long.

'And what were you up to, Will?'

The plague brought *Titus* to completion. And if you think it black, you've never known the plague. If there were reasons for these miseries, then into limits could I bind my woes. If the winds rage, does not the sea itself go mad?

'I'm not sure what you mean.'

I am the sea, Francis, I am the sea. Like Titus I supped full with horrors. I felt the cold winds go over me – as I do now. Hark how her sighs do blow.

36

'It's this pie I'm sighing for.'

Then sigh no more, fair Francis, here comes the harbinger of pie, if I'm not mistaken.

Alison's dark eyes peeped round the door and her sweet lips asked Master Collins if he'd care to come down to supper.

'And you, Will, can you make it?'

Alison can bring me up a small portion – if you can spare it, Francis. Tell your mistress that Master Collins will be down shortly.

'I'll be down right now, old man, if you don't mind.'

The lawyer was off the truckle-bed and standing between me and the door, rubbing his hands again, but now with a vigorous impatience.

Just a moment, Francis, before you disappear forever into that coffin down there –

'Don't! Not while I'm eating.'

You're not, not yet.

'I am in fancy, except you're keeping me from it. What's your question?'

Little Alison. I'd like to leave her something, in my will. What do you think would be appropriate?

The legal frown came on, intensified by hunger.

'Quite inappropriate, I have to say. She's just a girl. It would be appropriate to leave her nothing. Don't you have other servants – more senior ones?'

Yes, of course, you know I do.

'Well then, are you leaving them anything?'

There's no need – they'll be kept on.

'And the maid too, I presume?'

I suppose so.

'Then what are you talking about? I advise against it. Think of the questions it might raise, the whispers, after you're – '

Dead.

'After you're gone – which I am now, anon, for supper!'

Return post-haste, Francis.

'I'll return post-pie.'

And send Alison up with a slice for me.

'Will do.'

There it is again, the laughter from below, floating up from the world I'm leaving, shedding it stitch by stitch, like lendings coming off at last. I can hear Thomas Russell getting merry, and Susanna's laughter coming through, even above that voice, shriller than all the rest. Must you laugh, even as your father dies? Of course you must, they go together, no shadow without sunshine, our sweetest songs are laced with woe, my sweet Susanna.

'Master.'

My sweet Alison.

She was standing by me, holding a plate of Francis' precious pie. Her voice was ever soft – as even Francis observed, a lovely thing in woman.

Never mind that now, Alison, put it aside. There's something I want you to do for me.

She smiled shyly. Not what you're thinking, angel eyes, I thought. They were the eyes of an angel off duty.

Take this key – (I slipped it from round my neck) – and open the dresser, the big one over there, left hand door, top shelf. Bring me the purse that's there. Don't be afraid.

She was. She's a good girl. But she did as I asked, and I emptied the contents onto the blankets in front of me. They chinked and glittered.

Can you count, Alison?

'Yes, master.'

How many?

'Twelve, master.'

Twelve what?

'I don't know. I never seen them before.'

Crowns. Twelve gold crowns, and not a betrayer among them, all good and true.

'But what do you want me to do with them?'

They're for you, sweet one, to set you up, when I'm dead and gone.

Her tiny fingers flew to her face and she started to cry. I reached out quickly and laid my hand on her.

No, Alison, stop now, do you hear?

Her chest began to palpitate and I could feel the breast heave under my hand. I kept it there.

The little bird calmed down but shook its head over taking the money. I put on my sternest Stratford look – and voice.

Pick up the coins, Alison, put them back in the purse, and tell no one.

She obeyed – and held out the purse helplessly.

In your bosom of course, where else?

She looked at me with shining unsmiling eyes and started unlacing herself.

No need to make a fine art of it, lass, just squirrel them away.

But she wasn't preparing a nest for the golden egg, she was thanking me in the only way she knew how. And I couldn't have asked heaven for more. There they rose before me, the hills of paradise, at their most fragrant when sipped at by lovers or when babies nuzzle like bees. Thank you, Lord, for breasts. They are the round turrets of ineffable empires, to be taken only by the tongues of angels. They are the via lactea, doves on high perches, raindrops of flesh, grapes of Gethsemane, Christ's tears incarnate. They are the dreams of men.

And like dreams they come in a thousand shapes, of which I have seen many – little lemons with protuberant navels, peaches furred with down, melons like bombs, waiting to burst, wrinkled swinging wineskins, dugs hung so low you could paddle a wherry with them, row the queen's barge up and down the Thames. And the nipples staring like lobsters' eyes, pouting like pricks, nipples neat as rosebuds in spring or hard as crabs in a winter bowl, nipples like sea anemones clinging to the rock, made for the sea-hungry mouths of mad mariners, wrecked on strange coasts, avid for mermaids, exotic food of the ocean gods, and aureoles like the haloes around saints.

'Master.'

Forgive me, Alison, I was lost in thought –

Of other breasts. But none so lovely as Alison offered me now, leaning over me so that I could accept them with grateful lips and hands, none so lovely as the breasts that comfort the dying man. Alison's hung before me, not big, but round and firm, yet weightless to the eye, heavenly bodies poised, suspended in space, accidental apples, dropped elegantly onto Eve, onto the blessed Virgin herself.

There was a time I could have accepted their weight, drowned in that bosom, and gone to heaven. But now – now not a lustful tremor stirred within me after all, now that she stood there, so immaculate and calm. I reached out to the breasts and with fluttering fingers waved them away, like two frightened doves that were shooed from their perches. Alison looked at me sadly.

'I wish I had milk for you, master.'

Nipples like polished chestnuts, like two baby moles new come out, innocents under the sky.

I shook my head.

'What's wrong, master, are you angry with me? Is it no good for you?'

It is the milk of human kindness, Alison.

O, that this too too sullied flesh would melt. Yet I'll not scar that whiter skin of hers than snow, and smooth as monumental alabaster.

'Master?'

Lace yourself up, Alison, quickly now, put that money where my mouth would be, many moons ago, live well, and remember me.

'Thank you, master.'

No – thank *you*, Alison. And tell that fat lawyer to come up and finish the business. As it is he'll be back to Warwick in the dark.

37

'The fat lawyer will be here for breakfast at this pace!'

Francis came in grinning and looking, if possible, fatter than ever, just as Alison finished lacing up and hurried out.

The deep of night is crept upon our talk.

'And there are still things to settle. Why are you looking so pleased with yourself? You haven't even touched your pie.'

There are things sweeter than pie. Francis, I've been in paradise.

'Already? Then why did you come back? I thought no traveller returns.'

Ah, here will I dwell, for heaven is in these lips, and all is dross that is not Alison.

'Alison?'

I meant Helena – as in Helen of Troy. Marlowe's Helen.

Francis crossed his arms, jerked his head towards the door, and looked sternly at me.

'Have you been misbehaving, my boy?'

I've been reminiscing.

'You're a wicked old man. And after I'm done with you, you'd better settle up with God. By all accounts you'll have a few things to put right. And you've got the time, my lad. Marlowe didn't.'

Marlowe died of politics, Francis, the workings of which are even more inscrutable than the plague – though I can't imagine a world free from either, can you?

'I think you'd better start imagining a world without women, old boy. No sex in heaven, remember? Better get used to it.'

Then heaven's not for me, Francis. A world without women! What, no passion's heat? no carving in the bark? no cruel flame of love? no gods gone mad with mortal charm? Inconceivable. For if there's one thing worse than the plague – and believe me, Francis, there is – it's the plagues of loving. The pestilence saw you off in three days flat. But the plagues of loving set you on the rack.

'The plague of the pox you mean.'

That's different from love.

'Bad enough, I reckon.'

Well, I liked Lucy Negro's place. I liked Lucy Negro too and she liked me. Black Luce.

O thou black weed! Who art so lovely fair and smell'st so sweet that the sense aches at thee! would thou... would thou...

'Would thou get back to the real world!'

Her world was hell – black but aromatic.

'Murky.'

Would all women smelt so fair! Moorish whores. She got her girls to spice themselves up for me. O balmy breath! So sweet was ne'er so fatal!

'Then why did you go?'

The brothels were sanctuaries, Francis. No jealousies there, no doubts or fears, no visions of betrayal, the green-eyed monster that mocks the meat it feeds on, the damnèd minutes told o'er, the false friend's lies, the rank sweat of an enseamed bed, the wind, the bawdy wind that kisses all it meets, strawberry handkerchiefs, foregone conclusions, trifles light as air, paddling palms and pinching fingers, virginalling on knuckles, skulking in corners, whispering in chambers, wishing clocks more swift, hours minutes, noon midnight, leaning cheek to cheek, meeting noses, kissing with inside lip, speaking so nearly that breaths embraced, the tongue down the throat, all the way and into the tail...

'O Jesus, stop!'

Stopping the career of laughter with a sigh. Such are the plagues of loving. But the brothels were beautiful! Purged of the pestilence of lies, no vile spirit of love entered into the trade in human flesh. It was lust, pure and simple. You didn't sleep with a strumpet to get closer to the court. There was none of that in the stews. There it was cock and cunt, buy and sell, come and go, with not one syllable of flattery, hypocrisy, nor hope of gain. That, my friend, was pure beauty.

'Beauty truly blent.'

Let's not go back there. Anyway, the plague put all of that on hold when it put the whores out of work. You'd have to be weary of the sun to walk into a brothel during the plague years. It was safer to hold your piece in bed and crackle your sheets in the dawn.

'I think you should hold your peace.'

What else could a man do? Even the night-tripping ladies of the streets you never knew where they'd come from – straight from the whorehouses no doubt, ill-famed and idle. The stars of the stews put up their shutters. Even Henslowe shut up shop. Even the aristocrats had a hard time of it. You daren't mess with one of the Queen's Glories either.

'That sent her virgin Majesty mad, did it?'

Pembroke meddled with Mistress Mary Fitton once too often, and as her belly grew, so Pembroke's star waned, first in the Fleet prison and afterwards in exile. Such were the hazards, Francis, lining the route that wound up through a chamber-lady's petticoat. Not to mention the block. It just wasn't worth the risk.

'And there's nothing wrong with celibacy. Are you going to have that bit of pie, by the way?'

Celibacy was never the best of pastimes, but you can't be more celibate than when you're dead. My own ventures were not in one bottom trusted.

'I smell a woman – another one.'

Old Vautrollier had gone to sleep with his French forefathers, and in the risky spring of '93 Richard Field bolted back home to avoid the plague, leaving the lovely Jacklin – now his wife – to take her chances. And to keep the business running and the Splayed Eagle flying in the face of fear. When I heard about this I made straight for Wood Street. What would you have done, in my place, Francis, with sudden death lurking round every corner and liable to surface in your armpits? In any case, this Field was no eagle but a crack-brained cuckoo and he deserved the cuckold's fate that was coming to him. For if a man wanted an antidote now to the black death it was to be found jump between the Gallic thighs of black Jackie – a fiery wench to fire out the stench of death.

'No details, please! There were enough in Act One to outlast the play!'

Act Two was business, Francis. When I walked in under the sign of the Splayed Eagle I was carrying the intent of my quill as well as my prick – specifically the manuscript of a newly penned poem.

'Ah, your *Venus and Adonis*.'

A shut playhouse means an empty purse, Francis, and even an actor must eat. When Jackie saw me she threw decorum to the winds and leaped into my arms with a whoop. I grabbed her haunches and the pages of the manuscript slid from my fingers and littered the floor at our feet.

'Well! You weecked Weel! 'ow does your honour for zees many a day?'

'I humbly thank you. Well enough. Will is well.'

'And now 'ow famous you 'ave become zee talk of zee ceety!'

Still that broken music. I sucked it from her tongue and tasted French the way I liked and remembered. Then she shut the shop and we went to bed at noon, leaving Venus on the floor in disarray.

When we had put both Venus and ourselves in order, I returned to the manuscript.

'Inspired all over again no doubt.'

Which necessitated a return to Wood Street on the following day. And night. And every night thereafter while the plague raged in the city and the brothels begged for business. In the midst of the madness the Splayed Eagle hovered over us with its protective wings, gentle as a dove. Wood Street was an ark on a sea of troubles.

'And Jacklin was a good safe ride.'

It will not surprise you to learn, Francis, that I felt the need to check every syllable of my *Venus* as it went through the Field press – which entailed much labour under the Splayed Eagle, and between the splayed legs of dark Jacklin.

'I told you, I'm your lawyer, not your priest.'

I owed it to myself. It was my first work to appear in print. And I owed it to Field, who was not at hand to keep up his standard. So I kept it up for him. Nothing less than perfection would satisfy me, and Venus deserves and demands her due. By the time he came creeping back from Stratford, Jackie and I had done yeoman's work and a beautifully prepared poem was waiting for him. The sluggard took his time to give it the light of day, and eight months afterwards was stupid enough to sell it on – a move he lived to regret when he saw the sales. But there you have it, just as it fell out between the white sheets, pen and prick hard pressed but keeping perfect time together.

'A labour of love.'

As I say, my ventures were not –

'In one bottom trusted, as you said. Any others?'

Well, there was Elizabeth Daniel, sister of Samuel, the sonneteer. She married Florio.

'Ah, the Montaigne man.'

And the Earl of Southampton's tutor. And another writer who

never made it out of '92. But she soon discovered that Florio lived in a world of words. It was the very title he gave his dictionary and it was the maelstrom into which he plunged nightly, a world away from the black flag that should have drawn him like a moth to the moon. Night after night he left her sexless between the sheets, that word-mad mandarin of a grammatist, while he burned the midnight lamp over his Italian etymologies, and between you and me, Francis, I did the same for Florio in his ungentlemanly absence as I'd done for Richard Field in Wood Street.

'Performed his office.'

Betwixt the marital sheets. And warmed them up for him.

'Jesus.'

They needed warming – they were much too cool.

'But how did you – '

Southampton employed me, after I'd dedicated my *Venus* to him – to *him*! Henry Wriothesley, third Earl of Southampton and Baron of Titchfield! And it was accepted. The plague had been a blessing in disguise. So I entered his household. And there we all were – together.

'With Venus ascendant. What a crowd!'

Venus had to be ascendant. The theatres were shut. And the plague would have made a pauper out of me in no time had I not written the *Venus*. No, I didn't write tragedies during the plague, as you might have expected. There was tragedy enough piled up in the streets, in the houses, in the communal graves. People didn't need more than they'd already got. When you're up to your neck in excrement you don't want to be told how shitty life is. My *Venus* gave Londoners a sense of release and relief from the daily horrors that surrounded them. It was a window onto a world almost forgotten, a world of beautiful, classical, pagan love in a pastoral setting.

'And it worked. You were a sensation. Even I bought a copy – a boring lawyer.'

The young men loved it, the students slept with it under their pallets, even wrote me down in their diaries, considering it no baseness to write fair when W.S. was the subject. Suddenly I was sweet Mr Shakespeare, public plaudits and honour due. And a dozen editions speaks for itself.

'I think I preferred your next one, the *Lucrece*.'

The wiser sort did. Chaste Roman matron preferred to horny Roman goddess every time, when you're an egghead of acumen and understanding, as you are, Francis. But I'm willing to wager that these wiser scholars and sober souls were careful to keep last year's *Venus* slipped between the sheets for private reading – just in case the nocturnal urge took them unawares – and many a candle dripped and sputtered in the secret watches of the night.

'Jesus, Will, you're nowhere near ready for heaven.'

The plague years resolved me of one thing, Francis, that the play is most definitely *not* the thing. It's the thing of the moment. It always is. But as I hit thirty and looked at what I was – a playwright without a playhouse, I reached my decision. Not the play but the poem. The poem is the thing. That was the truth for 1593.

38

'Quite a career change, Will, from pleasing the mob to pleasing a nob.'

I was prepared for it, made ready for it, the previous year. It was early in the season, a dark dawn of '92, that the knock came to the door.

'Master Shakespeare?' the voice said, 'I represent a certain lady, whose identity will shortly be revealed to you. I also represent Sir William Cecil, Lord Burghley, the Lord High Treasurer of the Realm, and therefore, by extension, Her Majesty, the Queen. Do I have your full attention?'

He did. And so did my bowels. I'd known right away that he was a gentleman, rings and pearled ruffs apart, but when he came out with that mouthful I shook like the hare. The caller smiled and put his hand firmly on my shoulder, half easing me, half ordering me down into my chair. He was wearing very expensive gloves.

'Relax, there's nothing to worry about. Just listen to what I have to say, Will. Can I call you Will? Here it is, then. It's very simple. There is a certain young man who at this moment does not feel inclined to marry. Understandable enough in a lad of nineteen, to be unwilling to enter into the state of holy deadlock. Naturally he wants to live a little before settling down to raise a family and manage his estates. Holy matrimony has its drawbacks, as we all know, despite its undoubtedly blessed condition. Except that in the present case the young man happens to be Henry Wriothesley, third Earl of Southampton and Baron of Titchfield. And to speak plainly, his father has been dead these twelve years and there is no fourth Earl to speak of – not until the third one, our little Henry, does his duty and provides an heir. Which he can't very well do, legally that is, until he's married. Bastards don't count, as I'm sure you appreciate.'

'But what does any of this have to do with me?'

'I see that I enjoy your full attention, Master Shakespeare. Permit me to tell you.'

And that was how it began.

Enter into my life, just as the plague entered London, the Right Honourable Henry Wriothesley: beautiful as a woman, popular, self-admiring, ambitious. And rich, seriously rich, at least potentially. A golden lad without a girl was young Henry Wriothesley.

Actually the courtly messenger pronounced it *Risley* (with a certain sibilantic disdain, so I thought), though the young owner of the name always used the *Rye-ose-ley* slant, a euphonic preference which may have been a matter of vanity. To a wordplaying poet it was a matter of poetic serendipity – that thereby beauty's *rose* might never die.

'Nice wordplay, Will. You never miss a trick.'

He was beauty's rose, all right, was my young Harry.

'No bending and scraping, Will,' he'd say, 'unless I bend and you scrape. And you can count on my firmness, all the way to the end.' It was part of his charm, the silly schoolboy humour. But setting aside the jests he meant what he said, and was even better than his word.

He called himself Harry the Third.

'A lot younger than you, Will.'

Born in '73 – yes, I was only ten – his father was a Catholic and a queer (two dangerous dispositions) who'd done time for his part in the '69 rebellion of the Northern Catholic earls, and who'd died young and mysteriously – maybe not so mysteriously – after helping Campion, and left huge sums of money to one Thomas Dymoke, a mere manservant – how exactly he'd served his master seemed clear enough to some.

'I told you about leaving money to servants.'

Things moved quickly for young Harry after that. He became a ward of Burghley's, and Burghley was never a man to waste time.

'Poor old Harry.'

Poor little rich boy. Fatherless at eight, a freshman at twelve, a graduate at sixteen. Burghley sent him to his old college, St John's at Cambridge, brimming with bards and bumboys, then straight to Gray's Inn – where he benched with Bacon – to finish the business, with a marriage planned to follow hard upon. A quick march to the sacrificial altar.

'Old Burghley would have made a good executioner.'

He *was* the executioner. The marriage he had in mind was naturally to his own grand-daughter, Lady Elizabeth Vere, daughter of his dead daughter Anne (his favourite) and the wayward Edward de Vere, seventeenth Earl of Oxford, he who ruined himself and his estates. The marriage to Southampton was to be her consolation prize. As Burghley's grandchild the Lady Elizabeth wasn't just any young tart of the court whose arse you'd grope behind the arras. And Southampton was meant to be grateful.

'And wasn't?'

Alas, no. At any rate that was the Burghley plan: a wedding for his ward at sweet seventeen. The lady was just fifteen. Harry's mother was ecstatic – her son to marry into the family of the most powerful politician in the country. On top of which they desperately needed to secure the succession. A fourth earl had to be fathered, of that there was no doubt. And the filly was waiting for the foal, both to be groomed in the Burghley stables.

'Where refusals could doubtless cost you dear.'

It was to cost young Harry very dear indeed. Burghley blew up when this ungrateful milksop informed him he'd have none of it, not just yet, he wanted more time – a year at least – to think about it and to enjoy his youth while he was thinking.

'And you couldn't blame him, could you?'

What? Tutored since he was three, no childhood to speak of, head down at college for five years after that – and now straight into marriage?

'To hell with that for a lark at heaven's gate, eh?'

He wanted to be a soldier boy and march in triumph behind his model of gallantry, Robert Devereux –

'The Earl of Essex.'

Wedded himself, mind you, but glamorously so – to the fair widow of Sir Philip Sidney, dead on Zutphen field these four years, England's chivalric flower, immortalised by a bullet and a bouquet of sonnets. He'd bequeathed Essex his sword and his wife.

Essex sailed for France, commander of the Normandy expedition at twenty-four. But Elizabeth kept Harry at court with a few well chosen words, of the sort you don't question, not when they are wafted to you on the bad breath of ageing queens.

'For your intent in going to Normandy, it is most retrograde to our desire, and we beseech you, bend you to remain, here in the cheer and comfort of our eye. I pray thee, stay with us: go not to Normandy. And let thine eye look like a friend on England.'

'I shall in all my best obey you, madam.'

'Why, 'tis a loving and a fair reply.'

She brought him out of his dumps and raised his eyelids.

'But not his hopes?'

He gloomed again when she raised the subject of the succession. 'Your seeds are no use to us, sir, scattered over Normandy. Southampton House must come first for you.'

And so to my dawn caller with the expensive gloves.

'You see, Will, her Majesty herself talks of this. As for myself, I represent the Countess of Southampton, but the Countess spoke to Lord Burghley and Burghley spoke to the Queen, and her Majesty's wish – '

'Is an order?'

'Well let's just say that it is part of my job to translate wishes into orders and orders into facts. So what we want you to do, Master Shakespeare, (I'd better be formal here), is to take up your pen and write. It will be worth your while. Be in no doubt of it.'

'And so you became a sonneteer?'

In time, Francis. I was in no doubt of one thing: that right now I had to find an alternative occupation. The public that had poured into the playhouses were busy filling up the plague-pits. With the theatres shut I needed a patron. Now a patron had come knocking at the door. The highest in the land wanted me to write something for a young earl, something that might move his mind to marriage, not to war.

'So *Venus and Adonis* came out of politics!'

And money. Everything comes out of politics, and money. Especially when you don't have any. And you're a political pawn.

'I don't see how it fits, though.'

It's obvious enough, Francis. A young man rejects the lure of love, follows the call of action instead – and ends up dead, gored by a boar. The tusk is stronger than the tool. And you can call the tusk the plague of war or just the plague, or call it nothing but itself if you prefer. The point is that, for all his attractions and attributes, Adonis has left behind him no copy of himself for posterity to admire.

For he being dead, with him is beauty slain – and beauty being dead, black chaos comes again.

'But that was an exhortation to marry – just what he didn't *want*.'

I'd been asked – no – ordered to please an earl by persuading him to do the very thing he didn't want to, and the likelihood ran high that he'd object furiously to a bumpkin actor and untried poet having the temerity to take sides with Burghley in the matter of his marriage. I needed to make friends, not enemies. And to antagonise a theatre-lover like the third Earl of Southampton at a time when the theatre was in dire crisis, seemed hardly the best thing to do.

But I was under orders and I got away with it. I'd made the case for love, not war, to the satisfaction of his mother and protector, and even her Majesty approved.

'And he went for it.'

Straight for the sugar, ignored the allegory, accepted the dedication – and paid me handsomely. His mother paid me too, even more handsomely, if backhandedly. Maybe the Queen chipped in, or even old Burghley opened his purse and watched the moths fly out, who knows? It was all wrapped up in a fog and the same gloved gentleman apologised for that when he visited a second time. There was nothing airy about the purse of money that he slapped down hard on the table. In that silvery jingle I heard the bright ring of words. I'd made more in a month than I could have done in a whole year of theatre. Apparently I'd succeeded where others before me (Nashe notably) had failed. This business of writing for the rich was playacting of a different sort and much more profitable. Thank God for the plague, I thought – it had passed me by and raised me high.

'Lucky Will.'

It didn't end there. I was taken on as a member of Harry's household, went into service as entertainments man at Holborn and at Titchfield, where from time to time I rode out the plague with Harry – teacher, talker, friend. The theatres were out of business but now I had my own private theatre, and the Southampton circle loved it.

That's when I gave them *Love's Labour* and the *Shrew*, and early stabs at the *Merchant* and *Romeo*. And I gave them the *Two Gentlemen*, plenty of bachelor boy matter, female love and their conflicting claims. Through Harry I was even known at court. I was high on Fortune's wheel, and I floated like a bubble through the plague air. Little did I know the stage was set for betrayal. It seemed to be a golden time.

39

Seemed. How often have I used that word? And not for nothing, as things are seldom what they seem in this stage-play world. *Venus* had been a success in every way but one. It hadn't sent young Harry leaping up the Burghley balcony and into bed with the virgin Vere to tread the nuptial dance. Public acclaim was mine but the private job was still undone.

'And that's how the sonnets got started?'

'Several verses, if you will, sweet Will – or perhaps I should say Master Shakespeare, once again, as this is weightier business? – to sweeten the young bugger's judgement.'

'The same gentleman caller?'

The very same.

'And you'll be well paid for your pains.'

'Pains? No pains, my lord, I assure you, I take pleasure in singing.'

'Pleasure won't keep the wolf from the door when winter comes. And that will come soon enough if the young sod doesn't marry. We'll all be wolf's meat.'

Venus and Adonis was pastoral-classical-allegorical, all cloaked up, but now they wanted straight talking, with rhyming couplets pointing up the argument – for marriage. How to tell a not exactly straight young man in exact straight terms that it's high time he got his sex right and got married?

I began with the traditional arguments. Don't be a miser, a glutton and a hoarder, an enemy to posterity and to your fair self. Make a copy of it now, for when you're old and cold, nobody will remember how lovely you once were. Besides, there's a lady waiting, and her womb will be a wormery unless you plough it, a tomb, unless you break in there and people it with sons to carry on this proud world, and your own noble line. Otherwise, my lad, you're a lost day, a withered plant, a blasted tree, a blank page. And thou among the wastes of time must go. It's the only way. Even my verses can't do you justice. They're fruitless verses anyway and nobody will believe them in time to come, they'll say I was a barren rascal, a hanger-on, a hypocrite and hyperbolist, exaggerating for the sake of gain. At best, they'll say, it was a poet's rage. But if you were to beget children now, your offspring would confirm the claims of these poor poems of mine and you'd live again, twice over: in these here lines, and in the lineaments of your brood.

'Something of a lecture?'

It was. I even lectured him on wanking.

'You didn't!'

Why dost thou abuse the bounteous largess given thee to give? Fourth poem in. I got to the root of the matter early on.

'And incidentally complimented him on the size of his prick.'

And explicitly chastised him for having traffic with himself alone. After which I appealed to fear: fear of time, which is what we fear most. Fear of being forty when you're twenty. Fear of being fifty when you're forty-five. Fear of being fifty-one – but of never seeing sixty. Or even fifty-two. Fear of not being any age, ever again, of becoming a subtraction, a nothing – hid in death's dateless night.

'Frightening stuff.'

And a strong card to play. The young don't want to be old and the old don't want to die. Think about it: the blackness of the grave, the white silence of bones. Total extinction. Unless you beget that son.

'And did he?'

Breath into the wind. Waste of ink and paper. He was not to be quatrained and coupleted and rhymed and pentametered into a Burghley bed, and would not be sonneteered into marriage if you please.

'But you got paid?'

Sixpence a sonnet. Why do you think I wrote so many?

'It wasn't a fortune.'

Exactly. That's why I felt the close fist of the queen behind it.

'She got her money's worth.'

So did Harry. He didn't like the content but he approved of the art. And of the immortality. The sonnets would be his mausoleum, a monument that would eternalise his name though I'd tried to convince him of the opposite. My lines are illusory, I told him. Time's lines are all too real. A poet's are a mere make-believe, a melancholy sham, a desperate rhetoric, a freak of fancy, a trick of the brain. Posterity will dismiss my claims as a poet's passion, no more. My sheaves of verse will be straws in the wind, and I'll be classed as a stretcher of truth, an invalid babbler. A sad old stylist with an antique pen.

'Did you believe that? *Do* you believe it?'

Of course. But Harry didn't. He thought I was a genius. And from now on he wanted me to celebrate not matrimony but himself, in all his glorious youthful beauty.

'So the sonnets changed direction.'

You don't argue with an aristocrat when you're an out of work player and a sixpenny sonneteer. Make me immortal with a rhyme, he said – spell it out for posterity. And though I didn't believe in that kind of spell, I was under another. I was under his. I'd fallen for his charm. I tried to keep it from myself but it was no use. One day I woke up and spoke the truth: I worshipped him. I was in love.

40

'Shall I compare thee to a summer's day?'

Oh, Francis! I was using the language of the heart. I was writing from the soul. I adored the little bastard.

'So it would appear.' Francis fumbling in his pocket.

What do you mean? What's that you've got there?

'*O carve not with thy hours my love's fair brow.*'

Put that down, Francis.

There he stood before my bed, with Thorpe's pirated edition of the sonnets – as good as pirated – in his fat paw, and thumbing through what suddenly felt like a lifetime of love, though it was only the matter of a year or two, a little more.

Where did you get that?

'Mistress Anne.'

Ah, to twist the knife a little before I die. I see. She knows where I keep it. She can't even read, you know.

'It's pretty distinctive, Will – and there's your name, she can read that I suppose. On the title-page – *Shakespeare's sonnets, never before imprinted*. Unless there's two of you.'

There's one of me, shortly to be none. And they never should have been imprinted. They broke my own secrecy rule. They were private pieces.

'No pieces are private, especially if you put them on paper, and especially a public man's. Come on, Will, you know that better than I do.'

They were the inner man's, they were the key to my heart. They were me.

'*For thy sweet love remembered such wealth brings... O! know, sweet love, I always write of you... It is my love that keeps mine eye awake... I love you so, that I in your sweet thoughts would be forgot... After my death, dear love, forget me quite...* Love, love, love, what were you thinking of? I mean, if it had at least been a woman. Forgive me, Will, I'm a pretty straight fellow, forthright Francis, you know – '

With his eye on that last slice of pie, I know.

'But what sort of – I can barely bring myself to say it – love – are we talking about here exactly? I mean, how far...if you don't mind my asking?'

I don't mind your asking.

'Well then, in so many words – but not too many. You talk, I'll eat, how's that?'

Well then, as you say, I was smitten, and so was he. A self-smitten poser with a piece of petulance for a mouth. He was beautiful, sociable, selfish, susceptible, and proud, an arrogant sod who lapped up flattery like a cat.

'Nice choice. Congratulations.'

He was also generous, impulsive, accomplished, and full of fun. He could throw condescension to the winds and chatter with princes and gravediggers in the same breath. He was a fatherless youth exposed to temptation, under pressure, on the verge of plenty, itching for action and audience, and in need of guidance. More, he loved the theatre, praised my plays, accepted my verses, enjoyed my company, sucked in my talk, drew me right to the heart of his charmed circle. Do you know what it means, Francis, to hear the polished flagstones of the courtyards ringing to your proud hooves as you ride out with the great ones? To see the sparks struck from the cobbled streets fly upwards to the stars? An earl's hand on your shoulder when the oars dip and the sound of a lute sends a ripple over the Thames and a shiver up your spine? And even the queen's pale fingers extending to your lips? I'll tell you what it means, Francis. It's the taste and smell of success.

'But what kind of an affair was it?'

It wasn't any kind of an affair. It was a loving friendship. It was a beautiful attachment, a fair fellowship. And the truth is that if these poems you're holding there happen to survive, it won't be the sonnets that immortalise a dead earl, it will be the dead earl that immortalises the sonnets. And who knows, the earl may even immortalise the writer.

'Isn't that the wrong way round?'

No, it's what a writer wants most. Inspiration. That was his greatest gift to me. On top of which he gave me work, and much more than work – experience, circles I'd never have moved in, not in my best dreams. But for him I'd have lived on the fringes. Married too young, my father's financial fall, those early struggles, success snatched away by the plague, it was Henry Wriothesley who opened the doors of a new world for me, not to mention a special gift – the money that would buy me a share in the Lord Chamberlain's Men and put me on the road to business. Yes, of course I worshipped him. Cash inspires. But I owed him something greater than gold. He was a golden lad. I was inspired to write about him, that's all, words that bound the three of us together: myself, himself, the sonnets. He liked the idea of living forever in my verse. I liked the idea of my verse living through him. Not forever, of course, that's nonsense. But we made sense together. We were Mercutio and Romeo, Antonio and Bassanio, Proteus and Valentine, Horatio and Hamlet, Falstaff and Hal.

'O thou, my lovely boy!'

That says it all, Francis. Now give me back my book. And if you ask me to tell you why I loved him I can only answer, because it was he, because it was myself.

'Nothing else?'

There was something else. We were two men in a whirling world and an insane city, each of us lacking something in his life. Harry was a young man without a father. I was an older man without a son. I'd been away from little Hamnet these six or seven years, seeing him all too seldom. I'd traded a family in Stratford for success in London, and had become father to a family of shadows, sons and daughters of the stage given life for a brief hour or two on wooden boards. Walking illusions. In Harry I saw something of the son I'd set aside for those strutting shadows of the stage, a son left fatherless in Stratford. The shadows were to take him sooner than I knew. O thou, my lovely boy...

And in time even Harry became a shadow. Yet, there was a time when I did think him almost immortal. He seemed to stop the sand in the glass, the sun in the sky, the sickle as it bit yearly into the grass that was our sick flesh. That golden time between us was truly wonderful, passing the love of women, and our delight in one another unmixed with baser matter and incapable of corruption.

Or so I liked to think.

But how wrong I was, Francis, how wrong, how wrong, how wrong.

41

Do you smell a woman? Do you smell her coming? Do you have her in the nose? If you do, you're wrong. This is no woman, waiting to come on – this is a fiend of hell, this thing of darkness I acknowledge mine. And half of London's too. But you could smell her coming, long before you stuck it in. You could smell her off-stage, clothed with her aura, the stench of sex exuding from her before she even entered the room. And the whiff of foreign sperm in your nostrils. She was the bay where all men ride. The world dropped anchor there. Chaste as a cat and crazy as a cow in June. The heat was never off her – she itched for it, the bitch. God, Lucy Negro was the abbess of abstinence compared to this all-fornicating whore whose whole course and motive was the consumption of the male member. She was like that truckle-bed, always available, ready for use. Her petticoats went up and down like the moon and she went at it like a rabbit.

'Like the small gilded fly, Will, that lechers in your sight?'

No, she was no fly, not this one, no. I was the fly, and she was the spider, and the web was her sex. Look and see – how many came there. Closer, closer, come nearer, into the core, see the struggles of just another fly. This is where I died, Francis. And for years to come only the husk of me was left.

'Bring her on stage, then. Let her present her part.'

Her part was all of her – and she presented it to all. Francis, I give you Emilia Bassano, born six years after me, daughter of Margaret Johnson and Baptist Bassano, one of her Majesty's Italian musicians. Her mother gave her the ivory complexion but she took the blackness of her hair from her father. But by the time Burbage built the Theatre her father was dead and buried in Bishopsgate, and only days after I came up to London for the first time her mother followed him. I must have passed their corpses under the daisies on my way to Shoreditch.

'Fatherless at six and orphaned at seventeen? She warranted compassion, Will.'

I warrant you, music and sex ran in her blood, a witch on the virginals, on which she practised hard, attracting the attention of the virgin queen, also a virginalist of note. Unlike the queen she practised hard in bed too – you hadn't been fucked unless you'd been to bed with Emilia Bassano. It was official. And every young man wants his will.

'And every old man too, eh, Will?'

No one older than old Hunsdon, Anne Boleyn's nephew, Henry Carey, the Lord Chamberlain himself. He had half a century on her, but she became his mistress and he set her up lavishly in her own apartments and pounded her nightly. With one strict caveat. That if his ancient penis proved fruitful in her belly, she would have to abandon all and be married off. It was up to her to take good care of the Chamberlain's sperm. And if she didn't, and his old arrows hit the target, the unintended accuracy would be all her fault.

It lasted five years – miraculous, according to her maids, who rumoured it abroad that old Hunsdon could copulate till the third cock crew and any normal man's would have dropped off long before dawn, not to mention all those she lay with in between times, when his busy creaking back was turned. Finally she conceived, and had to be married off 'for colour', as the old fucker politely put it.

She thought little enough of the choice: William Lanier, a royal musician. Or, as she much less subtly put it herself, a fucking strummer – how she could swear! – a menial minstrel! She was back where she'd started, among the court lowlies, little better than the wife of a tradesman as she saw it, compared with what she'd known. By the time she wed she was already big-bellied and a sad laughing stock, in pod with Hunsdon's bastard and married to a player – sweet bells jangled, out of tune and harsh.

'And that's when you fell for her – when she was brought low?'

When in disgrace with fortune and men's eyes. And not only fell for her but felt for her.

'And good old lust?'

Lechery, by this hand.

It started at court, late one winter's afternoon, in one of the corridors of state. I was by my Harry's side, his hand familiar on my shoulder (that lightness of touch!) as we strolled idly past the portraits of the tight-lipped Tudors, having come from a conference with their current representative and incumbent of the dynastic chair.

As we ambled along, one another's best, my attention was arrested by something that struck me quite dead in my tracks. It was the sound of music, that's all. But what music! O, it came o'er my ear like the sweet sound that breathes upon a bank of violets, stealing and giving odour! Somebody was playing on the virginals. And that somebody knew how to play, by Jesus! The melody was wafting from some distant room, but seemed to emanate from heaven, so sweet and subtle was the strain. It was just some old ballad – but I'd never heard it rendered with such delicacy of touch, as if it were the finest needlework. I imagined some angel with golden hair, barely touching the keys, with fingers of liquid air. Harry laughed as he tweaked me by the nose, plucked at my beard, and knocked my hat askew.

'Come on, Will, it'll be dark soon, you're keeping our horses waiting.'

'No, wait a moment, Hal, what is it?'

'What do you mean, what is it? It's *Walsingham*, isn't it? Even hoarier than *Greensleeves*.'

'No, I don't mean the tune, you idiot. Who's playing?'

'How the fuck do I know who's playing? Let's go.'

'No, Hal, sorry my boy, but I've got to see the source of this.'

'Jesu!'

And perhaps if I hadn't insisted that day, that particular day, who knows? The fall of a sparrow, the wreck of a poet, the ruin of a man. So Harry suffered himself to be led by me along the echoing corridors, past frowning Tudors, dead but deadly, till we reached the open door of the room where *she* – it had to be a woman – was playing. And I looked in and saw – that my golden-haired angel was as black as a devil.

The instrument was placed in the middle of the room and the player was seated facing the door, but the coal-black wave of her hair washed over her face, obscuring it, as she bent to the melody. Behind her the low sun glowed an angry scarlet, silhouetting her in a sort of lurid last-day glare. The lady's gown was low-cut and the breasts were bare and bulging, benefiting from the fashion of the upward thrust appropriate to unmarried virgins, ill-suited to her case, but did I care? Even from where I stood I could see the tracery of veins, bright-blue, circling the ivory orbs. At the white pit of her throat there grew a large black mole, like one of Luce Morgan's nipples brazenly shifted, to give Satan suck – so old Granny Arden would have said. The torch flared in the testicles and spread rapidly – I was on fire.

'Who is she?'

I was reduced to a croak.

'Ah, now that is something you don't want to know, old fellow, I can assure you of that. She needs no Lad's Love laid under her pillow – it's rue she requires at the rate she mates.'

And my friend tugged gently at my elbow.

'But why, Hal, tell me why? Why wouldn't I want to know?'

He brought his lips up close and breathed the words like Sanskrit into my ear.

'Because, sweet Will, the strumpet on the virginals is no less a lady than old Hunsdon's cast-off – and she casts them off for anybody, don't you know? Drops them all over London.'

I made as if to speak, turning my head towards the dark lady, but Harry took my chin in his hand and gently compelling me, turned my head so that I was looking into his eyes.

'And one last item of information for your sweeter understanding, sir – *she useth sodomy!*'

I turned my head to her again and again he twitched me by the chin, insistently returning me to meet his earnest eyes.

'Open-arse Emilia, as known in the trade, so unless you want to be a poperin-pear to her medlar tree, don't meddle with her, old boy! You have been warned.'

At that point the virginal-strumpet reached the end of her piece. Her head came up, the hair swept backwards, and a pair of black eyes opened wide on me from a milk-white face. That was my first sight of Emilia Lanier, née Bassano.

'Don't stop,' I whispered loudly, my voice almost gone.

She looked back at me.

'That's for me to say, isn't it?'

A bold woman. A lickerish grin. A cunning whore of Venice.

'If music be the food of love, play on.'

Harry groaned.

'Give me excess of it, that, surfeiting, the appetite may sicken and so die.'

She half bowed her head in acquiescence, turning it to the side with the mock modesty of the courtesan, and played again the last bars of *Walsingham.*

'That strain again! It had a dying fall.'

A dying fall? It was prophetic. I was a dead man. And I entered the room like one bewitched, pulled to the source of infection as if by the Pontic Sea. No ebb tide in the world could draw me away. This was not love but lust – not the pure lust of Lucy Negro's place but something dark and dirty. I knew already it would lead to madness and despair, but I had drunk the potion and was past cure. It had the spider in it. Standing by a virginal on a winter afternoon, all I wanted was that long black mane falling over me like a cloak and brushing my belly as she came down on me with her mouth.

Without warning she went straight into *Greensleeves* at a roistering pace, singing along as she played. *Alas, my love, ye do me wrong.* The jacks leapt up to kiss the white insides of the nimbly flying fingers and under the barbaric black shock of hair her ivory cheeks flushed in the flickering light. The room darkened around us as she rattled through the entire eighteen verses – but at the last verse she slowed dramatically and drew it out with a plaintiveness that was remarkable considering her shortness of breath.

Greensleeves, now farewell! adieu!
God I pray to prosper thee,
For I am still thy lover true –
Come once again and love me.

And with these last words playing on her bright red lips, she gazed sadly, soulfully into my eyes. What an actress – and what a dupe. I knew it was show. And her voice had witchcraft in it. O, she would sing the savageness out of a bear! After that she rounded it off with the final refrain, delivered at the mad pace that had taken her through the piece in under five minutes. The hands rebounded from the keys with an exaggerated flourish and she sat back in her chair laughing and panting, the black eyes flashing.

Harry affected his aloof look.

'Don't happen to dance too, do you?'

He was still leaning in the open doorway and the irony matched the bored yawn. The candlelit echoes of the last chords were still trembling in the smoky air. Untroubled by the apparent disdain she leapt to her feet and went hopping and skipping round the room some forty paces, her arms in the air, hands and fingers twirling. And having lost her breath she spoke and panted, and with such excess of energy that she did make defect perfection, and, breathless, power breathe forth...

'I can dance any man round the clock, sirs!'

'If he's as old as Hunsdon, you mean?' Harry sneered.

That he wanted her was obvious and this irked and alarmed me.

'Or as young as you, *boy*!'

The earl ignored the insult to his immaturity and to his rank and retorted simply, 'To vouchsafe this is no proof.'

And with deliberate discourtesy, as if she wasn't there, he addressed me across the room in an exaggerated whisper.

'She made old Carey lay his sword to bed, you know – he ploughed her and she cropped.'

'And since then – ' Her wit was whiplash accurate in its quick return.

'And since then I've worn out younger ploughs than yours, young sir – in a single night.'

A snort from Harry.

'Why don't you show us what you've got, then? Bush and furrow!'

'Not now, ploughboy, I'm practising to play before the Queen tonight.'

'Did you think I meant country matters?' quipped Harry.

Her cheeks were still glowing in the glimmering candlelight.

'It doesn't matter what I think, *my Lord,* the court must come before the cunt.'

Harry smiled but I stood and stared. So devoid of innuendo. The actor in me came to the rescue.

'Lady, shall I lie in your lap?'

'What *are* you thinking of, Master Shakespeare?'

'Nothing.'

That's a fair thought to lie between a maid's legs.

'O!' Harry broke in, sniggering, and exaggerating the effect of the vowel. 'O! she knows you, Will – and before you've even known *her*!'

'That's because I'm a know-*all*, gentlemen.'

'Then lady, I desire to know you better.'

But Harry had had enough of word games.

'An apt enough player, madam, but a nimble-fingered whore.

Come on, Will, let's leave virginals to virgins and drabs to jacks!'

And he pulled me roughly from the room.

She was still standing there, her hands on her hips, head thrown back, face flushed, and laughing breathlessly. I could hear it echoing through the corridors of my mind long after we'd left Whitehall.

42

It was darker than desire, it was crueller than love. There was something evil about it. Lust? *She useth sodomy.* This was the dram, the leprous distilment that poisoned me, poured in the porches of my ears. As I rode off with Harry into the dark that night my whole being was bent now to one tortured quest. The plague had struck at last in its most virulent form. This was the black death.

I begged Harry to use his rank to write to her on my behalf which he did without a thought, to favour his friend. A rustic nobody and scribbler of scripts yearned for an hour with a high-class whore, to plume up his will. And why not? I'd have her, take my turn, withdraw, pleased with my triumph, and we'd get on with our friendship. That's how Harry saw it.

But he teased me mercilessly.

'O flesh, flesh, how art thou fishified! Poor Will, smitten by a brace of breasts, stabbed with a white wench's black eye, shot through the ear with a love-song! Death by a dozen quatrains to the tune of *Walsingham*, hung by a garter and drawn and quartered by *Greensleeves*, alas, alas! Who would have thought it? A blushing strumpet with the breath of a sparrow, one of the sluttish spoils of opportunity, a whitely wanton with a velvet brow, two pitch-balls stuck in her face for eyes, yes, by heaven, and one that would do the deed for sixpence and a song. A very good whore. And you to sigh for her! to watch for her!'

'Thy lips rot off, sweet Hal!'

'No, old fellow, but yours will – if she but once offers you her bluest veins to kiss. Why man, she's followed the sugared game long before you, as young as she is, she's melted down the lightfoot lads in different beds of lust, and has brought down rose-cheeked youth to the tub-fast and the diet!'

'Harry Hyperbole, come to court?'

'Believe what you care to, friend, and call me what you like, I tell you her activities spell the end of all fit members. A jigging fille-de-joie. A lisping loose fish. An ambling tart who loves it up the arse!'

'Peace, gentle friend!'

'Piece? Aye, you'll need to hold your piece with her, sir, but it will anger Hunsdon and husband too if you dare raise a spirit in her circle, sir, even if you let it stand there at the back door till she lays it down for you.'

'Enough, no more!'

'No more? That's but the text. You haven't heard the sermon yet.'

'I prithee, gentle Hal...'

'*And it shall come to pass that instead of sweet smell there shall be stink.* And we know where *that* comes from, don't we, Will?'

Harry was unstoppable.

'*And in that day the Lord shall discover her secret parts.* Therefore I conjure you, Will, by Lanier's bright eyes, by her high forehead and her scarlet lip, by her fine foot, straight leg and quivering thigh – '

'Have you done?'

'And the demesnes that there adjacent lie – '

'Eat your sock, Hal!'

'Make it a buskin, old man – and hung be the heavens with black. The stage is set for tragedy...!'

But he wrote the letter and the thing began.

The thing, the courtship – if that is what it can be called – proved successful, if that is the word to denote so dark a triumph. I sent her sonnets, naturally, though not letting her see the half of those I penned. *How oft, when thou, my music, music play'st... My mistress' eyes are nothing like the sun... In faith I do not love thee with mine eyes...* And she sent me back word. 'Stuff this stuff, sir sonneteer – write me something juicy!' She wanted bawdiness, not beauty. So I wrote about our two wills, and especially, about hers, and its capacity – to accommodate Will Lanier and Will Shakespeare and the wills of all the world.

Wilt thou whose will is large and spacious not once vouchsafe to hide my will in thine?

This whetted her desire and my suit was accepted.

Harry was the pandar, his letters providing the bridge prescribed by protocol even for the extra-marital fucking of a Jewish-Italian whore. Bridge? It was an archway over the abyss, but nothing in the world would keep me from it, blind as I was.

Why spin it out further? Emilia Lanier took me to her bed and fucked me just as frankly as I'd imagined it on that first plague-struck afternoon: the tongue down the tonsils and right up the tail, the mouth round the prick, the prick in the anus, up to the hilts, the lips of her will parted over my face, the beast with two backs inverted, on its side, upside down, inside out, its legs in the air everywhere at once. Emilia Lanier fucked me with the monthly blood in her, braving the smallpox and monstrous births. She sucked me dry and swallowed my sperm and I licked her wet and drank up her juice. Simultaneous. I came in her face and saw her lashes flecked with foam. I rammed my cock into every orifice, filling nostrils and navel and ear with hot spouting milk.

Offended, Francis? You stopped eating your pie!

'There's no offence, Will.'

Oh, but there was, Francis, and much offence too. Would you prefer a fig-leaf to fact? There's no dressing it up. We did everything a man and woman could possibly do together. And as I buggered her she screamed for me to fuck the harder and stay inside till I'd hardened up enough to give it her again.

'I can picture the scene.'

Acted out almost without dialogue, the soundless swinging of breasts and balls, the grunts and sighs, the mad moans, the brief muttered directions from one player to the other as the beastly drama unfolded. Words were not necessary. We had nothing to say to one another. She had an itch and I was mad to scratch it. No beast on earth went to it with a more riotous appetite. It was a shameful business, unembellished by any tender touch. No drop of decency was spilt, no milk of human kindness. *Triste post coitum* was the prevailing wind, the expense of spirit in a waste of shame. And I lived for months around that waist, well in the middle of her favours. Not that I was the only one of her privates, nor the sole lord of her secret parts. She was a strumpet and she shortened the lives of all who came to spend their manly marrow in her arms, and afterwards go mad. As mad as they had been both in pursuit and in possession of this fatal whore.

None madder than myself. No sooner had than hated. Had, having, and in quest to have – I was like a dog after a bitch, a mad dog, a cruel bitch. It was the season. It was always the season with her. Fuck was her word and the gutter was her cunt.

'All this the world well knows; yet none knows well – to shun the heaven

that leads men to this hell.'

Well chosen, Francis. Now close the book. It's an attack on myself, not on her. No-one knew the way to hell better than I – or less about how to avoid it. *Wide is the gate and broad is the way that leadeth to destruction.* The primrose path. That was her, all right – but without the primroses. She stank of sin.

43

'And so you broke away from her?'

Let's say I was broken from her – or just broken. The plague had kept the theatres shut most of the winter but we opened up again in April. Then in the summer of '94, when the heat brought back the plague, we were shut down again.

I remember that day, the day they came and closed us. I left the Theatre and wandered back to St Helen's. I'd moved from Shoreditch to Bishopsgate by that time. But I didn't go home. Instead I carried on walking down Bishopsgate Street, dropping in at the usual inns and ordinaries, the Dolphin, the Vine, the White Horse, the Saracen's Head, the Four Swans, the Green Dragon, the Angel, soaking it up at every one and throwing every one of London's weird beers down my throat – angels' food at the Angel, dragon's milk at the Dragon, mad dog and left leg and huffecap where I could get them. By the time I came to the Cross Keys my eyes were crossed.

'Unlike you, Will, to be cross-eyed.'

Unlike me, to be wandering at random on hopeless feet along Cheapside, by St Paul's, through Ludgate, all the way down Fleet Street and the Strand, past Charing Cross, and south again, till I came to Longditch, Westminster, almost to Whitehall. No, my feet weren't aimless. Who was I trying to deceive? And as I stared at my filthy shoes I heard again that voice from scripture. *Her feet go down to death, her steps take hold on hell.* The thing of darkness lived in Longditch and already I was entering the house I'd been drawn to a hundred times and more. I was climbing the stairs to the room where William Lanier had been cuckolded in every hour of the clock and under every star of the sky, and as I approached the room where I too had made one in that multiple cuckolding, I heard again the cries it made, the beast with two backs, at it, yet again, yes, why should I have been in the least surprised that she was even now about it, the deed of darkness, the age-old trade in which she was the witch, the queen of cunts, and ice-cold breaker of hearts? This was what she was for. This was what she did.

If only I'd turned round and gone away. But how we torture ourselves. I couldn't stop myself, inching up to the chamber door and easing it open just a crack, to feed my foul thoughts and fuel my jealousy the more. Just a touch more, then, they were so busy at it they wouldn't be aware of me, oh aye, just as I thought, she was flat on top, with her back to me and only the blind eye of hell staring at me as she thrust and thrust, but a different pair of hands were on her now, delicate and ringed and white, the fingers of a noble, what else, and strange how the aristocratic erection on which she fucked herself so fast and hard looked just the same as any other man's, player's, peasant's, even my own humble will, and it wasn't until the man cried out in his sudden ecstasy and I recognised that piping, scarcely broken voice, that I understood in the despair and fury of my very depths that this was not just *any* aristocrat, oh, no!

O, Jesus! Can it be so?

'Spare me the full details, Will.'

No scene with her in it was ever actually pretty but this one even less so. You can picture how it went – the uncontrolled sobbing I heard coming from somebody till I realised it was coming from myself, the startled servant girl running in, and me hurling a handful of silver at her for the keeper of a bawdy house, the flung coins clattering and rolling round the floor – You, you, yes you! There's money for your pains, they've done their course, I pray you, turn the key and keep their counsel! – the two of them disconnecting then and the awful indignity of it, indeed the pity of it, his prick unsheathed and on show, his seeds spilling from her, the look of black anger on her face, the shame and pain on his – he wasn't much more than a boy, for God's sake; and the start of the excuses, ah yes, the excuses, the serpent tempted me and I did eat, that filthy worm! But I'll not go on, I said I'd spare you. Let's draw the curtain.

'Please.'

But the play goes on behind it, all the time, in the mind, and behind the shut curtains of sleep.

'Was he just another fuck to her?'

Every man was another fuck to her, except this particular man. He was young, a virgin (take my word for it), he was handsome, he was rich, he was well connected, a peer of the realm – and he was unattached. How could she resist – she of all women? And how could a common player compete? He for his part told me tearfully much later that he was led to her precisely *because* she was my mistress. And, do you know, I believed him and still do. The feeling rang true. The boy was jealous, he was trying to get closer to me, his friend – in his own fashion he was being even more faithful to me than before. He was fucking *me.*

I do forgive thy robbery, gentle thief... Thou dost love her because thou know'st I love her... Then, if for my love thou my love receivest, I cannot blame thee for my love thou usest.

But that came later, that time of understanding and forgiveness – no more be grieved at that which thou hast done. He too found himself unable at first to struggle free, the fly to the web, the moth to the flame, such was her fatal allure – O! from what power hast thou this powerful might! And how could I grudge him the petty wrongs that liberty commits? A friend should bear his friend's infirmities. He himself was a walking temptation to any woman, and when a woman woos, what woman's son will sourly leave her till she have prevailed? Not my Harry. So I argued it out in my racked heart. She had corrupted his innocence and poisoned all three of us. The well had been defiled.

But it was the thought of losing *him*, not her, that was the real terror. And I made this known to him in the sonnets that poured out of me then.

That thou hast her it is not all my grief... that she hath thee is of my wailing chief.

I was writing stark naked as never before. And I veered wildly between humiliation –

Take all my loves, my love, yea take them all.

And hatred –

Lilies that fester smell far worse than weeds.

Until the storm subsided and I said, *I shall go softly all my years in the bitterness of my soul.*

But what do you think, Francis? Life goes on. It had been going on for months, so it came out, and it went on for months to come, in spite of the pledges. There were secret meetings, discoveries, quarrels, rumours, reconciliations, promises, broken promises, the whole catastrophe. What was I complaining about, she once asked me? I was breaking my own marriage-vows, after all. 'A long way from Stratford, you've come a long way from home, and you're just like all the others, so don't be so desperate, Will, don't be so dire.' Then she'd lift her dress and place my hand between her legs and say, 'Come on, old man, I'll fuck you out of kindness, for old time's sake' – looking with pretty ruth upon my pain. With those eyes of hers, those black and loving mourners. And I'd give in – what else? – and go to bed with her, whipping it up again, the ugly circle of lust, disgust, and jealousy – to follow still the changes of the moon with fresh suspicions, to tell them over on the rack, to long for sweet oblivion of their stolen hours of lust, as prime as goats, as hot as monkeys, as salt as wolves in pride, to find not Harry's kisses on her lips, grossly gape on, behold her topped, and my relief must be to loathe her, like summer flies that quicken in the shambles even with blowing...

And once – once only, as she lay asleep, after the inexorable deed and I looked at her white throat in the candlelight, the black mole moving almost imperceptibly with her quiet breathing afterwards... I thought of it, thought of murder. Put out the light. Strangle her in her bed. Even the bed she hath contaminated. But once put out thy light, I know not where is that Promethean heat that can thy light resume.

And I trembling, fled the scene.

Eventually, inevitably, she gave us both the clap, and so, sick in spirit and flesh, I went to Bath and took the remedy. And a sad distempered guest I was. Past cure I was, now reason was past care, and frantic mad with ever more unrest. Only by writing about it could I cauterise the wound, fight pain with pain. Weary with toil – I haste me to my bed. And so back I came to Harry, the wound in the heart not healed, but hidden.

How like a winter hath my absence been from thee, the pleasure of the fleeting year! What freezings have I felt, what dark days seen! What old December's bareness everywhere!

And he welcomed me with remorse. And with more than remorse, with money. A lot of money. He emptied his purse, it was his way of saying sorry. That was when I bought myself a share in the newly formed Lord Chamberlain's Men, just as the plague finally decided that London had had its share of misery and the theatres re-opened again. It was time to put the other plague behind me, and my two loves of comfort and despair. Two hopeless loves. I loved a man I couldn't have and I lusted for a woman I couldn't respect. As for my wife, abandoned and betrayed, the sonnets rubbed her out of my heart, banished her from my life. And yet she was better than the woman who betrayed me. She was false as water.

And Harry? In October '94 he came of age and had to pay piper Burghley for his breach of promise to marry grand-daughter. The fine was five thousand pounds, which crippled him. But his hour did come. He sailed off with his hero Essex in a company that included, ironically, William Lanier, and also the young Jack Donne. It was an anti-Spanish expedition to the Azores and he captained a ship. He took such a long farewell of his new love, Elizabeth Vernon, that he made her pregnant. Essex came home in disgrace, having let the Spanish fleet slip off without a fight, but Harry sank a man-o'-war and was the darling of the navy, and of his new wife.

He became a family man, grew a reluctant beard, and lost his looks.

He also lost something of his soul. He became a politician and a Privy Councillor, one of the cold controlling kind that eventually inherit the earth – without a hint of meekness. We drifted apart. It's the saddest thing in the world, is love gone – love gone, and in its place that sort of bare nodding acquaintance that is so painful because it reminds you of what you once had, what you once knew, what you once were, to one another.

I ask you again, Francis. All that love – where does it go to? All that beauty and passion? And when love begins to sicken and decay it uses an enforced ceremony. Better to have nothing at all than to be left with that bare politeness, the stiff and awkward recognition that saddens and embarrasses, don't you think? You meet in the street, you murmur something, nothing, you look at one another as if over an immense distance. There's nothing left, nothing there. This is what life does to us. This is what it did to me. And to the third Earl of Southampton, once my all-in-all, once my Harry.

So much for the lovely boy.

44

'Well, you didn't lack matter, Will.'

How do you mean?

'For your sonnets – quite a story.'

It's the oldest story in the world, the tale of three, the eternal triangle. And it went well beyond the sonnets. Where do you think Leontes came from? And Othello?

'That was later, wasn't it?'

You store things up. Sometimes they fester and break out. Right now I was flexing my dramatic muscles. I threw in my lot with the Chamberlain's Men, with young Burbage, now the player king, and Kempe the clown. And in that wet but plague-free summer of '94 the Admiral's Men settled in at the Rose while we took up residence at the Theatre. From my new quarters in St Helen's, less than a quarter of a mile away, outside the wall, I could hear the screams of the Bedlamites, inviting all-comers to the theatre of madness. Mostly they went unregarded. Who cares about the barking of mad dogs? But madness in great ones – must not unwatched go. And there was much madness to come.

So what do you think – by the rivers of Bishopsgate I sat down and wept? Wept when I remembered Harry? No, I sat down and set the scene. In fair Verona, in money-mad Venice, in easy golden Belmont, it didn't matter where. London was the real scene and the action was already in my head, past but present, waiting to leap into life, into the future, the play within the skull, the spectacle of a heart ripped out, a soul ground down in the mills of hell, but a mind ready to deal with all of that. The Chamberlain's Men were the stars of a bright new London, purged of pestilence and ready for taking. For the next twenty years business and busyness were the twin pillars of the new life. They propped me up. I stood between the pillars and like Samson I felt the power flow through. It was like being touched by God. I was inspired.

'Is that how inspiration comes – from God? Is that how it

works?'

Lepers are touched by God. Or so they may like to believe. Remember Lazarus? When you're a leper you're in a special relation to God. You've been chosen. I was a leper, Francis, be in no doubt of that. And when you're leprous you either carry your cross or pull out the nails, one by one. Every play you write is a nail withdrawn. No nail, no play.

'Are you saying that the secret of inspiration is suffering?'

Writing is a form of illness. Happy men don't write plays. Happy men play bowls.

'So your *Midsummer Night's Dream* is the work of an unhappy man? Come off it, Will!'

Ah now, Francis, that's why you're a lawyer, not an actor. Burbage knew all about life's dream, about the comic surface and the tragic core, how quick bright things come to confusion, when the jaws of darkness devour them up. He could dig deep, deeper than Kempe, and he could make Bottom sound like Hamlet in a world where carpenters talked like gods. You see, Francis, to realise the bottomless reach of Bottom's dream is to be wise. Burbage had that wisdom in his bones. He understood that a play with fairies and labourers in it only pretends to be a comedy. He understood that if there were a sympathy in choice, war, death or sickness did lay siege to it, making it momentary as a sound, swift as a shadow, short as any dream –

'Brief as the lightning in the collied night.'

Well completed, Francis, and apt to the purpose. Such is life, such is love, and such is the illusion of choice. Like the plague, you never know who, where, or when love will strike, but you know it will be devastating and you know you've no choice in the matter. Maybe the moon chooses, with its bow bent in heaven. Or the stars strike us with their spears. Whatever the answer, whatever the reason, one thing is certain – human confusion. So Pyramus dies in error and so does Romeo, Thisbe and Juliet too, while sterile queens like Rosaline die unmated, unfulfilled and chaste, free from the chaos, chanting faint hymns to the cold fruitless moon. Celibacy is rape. Better to die by Cupid's arrow. And a young girl's flower is purpled with love's wound. O, happy dagger, this is thy sheath – let it rest there. And so the *Dream* runs into *Romeo*, my first work for the Chamberlain's.

'*Romeo*. Now that's tragic.'

But life goes on, Francis, I told you. Old men babble about their age and ailments, servants squabble, families feud, and a long-tongued nurse wants her thirteen-year-old charge to have sex. That's not tragedy, that's life. In spite of tragedy the food has still to be put on the table and the family must dine. You above all appreciate that, Francis, don't you? As surely as you appreciate the mundane days of the week that keep love in perspective. You can't imagine Cordelia dying on a Thursday, for example – but Juliet does. Or Duncan being stabbed on a Wednesday – the murder is in Macbeth's mind and that's where he bleeds to death. But Mercutio dies on a Monday. Is that trite, Francis? Yes, it is, it's trite when a man can die on any day of the week, when life has become cheap and chancy – like that chilling thrust of Tybalt's under Romeo's arm, that gives the play its real-life twist.

All that, Francis, and the fact that you never really know who your family are, who your friends are, or who you are yourself, until it's too late. By the time tragedy has released the real people, the hidden identities, out of their own surprised skins, the stage is suddenly littered with corpses, like the stage of this wide world, and we're left asking, how did all that happen? And once more the fatal truth hits us. Free will is an illusion. At least it looked that way for two young star-crossed lovers, once upon a time in Verona.

45

'I don't know how you found the time, Will.'

Time for what, Francis?

'Time for all that subtlety – I mean, to put all that *thought* into your plays.'

Thought, Francis? No, there's no thought in them, not a scrap of rumination. Think for a solitary second and the thing goes dead. They were scripts, not plays, written by the hour and for the hour, they were lines on paper, that's all. No, if I'd stopped to think, I'd never have written a single script. They're plays now all right, but only because of what you or I can see in them, or choose to see in them. At the time I didn't do any choosing, there was never any question of choice, I was simply driven – driven mad, if you like, mad, possessed, fired and surprised. Whatever it was, it had nothing to do with thought. It was entirely instinctive – irrational, and even insane.

'Not stark raving Bedlamite insane, though, surely.'

No, that's the destructive and self-destructive end of insanity. Mine was the creative end of it, but it's the same stick, and it easily gets turned around. Things go wrong as you write – and for the better. If you'd thought about it you'd have put it right, and the play would have suffered. Take the *Merchant*, for example. Should have been a straight uncomplicated romance, complete with wicked Jew. But then look what happened – Shylock ran away with the play.

'You allowed him to.'

I couldn't control him. Maybe it was my own humanity I couldn't control, and it got the better of the playwright. Maybe it was because of what they'd done to Lopez.

'The queen's doctor? The one who tried to poison her?'

No he didn't, it was Essex poisoned her mind. But yes, Lopez, and those fine Christian Jew-haters of old England. Maybe it was because my own father was a money-lender and a butcher, good with both blades, cutting his pound of flesh from beasts and people, in order to survive. Maybe it was because there was some sort of fellow-feeling between me and Shylock. What's the difference after all between a dirty Jew and a filthy outcast actor? Whatever it was, he grew under my pen, demanding to be heard. Yes, he's avarice, he's anger, he's the devil from the old dramas, he's the killer of Christ and the tyrannical father too, but he's also got eyes, hands, organs, senses, affections, passions, and they're all abused. Ghettoed, garrotted, beaten, burned alive, murdered in mass, he's the voice of subjugated peoples all over the world and all through history. He compelled me to listen to him. Even the groundlings did. They left the theatre applauding but rubbing their eyes, a little dazed by what they'd just heard. They remembered Shylock long after they'd forgotten the moonlight.

I had Burbage to thank for that. Take another bow, Richard. He never came on like Barabas. It was a cut above Marlowe and he knew it. He could do you the cut-throat dog, the black demon whirling a cloak of flames, all that stuff. But he made you see and hear the fellow creature underneath the greasy gabardine, tortured, baleful, intense. He made you feel for him. And he went out with a howl and a whimper, like the dying Lear, like the dying bear, dragged from the pit, after the show for the Christians is over. They laid him on the rack and the gentle Portia turned the screws.

'The quality of mercy is not strained.'

The irony of it! Nobody marks that. Punish a man not by hanging, beheading or jail, but by making him change his religion. Now there's the ultimate twist of the knife, far surpassing anything Topcliffe could have invented.

'Yes, but that awful pound of flesh – '

Is emblematic, not essential. Flesh is living but weak, gold is dead but powerful, capable of corrupting the flesh, but incorruptible in itself. It can be weighed to the exact ounce and it doesn't bleed. Flesh does – and so does the heart, never more so than when betrayed, when love fails and its lily festers.

'They did show mercy of a sort.'

Not at Tyburn. No Portia in disguise arrived to save the day for Lopez, and nobody knew how many drops of blood were shed when the disembowelling was done and the quartering was over, or how much his innards weighed. Nobody was counting. Except Essex perhaps, who'd hounded him to his death like Gratiano, while the Christians cheered. 'Don't give his prick to the dogs – it's circumcised! They're good Christian hounds!' So: bloodshed, ballads, jests, a carcass torn for hounds, and a Jew died in agony – all in all a good day out. Nobody wanted to miss out on any of it, least of all the dramatist. Every man wants his pound of flesh. Especially the dramatist.

Yes, I hated the laughter, the mockery, the way Lopez was jeered all the way to his disembowelling. I hated the bloody, cynical Marlowe and his Jew of Malta play, hated all that. But I cashed in on it all the same, milking the myth for all it was worth. The Jews caught little Christian children and used their blood for bread. They poisoned wells and spread plague. Jewish women produced sperm. Jewish men menstruated.

'I saw the play once, Will – but I never saw it that way.'

Blood and betrayal, that's what I fed on. I'd tried all the other roads and failed, got lost. Failed as a husband, failed as a father, failed as a tradesman and as a scholar too, though that was hardly my fault. Failed as a martyr, you could say, not one of God's soldiers. And when a lovely boy and a dark woman have let you down, when pure friendship and pure lust have also failed – then what's left, I ask you, Francis, what's left to save and satisfy?

'You tell me.'

The stage. The stage was what saved me and kept me sane. It was banishment from respectability, exiled and reviled at first, just like Shylock. But I found great fellowship with the actors. We were a tight-knit family, bound by our common trade, illusion. And by our suffering, for sufferance is the badge of all our tribe.

And now I was in full flow – not in full control, thank God, for a writer in full control is a corpse, without the Promethean heat – I was inspired, if that's the word, by that very suffering, and my willingness to let it work, to get myself out of the way and give the crowds what they wanted. There seemed nothing now to cross me from the golden time I looked for.

Little did I know. There *was* more pain to come. A personal pain that divorced me from my time and made me madder still. Harry came back from Cadiz like conquering Caesar, the queen reached sixty-three – a portentous nine times seven – and didn't die, confounding her astrologers and drying Jeremiah's tears. The mortal moon had endured her eclipse and peace proclaimed olives of endless age. But the drops of this most balmy time, precious as they were, couldn't heal the hurt I was now about to endure.

46

I was sitting in St Helen's shortly before sunrise. It was the tenth of August, '96, the Company was on tour in Kent but I'd stayed behind and was struggling to bring *King John* to life, when the knock came to the door. I clattered downstairs, cursing, anxious to see off whoever it was and get back to the early thirteenth century. Perhaps I'd find a princely heart in the foxy monarch, as Holinshed had suggested, though it wasn't looking likely. When I opened the door and saw the horseman framed in the blue oblong of early Bishopsgate light I knew at once that King John's would be a heart that would never find a beat. My own skipped more than one.

Why do horsemen always call at dawn? He bowed slightly from the saddle but didn't dismount as he held out the letter at arm's length, as if rejecting all responsibility for it. I took it from between two gloved fingers. Then he wrenched fiercely, suddenly at the horse's reins and galloped away up Gracious Street, his crimson cloak fluttering like the streamers of the dawn. The cobbles rang to the hooves. He'd made no other noise, hadn't spoken a solitary word.

He didn't have to. It was Anne's hand all right. Almost illiterate when I'd married her, and still unable or unwilling to read, she'd made heroic efforts to scratch out this one and she was numerate enough to count the cost of a courier. The heart started its thudding as I broke open the red seal. It looked like a bloody splodge of sun, matching the Bishopsgate one that was catching the spire of St Helen's and turning its windows to fire. I was still standing in the open doorway.

Seconds later I was lying in the street, my legs buckled under me, my head swimming, in all that incredible blue emptiness, reaching unseen into ever more emptiness. By the time I'd risen stiffly and dizzily and found my way back upstairs like an old tired man, I was able to look at the letter again. I could see only the one tear-blotched line. *Our son, your Hamnet, sick unto death. For Jesus' sake come quickly!*

Every scrape of the pen had been a torment to her, physically and emotionally. There were no details. Was it a wasting? Was it a fever?

An accident? Either way I knew what to expect. I sat down quietly at the table and looked at the seventh scene of the last Act, where I'd left off. God help me, I couldn't help myself. I picked up the still-glistening quill and I carried on with the dying King's last lines.

There is so hot a summer in my bosom
That all my bowels crumble up to dust:
I am a scribbled form, drawn with a pen
Upon a parchment, and against this fire
Do I shrink up.

It was the first time I'd slipped into the skin of the unfortunate king. He'd been poisoned. What had happened to my son? How sweet it was for a moment to retreat into the unreal world of the play and shut out the terrible questions I knew must come. Not for long, though. Forty minutes later King John was dead, the drama was over, and I was on my way back to Stratford.

All the mind-filled length of the journey home I tortured myself with guilt. Was Hamnet's death a punishment for my desertion that day on Clopton Bridge?

I remembered the agony of poor Browne in the Boar's Head, that day he learned that he'd lost his family in the plague and wished he'd been there in London to die with them. 'And I must be from thence,' he kept saying, 'and I must be from thence,' before he crumpled up into that tight little knot of pain and was struck dumb with grief. 'Give sorrow words,' we kept saying to him. I remembered that advice bitterly now as I rode along in silence. Give sorrow words; the grief that does not speak whispers the o'er-fraught heart and bids it break. But there was no-one to speak to.

On the Chilterns I caught up with the horseman who had brought me the letter. We glanced at one another as I passed him in a dust-cloud on the blinding white road – staring into the eyes for a few strict seconds in the silence and the heat. I wondered for a moment if he rode a pale horse, but it was a bay. Neither of us spoke a word or twitched a muscle. Having delivered doom to my doorstep he was taking it easy on the return. I dug the spurs in deeper and hurried on northward with my heartful of horror and dread.

The rooks were cawing from the elms as I rode in and I knew they were singing his requiem. I didn't need the family huddle of five white faces out in the street to tell me that much. The shutters of the upstairs room were closed. Ten arms went round me from all sides, gripping me tightly. I took Judith and Susanna in an arm each and hugged them hard but the other arms continued to enfold me tightly, blindly. I thought of Laocoon and his two offspring, crushed by the monstrous sea-snakes that the gods had seen fit to send to suffocate them into silence. Nothing was being said here, just throat noises and tears. Then that old wordless air started up again in Henley Street, the one that only mothers sing, the one I'd heard Mary Arden singing for her dead daughter Anne, the one she'd sung before I was born, for Joan and Margaret. The one Anne Hathaway was singing now for our son.

'Let me see him now.'

I left them and took my grief upstairs. All grief is private. Jack Donne used to say that no man is an island. But every man is, especially when death comes. I opened the door quietly as I used to do, in case I waked him. Maybe he was only sleeping. That's what Jesus said, didn't he, about Jairus's daughter? *The maid is not dead, but sleepeth; therefore weep not.*

My son was dead, though. There was a terrible stillness about that little form beneath the blankets, a stillness that was not of sleep. Now I could re-speak sonnets in chilling whispers. Even so my sun one early morn did shine...but out! alack! he was but one hour mine. The region cloud had masked him from me now. Now I was Capulet. Alas, he's cold. His blood is settled and his joints are stiff. Life and these lips have long been separated. Death lies on him like an untimely frost. Upon the sweetest flower of all the field.

Juliet and Jairus's daughter got up again and breathed. They stretched and yawned. *Where have I been*? But here would be no miracle, no friar's balm for Hamnet, culled from the cunning fields, to make him wake as from a pleasant sleep. And, in spite of Christ's injunction, someone was weeping. I could see the scalding teardrops splashing the white sheets above the whiter face, and I could hear the strangled sobs coming from someone far away but painfully close – sounds harsher than the requiem of the rooks.

Stand with me a moment longer, Francis, while summer lasts and I commit that little body to the wet green earth of the riverbank. Stand with me still, while I sweeten his sad grave with thought.

It was the eleventh day of the month and I'd buried my only son, aged eleven. Through the slanting tombstones I could see the baby swans following in their parents' wake along the serene silvery Avon, and I could hear the silvery shouts of the schoolboys running home from school to play in the streams. Hamnet should have been among them, the son that had caught a raging fever that nothing would quench, and none could bid the winter come to thrust his icy fingers in his throat, nor let the kingdom's rivers take their course through his burned bosom, nor entreat the north to make his bleak winds kiss these parched lips and comfort him with cold. As I'd sat in St Helen's scribbling away through these long hot summer days and our blistering ships had cut their way into Cadiz, my cygnet had burned up and died. Now I was the helpless child, following the dead form of my son as he sped like quicksilver into eternity.

And still am, Francis. I am the cygnet to this pale faint swan who chants a doleful hymn to his own death and from the organ-pipe of frailty sings.

Where was my old Catholic God now? And all those sonnets to Harry about fatherhood and begetting a son – how ironic now they sounded in my mind. I was thirty-two and Anne Hathaway had forty winters on her brow and looked it. There had been a winter in her womb for the past ten years. The tree of descent had all so suddenly been lopped. Fleance had not escaped the stroke of fate. And my brothers – Gilbert at thirty, Richard at twenty-two, and Edmund at sixteen – standing round the graveside with me, they'd all be in their own graves before me, the whole line facing extinction. As we stood and looked into Hamnet's grave we were looking at the end of the line.

There was another irony, a bitter one. The Garter King of Arms was about to grant at last the family arms my father had been denied and had wanted so badly for nearly thirty years. And now no grandson to inherit the empty fame. The grant came not three months later – *Non Sans Droict* – the consolation prize for dead Hamnet's grandfather. Astonishingly, the honour made him happy. As for me, I'd have exchanged a thousand family arms for that one lost son, whose going left such an emptiness in heart and home. I knew there would be no more creations from my body. All future children would be the offspring of my imagination, conceived where fancy's bred, while the one child I'd cherished and deserted lay dead and cold in his little kingdom of Stratford clay.

Eventually you have to walk away. No matter how fond the farewell, how lingering the clasp, you have to walk away. I turned my back on my son's grave, came to Henley Street, and went back up to his room. I sat down by the empty bed on which his clothes were folded. The room filled up with shadows, then darkness. Still I sat on, unable to retire, unable to bring myself away from that bed. There was nowhere I wanted to go.

47

When I finally came back to my lodgings in St Helen's, I clumped heavily upstairs to find the script of *King John* scattered on the table just as I'd left it. I leafed through the pages till I came to Act Three Scene Four, where Constance, bereft of her boy, takes comfort from the Cardinal that we shall see and know our friends in heaven. 'If that be true,' she says, 'then I shall see my boy again.'

The ink in the pot had dried up in the sweltering August heat. The room smelt foul and was like an oven. I opened the shutters to let London in again, re-filled the inkpot, and with three strokes of the pen scored out the scene. Then I sat down and re-wrote it on the spot. This time the distraught mother found no comfort in the golden words of the church. As I wrote, I recalled those four empty walls in Henley Street that used to echo with his laughter and prattle.

Grief fills the room up of my absent child,
Lies in his bed, walks up and down with me,
Puts on his pretty looks, repeats his words,
Remembers me of all his gracious parts,
Stuffs out his vacant garments with his form.

Stuffs out his garments. I was remembering that little pile of clothes. And how I'd sat for hours in Stratford, turning them over and over, holding them up, crushing them to my lips. My own garments were stuffed out now with a stranger. I caught a sudden sight of myself in the glass. A ghost had come back to Bishopsgate to carry on the life of work and worry. There was nothing left for him to do. I knew he would throw himself into it, reap the rewards, bask in the glory, the honour, the fame. All of which he did. But he carried a long sorrow for his son and these were not the last lines he wrote for him. He spoke to him in his verses many a time to come. That's what the death of your nearest and dearest does to you, Francis – estranges you from yourself, from life. After the funeral you look at the world like the moon, with that vacant stare, and no one sees or knows what's on the other side.

Ben Jonson's son died too, of the plague, seven years later (the child was seven at the time). I poured drink into Ben that night.

'His life may have been cut short, Ben – but in short measure life may perfect be.'

He looked at me with red eyes. And later stole the line when he lost a daughter too and penned her an elegy. Never missed a trick, old Ben. But for his son he wrote a touching little lament of his own: *Farewell, thou child of my right hand, and joy – my sin was too much hope of thee, loved boy.*

My own sin had been the opposite. I hadn't thought of him enough. Not after that day I'd left him on Clopton Bridge. At least Ben Jonson didn't have that guilt to live with. But I buried my guilt between many lines. Ben's grieving love deserves to stand out clear.

Rest in soft peace, and, asked, say here doth lie
Ben Jonson his best piece of poetrie,
For whose sake henceforth all his vows be such,
As what he loves may never like too much.

It was nicely turned, don't you think, that verse of Ben's? But I don't believe Ben turned back to it after that. He moved on. Maybe I moved on too, or seemed to. But it didn't stop me, couldn't stop me turning back. Grief in its fullness doesn't always erupt at the time of death. It may take years to blossom, to burst into those blackest blooms of the heart. The black bile was always threatening me anyway, but Hamnet always kept it at bay, even when I only thought of him. And when I saw him, all too seldom, he cured in me thoughts that would thick my blood, with his child's matter made a summer's day short as a winter solstice. After he died came bleak December everywhere, every day; and every day after that, somewhere in every single day that followed, I felt the chill of that one awful day that would never go away. Every chill was that same chill, every day was that same day, the day we buried him.

What ceremony else? That's what I really wanted to shout at them that day, remembering my sister all over again, and those maimed rites. What ceremony else? The old rites were gone that could have comforted. We therefore commit his body to the ground. *Therefore.* It follows. Because we can no longer sing him to the saints with sage requiem and ministers of grace. Because we have taken away your old rituals, and therefore something of your beliefs too – for even beliefs are made of words.

Which leaves you with what? With a private knot of pain. Goodnight, sweet prince, I wanted to whisper – and flights of angels sing thee to thy rest. But no more of that, if you please. *Forasmuch as it hath pleased almighty God to take unto himself the soul of our dear brother here departed, we therefore commit his body to the ground, earth to earth, ashes to ashes, dust to dust, in sure and certain hope of the resurrection to eternal life through Jesus Christ our Lord.* Sure and certain? Nothing was sure and certain any more. They didn't even call him by his name, didn't even use a personal pronoun. Not a 'thou' was spoken. Dear brother? What brother? What impersonal being was that? Dear God, he was my *son*, my only son. They were throwing on the earth, closing up the grave, shutting off communion, sundering me from my dead child with their Puritan words, hammered like cold nails into his coffin. Must there no more be done? Can't we help them on, our lost lovely dead? Can't they be allowed to call out to us, to help us too, the ones that mourn? Can't we communicate? Must the bond be broken so entirely by death, and the starkness of that cold ground, those inflexible words? No, the dead boy is not in heaven, he is in the earth, he's dead, dead and rotten.

That's what you're left with on that terrible day, worse than the wrath of God. *Dies irae*? God's anger would be acceptable, divine ire heaped on your head, better than that emptiness, that coldness in the soul, and that rebellious anguish that makes you cry out in the bitterness of your heart. No, no, no life! Why should a dog, a horse, a rat, have life, and thou no breath at all? Thou'lt come no more. That's the closest words can come to expressing the pain of child loss. And ten years later, in *Lear*, the pain was still going on.

It went on in play after play. Sebastian was plucked from the waves and restored to his twin sister, Viola, the sea of troubles turning to salt waves fresh in love, in my troubled mind. And Leontes sees the dead brought back to life, a miracle before his eyes, and all pain subdued. But not the son, not Mamillius. The son never comes home again. Good night, sweet prince. It's the father's fault, always the father's fault. John Shakespeare's time was unjointed and I'd to set it right, an absent father, and I must be from thence, and Hamnet's life the price, aye, Will, lay thee down and roar.

So he died over and over as I lived on and wrote on and on, died in every play that filled up the space he'd left. He couldn't stop dying, even in the days of my best success. He had to keep on dying because I had to keep on burying him, laying him to rest – not in shattered Catholic rites but in the only rituals left to me, the theatre, the ones that plays provided. They could never take that away from me. What ceremony else? The play, of course, the play's the thing, once more, over and over again. It was a public burial, never ending, pulling in mourners from the globe, from the ends of the earth, but it was also deeply private too, it was that paradox of the self that only the player knows.

Hamnet's passing wasn't the end of it either. Death had us on his list, it seemed. Just after Christmas old Henry died in Snitterfield – the toughest tree falls in the end – Aunt Margaret just two months later, and that was the end of another era. Old Hunsdon had gone and while Lord Cobham briefly took over the Lord Chamberlain's office (but not his players) we were known as Lord Hunsdon's Men after our new patron, young Hunsdon. But within a year he'd succeeded to his father's office, and so when the queen appointed him as the next Lord Chamberlain after Cobham's brief slot, we were once again the Lord Chamberlain's Men.

'Don't confuse me, Will.'

Confuse? It was a fixed point in a wild and whirling world, and a brain gone blank and blue as that empty sky. This house – this was another fixed point, a piece of solid ground under slipping feet. Why do you think I bought it, New Place?

'You tell me, Will.'

I was trying to bury my grief by buying the finest house in Stratford, Clopton's old house. Sixty pounds for a sixty-foot frontage, thirty feet high, seventy feet deep along the lane, brick-nogged and lead-paned, three storeys, five gables, ten rooms, two gardens, two orchards, two barns, three-quarters of an acre – an easy bargain, you would think, Francis, you being a lawyer, except that the legal figure of sixty was to keep the Crown's fingers from dipping too deeply into my coffers.

'I didn't hear that.'

The real price of twice that sum was between myself and William

Underhill, whose father had bought it from another William, name of Bott, when I was three.

'I didn't hear that either.'

Did you hear that Bott poisoned his own daughter?

'Jesus, why?'

He'd married her off to a young idiot called Harper, under an arrangement that Harper's lands would pass to Bott should the daughter die childless. She did – Bott saw to that by poisoning her, thirty-four years to the day before I bought the house, and he used the law to keep his neck out of the noose.

Two months after I'd bought it, Underhill himself suddenly died – murdered by his own son, Fulke, another bad lot, the motive the same – inheritance of lands.

'And the method used?'

Poison again. Fulke went to the gallows but legally my right to this house wasn't finally secured until murdered Underhill's second son, Hercules, came of age three years later and secured the sale of it to me, confirming that the purchase had been properly made from the victim and not arranged with the murderer.

So along with the house I purchased a couple of murders, if you like – a daughter's by her father and a father's by his son, two dire crimes a generation apart, darkening the atmosphere if you cared to sense it, and linking it to poison, poison in the family. And it was poison poured into the ear of a playwright who'd lost a Hamnet and was seeking another. Across the road the chapel priests chanted prayers once for the repose of old Clopton's soul. But Chapel Lane out there, that's another irony – they sometimes call it Dead Lane. It was a dead man who bought it, and the purchase was a hollow victory. Death had triumphed instead. As always.

But I installed the family and took stock. I was thirty-three, the perfect age of man, a gentleman in fact, with a mansion, a coat of arms, my name starting to appear on the title-pages of the quartos, and men of taste and discernment about to elevate me to stand with Ovid. All that and my son lying dead by the river. The Lord had given and the Lord had taken away – without asking me which I'd have preferred. But as for John Shakespeare, he was happy as a cow in clover. He and my mother did their best to bring me out of the dumps, chiding me for my veiled lids, my nighted colour.

Thou know'st 'tis common; all that lives must die, passing

through nature to eternity.

Aye, madam, it is common. But I have that within which passeth show, these but the trappings and the suits of woe.

I left them in their brighter garb, to their arms and airs, and went back to London.

48

'You went back to King John.'

I went back to history. I told sad stories of the death of kings. Ben Jonson chastised me for this, naturally.

'Wasting your time with the dead.'

Maybe he was right. Maybe it was to elude the sad ghost of the fresh dead Hamnet that I buried myself so sweetly among the safely, famously dead, those on whom the worm had long ceased to feed. There's a massive certainty and calm about the past, a freedom about its finality. It's over. It was with a huge feeling of relief that I opened the book of history, from Richard of Bordeaux to Henry Five.

Henry Four was like Oedipus – he'd afflicted his people through a primal sin, in his case the killing of a rightful king. Henry was a better ruler than Richard but there was blood on his hands and it couldn't be washed away. He remained what he was: a vice of kings, a cutpurse of the empire. A king of shreds and patches. A common thief.

The cutpurse and the king. Bolingbroke with the measured talk and Richard, for whom life and language are intuitive matters. But the Richards of this world are the puppets of history. They come to pieces because in spite of their play-acting, they have no identity outside their public roles, no hard private core, no real selves. They are paper men, green reeds of weakness and sensitivity. Only in defeat and death can they find some sort of tough contentment, acknowledging that one last truth – that they are losers, shadow kings, meditating on the shadows that went before them.

'On worms and epitaphs.'

Not good listening for the ageing queen, who had just a few years left to live – and looked it. The end of century melancholy, the end of life gloom had already settled on her.

'Uneasy lies the head that wears a crown.'

Especially if it's a usurped crown. Elizabeth's was rightful and she shone under it. Bolingbroke never dazzled like his ancestors and his offspring. His reign was sad and he himself pathetic. As the main character he'd have been a bore – two such plays a double bore. I needed something to bring them alive.

'And that's how Falstaff was born?'

A liar, a cheat, a braggart, a fat drunken whoring coward – why did I love him so much? Because he isn't the Puritan who pisses in the ale, isn't the patriot who gets you dead for your country, isn't the soulless pious controller who wants to make you part of the state furniture. He's old Adam gone to podge, fallen humanity, Satan with a sense of humour. He's Tarleton, he's Yorick, he's the moral rebel and social renegade – and he's betrayed by his friend. Somebody has lent him a thousand pounds. It's spent and he can never pay it back.

Serve him right? Yes, the scrounging, thieving, work-shy ruffian. Why should we work and fight to keep the likes of him? A fat fraud without a conscience who digs you in the ribs at the tavern, and sweet talks you out of the price of the next drink. A filthy old bum and a corrupter of youth.

And yet. If you hate war, detest bullshit and Puritans and politicians, Falstaff is your man. He shows you that big bellies and nimble wits are not incompatible. He has the joy of life in him. He was born in the same sea as Venus, carries the tide of poetry in his head, keeps your feet on the ground and makes you feel the thrust of good old mother earth. And the various kings spin round him like remote and unreal moons. Without him the state goes back to being what it always has been – boring. Of course Henry Five has to reject him because the new king has now become public property. He has killed off his youth. And that killing is also the killing of poetry.

'But he sticks in the heart like a piece of old England.'

And that's because, Francis, the real hero of these plays is neither God nor King but England itself, and not the England of the great ones or even the England of John of Gaunt, it's the England of Shallow and Silence, the pathos of old men remembering their youth. It's Falstaff thinking of the fate of his three hundred conscripts after Shrewsbury, fit only for the town's end, to beg during life – the well-peppered poor sods that gave the Cripplegate its name. It's the image of somebody swearing on a parcel-gilt goblet sitting in the Dolphin chamber at the round table by a sea-coal fire upon a Wednesday in Wheeson week. It's soldiers shaking hands knowing they'll never all meet again, not like this. That was my England, Francis. It had nothing to do with St George or St Crispin or any Henry. *That* was for queen and country and Privy Council. It was for the Master of the Revels and the listening censors. It was for the dukes and generals and for the groundlings in their mindless patriotic passion. When all's said and done it was for the box. Maybe it was even for the drama. All I know is that nobody took down the names of the humble dead at Shrewsbury or Agincourt, only the names of the great ones. But it was the unnumbered ones, the nameless ones, that made up my England. Heaven rest them now.

49

'Heaven rest *us*, Will. It's growing late and I want a signature from you today, not tomorrow.'

You have till midnight, then.

'Jesus. I came here for your will, not your life.'

A man's will *is* his life, Francis. I'd best conclude the business.

'You mean the will?'

I mean the whole thing.

'In which case I'd best finish this last bottle of sack. A night-cap and a cat-nap much needed now, old man. Ten minutes, then back to work, how does that sound?'

Make it half an hour. I need to think.

And before the glassful had reached his belly he was flat out and snoring again.

How I envy him his fat contentment and easy oblivion. I never had that ability, never found the way to Lethe. There were always dreams. Even after a tiring journey I'd throw myself down to sleep, only to find another journey starting up in my head, to work the mind and keep the eyelids open, staring into the darkness, seeing but blind.

That's why you sympathized with Bolingbroke, Will, isn't it, old lad? You allowed him his moment – the ailing king who couldn't sleep even when he'd put aside that polished perturbation and golden care that kept the ports of slumber open wide to many a watchful night and many an English king. Envy Francis? The dying king envied those lucky thousands of his poorest subjects who at that very hour were fast asleep even in the hardest of states – in loathsome beds and smoky cribs, upon uneasy pallets stretching, and hushed with buzzing night-flies to their slumber – while here it was being denied to him, the highest in the land, even here in the perfumed chambers of the great, under the canopies of costly state and lulled with sound of sweetest melody.

Ah, Will, Will, how you long for it too, don't you, that oblivion, the common nightly balm of sleep, and your mind goes now to the wet sea-boy on watch on the high and giddy mast, in the middle of the storm. Deafened by waves and cuffed by winds, still he can close his eyes and be rocked in the cradle of the sea, while here in the calmest, stillest night, with all appliances and means to hand, the sleep the ship-boy finds so sweet and easy is denied you, as it was kept from the most care-ridden of kings.

Henry Bolingbroke couldn't sleep. Maybe that's why he fathered so many children – though perhaps the real credit should go to his first wife, Mary de Bohun, married at the age of ten, mother of Harry the Fifth at seventeen, bearer of six children and dead in childbirth at the age of twenty-four, a martyr to the principles of dynasticism.

Nineteen years after her death Harry became King of England, and also winner of one of the most famous fights in history. Absurdly outnumbered, the entire enterprise irresponsible and illegal, his assertion to France unfounded in fact, still he led his small force of Englishmen to a famous victory on the field of Agincourt. The light-foot lad of the Eastcheap pubs, Hal, the bosom pal of drunken bums and servicer of whores, had in truth seen action aged twelve – only Othello had beaten him, by five years – and he did well at Shrewsbury. Not that he really killed Hotspur there, but it made good theatre.

To temper these manly spirits he threw off his old unruly self and became the skeleton at the feast, even at his own coronation, where he frowned and ate like a mouse, while a terrible blizzard raged outside, warning of war and an implacable purity to come. The moody young king was making a public statement. He was a new man for a new play. About a famous battle and a band of brothers.

So he took five thousand killing machines to France. Five thousand six-foot lengths of yew and elm and ash – with a minimum draw weight of eighty pounds, many over a hundred and some above a hundred and fifty, and with a range of four hundred yards at maximum elevation, effective at two hundred, lethal at eighty – loosed their arrows in the same single second at the king's command. Three seconds later they shot again – and yet again in another three seconds, while the first volley was still in the air. Fifteen thousand thirty-inch lengths of poplar and ash, fletched with the finest feathers, had been launched into the air at frightening speed. The geese of England were flying again – but now they were making a blood-curdling song. It was not the song of the quill. The sky darkened under the storm-cloud, and from that storm-cloud there fell on France a terrible rain. The swallow-tailed arrowheads were made to inflict the most fearsome wounds, and the needle-pointed bodkin heads were unstoppable. They could bring down horses, pierce armour, penetrate helmets, vizors, dig deep into hearts, skulls, brains. So much for the little Englander with his little crooked stick.

The cries went up.

An iron army brought to a sudden and terrifying halt and introduced to agony, chaos and defeat.

Too famous to live long is what they said of him. But conquerors often lack humour – and maybe that's why they sometimes die young. Even death didn't make him grin. In his last procession on earth he proceeded unsmilingly as ever, to lie cold and alone in his tomb, and I gave his corpse a part to play at the start of Harry the Sixth. Dead Henry back on stage, his silent form lies in its black coffin, unspeaking but eloquent symbol of the huge task the political dwarfs have been left to fulfil. Some few of them will be touched by a brand of fire. Dogged York that reaches at the moon, the Earl of Warwick – proud setter-up and puller-down of Kings – Queen Margaret who stood upon the hatches in the storm. And Salisbury, that winter lion who in rage forgets aged contusions and all brush of time. But they're butchers in a shambles that was England. Brief are the days of glory.

Glory is what I went for, letting the play mirror the bellicose bustle of Henry's time and ours, as Essex got ready his force to crush Tyrone's rebellion in Ireland – and the city gave him his grand send-off. Ninety-nine, when all the youth of England are on fire and silken dalliance in the wardrobe lies. For now sits Expectation in the air...

I played the Prologue myself, like an old Greek, whipping up the atmosphere of valour, the heroic bustle. Naturally I didn't include among that symphony of sounds the screams of the hamstrung whores, carried kicking and yelling on board, tied like pigs to poles, as each ship received its quota – fucking equipment for use by English soldiers and sailors, and their needs at sea. Such sounds would have been out of tune and harsh. No, keep it clean, Will, hold hard to the poetic imperative.

Behold the threaden sails, borne with the invisible and creeping wind, draw the huge bottoms through the furrowed sea, breasting the lofty surge. O! do but think you stand upon the rivage and behold a city on the inconstant billows dancing – for so appears this fleet majestical!

This fleet majestical. Harfleur and Henry, Ireland and Essex. We put the play on in the summer, not long after Essex had left with the Irish expedition, and the audiences loved it. As they lapped up the glory of an illegal war Essex was about to show that in spite of his pride he was no Harry the Fifth, and that as the century had just a few short months left to run, so Essex himself was doomed to die at thirty-four, the same age as Henry. He copied him closer than he could have imagined, but never brought home the victory.

So *Harry the Fifth* was staged while Essex was still the fragile hero of the hour. I gave it to them all over again – the heroism, the patriotism, kingship, chivalry, the glory and cloudiness of war. I gave them aggression, expediency, betrayal, conscience, heavy care, the two faces of power and the loss of human life. That's where I humanised young Harry, showing how the conflict between guilt and glory in his soul went well beyond the conflict between the English and the French. You knew full well that the historical Henry never felt a single twinge of guilt. Kings don't think like that. They know that God is on their side and at Agincourt it was God for Harry, England and St George.

A play then for the ruling class – the band of noble brothers, the aristocratic élite. That's why they loved it. But so did the groundlings. You'd learned, hadn't you, Will? – to make drama a mirror in which each man saw what he always wants to see – a reflection of himself.

50

And he saw it in a circle, he saw it in the round, in a magic looking glass into which the people stepped, coming to see and to be seen: a new theatre. *Harry the Fifth* was its first play, along with *Caesar*, and *Harry the Eighth* was its last. And between two Henries it lived out its brief glorious life, with a high tide at Southwark for its birth, quickening the playgoers as they came from north of the river, and Venus and Jupiter appearing after sunset like new worlds in the sky.

'It was your world, my boy – it was *your* world, lad, wasn't it?'

Ah Francis, awake again, are we? My world. God was a carpenter and made the world out of nothing, but we were men and needed materials.

'They were there, Will, all the time, awaiting re-invention.'

Old materials, fresh ideas, new men for a new world. Old Burbage was dead, killed by worry. The lease on the Theatre had run out and the landlord was a grasping rat. He didn't want another lease, he wanted the land back, and not only the land but the theatre that went with it. Crooked contracts were his speciality. Giles Alleyn, yes, the Burbage sons were left to contend with him and Richard said he'd like to ram a pound of ratsbane down his greedy gullet.

It didn't come to that, though brother Cuthbert actually bought the ratsbane. They were Burbages and when their blood was up they didn't fool around. Old man Burbage had even appeared to them on stage, they said – the angry ghost demanding revenge, and he didn't have to come again to whet a blunted purpose, especially when Alleyn announced he was going to dismantle the Theatre and take its timbers for his own use.

We gathered in the Theatre for a council of war, and we looked at one another helplessly, a circle of fools on a dark and empty stage. There were plenty of words but no way forward. The ratsbane, it was decided, would improve the world by removing Alleyn from it but would not save our playhouse, and the Burbages would be done for murder.

'That's when you made history, lad, yes?'

Yes, by heaven, that's when I made my mental leap, the one that changed the future – or so they liked to tell me afterwards.

'Listen, friends.'

They were all ears.

'There is one way to prevent this bastard tearing down our theatre and it's the only way.'

A ring of eyes, staring at me intently.

'And that is – to tear it down ourselves.'

They all looked at me as if I were mad.

'And do what with it – light a bonfire?'

'No – do exactly what the execrable Alleyn has been proposing to do, convert it to some better use.'

'And what better use might that be, Will? Do tell us.'

'Why, build another theatre, of course – but in a different place.'

'What place, pray?'

The question had been put, but I noticed that all the eyes in the circle had widened – and brightened.

'Well, there is a site available, I believe – across the river in St Saviour's parish, not far from the Rose.'

They all stared at me. And then we all stared at each other. With a wild hope.

There was a plot of ground near Maid Lane. We moved fast, signed a lease – we, the Lord Chamberlain's Men – which meant that we could move in on Christmas Day. It was a mere matter of money, and that was no matter at all. Half came from the Burbages and the other half was made up by Heminges, Phillips, Pope, and Kempe.

'And you, Will.'

And me, Francis. Which meant that one tenth of the new theatre was mine, together with my share in the Company.

'You were inspired, my boy.'

There is a tide in the affairs of men.

And that was how, on the night of 28th December 1598, a dubious demolition mob with their hats plucked about their ears and half their faces buried in their cloaks, assembled in Shoreditch armed not with swords and daggers but with saws and hammers and all the weapons of the carpenter's trade.

O, conspiracy! Shamest thou to show thy dangerous brow

by night? Not Erebus itself were dim enough to hide thee from prevention.

But there was one old ally that did conspire to screen us from discovery. The winter of '98 had brought hard frosts, so savage that the Thames froze at London Bridge just before Christmas. It thawed the following day but on St John's Day was again iced over lightly. The miracle happened on the 25th. Jack Frost returned in force and the river was almost frozen again by the afternoon. The frost was followed by a ferocious blizzard that cleared the city streets of people – except for that small army of actors, going to war.

Darkness fell.

What a night, lad! What a night! 'Twas a rough night, but unforgettable. We had a new financial man with us, Will Smith, and a hired team of twelve workmen directed by master carpenter Peter Street. Heminges was there, and Phillips and Pope and myself and the rest of the Company. Kempe didn't turn up. 'Where's Bully Bottom?' somebody asked. But it didn't matter. The Burbage boys strode like generals, leading from the front, and took us up Curtain Road in a darkness that was weirdly whitened by the swirling snow. The flakes were stinging our eyes and lodging in our beards like bees out of hell. The ripping wind went through our cloaks, making them shake like the shrouds on a ship. We stood for a few seconds looking at our old Theatre, the Burbage sons especially staring at what their father had put up twenty-two years ago. Now it was coming down. A solemn moment. Wordlessly we went inside.

'Where are these lads? Where are these hearts?'

The shout came from the darkened stage. It made us all start violently. Had we been discovered? Had Alleyn sent the Watch? We clenched our hammers and axes.

'I have had a dream! I have had a most rare vision!'

Yes, it was Kempe, waiting for us in the dark, having his last hour on stage, all to himself.

'O sweet Bully Bottom!' we all roared, picking up his cue. 'O most courageous day! O most happy hour!'

Kempe bowed and spoke in a whisper, commanding silence.

'I have had a dream, past the wit of man to say what dream it was.'

'Tell us about it later, you ass!'

'Ass-*hole*, if you don't mind – I will hear nothing spoken against asses.'

This was turning into a performance.

'I will get Peter Street to write a ballad of this dream.'

But Peter Street was too busy for ballads that night. We took down our Theatre board by board, beam by beam, sweating and sliding in the snow, and under cover of darkness we carried it on carts down Curtain Road and Hog Lane and Bishopsgate, all the way down Gracious Street, past the Cross Keys and west of the bridge, to the Dowgate. Even in these fierce conditions we didn't want to take the risk of trundling our timbers openly over the bridge.

We didn't have to. It was the hour before dawn and the river was frozen solid.

'The Lord hath tamed the water!' yelled big Burbage, beating his boots on the thick ice and grinning delightedly, his breath clothing him like a fiery cloud. He stamped around like a child imitating a horse.

'And we are delivered out of the hands of Pharaoh!'

As it happened Master Giles Pharaoh Alleyn was out of London during the operation. And when the old Egyptian returned to the city he would find himself gaping in disbelief at an empty site in Shoreditch, shat on by dogs and deserted by the rats. He had no contract and no theatre.

It had taken all night.

As the snow suddenly cleared and the skies began to lighten over Deptford somebody said, 'We've just made it. Is that the dawn I see breaking over there?'

He was pointing at a pinkish patch downriver, streaking the grey skies of the third last day of the year.

'No,' Heminges said, 'you're mistaken, friend. Sunrise will be in that line there, closer to the Tower. Look how its stones are glinting already.'

'It's further downstream, I tell you, and yon grey lines that fret the clouds are messengers of day.'

'Gentlemen!'

Pope stepped forward.

'You shall confess that you are both deceived. Here, as I point my sword, the sun arises and the high east stands like the Capitol of Rome, directly here.'

He was pointing west, away from the light, at the huge pile of newly dismantled timbers. We all knew what he meant.

'Let's call it the Capitol, then,' said Kempe.

'Or the Dawn?' suggested Phillips. 'Or what about the Sun theatre?'

The Burbages looked at one another, then at me.

'What do you think, Will?'

I thought for a minute as the sun came up and warmed our faces, a huge blood-red ball over the river.

'Well, we're making a new world for ourselves, aren't we? A charmed circle? I'll tell you what – let's call it the Globe.'

'Will – you have been touched by God!'

And we all drew our swords along with Pope and pointed them at the pile of timbers that were lit up by the morning sun.

'The Globe!'

51

Totus mundus agit histrionem – all the world's a stage.

'Jenkins would have lashed you, lad, for that Latin gloss.'

An apt and antique motto. And above the Latin tag on the signboard Hercules bore the globe on his shoulders. A Herculean labour – and it had sprung up like Adam's habitat, a *tabula rasa* among the other worlds of London's theatre-land.

'You felt like God at the start of time?'

God took just under a week to make the world. Peter Street had said he'd rebuild ours in twenty-eight.

What a workman he was! Though the world had lain sick almost five thousand years, it was wonderfully altered. What a workman that could cast the globe of it into an entirely new mould! Peter Street had laid the stage so that it faced north, avoiding available daylight and allowing a little shade to help with the night scenes. You looked up at an upper stage that would be the walls of Harfleur, surrendering to Henry, but from which the owner of great Dunsinane, strongly fortified, would later look out undismayed on a moving wood and proclaim no surrender. I'll fight till from my bones my flesh be hacked! Your eye was drawn to the curtained inner stage where lovers would play at chess, not love, being of the same sex, and where Desdemona would be strangled, Othello end it all, and such heavy sights screened off when the tragic loading of the bed became a thing that poisoned sight itself. But in dreadful vein you could litter the main stage with corpses sufficient to impress even the battle-hardened Fortinbras. O, proud death! What feast is toward in thine eternal cell, that thou so many princes at a shot so bloodily hast struck? Take up the bodies, then. Such a sight as this becomes the field, but here shows much amiss. Not that bodies were ever unwelcome on the London stages, whether they got up again, bowed to the crowd, and walked off with pig's blood on their faces or spouted the real thing, sprinkling the heads of the Tyburn spectators.

Enter Hamlet, with a hell beneath and a heaven above, between which he would walk and meditate, in doubt about both, and unsure of action. The trapdoor on which he stood led to ghosts and graves, mysterious sounds, and was an image of the mighty world – London itself was a stage and you were all standing on a trap that might spring open any hour, any day, and catapult you to hell – the dungeon, the gallows, the block, the plague, the best known routes to oblivion. There goes Ophelia now, into that hole out of which Lazarus rose, but as for her, her death was doubtful.

With your feet placed here you looked up and saw the brave o'erhanging firmament, fretted with golden fire, and you informed an entranced audience of three thousand souls, packed into a wooden world of only a hundred feet across, that what you saw was nothing more than a foul and pestilent congregation of vapours. And breathing the same intimate air as you, they heard you murmur such a thought and heard you whisper suicide to a deaf grey sea of troubles. Groundlings in the yard, nobs in the boxes, they all heard you, as you stepped into this splendid world from the nutshell confines of a tiny tiring house, where you dressed for life's short comedy or tragedy, depending on the bill, the afternoon, or on how you chose to see life.

Such was the continent of the world, to which a world of beauties and of brave spirits resorted half the year when the elements were kind. They came over the bridge, under the swaying heads, along the High Street, through the alleyways south of the cathedral and the Bishop of Winchester's palace – and three hundred paces from the river they arrived at Maiden Lane, on the south side of which, west of Dead Man's Place, there stood the great Globe itself, conveniently plotted in a world of bears, bulls, and brothels and surrounded by drinking dens.

The world was their oyster – and ours. Harry was now Caesar, and French blood turned to Roman. It was the summer solstice. There was a new moon that night, auspicious for the opening of a new play, and a new house too, barely baptized. And a high tide too that ensured easy travel for the nobs who didn't fancy muddying their boots and staining their gowns simply to see an old Roman get it in the neck – as damnèd Casca, like a cur, struck Caesar from behind. An almost homely detail, like deafness and nightgowns and mislaid books, reminding you that terror is no dream – it strikes right to the heart of the real world. The one you live in.

Not everybody approved. Flanked by ditches and sewers and forced out of a stinking marsh – that was Ben's response. He'd gone off in a thundercloud, back to the Admiral's Men, objecting that we'd cut *Every Man Out Of His Humour.* It was much too long and should have gone to the barber's with Ben's beard, as I told him myself. Ben could take anything that came – except censure.

Nor did our rivals rejoice. Francis Langley, had built his Swan in the Paris Garden, but it was too far from the bridge and it was easier for swans to come to that theatre than people. We'd stuck close to the bridge in the parish of St Saviour's, and the dying Swan watched us come, and hung her head. To the west of us the bear pit – starring Sackerson, George Stone and Harry Hunks – later known as the building of excellent Hope. That made me laugh as well as weep, for the slaughter that went on there, the more so as it was owned by Henslowe. *Abandon all hope, all ye who enter here* – that was our motto for the Hope. If you were a bear or a bull or a poor old ape, or if you were a down-and-out, or an out-and-out hack, or an actor out of work, then No-Hope Henslowe was your only man, Henslowe whose helpfulness had decreased and his ruthlessness grown as the years rolled on. His Rose was just a few hundred feet away, also built on marshy land and fast withering after its dozen years on that ground.

The Swan sang itself out, Hope dwindled, and the Rose faded and fell – the Globe was the death of it. Henslowe admitted in the end that the Bankside was ours, and he and Alleyn decamped. They went back across the river, north of the city, and there off Golden Lane, close to the open fields of St Giles without Cripplegate, Finsbury Liberty gave them their site, about half a mile west of the Curtain. On it they built their successor to the Rose, and when they finally ran up the flag in 1610, it was the flag of Dame Fortune.

Now we were the lords of the south bank, and to be close to the Globe I shifted my lodgings again across the river to Southwark, idyllic with wildwoods and flowers, babbling with streams – and imbued with the leakage of cesspools and graveyards that seeped into our houses, breeding fevers in the flesh and agues in the bone.

'More money in your purse, Will?'

Yes, it was time for serious business, and it was on 21st February 1599 that I entered into an agreement with the Globe syndicate, binding for thirty-one years.

'What was the agreement?'

You don't want the details, Francis. They're boring.

'I'm a lawyer. I live by details. And by boredom. Tell me.'

There were seven of us including myself, Will Kempe, Augustine Phillips, John Heminges, Thomas Pope, and the Burbage brothers, Richard and Cuthbert. We split ten shares among us – five to the Burbages and one each to each of the other five. Which meant that as one of the housekeepers to the Chamberlain's Men I owned ten per cent of the whole. When Kempe left (as he did right soon) my share rose to an eighth, but when Harry Condell and Will Sly came in with us it fell to a twelfth, and later to one fourteenth when William Ostler bought in. But by that time I'd been earning up to seven hundred a year for more than a dozen years in the business. Even in the early days I was taking in a couple of hundred. The Company took half the income from the galleries but the other half went to the housekeepers, plus the takings at the door. I was writing plays, acting in plays, and selling them to my own Company, an actor business-man, helping to run the theatre I played in. As long as the theatre stayed open I couldn't lose.

'And you didn't.'

Gradually the spectre of debt withdrew to the rear, though it never ever left the stage. Not the stage of my mind. The worry was always there – that it could all crumble away, just as it did with my father. I just couldn't shift it – the uncertainty, the unease. I became what Hamlet doubly despised – a great buyer of land, spacious in the possession of dirt. A strange compulsion – to purchase acres of what you need only six feet of, to amass money for other people to spend.

'Ah, very well mentioned! You have indeed amassed a tidy amount of money. Now let's get back to giving it away. Back to the will for a moment, if you please. Mostly it's covered. We haven't entirely wasted our day.'

And you've fed well on me, Francis. You'll feed even better when I'm gone.

'I'll ignore that quip. Now, these fellow actors of yours, your second family – '

My only family.

'If you all got on so well then you may wish to leave some small bequests – to a chosen few, that is?'

A very choice few.

'You mentioned Kempe, for example.'

Left us. And left the world.

'Phillips?'

Left me a thirty shilling gold piece in his will, he did. But sadly – he too has left the great stage.

'There was Tom Pope.'

Stone cold.

'Sly?'

Dead and rotten.

'Jesus, how many others have gone?'

Ostler, Bryan, Cross, Gilburne, Cook –

'Enough, no more! What *was* it about acting?'

On the contrary, most of them did well for themselves. And they had another thing in common. Almost to a man they were married men, and family men, with lots of children. Heminges has fourteen! Condell's got nine, Dick Burbage can account for seven that I know of – I'm counting down – Cowley's got four. Phillips had five before he died. They were busy men. And they had property, lots of it, in and out of London, town houses, country houses, estates. They lived in a world of make-believe, rattling through rôles at battle-speed, growing and shedding skins that left ordinary mortals standing gaping, but they were realists to a man, and they had a strong nose for the three facts of life.

'Which are?'

Land, lucre, and loads of kids. Don't you be fooled, Francis. Dick Burbage may have been the doomed hero of the stage and died a thousand tragic deaths, but when he makes his last exit he'll be leaving his wife and children a rich legacy.

'Talking of legacies – '

Right, let's do it. *Item, I give and bequeath to my fellows John Heminges, Richard Burbage and Henry Condell, thirty* – no – *twenty six shillings and eight pence apiece to buy them rings.*

'That's it?'

It's a token. They're well-off men, as I said. If you want to know how close we were, you won't find it in a funeral ring. Look at the names Burbage gave his children. He had a daughter called Juliet – she died young. There was another daughter called Anne. Ring any bells? And he had a son called William. There's a better token of how close I was to Richard Burbage.

'What about Cuthbert Burbage?'

Sly left him something, as I remember...but no. He wasn't an actor, he was a manager, that's all. Richard had some soul.

'What about Henslowe?'

What! What *about* Henslowe?

'It was a joke.'

A bad one. He died the month before last. Hadn't you heard?

'God rest his soul.'

Too late. The devil will have snatched it already. No, Francis, that will do for my fellows in the trade.

'Very well, Will. Were you really so close to them? All that family stuff?'

Yes and no. Oddly out of step, I suppose, with these fellows – living alone, shifting from lodging to lodging, Shoreditch, Bishopsgate, Southwark, then back across the river to Cripplegate.

'For I myself am best when least in company, eh?'

You never fail to astonish me, Francis. But yes – that's when I wrote my plays, after all, in solitude. That's when I came alive. And that's how I made my living – bought my own scripts and shared in the profits. A good system if you keep scribbling. Which I could and did. And we were lucky not to be controlled by the likes of Henslowe. He kept his company under his thumb and he treated all writers like hacks. Even good hacks like Dekker had to be rescued from prison within a month of starting to scratch for Henslowe. Thank God I was under no such bad angel. Nor was I under the influence of any aristocrat and his pack of chattels and toads. I was myself alone. And free to write for the company I chose – and as I chose. I should have been a happy man.

52

Happy? Call no man happy until he is dead. Only then is he free. Never really free, was I? Only as free as the Company allowed me to be, fashioning scripts to the available talent, or lack of it. Kempe was so coarse he didn't even catch on that he *was* Bottom, a part specially created for him. It was self-parody without self-knowledge – the playing up to the audience, the interfering with the script, the self-importance and wanting to take over every rôle in the play, especially the lead, and steal its thunder. Not to mention the massive hamming and crude antics. Good for Bottom, you would think – and on its own level it was. But when he fell ill, Burbage took over the part for a single performance, investing it with a subtlety and depth undreamed of by everyone, except by me, and turning the ingenuous weaver into a half-tragic character, to the Company's amazement and Kempe's disgust. That was the start of the rift that led to his exit.

I was glad to see him go. He danced himself to Norwich – and from thence to death, when he borrowed money from Henslowe. Indebtedness to that implacable creditor was always the kiss of death. They said he faked his own demise so as to escape him, and that he lived on in poverty and secrecy for another five years. Others said that the queen who'd let old Tarleton die had also seen out his fat successor. Nothing sadder than a spent jester shaken by the pangs of death, infirmity that decays the wise improving his gags by bringing them to an end.

And along came Robert Armin, the genius of the tear behind the smile, the wistful irony beneath the wit, the subtler strain of comedy, written not for a straight clown but for a witty fool, even a bitter fool, Touchstone, Feste, Lear's loyal boy, he took on the lot. By the time he'd done Thersites and Caliban he'd left comedy far behind. But then so had I. We'd all come a long way from the days of tubby Tarleton. And from a queen who put plays on a level just one up from the torture of bears, as public entertainment. Why do I flatter her? Probably she preferred the bears to the actors. Clever she may have been but she had not an ounce of art, except for politics. She was bloodless, you see. She was a Tudor. The Tudors were the shopkeepers of the realm.

So Essex made his bid to turn a tired old shopkeeper out of her stall. But he understood one thing too late – that Englanders are content with shopkeepers, not with stars. Shopkeepers go to bed – stars fall from the sky.

Impossible to say – but not to speculate – what went through the Earl's mind that cold Ash Wednesday morning on Tower Green as he mounted the final steps to embrace the block, his last lover. It must have been clear to him at last that the play-acting was over. This was really happening and even his old red flame Bess wasn't going to step in and save him. She'd never received the ring he'd sent from prison – her own gift to him – and he knew that was his last card. Probably he was just glad he was going to die with his bowels still in, and his privities intact, and that he wouldn't be jeered from the stage by the mob whose hero he'd once been. He was turning down his red waistcoat as he recited the Creed and the Lord's Prayer and prayed for the queen to have a long life. She had two years left.

Nothing in his life became him like the leaving it. He died like one that had been studied in his death, to throw away the dearest thing he owned, as it were a careless trifle. Rebels and traitors may yet die well and give a good performance. Ralegh apparently wept – and those standing close by saw crocodiles falling to the ground, sweet ones, they said. Even the Ralegh tears were perfumed.

The Earl's last words were to thank God that he had been thus spewed out of the realm. The axeman didn't succeed in getting him out of it immediately. It took three attempts and the handsome head parted company from the body only on the third. He was thirty-five years old. Young Burghley was watching, rubbing his rubbery little hands. He might have remembered what his father once said about Essex, prophesying his end: 'Bloody and deceitful men shall not live out half their days.'

On the eve of the execution the queen passed the time at Whitehall by watching a play. It was a command performance and the players were – yes, the very men, the Lord Chamberlain's. And not only had she asked for us but she particularly requested the play she wanted staged. It was the contentious Richard the Second, the very play we'd put on to promote Essex's failed coup. Not only that, but she wanted it complete with deposition scene. And she had one further request, that the part of King Richard himself be taken by none other than Master Shakespeare, that he might know what it was to be a prince and to be deposed. What a hag! And I sweated through that performance – for which I was unfitted anyway – conscious of those cold eyes glittering at me out of what was left of her face.

After the execution she paced up and down in her privy chamber for days on end, stamping her feet, fretting and fuming, and thrusting her rusty old sword into the arras in a fantastic rage, a madness. How now! A rat! dead for a ducat! Dead!

The evil that men do lives after them, the good is oft interrèd with their bones. But in Essex's case the people chose to forget the moody cruelty, the procrastination, theatricality and instability, the wild-eyed boy who'd burst into the queen's bedchamber, mad as the sea and wind. They remembered after all that he was frank and free by nature, cultured, witty, loyal, gracious, kindly to inferiors, generous to a fault, a devoted husband and a brave soldier – but no general and a political dunce. Strange how death alters a man's character. But nothing much wrong with that in a world of self-seekers and cynical clever climbers up back passages. Better to be a failed idealist and be lamented by the people, a noble mind o'erthrown, the expectancy and rose of the fair state, the glass of fashion and the mould of form, the observed of all observers, quite, quite down. Better to have a poet write your epitaph – *truth and beauty buried be* – and to live again in The Phoenix and the Turtle – *for these dead birds sigh a prayer* – or just to be remembered even by your enemies in a wave of warm nostalgia, as an embodiment of the old classical virtues. This was the noblest Roman of them all...this was a man.

53

'A melancholy mood, Will. And yet you wrote more comedies.'

They darkened round the edges. And tragedy ran into comedy.

'But Illyria – '

Not so much a place as a state of mind, a dimension in which you can go disguised until you've discovered your true self. A place where you have to fall in love with the wrong person so that you can find the right one. It's the Forest of Arden, the wood outside Athens, the comic opposite of Lear's heath on which things are as they are and people are seen for what they are: angels, sharks, dragons, worms. In tragedy people don't put on physical disguises, they assume inner costumes instead – the wickedness wherein the pregnant enemy does much – to hide their true selves from themselves, and others, and it's hard to see through the veil. But in comedy you simply remove the doublet and hose and say, 'Look, I'm a *girl*!'

Of course the conventions we followed added to the comic situation. Viola is a boy actor playing a girl pretending to be a boy and dressed up as such. Rosalind took it one stage further by asking Orlando to imagine her – or him – as a girl, which she both is and isn't.

So what's real and unreal? Sebastian seems to be Viola; Orsino seems to love Olivia, who thinks she is loving a young man, Cesario, and also imagines herself as a grieving sister and perpetual spinster, though that role now seems to have worn thin; Viola and Sebastian think themselves bereaved; Malvolio thinks Olivia is in love with him; he thinks Feste is Sir Topaz; Sir Andrew thinks Cesario a demon with the sword; he thinks he can succeed with Olivia; he thinks Sir Toby is his friend. None of them is actually mad but illusions can come close to madness and Malvolio teeters on the brink.

To arrive at happiness you have to throw off all this illusion and live life genuinely. People like Jacques and Malvolio – cynical, Puritanical, disfigured by misanthropy and sick of self-love – they're unable to do this because in spite of their lofty opinions of themselves they too are playing parts which they can't get out of – the part is playing *them* – and so they prolong their solitary off-beat retreats, ending in sadness and solitude, eating sour grapes or plotting revenge, surrounded by married couples whom they will pity, ignore, sneer at, or be revenged upon. Their high-minded superiority is another envious illusion and they don't have the prerogative of truth that they think they have. What they do have, however, is a point of view. All the world's a stage. No more cakes and ale. For life is never simple.

And so my last real comedy was already looking to Hamlet – who may be dressed in black but is brighter than anybody in an Elsinore that would be a poorer place without him, all sex and flattery and alcohol and a plentiful lack of wit. Viola isn't lacking in wit. Out of the sea of troubles that starts off the action, she comes alive and kicking, interested in rich bachelors, and finds herself in an Illyria that, unlike Elsinore, is dressed in crêpe – a world whose leaders, are busy playing parts, sad ones. It's a languid society, apart from the hangers-on, a society where Puritans thrive and clowns are low on work. It's in need of livening up and releasing from its restrictiveness and she's just the boy for the job. Into this melancholy, half-dead, self-deluded world of mourning, repression and frustration she comes, breasting the surge, with the tang of the sea about her, to regenerate and replenish. Oh yes, I was already looking beyond even Hamlet, to Pericles and Prospero. Tempests, it turns out, are kind, and shipwrecks do save souls. As Prospero's family and friends find out – and his enemies too.

But not Malvolio. He won't be pacified by life from the uncivilised sea. The fault is in himself, not in his stars, though there's cruelty here, and torment, and the shadow of revenge, and he's notoriously abused. So, like Jacques, Malvolio resists the neat and friendly closure – marriage is denied him. Not that he could ever have had a true marriage. His own mind was impediment enough to that. And yet there's a dark truth that sticks to him, uncomfortable as it may be for us to admit it. You can play your way through life to find an otherness that can free you from yourself, attach you to another half or integrate you into society – but the self is always incomplete. And uncertain of itself. Viola is still dressed as Cesario, Malvolio has stalked off, and Feste is out in the cold, Belch and Aguecheek deprived of their melancholy minstrel and of each other. Their illusions have been ripped away. An ageing drunk with a broken head has discovered he can no longer fight like he used to. And an antique idiot finally realises he has been strung along. All along.

Yet they needed one another. It was their desperate glee, their melancholy need that made these hangers-on hang out as one, threw them together with the even sadder Feste and the unholy Maria, the mistress with the streak of cruelty, whose relationship with Toby hardly goes deep. They're failures in fight, failures in drink, in love, in life, in everything. They have no work to go to, no worldly hopes. They live in, but they are outsiders.

The extreme outsider is Feste, put out of doors like poor Tom, back to his almshouse by the church if he's lucky, or in harder times abroad to beg his bacon, to face the hag and hungry goblin, nothing but his songs to clothe him in his nakedness from the spirits that stand in the book of moons. And only the flaming drake and the nightcrow make music to his sorrow. These are his new companions as he barks against the dogstar and crows away the morning, the moon his constant mistress, the lonely owl his marrow. Sweet mistress his exists only in his songs. And though he's not disfigured by Malvolio's self-love or by Jacques' aloofness, still he stays unloved and lonely, a sad figure with his wistful songs that sound as if they belong in a play – which of course they do! A player then, an entertainer – removed from the married estate back in Stratford, if you like, and lying down alone under a roof that is not his own.

Yes, yes, easy enough to feel with him. I always said I'd hate to end up like Feste, and all my life I strove to build my scripts against the spectre of a jester's ruins. And succeeded beyond the dreams of all security. All the same it's Feste I stand with in the end: the Fool who stands outside love, stands in the wind and the rain and sings of all three sadly. Love is like the sea, endless in capacity but it's water through the fingers in the end – it's the wind and rain that are the true elements, those counsellors that cannot disappoint, whether you're king or clown.

I remember the early days, when I believed in the illusion, that I could come in from the wind and the rain and join the cakes-and-alers in the castle. Now, years later, as I come to die, I know the truth of it. Sobriety bores, but revelry is a belch in the face, ripe with pickled herrings and the plague. Olivia's beauty is truly blent and won't outlast wind and weather. Youth's a stuff will not endure. So beauty fades, the cakes go mouldy, the ale turns sour. Nothing is certain except death.

Shallow and the Psalmist have their say. Even the opposites, Viola and Olivia, are almost anagrams of one another. Work it out.

'And love?'

Well now, Francis, a good fuck is still better than a good belch but even there desire outlives performance. And it *is* performance. All is performance, especially love: foreplay, development, complete with climax and untying of the knot and plenty of cunt and thrust – and love itself the romantic spectacle, the grand and noble lie. For what is love? 'Tis not hereafter. Present mirth hath present laughter. And women are as roses, remember?

'As you said. Whose flower, being once displayed – '

Doth fall that very hour. They die even when they to perfection grow. The spinners and the knitters in the sun, and the free maids that weave their thread with bones, they chant a song that dallies with the innocence of love and promises old age and death.

So come away, come away, death. Feste says it all, with his two songs of love and dissolution, comedy and tragedy, the one commending Venus, sex, and laughter, the other draped in crêpe. Feste is inconsolable. His sadness is the artist's, who knows that by singing a song for sixpence he's merely helping you pass the time before you die, in a world that began a long time ago and has not got much better with age or practice. Still the swaggering and the knavery abroad, cutpurses and punks and the roaring boys' bravado. Still the disillusion of love and the black coffin coming after the cakes and ale.

And always the fucking rain.

No, I was in no mood for clowning, or for any of those comforting fairy tales by which human beings try to run their lives. I come no more to make you laugh. Things now that bear a weighty and a serious brow I do present. *Twelfth Night* was my farewell to comedy. The death of Essex had put an end to all that.

54

'More sad stories, Will?'

Of the death of princes.

'And enter Hamlet?'

Essex's was the most famous death of 1601.

'But your father's now, was one of the more obscure, in spite of that coat of arms.'

The king my father. Having achieved his dream, he began to dwindle, subtly, and by slow stages. It was as if there was nothing left that he really wanted. Maybe he was more affected by his grandson's going than I gave him credit for. People grieve differently – some store it away, some start to die themselves. Even before Essex embarked on his last venture, John Shakespeare's death ran up like a flag in his face and it was against the fading light of these two stars, one the brightest luminary, the other a dim glimmer, that I began to write *Hamlet*.

Sons and fathers. I had lost one and could see the other receding from me – ineffectual, mysterious, and pale. Where do you stand exactly when the pillars topple, when your past and future fall away from you on either side? It's hard to stand upright on the empty heath, when you're a man in limbo, when you're a ghost. And what better part to play in your next drama than the ghost of a father? The husk of a king, and the eggshell of John Shakespeare, who could kill an animal with an impatient shrug and leave you with an image of a life lived without the shadow of a doubt. So frowned he once when in an angry parle he smote the sledded Polacks on the ice. 'Tis strange.

Strange indeed. When someone dies whom you've dearly loved, you understand as never before that your own being was rooted in that relationship, partly, largely, it depends on the person, and now that he or she has gone, something of you has gone too, along with the dead one. You don't know who you are. Identity? It's amputated. That part of it will never grow again. It needs must wither. You have to find a crutch – and hobble on, to silence or survival. Some never make it, do they?

'And you, Will, did you make it?'

A piece of him, perhaps.

'Who are you, old man?'

I'm nobody, I told you. A ghost, no more. I'm the man who wrote *Hamlet,* that's all, an actor, a player playing a ghost, twice unreal. I don't exist. Where is that Stratford lad, my lost son, the grandson of the father who was himself now disappearing like the ghost into the dews of dawn, through the eaves of Henley Street, where his Testament lay lodged, hidden, but not forgotten. The glow-worm shows the matin to be near and 'gins to pale his uneffectual fire. Adieu. Remember me. Say masses for my soul, pray for me in purgatory. Yes, father. And O, my son, my son, while memory holds a seat in this distracted globe – yes, by heaven. The voice of a dead father, the voice of a dead son, my own echoing voice, crying Hamlet, Hamlet! Every time I wrote that name it was a stab in the heart from my own quill, the life of the quill that had taken the life of the son, the absent father, and my own father still crying out for reparation. I was father and son and my struggling self, caught between them, three generations fused in a single play, Hamlet, Hamlet, remember.

Remember? How could I ever forget that awful duty he'd laid on me by his own failure: to win back from life what he had lost. And to fulfil it I'd had to leave them, all my pretty chickens. This was my task and its completion was a coat-of-arms and a play – the deepest statement of my entire being, and a bloody revenge, bloodier even than a father's that cost a son's life.

Revenge was in the air. Dead Kyd was enjoying a resurrection with his *Spanish Tragedy.* His own old play of Hamlet had been around a dozen years or more and had been done to death at Newington Butts. But Marston was the man of the moment with *Antonio's Revenge,* Tourneur and Webster were on the way with tragedies of white devils and duchesses and atheists and other revengers. And there were shoals of small fry around, swimming in and out of skulls. It was time to show them the way a revenge play could go – a direction never dreamed of, not even by Seneca's ghost. Now my Hamlet stepped out onto the stage with a problem that the stage had never known before, a set of crippling anxieties, hesitations and doubts, displacing the revenger and putting a thinker centre stage. Now the interest lay not in putting another person to death but in the very nature of death itself, and in the nature of that soul-sickness that makes you long for death when your dearest loved one dies and you suffer the worst of the thousand natural shocks that flesh is heir to, the worst one of all, a father grieving for a son, and watching a father die.

The time was anything but out of joint. We knew we'd have a Danish queen in London when the Scot succeeded to the throne. And something was rotten in the state of Denmark, traduced and taxed of other nations. A Scottish play might yet be needed, but for now the Dane was the man, his story reaching down to the roots of history and human life, the darkest tangles of the jungle, the first corpse, the curse of Cain, and of Oedipus, incest, adultery, suicide, revenge.

Stage versions were dire. Glaring at the groundlings, a filthy whining ghost lapped in some foul sheet or leather pilch comes in screaming like a pig half stuck and crying *Vindicta!* Or, in Kyd's old case, *Hamlet, Revenge!* Vengeance is not yours, he says to God, it belongs to the hero, who will kill the killer, and the filthy ghost will turn up like a groundling to the moment of reckoning and will enjoy every second of it, gloating over his murderer's final demise. The revenger is unlikely to survive and his corpse is added to the shambles that litters the stage. Pig's blood has been bought in by the bucketload and adds to the general smell of mortality and crime.

That was the formula faced.

The abominable Bacon once said that if you begin with certainties you will end in doubt, but that if you will be content to begin in doubt you will end in certainty. And as a law of life that rings rather true. But not for Hamlet – who begins in uncertainty and ends in even greater doubt. The play's the thing. But the play is unreal. Fill it with questions, Will, questions that question the action and the actors, questions that obliterate in their range and depth the one absurdly elementary objective, to kill the killer. Why, this is hire and salary, not revenge. There's some greater task afoot, something bigger than revenge, something to stop the action and give us pause. What is it?

It has something to do with death.

Death is certain, did I hear myself say? Some time ago, but yes, nothing else is fixed, not even birth, for you may be born dead, die in the womb, never be born at all, joining the billions of spilt seeds that went among the wastes of time. To be or not to be? That was the question, and *not* to be – the likelier of the two, the surer fate, not to have been in the first place, never to have been at all. But once born you will surely die, and though all your life you will shun this certainty, you draw towards it day by day, faster and faster as you age. Work, play, politics, love and money, music, friendship, wine – you will find a thousand corridors to avoid the one that leads to that dark door, and you will never be happy because you can never forget it quite. It will always be there, that door, opening on that one question: what is it that waits for you at the end of the last corridor? An end of flesh, yes, and rotting in the earth, but after that, what? Translation, torment, extinction, oblivion? A next world? And if so, Catholic or Protestant? Hell or heaven? Or Greek shades. A dreamless sleep perhaps, and an end to heartache. Or an endless troubled night, with the days' affairs running riot in your head, a lifetime regretted and a restless eternity all around you like the sea.

No, Will, no. Other than death there is only one certainty: that action is futile, momentary and absurd, that suffering is long, infinite and obscure. You know this for a truth but you know also that nothing can alter it, and so you work on, killing yourself, shortening the process, the madness, striving to forget – and lose the name of action, but unable to escape the treadmill of existence and the thousand grains that issue out of dust, afraid to take the forbidden route to resolution, the bare bodkin, the watery plunge. You know only that truth arrests all enterprise, that understanding kills action, that in order to act you need the veil of illusion. You know that Hamlet was the only one to face it, flat on, to see it squarely, to get it right, irrevocably and whole. You know that his call to self-slaughter was the right one for his philosophy, but that you will never take up arms against that sea of troubles. And so you will carry on courting illusion after illusion. And for you the best illusions are the purchase of properties and the penning of plays.

'It seems you never knew what else to do.'

I couldn't find the other way, Francis. Native – and to the manner born, as somebody once said. I did what I could, what I had to. And life passed – and here we are.

55

'If you'll forgive me saying so, Will, for someone who was only apparently filling in time, you filled it in rather well. How many plays did you pen altogether?'

Heaven knows, there were so many hands in the kitchen at one time. About forty, I suppose.

'Well, don't you want to let me have a note of them, some sort of list? They're your works, after all. They should form part of your estate.'

Trash, Francis. Who'd want them? They're afternoon entertainment. And their day is past, I fear. Anyway half of them aren't even in print. They don't exist – as good as not. They're the footnotes of history. Concentrate on my properties.

'Yes, you've given me careful notes about all these. Henley Street passed to you when your father died?'

Death always enriches somebody or something, even if it's just the earth.

'And half of it's let to sister Joan.'

The other half I let out.

'Yes, and 107 acres of arable land in Old Stratford to the same man, Lewis Hickocks.'

Along with John Hickocks. That was the following year, 1602. And I bought twenty acres of private pasture.

'The Chapel Lane cottage you purchased in the same year. Why did you buy it?'

I needed a gardener and he needed a house, simple.

'And the rents came rolling in, I see.'

The ledgers grew thick with figures, like the plum trees in my orchard.

'Then you bought a half interest in the lease of tithes of corn, grain, blade and hay.'

From old Stratford again.

'And from Bishopton and Welcombe. You kept your eyes open.'

Slight risk. It was £440 down and an annual rent of £22, but the guaranteed return was sixty pounds a year. On top of which, the purchase of these old religious tithes made me technically a lay rector, with the right to be buried within the rails of the Holy Trinity chancel, where I already had a pew, not outside in the anonymous earth, like Yorick, along with my father and my sisters and my poor lost son.

It would have mattered to my father though, and with him in mind I looked on the prospect of a very respectable death, if not a glorious one.

Glory? What am I talking about? Even Gloriana died like any other ill old woman – by stopping breathing and entering the rest of silence. Nobody followed her into that silence – except a few hack writers, among whom I did not number myself, I have to say. By then she was past her time. She was in her seventieth year. Three thousand gowns gathered dust in her wardrobes. Always stingy with the state but ready to spend on herself, she grew tired at last of display. Vanity palled, melancholy fell, appetite went. She was dying. She'd gone lightly dressed through a bitter winter, eating little and wandering a little while her courtiers huddled in furs and hugged the fires, shivering and swigging back mulled wine. It was as if she was summoning the king of terrors to come to court and face her rages.

He came first for her old friend and cousin, the Countess of Nottingham. And when one of her own ladies of the Privy Chamber, Katherine Carey, lay on her deathbed, she whispered a terrible confession. It was she who'd been given the ring to pass to the queen, which she had deliberately withheld. That was the one sent by Essex the night before his execution, and it was the ring the queen had once given him as a token of her protection. Essex's last plea for his life had gone unheard.

'May God forgive you,' said the queen, 'because I never can.'

This plunged her into the melancholic fit out of which she never came. She didn't want to – she had finished with life and started to die, refusing all physic or entertainment. You know, Francis, there comes a time when an organism is like an age – it dies because it wants to die. It's had enough.

We performed before her for what turned out to be the last time on Candlemas Day. We might as well have played for a corpse. Nothing registered in those black eyes, sunk deep into the shrunken white face. And the black teeth stayed hidden, though Armin jested and even Cecil cackled to encourage her. Nothing. Not one crease added to that hideously wrinkled mask. When I saw her like that, I knew only death would make her grin again. And maybe she was the best critic, in her coldness, of that particular play we gave her. Maybe she sensed the irony of the title. *All's Well That Ends Well*, a cold story of rings and wrongs and a lame attempt to sweeten the bitter past. And when the play is done and the costumes taken off, what is a king but a beggar? That's the epilogue to even the greatest life. When her godson Harington tried reading her some of his witty verses she told him stonily, 'When thou dost feel creeping time at thy gate, such fooleries will please thee less. I am past relish for these matters.'

The year moved gloomily into March, her last month.

She still wore a small ring that Essex had once given her but the coronation ring, embedded in her flesh and impossible to twist from the finger, was filed off. It had been there for forty-four years and five months. She'd always said she wouldn't wish to outlive her usefulness to her subjects or her country and now she was acknowledging that the bright day was done and that she was for the dark. Her life's long task was over. She fell into her final illness.

It was the quinsy that stopped her eating – but that's a medical matter. The taste for life had gone. And yet she wouldn't lie down but stayed propped up on cushions, for fear she'd never get up again if she took to bed. For four days she sat, and even stood, simply stood there dying, such was the will – not to live, but to fend off the fearful skeleton that grinned at her in the mirror, humouring her, looking over her shoulder, scoffing her state, allowing her a little breath, a little scene, death keeping his court. Yes, now she *was* Richard the Second. Now she was all kings and queens.

There were stories of visions heralding her end. She saw her own body gloating down at her from above, emaciated, horrible, surrounded by the flames of hellfire – hallucinations that attend the dying, antics of the brain, of course, but still there were necromantic exercises performed, just to make sure, to exorcise the devils that had been sent to torment her in her last days. As devils are. As devils do.

'Well, we've all to come to it.'

And what of other visions? Did she think of her mother, accused of adultery with six men including her own brother and executed when her daughter was only two? She didn't have it easy. Offspring of a notorious whore, bastardised, scarred by watching women go to their deaths at the hands of men, the bed and the block fused and confused in her damaged mind, barred from the throne since she was two, forced further back by a pale cold-hearted brother, coughing his black life up against the pillows for Lady Jane Grey, bastardised again by Bloody Mary and accused of treason, the gibbets strung with rebels and she herself rowed through Traitor's Gate in the pouring rain and into the Tower.

Even as Mary lay dying she swore that her sister was a theological bastard and the bastard of an adulteress and a whore, not even Henry's child – though a blind man could have spied the father, from a mile away, of that pale-skinned, red-haired, hook-nosed, and black-eyed beauty. Only at her last gasp did Mary give in, acknowledging Elizabeth as her heir. She had made it.

Made it into forty-five years of stress, the sovereign born cloven, not crested, much to the chagrin of her father, who little realised she'd be more of a son to him than most sons could ever have been, and who declared that if she were turned out of the realm in her petticoat she could live in any place in Christendom.

What lay under that petticoat? Venus or Vesta? Brown-nosed Lyly, who licked anything that faintly resembled a royal rear, called her better than both. She was in her sixties by the time I first played before her and saw the famous facial inventory at close quarters, the corpse's skin, the bill-hook, the black eyes, the sugar-black teeth to match – the queen who wouldn't look in the mirror because there she saw a death's head wearing a wig. Beneath that red wig the red fires of the follicles had long gone out but the red temper still raged and burned and ate her up.

Was the coronation, I wonder, the brightest memory of all? The crisp winter morning with the hint of snow in the air? The ermine cape, the cloth-of-gold gown, the crimson-covered chariot, draped with velvet, the long loose hair, worn like her mother's a quarter of a century ago, before it was pinned up ready for the block? Or did an oak-tree spread itself out instead in her failing brain while, standing beneath its canopy, already royal with expectation, a young girl of twenty-five, watched a messenger draw close, knowing his message would be wordless, waited for the proffered ring, drawn from the dead finger of an unwilling bitter sister?

What did she really believe in by the end? Loyalty? Love?

Friendship? Religion? Difficult to say, but not much is the probable answer, outside of duty – meaning England, the anchor she clung to perhaps when her eyes began to swim.

Carey heard her sigh forty or fifty times – such deep sighs she fetched as he had never heard since Mary Queen of Scots went under the axe. On the 23rd she asked for a little rose-water and some currants, then the inflammation in her throat prevented her from saying any more. Wordless, still she refused until the last possible moment – by putting her hand to her head when James was mentioned and making her fingers into the shape of a crown – to name her successor: she had reigned for nearly half a century without one. Word was sent all the same to James in Edinburgh to watch the Tudor clock. It ticked as all clocks do. She turned her face to the wall and slipped into the deep sleep, and on 24th March, between two o'clock and three in the morning, died without further fuss – mildly, it was reported, like a lamb, easily like an autumn apple from the tree – at Richmond Palace, after a short illness, bravely borne, Elizabeth, Queen of England, 1533–1603.

What more can you say? Ripeness is all. The ancient overdressed woman who'd been monarch of the realm for as long as most of us could remember – bewigged, beruffed, bejewelled, begotten a bastard in the eyes of her enemies but ultimately betrothed only to her country – was dead. And those black moth's eyes which looked as if they'd never slept beneath the hollow crown that rounds the mortal temples of the uneasy head, were closed at last. James was proclaimed in Cheapside and few wished her alive again – the decades of uncertainty had gone, and the gloom of those last years and melancholy months.

The body was brought by barge from Richmond to lie in state at Whitehall: a dead body ablaze with jewels, replacing the fire of England that had gone out. Up in his turreted study, that night, high above the Thames, Ralegh wept more scented crocodiles from his window as he watched the melancholy line of boats go by with muffled oars, their torches glimmering on the water. The chief cargo was the age itself, the chief barge carrying the embalmed body of the ancient virgin, seduced at last by the invincible bridegroom. Her old Captain of the Guard had greater reason to weep than he could have guessed. His protectress gone, the wolves were already gathering at his gate, baring their teeth. There were tears in their eyes too, but like Ralegh's for Essex, they too were crocodiles. The fall of a falcon usually involves a sparrow or two, even those who acted like eagles before worms.

But there was only one great one the people of London had come to mourn. Westminster was awash with people, in the streets, houses, windows, leads and gutters, a multitude of all sorts who'd come to see her make her last progress. And when they saw the effigy over the coffin a great groaning wave of grief went up that washed the spires and shrunken skulls of London. Soon the sweet regret set in – it always does as people remember the good days – which is what people do and what good days are for. There had been heroism enough in her time to eclipse the cruelty. But Dekker exaggerated as usual when he wrote of showers of tears raining down for the old queen. Down she went into the vault in Westminster Abbey, over monumentless Mary, the half-sister but full-blooded and well-bloodied Catholic. All one now. Emilia Bassano's much cuckolded strummer was one of the musicians that saw to her obsequies – at which there was much professional sighing and no real grief. Nothing worse than becoming too successful and living too long.

The poets kept their silence. Mine was noted by Chettle, among others, and the Stratford shepherd was urged to remember Elizabeth and sing her rape, done by that Tarquin, death. Chettle himself took me to task for not responding to the honourable task.

Nor doth the silver-tongued Melicert drop from his honeyed Muse one sober tear to mourn her death who gracèd his desert, and to his lays opened her royal ear.

Melicert indeed. Silver-tongued if you like. Silence is pure gold, they say. Mine was, compared to the plays that followed now. You won't find much nostalgia there for a life well lived, nor much to celebrate in the life of the times, nor in the life to come. I was going my own way in an age that had shaken the certainties. Tragedy was the tool I would use to explore the new incoherence. Chaos had come again. I was entering the tunnel. Out went the lights, as they'd done in Henley Street. And once more we were all left darkling.

56

It took the new king six weeks to get from Edinburgh to London. Robin Carey had done it in three days – at breakneck speed, and on the third night he came thrashing into Edinburgh, bruised, travel-stained, and torn, and gave James a blue ring from a fair lady. The man he'd come to see, though keen to take up his crown and toss the old one into the gutter, was not so keen on physical exertion, but he was anxious to make a big show of it. This would be no mere journey, it would be a triumphal progress.

And it was – except that the new arrival was terrified by the sight of his own subjects clamouring to come close, and wasn't over eager to stage him to the public view. As the people screamed to get a better look at him, he showed every sign of anxiety and alarm, but managed to carry off his nervousness with a jest.

'Good God Almighty, how much nearer can they get? Would the bastards like to see what I had for breakfast? Do they want me to pull down my breeks so that they can gawp up my arse?'

This was Elizabeth's replacement – a man with the body of a weed, the heart and stomach of a coward, and the manners of a boor, though a scholarly one and a pompous and pedantic ass. An interesting oddity of a new ruler and one who would suit well in some strange new play methinks – God's vicar playing God himself, a duke of dark corners. But he resembled his predecessor in one respect – he enjoyed cruelty to animals as turned into sport. Animals were for cruel fun – and for stuffing down your gullet. In vast quantities. He was a glutton.

But he arrived from his rainswept Scotland and its dark theology remarkably affable and oddly robust for a man whose frame spoke of physical frailty. Would you care to take a closer look, Francis? Truth to tell I do not recommend it, but I expect you're curious, and there's no need to go as far as craning up the royal arse. Let me show you what I saw in the May of 1603.

'I've heard he's no picture.'

A big head and a scraggy beard, bulging hare's eyes staring at you moistly, curiously, warily, summing you up. He was nobody's fool in spite of facial evidence to the contrary. A slobbering tongue, too long and loose for the wet mouth – it was true what they'd said – the spittle hitting you in the eye and spraying the air about you the moment he started to speak. Later you noticed that he always seemed to be eating his wine rather than drinking it, so that it dribbled out on either side of the mouth and back into the cup. There must have been a good quarter's worth of backwash – the goblet got fuller rather than emptier, the more he drank – or rather slurped. And when you lowered your eyes, affecting humility but actually trying to avoid the spray, what did you see? A pair of spindly legs sticking out clownishly from an armoury of heavily quilted clothes. All that padding was fearfully intended to stop, or at least to slow the course of, a sudden stiletto or an assassin's dagger. The poor man lived in perpetual terror of his life.

Sadly he hadn't inherited an ounce of his mother's notorious beauty. It was the father's wretched physique that had come through. He was still in the Mary Stuart womb, and technically therefore in the same room as his mother, when his father and his drunken thugs murdered Rizzio before her eyes. He was not long out of the womb when Darnley was murdered in his turn by the mother's next lover. And even after he came to the Scottish throne witches were after him, waxen images of himself, live cats tied to joints of corpses and hurled into the yeasty sea to raise storms to drown him as he made his way to Denmark to marry Anna. He was a king of terrors, stalked by the King of Terrors himself. Satan was alive and well in Scotland. Plots to destroy him multiplied in his mind. Even as a boy he'd had a hard time of it – he was a target for the rival Scottish nobles bent on kidnap (the hand that keeps the king controls the realm), and his bent backside was a butt for the erudite lash of George Buchanan, who schoolmastered him mercilessly. The Bible was his entertainment, though he took refuge in books on history and witchcraft. No wonder he looked as he did, and looked at you as he did – with those abstracted and always anxious eyes. He was never sure of the English crown but by the time it came his way he was ready to go wild. And he did.

Not everybody benefited. Ralegh went straight to prison. Jamie hated him down to his earring, hated him for introducing tobacco to the court – a vice he blasted in one of his books – hated him for making the Spanish merchants rich and the court unhealthy, hated him for bringing savages to England. Two months after the accession old Stinkweed found himself deprived of his captaincy of the Guard, then of his income, then of his house. He no longer needed a house, quipped the king, bound as he was for the Tower, like Harry. He was confined there in the summer, charged with treasonable conspiracies, and tried in November. The court condemned him to be hanged, drawn, and quartered. He must have sweated. He knew what that meant. But such is the mind of the mob – the poor who'd have gone a hundred miles to see him hanged now went the extra mile to save him, and the king gave in to the popular mood and reprieved him on the scaffold. But his days are numbered.

Whereas young Harry – now ageing Harry, to speak true – was set free and given double compensation for his time in the Tower – Essex's sweet wines' revenue and Knight of the Garter. Jack Donne was another. Bess sent him to the Fleet for running off with his employer's niece – she was only sixteen at the time, Anne More. But he was forgiven and became a better boy under Jamie. Some said Jamie would have liked Jack under him too – a handsome piece of haunch, if not a stripling at thirty. But you can't bugger the Dean of St Paul's – a plum post for the court's most popular preacher – though Jack never was at heart's ease with himself or his position, always feeling in disgrace with fortune and his own eyes. Self-envious was our Jack, his own worst enemy. He was lucky to have the king as a friend. Same with Bacon – the rubbery little turd got a knighthood.

But Jamie's best move, only ten days into his reign and by far the greatest act of that reign – says your impartial client, Francis – was to take over our Company and issue us with a warrant for Letters Patent under the Great Seal. The warrant went under the seal only two days later. *His good servants William Shakespeare, Richard Burbage, Augustine Phillips, John Heminges, Henry Condell, William Sly, Robert Armin, Richard Cowley, and the rest of their associates were permitted freely to use and exercise the art and faculty of playing comedies, tragedies, histories, and the like as well for the recreation of his loving subjects as for his royal solace and pleasure when he should think good to see them during that pleasure, etcetera etcetera.* It was a bitter pill indeed for the City Fathers to swallow but they just had to gulp and bow. Jamie the Sixth's the man!

Furthermore, the said comedies and tragedies and suchlike were to be shown to their best commodity as well within their now usual house called the Globe within his Majesty's county of Surrey, as also within any town halls or moot halls or other convenient places within the liberties and freedom of any other city, university, or town.

And more words to that effect.

We were now the King's Men.

Forgive the parliamentary language, Francis, but that is exactly what it was. It had a certain ring to it, you will admit. The King had done us proud. Starved of theatre culture during his colourless days with Calvin, he'd determined to make up for it with drums and trumpets. Less than a fortnight as king and he had his own theatre group. At the stroke of a pen the rate of pay was doubled from ten to twenty pounds per performance. We were up to our balls in clover and all we had to do was bend a little and browse.

We weren't the only men. After Henslowe leased out the Rose to Pembroke's and Worcester's, these lads went to the Curtain and joined up with what was left of Oxford's to become the Queen's Men, with Thomas Heywood as resident poet and actor, Will-style. And Alleyn was still the star of the Admiral's, who became Prince Henry's Men. But we were the premier company in the country and our performances, as things turned out, numbered more than those of all the other companies combined. We did not fear the Greeks. We were men of the hour.

The King's Act had made me into a Groom of the Royal Chamber, and though I never went near the royal chamber (nobody did if they could help it) I had to look the part for the coronation the following year and was duly awarded four and a half yards of scarlet cloth by the Master of the Great Wardrobe. And so, in a resulting red livery of doublet, hose and cloak, with the royal arms emblazoned on the sleeves, I walked in the procession through the streets of London, bound for Whitehall. I couldn't help thinking as I looked at the roaring sea of faces, how I'd stolen here all those years ago (sixteen was it?), a frightened shadow from Stratford, slipping in anonymously, and now here I was, one of the chosen few, proceeding publicly and with great ceremony, my will well plumed up under the red plumage, proud as a peacock – or so we were instructed to appear. That wasn't difficult, after all, for an old actor, and though I couldn't give a tinker's toss at the time, a part of me was just sorry my old father wasn't there to see his son swanning along behind the King – it would have flushed him up with sheer pride to have spotted me just below the sergeants and yeomen but still above the boys and pages, following the cynosure of the nation, a Scottish scarecrow on a white mule. It took half a day to reach Westminster from the Tower and my legs were killing me.

But there was a bright March sun in our faces and it was a far cry from those never-to-be-forgotten bad old days trudging behind the cart in the wind and the rain, only to be spat on by jumped up jacks-in-office and have the sticks and halters shaken in our faces. No more o' that, I thought, no more o' that, and as I joined in the prayers for God to protect our king and grant him a long safe and happy reign, I meant every word of it – well, almost. Never mind about the happiness, I thought – just make it long. And make it safe.

The Powder Plotters were thinking different thoughts. They'd had a year to think them and behind the mouth-honour there was whispered discontent. But let that wait. I shall be faithful, Francis. I promised to be faithful that glittering March morning, a faithful subject all my days, and to mine own self to be true. My personal faith was no child of state, was builded far from accident, suffered not in smiling pomp and feared not policy, that heretic which works on leases of short-numbered hours, but all alone stood hugely politic. Stood above it all, if you like. Stayed out of it at least. A quiet life is all I wanted.

A quiet life? James wasn't the only famous visitor to London that year. Our old friend the plague returned, and after almost a decade away he'd gathered strength. There were over a thousand deaths a week that first summer, rising to three thousand by September, with thirty-five thousand dead in the first year of the new reign, a sixth of all souls. In the Cripplegate where I'd been staying, it was a lot worse, nearly five-sixths, if you fancy it in fractions. Put it another way. Out of three thousand folk there were barely six hundred left alive. I was one of them, but I wasn't there in Silver Street to be counted among those still standing. We were much in demand outside the plague-ridden city.

After it passed we never really stopped playing for the king – who paid well. I'd ample reason to be grateful to him. His predecessor never rated a play much higher than a cock-fight or a jig. Hers was a prose mentality, clever but dull, devoid of fancy. Now it was farewell, sour annoy! For here I hope begins our lasting joy!

Lasting joy. Was that what I really felt in 1603 and after? Joy had fallen from the air during the queen's last days, along with the brightness.

Gloriana had got tighter, coarser, colder, more of a close-fisted old shrew. I felt a surge of hope now that she was gone. And yet and yet – in Jamie's time the gloom somehow deepened, the sourness thickened, plots and plays curdled. Something was indeed rotten in the state of Denmark's partner. The golden time I'd looked for – and got – had somehow gone, trickled like water in the desert, right through my fingers.

And so. You strive all your life against your lot, against fate and circumstance, against your own faults and follies and those of the times; you win through to security, stability, recognition – and yes, Francis, yet more money in the purse. And then? Suddenly you start to age, to sicken and slide into doubt, along with the times. Maybe it's got nothing to do with kings or queens, who's in who's out, it's just you and history going grey together, not even gold with grief, just drab with disenchantment. The days of drums and defiance are over. Men are no longer heroes – the toads are croaking thick on the ground. The soldier's pole is fallen, and withered is the garland of the war. And there is nothing left remarkable beneath the visiting moon. Even sex no longer attracts. Something has gone out of that too – the thrill, the passion, the fun and folly. Even the guilt. And all that's left is a sudden coupling. Underneath a brothel roof. And a cynical uncoupling. An uncoupling too of morality and manners from life. Tragedy is no longer grand, history no longer healthy, comedy no longer corrective or even funny. Nothing works any more. Self-doubt takes tighter hold, closes round your soul. And if you happen to be a playwright, you may lose the plot. Or you may go to plots and places you never dreamt of. And you write *Measure for Measure*.

57

It was the first play I gave the king and in so doing I was giving him a glass in which he would almost see himself. Playing does not exactly hold the mirror up to nature, as Hamlet said. It holds up a distorting mirror instead. Plays are not copies but illusions of reality. And Jamie always saw what he wanted to see. He was an easy target for a new and subtler kind of writing, one that reflected the spirit of the new age without fear of being seen as critical.

Look at the way he played cat and mouse with conspirators. In Elizabeth's time they'd have been tried and gutted and that would have been that. But he enjoyed the torture of the mind, granting brief reprieves, two-hour stays of execution, sudden pardons, keeping his guessing subjects on their toes and playing God. An excellent candidate, you could say, for a duke in disguise.

A story with a beard. The disguised king goes among his people, righting wrongs. But there was also the story, not inappropriate, of the corrupt leader who abuses his power to slake his sexual lust. Bring in the other bearded legend of the wronged wife who uses the bed-trick to regain her husband – and you have a triple plot under way.

Jamie was free to see the Duke as a flattering image of himself: benevolent authority, caring king, kindly father, the master of munificence, life's scripter, destiny's dramatist, actor in and director of his own creation, a healer of his sick and seedy city. Not too hard in fact for James to glance into the glass of art and see himself as something even greater than an earthly king – God himself, divine mercy, heavenly grace, Christ the cauterising sword and forgiving redeemer – with Angelo the Old Testament letter of the law, Isabella chastity and righteousness, Lucio the Devil, and Claudio unregenerate man. It was the kind of scheme designed to appeal to a king who really believed he had private audiences with God. He'd even written a book about it, confirming his authority as God's deputy.

What he chose not to see was the other side of the Duke: a man remote from his people, a people he doesn't love, in spite of what he says, but sees as his concern and source of his power. A king without subjects to control is a king of shadows living in a paper palace. The Duke has neglected his kingdom and allowed moral chaos to reign, so draconian measures are required. But if you don't want to be the unpopular reformer – if you want to continue to be flattered and admired, make somebody else stir the moral midden. Angelo's the man, the assistant doctor to lance the sore – while the Duke questions the distempered part in secret, revelling in the play, plotting real people on his stage, extracting actions, dialogue, giving them set speeches, but giving little away. A controller who hated to get too close to the crowds he controlled.

I love the people, but do not like to stage me to their eyes, I do not relish well their loud applause and aves vehement. Nor do I think the man of safe discretion that does affect it.

In the end he's a stage duke, a theatre puppet himself, created to put a play before a king, that's all, and yet this thin but intricate figure gets the girl in the end, in spite of his insistence that he was proof against the dribbling dart of love. Yes, that's how he described it: *the dribbling dart of love*. A reductive image of the prick, you'd say; and people like that who pontificate, tuck back their balls and deride the penis are usually the first to end up with an erection. By the time I'd finished with him he was hot for Isabella – she turns on the men of power – and she goes off-stage to get what nature intended for her, a better image of the dribbling dart.

Picture, if you will, dear Francis, the Green Room at the Globe, and poor Sam Gilbourne, who had to play her, smashing his head against the stage and asking me the way. How to play her, this novice nun who makes the snow-broth blood of Angelo boil over?

Poor Sam. Whatever you do, I said, with tongue in cheek, don't make her likeable. She's a damaged Diana howling for sex, the very words she chooses exuding a longing for rough stuff and penetration – the keen whips she'd wear like rubies – and strip myself to death as to a bed that long I have been sick for. Oh yes, she's hot for it, Sam. Let Angelo get an erection in her presence and make our Jamie roar. The wanton stings and motions of the sense have come to plague him.

'A little harsh?'

Served him right, Francis. Angelo the fallen angel, the counterfeit coin, a nasty piece of work, a Puritan. And an indication of how things would have run had they got into power – decent people punished, adulterers even to the death, while the pimps would be untouched because they went with the unregenerate and were therefore acceptable, like imps on lettuce leaves and turds in privies – part of our fallen nature and part of God's plan. But Puritan Angelo is punished where he most deserves it. Malvolio I punished merely in the mind. This kill-joy gets it in the balls, and the critic of lust now burns with it himself and is exposed for the hypocrite he is.

But what does it mean, Will? – more anguished back-stage squawks. Actors always want to know what they're doing. So you hand them the script and say, don't ask me, I only wrote the thing. Words, words, words. They come from deep within – or far without. Either way you can't reach the source – what they actually meant as they came to you. And that too is inspiration.

'What did it mean, Will? Did it mean anything?'

It seems to be a comedy – much disguise, much confusion and confrontation – but there's no friendly wildwood here in which it all gets disentangled, no leaves and lyrics. Something less healthy than nature sorts it out – sorts it out in the corner, muffled and shuffled and feeling dirty. Dilemmas, disturbances, dubious ideals, a loss of bearings. And a feeling that people are not so nice any more – the absentee ruler, the hypocrite judge, the chilly sister, the lax brother, the whores and pimps and bawds and murderous convicts, the state itself that sentences a man to death for sleeping with his girl. Life has lost its lustre but death still horrifies and the prospect of any redemption is remote and unreal. Sex is a mire and marriage a punishment – the wedding bells jar at the end, jangled and harsh yet again. Angelo's nuptials are an alternative to execution, Isabella is stamped as the Duke's marriage property, and Lucio is made to marry his whore.

A play for an anxious era and for melancholy middle age. A thing of darkness, twisted and wrung into a suspect structure, of uncertain essence. It leaves you disturbed and divided, less certain of your ideals, a little cynical perhaps, even a little disgusted with life, a little weary. Meanwhile the plague sweats on and on, death's messenger, wedded to sex, and the king pulls down the brothels. And maybe you can't come closer than that, to any sort of belief. And yet once more – it's something to do with sex. And yet once more it's something to do with death. It's what it always comes back to in the end. Death is the end of every story.

58

'The best antidote to death is birth.'

Still with me, Francis? Well, I remember one of my Silver Street neighbours, William Taylor, asked me to be godfather to his baby girl at that time. She was christened Cordelia.

'Ah.'

Ah, what?

'Nothing got lost on you, did it? Nothing ever went to waste.'

You weave into the tapestry everything you can find. Some of it's from books but much of it just straws in the wind, thistle-seeds, the gossamer of gossip. A dropped feather turns into a quill.

'You've got to start somewhere.'

There were other beginnings just then. I was in Silver Street, in the Cripplegate, cornered with Muggle Street, in the north-west of the city, almost at the wall, where from my upper room I could look out over a sea of rooftops to St Paul's, and with St Olave's a spit of the mouth away. Not that I was a church-going man in London, though I showed face at funerals and baptisms.

I was lodging with the Mountjoys. I'd met Monsieur Mountjoy's wife, Mary, through Jacklin Vautrollier – Wood Street being just around the corner, running down to Cheapside. Do you want me to spell it out for you, Francis?

'Not another dark lady!'

I was up to my ears in them.

'Not the anatomical image I'd have chosen.'

True, Francis. But Mary Mountjoy – you'll recognize the name from Henry Five, and it does have a certain vulgar aptness, you'll admit – also fucked elsewhere. In particular she'd been joyfully mounted, hoping to make me jealous, by one Henry Wood, mercer and cloth-trader in Swan Alley, and she thought she'd joined the pudding club, so she went scuttling off to see Simon Forman, as they all did. It turned out she was no more pregnant than I was. Or than Henry Wood was, for that matter.

But old Christopher Mountjoy suspected she was having it away with somebody and ironically poured out his woes to Will – whose will had been most active in his good lady. So I gave him the Iago stuff. I'd watch out for Wood, if I were you. Note if *la belle femme* strain his entertainment with any strong or vehement importunity. Much will be seen in that. In the meantime, hold her free, I do beseech you. I then warned Madame to stay well away from Swan Alley and make sure to give Mountjoy the time of his life for the next few nights. She was so grateful she fucked me too for old time's sake and present thanks – I'd given up brothel-creeping by that time. Doubtless Forman fucked her too. He fucked most of his clients.

'You make Cripplegate sound like a fleshmarket.'

There were almshouses and autopsies within fifty paces, and poor old buggers living on seven pence a week, five sacks of charcoal, and a quarter of faggots a year. The Barber Surgeons opened up the corpses of criminals four times a year and let you see what bred about their hearts if you cared to sit through the lectures. After I'd seen that I needed a drink in the Dolphin in Milk Street where for tuppence you could browse and sluice in your private snug and if you wanted to write, the candles were free.

'They made wigs there, didn't they?'

And tires. That was Mountjoy's trade. Old Ben once said of the queen that her teeth were made in Blackfriars, each eyebrow in the Strand, and her hair in Silver Street. Mountjoy's shop was one of several and he devoted his days to beautifying the heads of ladies. It wasn't far off being a fleshmonger's, though, as you will hear, Francis.

'All ears and no choice.'

Mountjoy had a daughter called Mary, after her mother, and she – young Mary, not the mother – was being fucked by one of the apprentices, Steven Belott, unknown to the parents. I knew about it, though. The shop was on the ground floor and everybody slept upstairs. Her room was next to mine and if the walls didn't have ears, I did. French women come like it's the end of the world – trumpets and tambourines and the crack of doom, that sort of thing.

Belott, like Richard Field, was a young bugger on the make. He had business plans and wanted a bigger dowry than old man Mountjoy was prepared to offer. They dragged me into their wrangling, and for the sake of peace in mine inn and paying my sexual debt to Madame Mountjoy, I became a judge, settling on an arrangement to everybody's apparent satisfaction. Sixty pounds down as soon as the knot was tied and a further two hundred jinglers as soon as Monsieur Mountjoy had said *bonsoir* to this world. The unwritten assumption was that the apprentice would also inherit the family business, especially as young Mary was the sole child and daughter and thus his heir. Belott was onto a good billet. All he had to do was wait. They were married in St Olave's and I looked forward to the sounds of legal shagging shaking my chamber wall. And as legitimate sex invariably settles down to being a lot less vigorous and a lot less frequent than the illicit variety, I also looked forward to a lot more sleep.

Things took an altogether different turn – though I did get the wished-for sleep. To my surprise the shagging ceased altogether and the sounds of stifled sobs came faintly through instead. I could live with that. And sleep with it too. If young Belott was not seeing to his husbandly duties and young Mary was being denied her conjugal bliss, it was none of my affair – though if I'd been his age and betwixt the sheets I'd have done his office gladly. Mary minor was a pretty thing, dumpy and plump and with a dusky little rump which I'd glimpsed in action one summer's midnight when her door was ajar and she on top, thrusting merrily. But now it seemed that Belott was coming out in his true colours. Not willing to wait for the death of his employer, now his *bon-père*, Belott haled Mary from Silver Street without so much as an ave or adieu, to set up a rival business of his own, expecting to use the promised sixty pounds to the purpose.

It didn't work out. Mountjoy went wild and gave them only ten pounds, palming them off with some old rags and sticks of furniture thrown in. '*Voila!* Set up your 'ouse and shop wis zat, if you can!' After all, if Belott could renege on the deal, so could he. But then what happened? Madame Mountjoy suddenly died (of one of Forman's concoctions no doubt) and the prodigal couple came back to the sad fold to look after father and to become his partners.

Not for long. The old squabbling started up again and the couple stormed off, leaving the ageing wigmaker to turn to Bacchus. Belott heard on the breezes that his father-in-law had every intention of putting away down his neck as much of the inheritance as he possibly could before cutting off son-in-law without a penny piece. 'He won't even have a nail left to claw his English arse with by the time I'm done!'

The saga ran for years. By the time it came to court I was retired and had to leave Stratford and go up to London to summon up remembrance of things past. There I was obliged to inform the Court of Requests that I found myself unable to remember all the details of the case. Yes, I did recall Stephen Belott, who had struck me as a good enough worker, and yes, I recalled that a sum of money had been agreed on. It might have been about fifty pounds. (It was sixty if it was a penny but it wouldn't have done to remember too precisely.) And I recalled nothing of the two hundred pounds. Two hundred is a lot of money. But Belott had been a good worker, was that the phrase? Well, yes, good enough, and valued by Monsieur Mountjoy for his services as an humble apprentice, but at the same time I hadn't heard Monsieur say that he'd made any real profit out of him. And coming back to the crucial matter of the money, the actual sum promised? Ah! Now there I simply couldn't swear to an exact figure. Couldn't swear that there ever was such a thing as an exact figure – more of an honourable agreement, perhaps, if even that. There my memory simply failed me.

'You old fox.'

I'd had enough of the Mountjoys and the Belotts and I wanted no more. I wasn't going to come down neatly on either side for the benefit of one of the parties. Life's not so simple, is it? And discretion is the better part of witnessing. I left it to other parties to sort out. It turned out to be the elders of the French church, when the case was turned over to them. They found for Belott and ordered Mountjoy to pay him twenty nobles – which as far as I know he never did. They also added that both father and son-in-law were a couple of drunks – something they didn't get from my studied ramblings on the stand, though I could have given them chapter and verse on that old score. I could have given them the whole volume if I'd wanted. But the older I got the more I valued silence, suspension, keeping my thoughts to myself.

Or putting them on the stage – in such a way that questions of innocence and guilt were swallowed up in the spectacle of sheer human suffering.

Nowhere more so than in the plays that had poured from my hectic pen for those past ten years.

59

The plague, the Powder Plot, the great eclipse, murder and mayhem calculated on a cosmic scale, the sheer diabolical ruthlessness, wickedness and immorality, of people prepared to blow up their fellow human beings in London for a religious cause. To maim, mutilate and murder in the name of God. Jesus Christ, Francis!

'I know. You wrote *King Lear.*'

Among others.

'Well I may be a humble lawyer and you are the English Ovid, but there I take issue with you, if I may.'

You may, Francis, but on what account?

'On Cordelia's account. You killed her, Will. You didn't have to. You hanged Lear's only remaining daughter – and you made him see it. The only good thing he had left, the only one in the world he had ever really loved. And you crushed them up together.'

I did.

'But why? I mean, surely, it wasn't necessary!'

Francis?

'You changed the plot. I've heard it said. You altered the facts of the story. It didn't have to be that way. What on earth was the point, I ask you?'

What's the point of anything, Francis? It was putting on the agony, putting on the style – the tragic style. But it wasn't only the characters I tortured. I wanted the spectator to suffer too. The cruelty is calculated, you can hear it, Francis, in the actual writing, a ferocity that kept me sane – just.

'Well, that's a riddle!'

I'd reached the stage where the play was the rack and the playgoer my victim and I was ready to play my terrible game with him. Even when the play was over the pain wouldn't go away. He'd never be the same man again. Even you, Francis. It's under your skin. The old *Leir* has a happy ending like the Book of Job – but my heath wasn't the forest of Arden any more, and was far from Arcadia. In *Lear* the plot is there for the pain, nothing more, just the absolute agony of living.

And so I piled on the agony, added to it by draining the play of domesticity – in spite of the flax and the whites of eggs, in spite of home's dull cruelties and slimy smallness, there's no background of real living here, no familiar quotidian routines, no comforting ordinariness. You can imagine Lady Macbeth dressing for dinner, or Desdemona hurrying back from the privy to hear the rest of Othello's travels. In *Lear* life is lived out in a bear-pit of a world, loud with howls, a world away from the little loyalties of Stratford, the tough kindnesses of Snitterfield, the Christian values, the pastoral ethics, the human knots that bind. Lear's men and women are merely players, strutting symbols on a propless stage. Their words reverberate in the encompassing emptiness, their actions have no continuance in time.

'All right, all right, you had your reasons, obviously.'

As for the Green Room at the Globe on a *Lear* day, you can well imagine it.

'Man, you're ill!'

'Is it the pox or what?'

'Tell him to take a holiday, go abroad. Haply the sea and countries different with variable objects shall expel this something-settled matter in his heart.'

'*Were* you sick, Will?'

In body and in mind, Francis. And it came out in the play. Was it a tale told by an idiot? an absurdity? Was Cordelia's hanging *after* the death of her enemies, in the midst of friends, the last hideous joke of destiny? And Lear's last words as he sees her lips move, a last trick of the tortured brain? Does he die from a broken heart or a surge of joy? Or was it about the corruption of the court and the aristocracy under threat? Or a great cry of outrage against all forms of injustice, ingratitude, ignorance and suffering and violence and cruelty and pain? Especially the pain of the martyrs that makes you want to speak what you feel, not what you ought to say? Was it an image of doomsday? a parable of pride, power, blindness and sight, madness and sanity, the forces of darkness, the need for self-knowledge? Or the need to be human in a state of nature where the human condition is a condition of war, everyone against everyone, and life a bearpit?

Not quite. Yes, Cordelia was pure love and there she lies, dead on stage, and will not come again. Never. The cold core of the play's statement. And yet, in spite of all the evil – the ingratitude, the greed, the lust, the ambition, the treachery and cruelty and the rest – in spite of suffering and injustice and death and extinction, she has been, she has existed, and her love got through to her father in the end, at no point more movingly and unbearably than when he sees her dead, imagines her alive, and dies himself. I could have denied the audience that last wild flicker of hope before the end. And then it would have been a ticket to hell. But instead I gave them that flicker of a candle in the dark.

'Is that it, then?'

That's it, Francis.

'Must there no more be said?'

No more. Not publicly, anyway. But I'll tell you in confidence. It's a play about fathers and children. The Fool is the son Lear never had, the son he only pays attention to when it's too late. Cordelia and the Fool were doubled by the same actor. *And my poor fool is hanged.* Yes, that's Cordelia. But the trick of language and the fact of doubling has you looking down at a dead boy – and there's a chilling affection in the tone. You recall the king's other Fool at that point, the boy who went to bed at noon and never got up again, vanished from the action – just like Hamnet.

'You suffered, old man.'

As time went by the dead son died over and over. After Lear's bitter boy, young Macduff, Marcius, Mamillius. And all the lost daughters were reclaimed: Cordelia, Perdita, Marina, Imogen, Miranda.

Meanwhile Susanna and Judith were twenty-two and twenty and the best catches in Stratford. Their father could have retired at forty and re-joined them in Stratford. But right now he had more on his mind. And in his sick carcass and ailing soul.

60

The fires of Venus had been lit – in my genitals and all other lubricated places, the eyes, the mouth, the nostrils. Most of all the mind, heating it up with horrified contemplation of the body's rotting. I knew very well what could lie ahead for me; baldness, blindness, lameness, madness – the multiple wages of sin in many a brothel and the hell of many a dark-skinned whore. This was the stake I'd sharpened, and chained myself to stand there. I cannot fly, I said, but bear-like I must fight the course.

And what was I, for God's sake? Early forties, that's all. Sounds young, a man in his prime. But not in London. There I was five years past the average for a city drabber, and deep in its hell. Nashe penned a piece he called *Christs Tears Over Jerusalem*, but it was Nashe's over London, a lament for its vices. He called it the seeded garden of sin, the polluted sea that sucks in all the scummy channels of the realm. What are thy suburbs but licensed stews? Whores were syphilitic at fifteen, lethal at twenty, skeletal at twenty-five, and dead at thirty – often sooner.

'A real Jeremiah.'

He did not exaggerate. Three-quarters of the sodden stream of humanity that sludged into St Bartholomew's were venerally diseased, the result of sex for sixpence – and cheaper with the pox on offer – among a population that had quickly spilled out from the country and fetched up trapped in the capital.

'You being one.'

Who was I? Where was I headed? Son gone, father gone, the age gone, a strange new epoch in progress, the inner life dead. Only plays left to live for.

And driven, Francis, driven. Burning out my brain in building all those other worlds. Where does it come from, the energy? Where does it reside? Deep in the nerves, I suppose, and somewhere in the sick soul. I told you, inspiration is illness, that's all I know. I don't know where it comes from. I know where it went to, though – into those other worlds. And I know what it left behind. A man who'd lost the taste for living. A man stuck in lodgings for half his life, no longer needing to make money but who just couldn't stop writing, not yet. Because work was all there was. It was what was left. You know how it happens, Francis, one day you're taking a piss with a group of younger bloods and you're suddenly horrified by the gush they're producing, the strong steaming waterspouts, in contrast to your sickly trickle. Gloom descends.

'Oh come on, Will! Put off by a piss! You're not serious.'

And yet more work becomes the substitute – for the healthy life. It keeps you going, day after day, in the fly-infested, plague-prone, stinking city which has claimed you for her own. She gives you all she's got and you're utterly dependent on her, she's your infected mistress, you're her hag-ridden man-whore, and you sing to her in the sickness of your soul. I loathed London. She made and unmade me. She was the real Dark Lady. She was a Muse – of hellfire.

I'd reached the age too where loan oft loses both itself and friend. The knock on the door, the urgent letter – I'd come to dread them. Always amounting to the same thing. Will you lend us thus much moneys? Now that you're successful, friend, and free from care.

Free from care. Did they think Lear was written one carefree afternoon? Did they think adultery lay simply in the script, and the stench of cunt only in the ink? Burning and consumption a figment of the mind? And an ounce of civet, good apothecary, to ease my imagination? Sweeten it away? Begone, bloodsuckers! There's money for thee! Now go – and get me surgeons.

Add to that the pox and there's your Timon, Francis. I had him on my mind with Lear. Once you're infected you want companionship in misery, you want the effects of it to multiply and so contaminate the stinking city from wall to wall, strike the whole world. You write hymns to syphilis, to blast the ingrates out of being. No, Lear was too kind. Call down on them instead all the horrors of the dreaded disease, hail down on all men, consumptions sow in hollow bones, crack the voice, hoar the flamen that scolds against the quality of flesh, down with the nose, down with it flat, take the bridge quite away, shrivel the privates, turn piss to fire and breath to agony, make bald the pate and let the unscarred braggarts of the war derive some pain from you! Plague all, that your activity may defeat and quell the source of all erection! There it is again, erection, erection, that furtive fucking, fully clothed, a short and secret act, and a mere spilling of animal spirits and filthy stinking fluid. Love is the door that opens on disease...

So Timon turned his back on Athens, as I'd turned mine on London. Already I was going home. In my mind's eye. A breath of country air was all I wanted now, the soothing balm of Stratford. But I could never go home like this, laden with London's lethal gifts, a surfeit of deadly sin that had damned both body and soul. I didn't even finish with Timon, I banished him instead to his everlasting mansion upon the beachèd verge of the salt flood, where once a day with his embossed froth the turbulent surge shall cover – lines already tangy with the fresh and eager air of the last plays – and there I left him. And my ruined self – the two of us unable any longer to stand the pain of being.

And went not to Stratford but to the consulting rooms of Dr Simon Forman, the last resort of diseased bodies and ignoble minds, out beyond Cripplegate.

61

It was the plague that made Forman. Somehow he cured himself – and others – so successfully that he was prosecuted by the Royal College of Physicians, who couldn't tolerate any form of medical success in a case where the doctor in question didn't even have a degree to his name. There was no lack of quacks, imposters and charlatans who set themselves up as physicians and astrologers, raked up dunghills for dirty boxes and plasters, and out of some toasted cheese and candle-ends tempered up a few ointments and syrups with which they sped into the country and gulled the rustics. Forman came to the capital, and very soon there wasn't anyone who hadn't heard of Simon Forman. By the time royal Jamie came more than half of London's paying population had been to him. That'll give you some idea of his love life, because most of those who came to him were women and by all accounts including his own, he seems to have fucked them all. Only the chosen few left him unadulterated, or virgo intacto. Ben had a list pinned up in the Mermaid, which he added to week by month, and the roll-call of seductions unfurled with astonishing speed and to seemingly infinite length.

'I don't believe it.'

Carved in my memory. You want names? Sarah Archdell, Appelina Fairfax, Anne Waller of Ashby, the widow Boothby in St Lawrence Lane, the widow Calverley at Holborn, Mrs Withypoll's daughter at Stourbridge Fair, Katherine Gittens, Anne Eglesfield, Mistress Lee, Captain Monson's sister.

'Stop, stop!'

Anne Nurse, Judith Ankers, Joan West, Elizabeth Hipwell, Mrs Anne Condwell, Frances Hill (his own maidservant), Bess Parker, Actaeon Dove, Aquila Gould, Temperance Slaughter, Cognata Stocker, Cassandra Potter – to name but a few. Ben said he liked men too, though he was as old-fashioned as Old Street in my opinion. And this was quite apart from the various loves of his life, Anne Young and Avis Allen and Jane Baker. And so they came. And came. Emilia Bassano's name was not on the list but that meant nothing.

'But what did they come for?'

What does any woman come for? Pregnancies, false pregnancies, deliveries, stoppages, averted miscarriages, arranged miscarriages, in the course of which he wandered deep into necromancy and infamy and horoscopes and forbidden realms. He was London's very own Faustus. They said he knew something about everything under and including the sun, and that what he didn't know he was ready to guess. Sometimes his guesses were inspired. As for me, I reckoned that a man who'd danced with the Black Death and lain with a third of London must have had the pox at one time or another and was surely worth a visit. There he was, living prosperously and healthily just upstream from me in Lambeth. What could I lose?

'Reputation, Will?'

Well, I knew he kept case-books – and held more intelligence in his pen than the recording angel. But I went loaded with gold and told him I was ready to pay not just for cure but for anonymity even in his deepest files. Quill shall not whisper to paper, etcetera. He said he admired my plays, had been to hear some of them, and would show me the respect one seeker after truth accorded to another. There was something I rather liked about the red-haired little runt with the frizzy beard and freckled face who looked directly at me across piles of text-books and case-notes and in between leaning towers of pill boxes and dangling animals, long dead, but bright-eyed and knowing in their stuffed secrecy. Something rather reassuring, really. It wasn't the trappings, the planetary charts on the walls, the unicorn's horn, the relaxing fragrance of remedy, the comforting authorities bound and stacked on the shelves – Hippocrates and Galen and all the medical giants – it was something about the man himself. Maybe it was because he'd started off talking about my plays. He had a good bedside manner for sure, and before I knew what was happening I felt so much at ease I was exchanging small talk with him about our respective trades and enjoying the stream of cases he referred to without dropping the name of a single patient or client.

Her menstrual blood is running to her head, she has a wolf at the breast, he's afflicted by melancholy and wind. And the endless questions they brought to his door: what about her husband who sailed to Russia in the *White Lion*? what does a dream of swans signify? is she pregnant? has he been poisoned? will the ship or the child miscarry?

is it a changeling? is she star-crossed, planet-struck? should we sell up? stay in London? go to the country? can you deal with a suicide sprite? – it's offering knife, rope and water – can you find buried treasure? discover a lost dog, a little bitch with six silver beads about her neck and a greenish and blueish velvet collar? And so the curious callers came to this curious little man, who saw, found, predicted, diagnosed, and sometimes cured. Richard Field went to him as I recall, when he swallowed a Portuguese coin, though he could have saved the coin he paid Forman and simply let nature take its course. Mountjoy consulted him to find out if his wife was lying with other men – and Forman didn't require specialist knowledge for the answer to that one. I still kept wondering if he'd had Emilia. Not that I cared nowadays, though it seemed a likely scenario, given the natures of both doctor and client.

'But mostly,' he was saying, 'it's the usual stuff, you know, the humdrum of a doctor's days. Can't sleep, can't stop sleeping, can't eat, can't stop eating, can't shit, can't stop shitting, can't shag – '

'Can't stop shagging?'

'Well, yes – and no. Not many men find that condition a cause for complaint. But their wives do, naturally.'

I smiled slightly, suddenly anxious to get on. Which he sensed.

'And now Master Shakespeare, let's do something about this pox of yours.'

I hadn't given him the least indication but wasn't in the least surprised that he knew.

The interrogation began. How many whores? How many times? How long ago? Their complexions, please, their years, the addresses of the stews. Had I tried hard pissing at any of these? (The best brothels, Francis, kept two chamber-pots beneath each bed for pissing into fiercely by the client, to piss out the poison, immediately after sex and while his prick still retained some erectitude.) Did I still get erections, by the way? Apart from morning erections, that is – how was my old Adam, in other words, and were stiff ones painful? Was pissing laborious, difficult, sore? Did I feel as if I were pissing blades of Spain?

What I did feel was as if I were a gigantic prick, nothing more, burned up with sin and syphilis from hilts to slit, and all the other parts of me – arms and hands and legs and head – just didn't exist. You know the feeling, Francis?

'I most certainly do not.'

Your entire body and being have become reduced to that one

distempered part of your anatomy and you are now an object of curiously unhorrified analysis by one who has seen it all.

'I can introduce a thin lead pipe into your penis, Master Shakespeare.'

The bland voice, announcing torture, hardly seemed real. The whole thing was a dream, for sure.

'Since the Armada year some of my colleagues in the field have been using a slender stalk of parsley or mallow instead, but there have been cases where these have snapped, leaving the patient in considerable trouble. Personally I prefer the lead. Excruciating, of course, but no worse than syphilitic constriction during involuntary erection or necessary urination. And of course stricture of the member can eventually kill.'

Kill, kill, kill, kill, kill.

'I think I'd better examine you now.'

Sweet Mr Shakespeare, the English Ovid, honey-tongued Melicert, star of the stage and genius of the Globe, removes his breeches and lies on the table. Dr Simon Forman, physician extraordinaire, bends down and peers at poor Percy, pursing his lips and reaching for his notebook, which Will waves away.

'Ah, no notes, of course, I had forgotten, very well. It's no matter, this is far from fatal, I can assure you. I think you're oversensitive, my friend. All the same I'm going to suggest the lead pipe and also as a precaution the mercury fumigation.'

And so to the powdering-tub of infamy in which I'd placed Doll Tearsheet, dying of syphilis in Henry Five. She was exposed to the fumes of cinnabar heated to smoking on a hot plate and the remaining powder used to dust the suffering body. This is the treatment she underwent at the hospital of St Mary in Spitalfield, once used by lepers. Now it was the turn of her creator, lying in Lambeth with the smell of the sea from the Thames killed by the combined stenches of mercuric sulphide, vermilion, and mercury ore. That was the start of it for me and it went on from there in the usual way, first the ointment applied, and then I was wound up in sheets with winter warmers, hot bricks and heated stones, for hours a day over many days, to sweat out the disease, fighting fire with fire. Some died in the sheer hell of the cure. Others simply succumbed to the slow rotting that was taking them apart.

I dreamed for years afterwards of those benchfuls of men, their legs swathed in spotted bandages, their flesh pitted with sores. And still I dream of them, and instead of waking up in Stratford I'm in the terrible stews again, being helped out of my clothes, sleepwalking my way to the smoking rooms and the tubs and the rows of corpses. The temperature soars, visibility plunges. Silent forms glide past, half hidden in skeins of steam, applying the poisonous concoctions, filling up the wounds on backs and bellies and privities, gilding the skin with the silvery-coloured cure that floods into the system and causes more pain and poison than the disease itself, fighting hell with hell, just as Hippocrates advised, little to distinguish between the fires of Venus and the fires of the physician. The blisters spread, the gums begin to bleed, the body bakes and suppurates, consciousness collapses, and in your struggle for sanity you try to remember a doctor of Verona who wrote a poem before you were born: a poem in which Syphilus – the name sounds innocent and idyllic – insulted the god Apollo and was punished by a pestilence that could be cured only with quicksilver – the quicksilver that was killing you quicker than the pox and dividing the spoils between them, body and bones and brain, sans eyes, sans teeth, sans nose, sans everything, except the peace of death. But it could be many years before the man finally died. A night with Venus, a lifetime with Mercury – so the saying went.

Somehow I came through, the survivor of just one of the cures for those that breathed the air of infection, made love to a killer, and lived on the slicing edge of death.

As did we all.

'But some of us don't help ourselves,' tut-tutted Dr Forman, 'by our general way of living, Master Shakespeare. Nothing to do with sex – you have assured me that's all in the past. You clearly don't look after yourself properly.'

And that was true enough, too. Meat over-salted, over-spiced, red-hot bowels in winter (whip me, ye devils!), an angry liver, an itchy skin, and carious teeth. Generally I ate with one hand and wrote with the other, ate on my feet, pacing up and down between speeches, speaking the lines trippingly over mouthfuls of pippins and cheese. That and the brief sleeps and buzzing slumbers, waking early and unwashed in dirty dawns to escape the scorpions of the mind, and moving at once to the work that crushes even as it relieves. Work was what it was all about. Work was what London was for. Was it why I had come here, then? Not exactly. Work isn't what Adam dreams about, it's what he's been assigned to. No, it was something other than the notion of work that had sucked me up into the city all those years ago, but whatever it was, it had been largely forgotten. As it always is. All I wished for now was a little rest in Stratford, rounded off with a good long sleep. Followed by a never-ending one. The consummation devoutly to be wished? Years away. I still had plays to write. And money to make. And health to ruin, in spite of Dr Forman's advice.

'Go home,' he'd told me, 'go home and get some sleep.'

62

But in the year 1606 Macbeth put an end to sleep.

He did as the Powder Plotters did, the year before, when sleep stole from my pillows, and I began to fear the knock at the door at four in the morning.

The true begetter of the Catholic plot may well have been none other than Robert Cecil, but as far as the world was given to know, it was another Robert – Catesby, an old friend of my father's, and not only a friend but a deep religious one to boot. My father was safely in his grave – nothing could touch him further. But his son wasn't. And the conspirators were on the run. They tracked them through the November glooms, the rain-drenched lanes of Warwickshire, where Catesby died with harness on his back. But others were taken for the torture – under which anything could be said, true or not, it didn't matter. The rack spoke with a tongue that always told on somebody. And sleep was the first casualty. The old Warwickshire ghost was back again, putting paid to that.

Night after night the restless ecstasy. Morpheus slipped out of Silver Street and never really returned. Names were being cut out of the conspirators, literally, before their very eyes, and before their slow deaths. Names were being roasted, wrung, squeezed, twisted, teased, and torn out long before the ripping of the actual heart or the prolonged burning. Names that come out during torture don't have to mean anything, don't even have to exist, except on the tip of the terrified and half-torn tongue. But once uttered – oh, then they will become confirmations strong as proofs of holy writ. And will be found to fix on someone, like the slime that sticks on filthy deeds. Yes, I often heard it, in the dark, that terrible knocking, and lived out the following scene in sleepless fear and memories of Hartley. Bind fast his corky arms. Out, vile jelly! See shalt thou never. You don't know anything? Of course you don't. You're dead. The dead know not anything. Don't you read the Bible?

It was a fearful time.

And the next play was drenched not only in blood, but strung with that terrible sleeplessness, and haunted by witches, witches that perplex and prey upon the brain, releasing your deepest darkest fears. Is your manhood certain? Are your friends true? Is your future secure? Are you sure of your wife? Can you trust your dreams? the double-talk of destiny? the meanings of words?

'A play to please a king?'

Please him, yes, butter him up, work by witchcraft – his favourite study – revive the old terrors, Satan stronger than gunpowder, the evils he adored, tickle his childhood fears, flatter his ancestry, derive him from Banquo, not father Darnley but the dauntless valour of the incorruptible – hedge him with divinity too, and he'll lap it up.

And he did. Macbeth killed Duncan not on the field but in his bed, while acting as his host shattering the sacred duty of the host. His reign was brief and brutal, not the stately seventeen-year affair it really was. But I wasn't writing history now, I was putting a king-killer on show – and showing what happened to king-killers.

'Which is?'

Brooding discontent, murderous ambition, your secretest thoughts spoken aloud, suddenly, on a blasted heath, not by yourself, but by three weird women, who disappear like the words themselves, breath into the wind. You're ready to renounce the life to come, but even as you spur your horse to jump your conscience, you start to hear the voices in the night, to see the pictures in the dark – a sleeping king, his innocence pleading with you, trumpet-tongued against the deep damnation of his taking off, the world spread out at angels' feet, heaven's cherubim horsed upon the sightless couriers of the air, the naked babe, sweet Jesus, striding the blast, tears on the wind, terrors in the sky. *Et sepultus est in inferno.* And now you falter. But not your wife – bring forth men children only, you gasp, as she takes out her breast and bares her nipple in your face, saying the unsayable. Appalled by her undaunted mettle, you drown the voices, tear the pictures, suppress your conscience, sell your soul. Now you're Faustus. Worse, you're Judas. *That thou doest see thou doest quickly.* And all goes down before you – your best friend, your king, your marriage, golden opinions, eating and sleeping, the wine of life, self-respect, peace of mind, old age, honour, love, obedience, troops of friends, all for your few years of power, your circle of care, your paltry pieces of silver. And you're left with what you have accepted instead – the curses, not loud but deep, the mouth-honour, the scorpions of the soul, the mind diseased, the written troubles of the brain, the stuffed bosom, the perilous charge which weighs upon the heart.

And it's only the beginning. Add to that nightmares, demonic possession, strange intelligences, air-drawn daggers, deceptions, delusions, broken promises, mysterious messages, mocking echoes, gouts of blood, rooted sorrows, uprooted branches, moving woods, dead men dining, ghastly concoctions, poisoned chalices, drugged possets, vaporous drops, stolen garments, insane roots that take the reason prisoner, Satan himself – *Seyton, I say! Seyton!* – and the gashed king's skin, all silver, laced with that golden blood.

What else? No end? No end of it, never an end, the apparitions, glimmering killers, spies, night-borne beetles, gory locks, strewn brains, strange screams of death, accents terrible, someone weeping in the dark, that nipple plucked from boneless gums, a woman wringing her hands, a knocking at the south entry, always the south entry, the rack, the rooky wood, the torture of the mind, the walking shadow, the bloody child, the great bond of destiny, all of nature's fluids foaming like the sea, blood and milk and tears and wine, and all great Neptune's ocean turning red, the multitudinous seas incarnadined, everything laid on, courtesy of the instruments of darkness, a feast of horror for a soul in torment, a heightened state of feeling that I never touched again in any play. I wouldn't have wanted to. You don't write plays like that and know a good night's sleep.

Othello never charmed the king quite as well – no ghosts or witches here, no consequences hanging in the stars, no metaphysics, cosmic meditations, voices from the grave, from worlds beyond, all that predestination. The wickedness is exclusively human. Unbelievably human. And a private agony made public is what makes the play unbearable. In torturing Othello I was remembering the rack and how I lay on it in the Bassano years. Desdemona now, was she so innocent after all? She betrayed her father, dallied with Cassio. She sang of loose loves and eyed up the handsome Lodovico. One thing she was not. She was not Ophelia. Or any of the string of innocents to come: Imogen, Perdita, Marina, Miranda.

And she was not my Susanna – though how did I know exactly how it was with my daughters down in Stratford, while I'd lived the guilty life in the capital? An absent father. One who'd whored his way to forty and whose next stop was fifty.

The fires of Venus were dying down. And no more storms on the heath. You can see the difference, Francis. Cleopatra was calmer, Coriolanus colder.

'You were mellowing.'

A nice euphemism, Francis, for decline, the slow ripening of the plum that goes before the drop. Perhaps Cleopatra was how I'd have *liked* Emilia to be – everything there except the infidelity.

'You were no Antony, though.'

A soldier in decline, an ageing lecher who just wouldn't, couldn't give up, infatuated to the last gasp by his swarthy goddess, and he himself a onetime god, now become a pair of bellows and a fan to cool a gypsy's lust. These strong Egyptian fetters I must break, or lose myself in dotage. Easy to say, Francis, but time passes, the hair grows greyer, thinner, the beard more grizzled, the sap not so rich and thick as it was wont to be in your salad days when you were a cannon on the loose and firing fourteen-pounders. And for Antony there's the knowledge that this could be his final fling. She is it.

And what a woman! Death for her isn't the end of a tale told by an idiot, isn't a descent into dreams or sleep, a slipping into silence or rottenness – it's an orgasmic adventure. Husband I come! As she must have said often on the Nile, and to the sound of music, moody food of us that trade in love. And they'll be going hand in hand where souls do couch on flowers and with their sprightly sport make the ghosts gaze. She's echoing Antony's own erotic farewell to life. I will be a bridegroom in my death and run into it as to a lover's bed. The bright day is done and they are for the dark. But darkness is the door to love as well as death.

Even the dreaded end is eclipsed by love, as Charmian says. Now boast thee, death, in thy possession lies a lass unparallelled. Downy windows, close, and golden Phoebus never be beheld of eyes again so royal.

My own mother was dying at the time. It was 1608. I wrote *Coriolanus* here when she was ill, and you can find Stratford in it, if you care to look: the shepherd's pipe, the hunted hare, the burning stubble, dogs chasing sheep, the boys pursuing summer butterflies, the butchers killing flies, the graves wounding the churchyard grasses – my mother's soon to be one of them.

Stratford. I'm growing tired, yes, and some memories of first love even crept in, and marriage to my Anne, when our nuptial day was done and the tapers burned to bedward. No more o' that, Francis. No more. *Coriolanus* was the closing of a door.

And the death of tragedy.

63

'How many did you write?'

Tragedies? Some dozen.

'Didn't it depress you?'

Not professionally. I got better at it – brought it on a bit. I inherited the groundling's version, the medieval model, the turn of the wheel stuff, inhuman, mechanical and immoral. Any saint or sinner can go down, though by definition they must be high up on the wheel in the first place. And the downturn is tragic. On this model failures and vagabonds can't have tragedies – they're already in the privy. And when you're in the privy what can you expect? That's reality, not tragedy. But to see a great man go down – it satisfies the envious streak in all of us, and our need for spectacle, to colour our colourless lives. Even the recording angel feels a glow of pleasure as he scribes. And heaven stops the nose at it.

'So how did you improve on this?

By making the wheel turn not by chance but by the influence of some prodding finger on an evil hand – a wicked woman, a witch, an ungrateful daughter, a hard ambitious bastard, a psychopath. And by allowing another invisible hand to add its weight to the wheel – the hand of circumstance, accident, ill-luck, call it what you will, call it destiny, fate, the stars – or lack of stars, if night's candles are all out – darkness, the fly-killing gods. In this scheme trifling incidents may turn the scale, as happens in life – tittle-tattle, a letter delivered or undelivered or intercepted, a chance meeting, a handkerchief spotted with strawberries. Or simply being thirty seconds too late to prevent a hanging. As terrible and trivial as that.

'I prefer to keep the trivial trivial.'

One thing you know from the start – your hero is doomed. There is no cheap suspense deriving from any vulgar possibility of rescue or escape. None of us escapes death in the end. And so there is a greater tension in tragedy – the tension caused by your certain knowledge of the hero's approaching death and your fascinated glimpses of the inevitable stages by which it is arrived at, as the cat comes closer to the mouse, or the mouse to the cat. The wheel slips through Fortune's fingers and fate's grip is inflexible.

Still too simplistic? I see the look on your face, Francis. But supposing I were to make the hero lose his own balance on the wheel, thereby adding to its downward motion and lending an unfortunate hand to the forces already militating against him? And this is precisely what happens. Some vicious mole of nature, the stamp of one defect, being nature's livery or fortune's star, some error of life, some habit, if you like, the o'ergrowth of some complexion, some flaw in his character, his imagination, his arrogance, his greed, his ambition, vanity, credulity, jealousy, blindness, lust, even his idealism and intellect, an honest carelessness and freedom from suspicion – the very things we value and respect, in other words – may contrive against him in the peculiar circumstances in which he finds himself; wrong place, wrong time, irony of fate. And all the other virtues, be they as pure as grace, as infinite as man may undergo, shall in the general censure take corruption from that particular fault.

And so what happens? All these forces, external and internal, combine to produce a catastrophe in which not only the hero but his friends and loved ones as well as his enemies perish. Even innocent bystanders get sucked in – or relatively innocent. I wanted to leave the audience with the feeling that everyone is guilty. You can't wholly blame the hero. You can't fully sympathise with him either. After all he was free to choose. Or not to choose. And even not to choose is a kind of choice. He's got it coming to him. You feel sorry for him but you grant the rightness of what's happening even though it feels wrong. You've been caught up in the rich complexity of life itself – which somehow you feel you understand better now, though that's an illusion. You have been reconciled – not to a single point of view but to an admission that one truth does not exclude its opposite, and that today's answers may not be tomorrow's.

That doesn't mean it's not hard to bear. A son suspects his mother of adultery with his uncle and then finds out it's worse than that, it's murder. He's betrayed by the girl he loves, by his friends. He loses his taste for living. An older man is torn apart when he thinks his wife is sleeping with his friend. Another woman walks alone in the night, wringing her hands for a killing she thought her conscience would let her get away with. Her marriage has floundered and her husband has given his soul, his eternal jewel, to the common enemy of man. Just like that older man – who strangles his innocent wife only to realise that like the base Judean, he has thrown a pearl away richer than all his tribe. O, insupportable! O heavy hour! And a father finds that children can turn into monsters. Monster ingratitude! When all that happens, there should be huge eclipses of the sun and moon and the affrighted globe should yawn at alteration. But there aren't. And it doesn't. Instead it's human goodness that for a time appears to be eclipsed.

But not human greatness.

That's the unexpected thing. The fading stars have seen something before they fall, something that places them on a higher plane which momentarily you are allowed to share with them. Only momentarily. Together you take a cosmic view of things and feel that wave of cosmic nonchalance wash over you, however bleak the business. You know that life is a succession of meaningless tomorrows going down to dusty death, and you review it all in your head, the brief candle, the walking shadow, the poor player, the pitiful tale – and gradually, magically, the sound and fury die away, leaving you unafraid to face the nothingness that awaits us all.

And it's this, this combination of the real and the ideal worlds in the single new world of the play, autonomous, untouchable and true, but at the same time fragile, transient, tender and sad, that makes the theatre itself so magical and the tragic moment so mysterious and profound. You go home by Dead Man's Place knowing that man is nobler than you thought him, but knowing that his defiance will be crushed by the cosmos anyway. It doesn't seem to matter. You are on a cloud with a candle in your hand, a little closer to heaven, having just been through hell. A spark of hope in the darkness, then? Yes, in spite of everything. Even if for no other reason than that some mad dramatist in the fury of his heart actually took the time to sit down and put it all into words, simply for playing on a stage. There must be some good in us somewhere. And maybe even some meaning to it all.

One last thought, Francis. The hero has to die – we know that. It's a fixed law of tragedy and I never tried to change it. But it's the mental suffering that constitutes his real tragedy, what he has undergone. Othello has died inwardly long before he kills his wife, or indeed himself. Macbeth has long wearied of the sun and is tired of tomorrows. Lear dies on the rack of the tough world away back in the third Act – it's a dead man who walks on stage holding a dead daughter in his arms. And Hamlet – his death is not due to poison – he gives up quietly on life shortly before he enters his silence. And yet he has to die.

Not because death is the end of all stories but because the death is artistically satisfying, that's all, rounding off the sense that the wheel has truly turned, the clock has ticked, while on a more basic level than that his death quite simply satisfies the spectators' taste for blood. It will have blood, they say, blood will have blood. They saw plenty of it and they could never have enough. Liver of blaspheming Jew, finger of birth-strangled babe, ditch-begotten by a drab. Not nice? No, but that was their England, take it or leave it. They had no choice. Life was still a bear-pit and they wanted their penny's worth, and that's the truth of it.

64

As you get older you outgrow tragedy. You've become so used to it, if not inured to it, during the course of a lifetime, that now suddenly – contrary to all that experience has taught you and which you know to be true – you begin to hope that there's something beyond tragedy, as life may exist beyond death. Some sort of redemption. You know it's not so but you indulge yourself nonetheless. You can't help it.

The odd thing is that this new mood, superseding the tragic, occurs at that time in your life which in one sense is the most tragic of all – the time when all your friends and family start to die, leaving you naked in your age. You find yourself attending more funerals than weddings. Seven funerals and one wedding in a three-year period gives you some idea of what I'm saying. And the three family funerals were practically within the same year. Even the occasional christenings, which ought to be occasions of pure joy, sharpen up instead your awareness of the gulf that divides the generations. Yes, Francis, you are a passenger in a fierce chariot, a journey going every day. And you're heading away from the earth, with all its shapes and scents and sounds of beauty. You're heading into the dark and you want a candle to take with you.

The deaths of colleagues are worse than family bereavements. Family losses are more affecting, naturally, and are harder to bear. But there's something more chilling about the death of a business partner that makes you stand back a little and look at your own life and what's left of it. All that work and worry – and for what? You start to measure out the grains of sand that remain in the glass.

Tom Pope had died back in the year of the new king. He'd retired by then, but Gus Phillips was still working when he fell ill in the spring of 1605 and drew up his will. He died in May, leaving a wife, Anne, and four daughters. Young Gus, the son, had stayed always young, dying in childhood, so as with Ben Jonson there was a bond between Gus and myself. Such kinships were hardly uncommon.

Gus and his family had lived close to the Bankside theatre district in Horseshoe Court in St Saviour's in Southwark, but he'd moved into his splendid new house at Mortlake in Surrey just before making up his will. This was the house I went to along with Condell and Cowley on a fine summery May morning to hear what Gus had to say to us from beyond the grave that hid him so well from the searching sun.

Something of the old Gus couldn't be hidden, however. To his late apprentice, Samuel Gilbourne, he left 'forty shillings, his mouse-coloured velvet hose and a white taffety doublet. Also a black taffety suit, my purple cloak, sword and dagger, and my base viol. And to my other apprentice, James Sands, also forty shillings and a cithern, a bandore and a lute at the expiry of his indentures.' Yes, that was Gus, all right. You got the picture of him there, ruffing it well and cutting quite a caper in his dashing coloured clothes and his accompanying instruments. And that's how we remembered him, resurrecting him for the sake of his widow and children in anecdote and accolade.

Five pounds went to the hired men, thirty shilling gold pieces to me, and to Condell, and Chris Beeston, and twenty shillings in gold to Fletcher, Armin, Tooley, Cowley, and Cooke. Heminges and Burbage each got a silver bowl worth five pounds. Tim Whithorn was left one worth twenty pounds. His sister Elizabeth came in for only five pounds but she'd married into the Company two years ago and was well provided for. Five pounds went to the parish poor. (Ten from me did we say, Francis?) And finally, on the strength of his newly acquired Mortlake property and land, Gus wanted to be buried in the chancel of the church, like a gentleman. How's that for a will?

Will Sly also got a five-pounds silver bowl. He had three years left to enjoy it. Unmarried, he'd buried his illegitimate infant son not two weeks old in St Giles Cripplegate. He himself was buried in St Leonard's Shoreditch in a blinding August sun in the plague year of 1608. He left his house in Holywell Street to the daughter of our fellow Robert Browne, the one whose whole family had succumbed to the plague back in '93. But Browne had married again, if you recall, and Sly remembered him through his daughter. He remembered him for himself too, bequeathing him his entire share in the Globe. James Sands did well again – Sly left him forty pounds, no mean sum. Cuthbert Burbage didn't need much; he inherited Sly's hat and sword. And the parish poor got the forty shillings that were left.

And so, as the fellows die off and the bequests are read out, you begin mentally composing your own will, hoping there won't be any need actually to call in the lawyer for years to come – and yet here you are at last, Francis – but all the same starting to turn over in your mind the bits and pieces that form the material mosaic of your life – houses, investments, furnishings, and how the whole is to be broken up and distributed and who gets what, even down to the silver bowls and the doublet and hose.

Whispers of mortality. They buzz all the louder about your ears when you help put into the ground somebody you slept with not all that long ago. Madame Mountjoy died the year after Gus and we buried her on the second last day of October, among swirling leaves that were already driving like snow into the cold hole that awaited her. I looked guiltily at the blind shrouded thing we were about to put away from us and remembered the rank sweat of the bed, a few furtive fucks in the Silver Street chamber above the shop, listening for noises from beneath, and the armpit smell of adultery. The haunches that had reared so wildly beneath my reining hands – so still and cold inside that stiff sackcloth that was being lowered now into the silence and the dark. And all that excited French whispering and kissing, her tongue never idle. It was now, though. Jesus. In went the earth and we walked away and left her with the leaves flickering on her grave.

But sun and shadow are always at it, dancing down the years. The following year, 1607, my Susanna was married on 5th June, and in the February following I was at the christening of my first grandchild – her daughter Elizabeth. My mother had only half a year to enjoy her great-grand-daughter. She died two weeks too soon to see the arrival of a new grandson, Michael Hart. My sister Joan had married the hatter, William Hart, whose only accomplishment was to produce four children. Their three-year-old Mary had already died the previous year. We buried my mother on the 9th day of September, and infant Michael was baptised on the 23rd.

'What a brain for dates!'

What a *brain*, Francis! Never mind about dates. By then Mary Arden was one with the forest that bore her name. She had gone back to nature.

She who had borne eight of us and lost an early three, now lay unringed for us all to see, the winds' blown toy in time. She had fed us, clothed us, wiped our noses, bandaged our bleeding knees, dried our tears. She couldn't dry them now. All that exuberance and love reduced to a grey starch over lips, over lineaments that were no longer hers – they were the earth's due and it was waiting for payment. I looked dumbly at the hands' knot, the hands that had provided an arch under which we had all stood protected, to her best ability, for half a century of motherhood. An awful moment and a point of no return, when you confront the corpse of the one that gave you life, knowing that the knot intrinsicate of life itself has been unravelled and nothing will bind it up again.

But there weren't five children standing round that stillness in the best bed in New Place that September day – only four. One had followed me to London to be an actor. And it was the loss of the twenty-seven-year-old Edmund, her youngest child and her favourite, that had begun the slow invisible unravelling of the knot over nine mysterious months. It was the reverse of her final pregnancy – a nine-month maturation of the wolf in the womb, at the end of which she herself was delivered, to death.

Edmund died in the big freeze of 1607, the hardest frost in my lifetime, the hardest to crack my heart. The Thames donned her stiff coat again and the ice piled up against the piers at the bridge. The river turned into a white marbled road, women crossed from bank to bank, as safe as in their parlours, fires blazed on the huge tract of glass that had been London's waterway, and hawkers offered you pans of coals to warm your bitten fingers as you travelled by. Even the archbishop of London made this his route, passing from Lambeth to Westminster over water that Christ could have walked at any time and the archbishop trusted well enough in its frozen state.

A carnival atmosphere it was. Bowling on the frozen river, archery practice, skating, wrestling, football, booths with fruits and hot pies and roasted chestnuts. Barbers with their chairs set down on the ice and their signs hung out, cutting the hair and tearing out the teeth of any who cared to stop and be trim or toothache-free for the New Year. Blood spattered the ice around the benches but a good fire was blazing at their backs to comfort the clients in their pain. Most folk just stopped for the haircut, accepting a glass from the youths who burned wine and sack on the ice and made partakers out of all those with wintry stomachs that passed their way. A temporary tavern was even set up on wheels. It was all a festival.

Only the watermen, the fish, and the poor were losers. The

ferrymen furled up their smoky sails. The finned population of the city, unused to lie under such thick roofs, were stopped in their courses in the frozen stream. And the poor froze too, as woodmongers and chandlers put up their prices when supplies fell well behind demand, even though fuel-laden barges coursed slowly over the ice, drawn by engines and pulleys. But the poor are always losers – poor folk are soonest pissed on, my mother used to say. And rich men never had more money and covetousness never less pity than at the time of the big December freeze.

It was an odd time for Edmund to die, especially of the plague. It had raged hard between July and November that year, killing his base-born son in August. We buried the infant in St Giles without Cripplegate, another anonymous number without a stone to his name, all the more anonymous for his illegitimacy – in the eyes of a cold church. But even the freeze didn't kill the plague entirely. As a killer it vied with the frost, and the gravediggers ran with sweat, hammering at the iron earth with their picks and cursing like madmen, unable to crack a crust which they swore went deeper than six feet. Many went into graves so shallow they protruded soon after the first thaw and had to be reburied in the spring. It was in this abandoned atmosphere in which life danced with death that Edmund died of a last mad fling of the plague. While he was still together he begged me not to commit him to one of the shallow frost graves. I promised him I'd do better than that. He'd lie inside the church, like any gentleman.

He died on the Wednesday morning, 30th December, and was buried quickly on New Year's Eve. And before the city bells tolled out the passing of the old year, a forenoon knell of the great bell tolled for the passing of my youngest brother, little Edmund. It was eight shillings for that knell and twenty shillings for the interment within the church. The lesser bell would have cost only twelvepence and what did it matter as he couldn't hear it anyway? Well, it did matter. *I* could hear it, and that's what mattered. Two or three shillings would have bought an earth grave in the churchyard but I saved the sexton's sweat and paid the extra to pacify Edmund's soul – and my own. Why do we spend good money on the rubbish death leaves us with, the churchyard remains? Money that's grudged during our lives but that flows readily enough when death opens the floodgates. Guilt? Of course.

Tons of guilt, years of it, yes, years, years. My little brother who was so proud of me, who was always in my shadow and never needed to be, because he was a better man than me. Edmund, who shadowed me to London, wanting to be a player, wanting to be me. He was betrayed by a bitch, you know. She broke his heart. And I should have looked after him, shouldn't I? Of course I should, I was his big brother, but something got in the way, life got in the way, didn't it, as it always does, my own sodden life, and now he's dead, and love that comes too late is the last futile flag of our humanity, run up in anguish to signal to a vanished soul that this is what we meant to say, for years and years – and never did.

And so instead of the gravedigger's sweat on that last day of the year, it was the sweat of the lone bell-ringer who went up the tower of St Saviour's, Southwark, and began to pull on the forty-six hundredweight of bell suspended above his head. His hands would have been blue up there in that freezing white air. Far beneath him the people on the Thames looked up – the foodsellers and football players and barbers and bear-keepers and the cold whores. The whores would have paid little attention. It was only the sound of another rich man's funeral, apparently, if only they'd known, someone fat enough to have lain with flesh less diseased than their own, someone with sufficient cash to have paid for the knell of the big one. No whore's ghost would ever hear that sound as the poxed corpse was shipped into the anonymous earth to the sound of silence broken only by the sextons' spades and curses.

Edmund was buried in the actors' quarter of the church, a shadow who never offended, a poor player who'd strutted less than his hour or two upon the stage. Just three days earlier we'd performed before the king at Whitehall. Our lines were still in our minds as we stood there thinking about an afternoon performance at the Globe that few would come to because of the cold. Players were a little better off than the fish stilled in the ice – at least we were alive, we who came away from Edmund's grave that morning. But as for trade there was not much between us and the cursing watermen. It didn't matter to me. Nothing much mattered to me after my little brother's death. After that I was merely marking time.

65

Jack Frost was not the only enemy to our livelihoods that year. There was a theatrical freeze on as well, a frost of fashion, Francis, settling on the kinds of play that had made my name, and tightening its white grip year by year. The stage had faded from the heyday of Faustus and Harry the Sixth. The grandeur and glory days had gone, and the drama no longer opened out for you a window onto the universe. It closed all the shutters instead and made you look in on a confined world, socially confined as in Ben's plays, or spiritually, as in Webster. God and the Devil were no longer on stage. Nor were all their heroic opposites – just a collection of horrible or petty human beings, beetles with brains, and without souls.

Take Beaumont and Fletcher. They were the waterflies of the theatrical current. They'd written plays together and separately for the Children's Companies and now for us, and they gave the middle classes the dreamy nonsense they wanted, weaving their pretty yarns and working the trick. Superficial writing is an easy winner with an idle and ignorant public.

These two set up bachelor lodgings on the Bankside and shared everything: one house, one cloak, and one wench – whom they did so admire as they lay together! But Beaumont married in 1613 and died this very March. They used to drink in the Mermaid with Ben and Donne, and Ben said Beaumont had died of marriage, for not only had they shared everything but they were so wonderfully attuned. And the knave was only thirty-two. So much for them. They'd waltzed their way to stardom and had drifted apart on a floor of glass. Fletcher carried on, collaborating with me on *Henry VIII* and on *Cardenio* after I'd retired, and later I lent a tired hand to *The Two Noble Kinsmen*, which was mainly Fletcher's. His hand crops up in many a play and still he writes his own. But the partnership with Beaumont was the great thing.

Partnerships often are. While Beaumont and Fletcher were deep in their dramatic union and in their one wench, my daughter Susanna was busily accepting the attentions of the doctor who came to call and stayed to court.

Dr John Hall – a marvel of a man, if a little unorthodox.

'But well qualified, Will?'

He took his B.A. and his M.A. at Queen's, Cambridge but didn't graduate as a doctor. He trained in Switzerland, according to the school of his ultimate authority Paracelsus, who'd written about syphilis. Not a bad man to have in the family, then. He was also impeccably Protestant, if inclined to Puritanism. It hardly mattered. Or the fact that he was only eleven years younger than me. For that matter he was only eight years older than my daughter, the same age-gap as I'd known with Anne. I gave my blessing and Susanna has never looked back. They have a good house nearby and he owns land at Evesham where he grows his plants. He cures with many concoctions of these and they're a far cry from the backstreet bullshit of barmy old Simon Forman and his ilk.

Bullshit is almost literal, Francis. A hot cow-turd clapped on for a bad knee. A lye of ashes burned from dog's dung for baldness, or the ashes of little green frogs instead. And to cure the toothache, application to the tooth of several of these many-legged lice that you find beneath old stones and rotting wood, each insect to be pierced with a bodkin before putting on.

'You just love it, don't you? – ailments and antidotes, the diseased human flesh, all that medical chatter.'

Talking to John, though, that was like getting back into the innocence of Warwickshire, and a long way from London. I loved his talk when I first heard it – it was full of healing. Conserve of red roses, syrup of violets, raisins of the sun stoned, sugar candy, fumes of frankincense, juniper, storax, distillation of coltsfoot, ground-ivy, speedwell, knapswood, scabious, hyssop, herb trinity, great figwort, maidenhair, roots of orris, angelica, soapwort, water-betony. For greensick girls round here he makes elixir of rosemary, borage, fumitory, and winter savoury, simmered in white wine, boiled and strained, then mixed with cloves, powdered cinnamon, nutmegs, raisins, figs, saffron, and white sugar, all reheated, stirred and thickened – a pleasant and expensive remedy that sometimes works and sometimes doesn't. If they can't afford it he gives it to them anyway. A feverish young lady in Bridge Street was coughing herself to death. He gave her back her strength with chicken and veal, lettuce, frogs, snails and river-crabs mixed with women's milk. Susanna surrendered some of her breast milk for the purpose after Elizabeth was weaned. He lengthened out the young lady's life by a year. A doctor is not a god, and a year is a long time in an uncertain world.

Certain young men of Stratford come to him for impotence of their members.

'How come young men can't get it up these days?' I asked him.

He frowned at my language, unseemly in an invalid like me, old before my time, and ill again with you know what. Getting it up was never my problem. I asked him again and his frown darkened. A bit on the prim side is our family doctor. But he told me his remedy. Civet, potato roots, and sea-holly from Colchester, its long pokery phallic roots boiled, cut up, and candied. I'm still curious about life, as you see, though my own is ebbing away from me. Faster every day. This is one thing the good doctor can't cure, though he's tackled everything from measles to melancholy hereabouts, the whole range of medical miseries: colic, cancer, black stools, pleurisy, pneumonia, the French pox. He treated and cured a chambermaid of ours when her arse-gut fell out. He cures young folk prone to pissing the bed. He fights scurvy with his scorbutick beer – watercress, brooklime, scurvy grass and a concoction of herbs and roots all boiled in beer with sugar, cinnamon, and juniper berries. When Susanna had the colic and was in agony he fixed her up with a pint of hot sack pumped up the arse, which he said produced a massive blast of wind but immediate relief from the pain.

'Did you ever hear your wife fart before that?' I asked him.

The frown, the pursed lips, the shaking of the head.

'Health comes from God, Will. If a fart is necessary it is a blast from heaven, not hell.'

'I never thought of it in that way.'

Nor me, Francis. But John's one of those zealous church-goers who scolds latecomers or those who nod off or keep their hats on, and let their hands wander into ladies' plackets. Religion hasn't disfigured him, though. He still ministers to lords and their servants alike, to poor folk, barbers, children, Catholics, Protestants, even animals. He'll ride forty miles a day to see a patient, and he's already declined the offer of being elected a burgess because of the needs of his practice. A son-in-law to be proud of and to be grateful to. And for.

'And yet his God has not blessed this upright man with a son. Or his father-in-law with a grandson. What does that tell you?'

It tells me many things, Francis. But you'll find them written already – in my plays.

66

I'd few left to write. And little more that I really wanted to say. John's concoctions included coral and pearl. Isn't that surprising? Ariel remembered that and put it in a song. And I slipped a Paracelsian doctor into *Pericles*. But if a new type of play was needed to suit this last mood of mine, a new theatre was required in which to stage it. And that's exactly what the Blackfriars provided when we recovered the lease.

We got it for twenty-one years, longer than I knew I'd need. Apart from our summer quarters on the Bankside, we now had our winter theatre – the Blackfriars was enclosed. It had a roof, darkness if you wanted it, candlelight, magic tricks, and an altogether smaller arena for the chosen few, seven hundred spectators to savour the strange new flavour of these last plays. The days of huge heroes and actions bloody were over. So were the days of vulgar laughs and a penny a seat. The Blackfriars prices ensured a higher class of spectator. Entry to a gallery, sixpence; a bench in the pit, one shilling and sixpence; a box, half a crown; a bench on stage, two shillings. And as many as ten tobacco-puffing peacocks could parade themselves on stage under their plumes of smoke and huge feathered hats.

We celebrated our success at the Mermaid, toasted ourselves deep in wine, don't ask me why – we were toasting the demise of my kind of drama, the plays that had shot us all to fame. Marston and Middleton and Massinger were now the masters, Jonson the master of the masque and the uncrowned king of the court. The discerning sort now approved of him more than of me. I was beginning to feel I'd outlived myself, but not yet ready to give up. We were a private company taking over a private theatre and in the process we were moulding ourselves to the changing tastes of the new audiences, exclusive and expensive, expecting to see plays that were more exotic, less representative of the great sweep of life that had brushed the boards of the Globe with such gusto. Our new theatre was eminently suited to old romance. And these were the last offerings from my suddenly antique pen. To the last, and as far as I was able, I went with the flow: *Pericles* in 1608, the year we got back the lease; *Cymbeline* and *The Winter's Tale* in 1610, and *The Tempest* in 1611. Nothing in 1609 – the theatres were shut for more than a year. The plague, the story of our lives, had not done with us yet.

And so to the few final feathers from my plume.

'A last statement, Will? What were they saying?'

For me, they say something about an author on the retreat from time. The ancient enemy is breathing down his neck and the fleeing dramatist is feeling the gulf, now yawning hard. The old family is being folded up one by one and put away from him. Friends have gone into the dark. Your author is not old but he's increasingly isolated. At the same time he clutches at the hope offered by youth and regeneration. He's returning to the themes of the sonnets – love and begetting – but this time round it's not an exercise, it's personal. His grand-daughter Elizabeth has been born in Stratford and the old home he wanted to be away from begins to call him back again. Old longings and memories are always quickened by new births. The heroines that will grace the last plays like beautiful flowers stem not just from the new-born child but from the dead one. They have their roots in a poor dead son, deep in his fathom of earth, deeper than did ever plummet sound. And a youngest brother is almost like a son. The girl-heroines are re-inventions of Hamnet, of Edmund. Over and over your author is asking a dead boy to forgive him for letting him die, for not being there for him, for not being there at all. The pain never goes away.

The last plays are an antidote to pain, to tragedy personal and theatrical. Improbable plots, unlikely characters, exotic settings, shipwrecks, storms, separations, reunions, revelations, reconciliations – all brought about by the unlikely interplay of chance, nature, the gods, and the overpowering drive of human love, leading to ultimate hope and harmony. Faults are forgiven, discords dissolved, lost love restored, lost children found, parents re-united, the hearth become the new kingdom of the heart.

'But what are they all *about*?'

About a state of mind. And a need. Job recovered his peace of mind not by listening to philosophers but by contemplating the beauty of the world – the glory of the stars, the wonder of a snowflake, the grand simplicities of nature. I think I understood something about this at last. I'd been ill. And to tell you the truth, Francis, not, I fear, in my perfect mind. I needed surgeons. And I looked back to Stratford as the medicine requisite to sweet sleep.

But not quite yet. There was still one last thing I wanted to say.

Not so much with *Pericles* – not all mine in any case. An obscure hack started it and I finished it off – a step back twenty years into the past. It was a long time since I'd tried my hand at somebody else's play, a sure sign that the blaze of energy was dying down.

And yet I liked *Pericles* and still do. Maybe because the story goes back to old John Gower. I was always fond of him. St Mary Overy wasn't far from the Globe. Many's the time I used to stop off there and stand by Gower's tomb and effigy, in a silence not so much reverential as affectionate. I liked the monument too – the old poet with his head resting on a pile of his own books, *Vox Clamantis, Speculum Meditantis* among others – and *Confessio Amantis* from which some of the story of the play is taken. Not a bad way to be remembered, I often thought. I even played the part of Gower myself and enjoyed the easy beat of the tetrameters in the Prologue, with its talk of ember-eves and holy-ales that evoked for me again old Warwickshire and an older England, changing fast.

To sing a song that old was sung
From ashes ancient Gower is come.

Yes, it was a great moment, to stand there before an audience of the elect and break the candlelit silence of the Blackfriars with a song of the sea – to fill the theatre with it, the surges which wash both heaven and hell, the brine and cloudy billow that kiss the moon, the belching whale and humming water, and how that same ocean makes raging battery on shores of flint forever. To give sea-room to a tiny stage was the task in hand, to make every line wet with surge, and I knew I'd made it work. As old man Gower has risen from his grave to tell the tale, you can expect it to be a tall one, and I can get away with the unlikeliest episodes that evoke and fulfil the playgoer's sense of the miraculous, his longing for the wonder of life. It's not primarily his, of course, it's the author's – an author now turned from tragedy and history and comedy, and looking increasingly to magic, as all old men do, even Homer. Your old men shall dream dreams and your young men shall see visions.

The vision I'd had as a young man entering London twenty years ago had passed. And in a sense had been fulfilled. Not quite as I'd expected, perhaps, because we constantly expect happiness, knowing it to be an illusion of the tomorrow that never comes. I had achieved only two things of which I was absolutely certain: premature old age and absolute exhaustion. My next play, *Cymbeline,* another collaboration, was a tired man's play, the tinkerings and fidgetings of a man suffering from nervous fatigue. It's not the imbecilic plot that matters, its thrills and spills taken from all over the place and ending up all over the place. Not guilty, Francis, I assure you – it wasn't mine in the first place, this stagy trash, and I wouldn't have taken it on if I hadn't been so spent. But now I see a writer tying himself in knots. He's lost his power of expression. He's written too much and in too short a time. He's still trying to say something but the utterance is nervous. He can either have his breakdown or go back to Stratford for a rest.

I went back to Stratford – where rest indeed awaited me.

But so did the ghost of dead Hamnet, still haunting my plays from his still empty room.

Fear no more the heat o' the sun
Nor the furious winter's rages;
Thou thy worldly task hast done,
Home art gone and ta'en thy wages.
Golden lads and girls all must,
As chimney-sweepers, come to dust.

A dirge for a dead boy had been playing in my head for nearly fifteen years. He should have been twenty-five. Instead he was tetrameters, he was imagery, he was rhyme. He was Fidele.

And he died again as Mamillius, a boy who fell ill and died because of the absence of a beloved parent – his mother, as it happened. But it was the father's fault. Of course. And I punished him in the play.

'You were punishing yourself?'

Who else?

Mamillius says before he dies that a sad tale's best for winter. And there's nothing sadder than the death of a child. Nothing more useless either than our vain attempts to resurrect that child in the person of a sibling, though the boy-actor playing Mamillius appeared later in the play as his long lost sister, Perdita. I had a Perdita of my own, Judith, living among the sheep and flowers of Warwickshire, unmarried, lost to me, an absentee father – London, Bohemia, what did it matter? – and the twin of lost Hamnet, so always associated with lostness, with the missing one. It's the penalty a twin always has to pay, and sad and loving and vulnerable creatures they all are. So I have observed.

So Hamnet lies in his grave, Susanna is married with an infant daughter –

'And Judith?'

Ah, Judith's a story that can't keep much longer. Let's say for now that Dr John Hall may now be the only suitable begetter of Hamnet's substitute, a male heir to gladden my age and fulfil the golden promise of my own destroyed loins and the eternity outlined in those sugared sonnets.

What fools we mortals be. They may be old romances, these last plays, but they come close to home. A dead wife quickens, a lost daughter comes back across the trackless seas, a mad husband is restored to sanity. It was he and not his wife who was the unfaithful one, unfaithful even in his thoughts. Now he is himself again. And everyone comes home.

'But there is that penalty – the dead son.'

I would most gladly have forgot it – O! it comes o'er my memory as doth the raven o'er the infected house, boding to all. The dead son. This is the punishment visited on a shaky father, an unbalanced, overwrought, sinful character, always asking himself the question: was Hamnet's death the retribution for my crimes? Hermione's infidelities were unreal, imaginary, all in the sick mind of her insanely jealous husband. Mine were real. Is this how the gods punish us, then? Or God? A son dies. The faithless father is smitten with disease. Job again. Your son is dead – and Satan strikes you with those hideous whips, those scorpions that bite into the bone and turn you all to ugliness. And pain.

Pain, self-torture, delusion – it's all in the play. But it's only an old tale, after all, nothing more. A stage play, taken from Greene's *Pandosto: the Triumph of Time.* And my own triumph over the man who had poured so much ridicule over my arrival on stage twenty years ago. I suppose I was allowing myself a sort of revenge over Greene, long dead and defenceless, augmenting the sound of the verbal echoes, the borrowings. Thefts, Greene would have called them, and I'd have reminded him that poets are magpies. I enjoyed beautifying his dull feathers and turning his old argument against him, turning his mediocrities into a marvel. He wasn't entirely devoid of talent, he just didn't have a lot of it, that's all, reading matter for a chambermaid and nothing more. *Pandosto* re-appeared in 1607 but I used my original 1588 edition, one of the first books I bought when I came to London, and took from it what I wanted, settling an old score. Eat your heart out, Roberto, and may your ghost revolve in its grave.

Such was *The Winter's Tale*, my last look at the life of Warwickshire and the England I'd known: the songs, the shepherds swooning for Sylvia, the lover and his lass, kisses sweet and twenty, all the flowers and gardens of Stratford, flowers that nodded to me as retirement beckoned. And the wind and the rain, not forgetting them. Or the thieves and wanderers that walk in them. Or those that milk their ewes and weep. The drama has its dark side; there's no denying the cruelties of nature, no escaping my own inadequacies as husband and father. It was time to make up for all that – time to return to flowers and roots and family and friends, yes, friends.

But I'd still one more play to write. My swansong to the theatre and my return to Stratford and the swans of the Avon.

67

It was an exotic enough source that took me home. A sea story, like *Pericles*, beginning in 1609 when an expedition set sail to succour the Jamestown colony. Half the Virginians were dying each winter. So a little fleet of ships set sail from Plymouth on 2nd June and they all reached Jamestown – except for their flagship, the *Sea Adventure*. The fleet had been scattered by a storm and the flagship disappeared – into the white throat of the sea, so it was assumed, the vessel and all her hands.

Ten months later, almost to the day, two little ships put in at Jamestown. On board were the full crew of the *Sea Adventure*, not a single man missing or harmed. It was miraculous. They'd run aground on Bermuda, the Isle of Devils, where they'd expected to be eaten by tribes, or at the very least to encounter horrors as bad as anything experienced by wandering Othello. On the contrary they found the island to be a haven of shelter and natural resources. And they survived for all those months on wild hogs, game and fish, roots and berries. Their only fears were caused by the certainty that the island was haunted, it was so full of noises – spirits and devils for sure – and there on the Bermudas they built the two small craft that took them to Jamestown.

Soon the stories began to circulate like sea-fire in the shrouds, shooting from sail to sail and running along the rigging. And so Ariel was born. I flamed amazement: sometime I'd divide and burn in many places; on the topmast, the yards and bowsprit would I flame distinctly, then meet and join. They were seeing St Elmo's fire, that's all, but a spirit makes for better spectacle, and who's to say that spirits don't inhabit nature? The fear of human flesh-eaters gave birth to Caliban – as close to cannibal as a name can get. A pamphlet described the miracle of mariners fallen asleep where they lay at their working positions on the ship, while the storm howled about them, and yet not a man among them come to harm.

And so *The Tempest* – in which a storm turned out to be less destructive than it seemed to the terrified sailors because it was called up by the art – or science – of the king of a New World island, Duke Prospero who'd already brought the natives under his control and raised his banner. Caliban and Ariel would play elements of that unspoiled world and the play would put the question of whether these were superior to those of the better-taught.

And so it went off again: storms, shipwrecks, abandonment, lost children, dearest believed dead, adults at odds, pure young lovers having their difficulties, deities, songs, the supernatural, split people, split time, all working towards reunion and reconciliation and the fairy-tale ending – in spite of dark continuing undercurrents to give us pause. Sounds like a hotch-potch, doesn't it? But it isn't. I'd recovered from the fatigue of *Cymbeline* and I knew I could end on a strong note and with classical concentration.

Caliban had come a long way from Shylock, and even further from the fairies in the forest. He'd been dispossessed and exploited and there's a warm-bloodedness about him that could trap you into thinking him innocent, or even noble. But dispossession and exploitation don't alter the fact of his nature: bestial, primitive, ugly and gross. He's not your unspoiled innocent who eats berries and likes music. He's the Wild Man who rapes your daughter. He made little enough of his island before Prospero came, and when the colonists withdraw you don't have to be a seer to see what's going to happen when the natives regain control.

Prospero himself was hardly the perfect ruler, either on his island or back in Milan, and you start to warm to him a little only when he takes off his cold robes of office and learns a little humanity, humility, compassion, starts to think about dying – the vision every ruler should start from, the vision I have before me now.

It's a drama about power, natural and supernatural, temporal and spiritual, power over the self. Prospero has to learn to be a better ruler in all senses. It's about atonement, regeneration, planes of truth, the need for some kind of belief – but not belief in any form of dogma, rather some kind of natural magic, without which even the comedy of life is no longer tolerable. Call it prayer, if you like, as Prospero did. And my ending is despair, unless I be relieved by prayer. But he didn't mean an Anglican prayer. That last play shows how little I'd left in me of formal religion – it was fairy-tale stuff and I knew it. We are all islands. And no island is more enchanting than that of the theatre.

Nor more desolate and sad than when the audience has left and the playwright has no more scripts. Then it's time for him to go back home, renounce the magic that made him the demi-god of the theatre for twenty years and slip back again into the comfortable clothes of ordinariness, his preparation for death. That's what I ask you finally to confront: the vulnerability, fragility, and impermanence of life. It's a tough play but it's about things that are tender and transient and infinitely touching.

And true, Francis. And true.

'Our revels now are ended.'

These our actors, as I foretold you, were all spirits, and are melted into air, into thin air: and, like the baseless fabric of this vision, the cloud-capped towers, the gorgeous palaces, the solemn temples, the great globe itself, yea, all which it inherit, shall dissolve, and like this insubstantial pageant faded, leave not a rack behind. We are such stuff as dreams are made on, and our little life is rounded with a sleep.

Rounded, not ended, if you care to see a circle there. Or you may prefer to see this life as a brief awakening from the oblivion that surrounds us.

'Well, well, well.'

Forgive me, old friend, this assumption of your indulgence. My story will soon be over. That last speech was the breaking of the staff, the drowning of the book. The magician abjures his astonishing magic, his visionary gift, and goes back home. He who had imagined so much must embrace ordinariness again. But it's what he started from, and never lost sight of. Now I was an actor without a part – nothing sadder – a magician without a wand. This was my farewell to my art. I bought London property after writing it, but the play was my farewell to poetry, not property. As far as I was concerned at the time, these were the last lines I would ever write, and they came from the heart, as poetry does, not from the arid intellect, which makes a writer scribble on and on in vain as I did for a bit. I *was* burnt out, Francis, but I'd summoned up a burst of the old magic for that one last performance.

The King saw it in the Banqueting House at Whitehall on All Saints' Night, when the Revels began in 1611.

'Ah, I see, of course – the Revels.'

Yes, and I came up from Stratford for the performance, having written the swansong some little time before then. Because by then, I'd retired to the swans of Avon, and here I am – with every third thought my grave, and my long suffering lawyer come from Warwick, to round off my life with a nice tight will – and a good long sleep.

68

'I'm all for a nice tight will – and we could both use a good long sleep. But I'd like to round off with a last bite of something for the road. I fancy a bit of toasted cheese, how about you?'

Not for me. It'll make you dream, Francis.

'What dreams may come, I'm ready to face them – on account of the cheese!'

And Francis lumbered off downstairs, gone quieter now, to find little Alison – now rich little Alison.

What dreams may come.

There was a story about an emperor who dreamed he was a butterfly, and when he told it to one of his sages, the wise man asked him, how do you know you're not a butterfly dreaming you're an emperor? Good answer, Will. How do you know you're not a butcher's boy dreaming you're a dramatist? Or *were* a dramatist. It feels like a dream now, though it was only yesterday. But that's what happens as you approach the end of your time. The life you had drifts past you and away from you as if you were a drowning man. You see it as a sea of troubles, flecked with bright heads lolling slowly in the wishless deep, all those you knew and loved, gone from you now, irretrievably lost. Of his bones are coral made. Those are pearls that were his eyes...

Eyes. Alison briefly came in with shining eyes – and a platter of cheese.

Nicely toasted for Francis, Alison, to make him dream of fees. Queen Mab will be visiting.

'What's that you say, Will? Queen Mab? What are you talking about?'

Oh, nothing. I was dreaming.

'Still on about your dreams. Have a bite of cheese.'

Thank you, no. You'll have every mouse in the house here shortly, to share it with you. What an odour!

'Delicious. Excuse me while I munch and talk. Now then, let's get this will in the bag.'

In the bag. You know, Francis, I remember packing to leave London. Prospero was my last complete play. New Place awaited me. Like Ariel, I'd flamed amazement and like Ariel I longed to be free – to embrace the elements again. I'd lived light in London, for I didn't even live in rooms, I lived in plays, and I was taxed at only five pounds. Of course I squirrelled some things away, out of the sight of the assessors, not that it would have made that much difference. So I put all of the London life into a bag – the work of ten minutes for this sudden stranger I'd become to myself, a man with no continuing city. I never had possessions in London. I'd lived out of a bag. And I closed the door behind me with the toe of my boot. The truth was I didn't dare look back. I might have wept.

Stratford in September. It was 1611 but it could have been 1601. Or 1581. The place looked much the same. And some of the familiar folk had survived into grizzlement and either corpulence or spindliness. Most were dead.

The mad Puritans, were all too alive. They'd banned all dramatic enactments in the parish. Let nothing about your Puritan surprise you, Francis, least of all his fear and hatred of the theatre. Maybe I welcomed the anonymity, the oblivion, the freedom from the dust and heat of the race. The curtains were drawn on all that. It was past, it was over.

'Or was it?'

Stratford didn't have the exciting unpredictability of a London that kept a man on his toes when he'd rather have been oftener on his back, or his backside. I'd imagined that the Stratford retreat would at least bring me the remote balm of breathing-space, the opportunity to relax a little and calm myself, far from the clatter and the chatter of the city, its filth and fury, the hectic rounds of writing, rehearsals, meetings, management, and the mad and manic business of making more money. But that was the very trouble. A man becomes addicted to overwork. Without it – such is the mad paradox of this life – he relaxes even less. Inside his own mind, that is, the beating doesn't cease but grows louder than ever. His fingers twitch – fingers without a pen in them – his eyes dart anxiously in all directions. He catches sight of the haunted stranger in the glass, staring back at him, and asks him the question he was afraid to ask himself. Is this it, then? Is this what it was all for, this half-oblivious existence? Surrounded once again by the infinite pull of skylines, insistent as the tides, as the tugging of the moon, he shuts his eyes on them and tries to pretend they don't exist, or that he can continue to ignore their beckoning, the long low lure that drew him away a quarter of a century ago.

And so I pulled fruit, fed cattle, wondered what the late sunsets meant, pondered the spaces round the poplar tree. Prospero had come off his island of art and had found that Milan was as irksome and insipid as ever. I was bored. I rose early in the mornings, as was my wont – couldn't help my nature – and sat in a chair staring into space. What was I supposed to do? Count the plums in my orchard? Yes, said, Anne, that's exactly what to do, count the plums in your orchard. Do something useful.

Useful? What's useful? I'd written forty plays and a hundred and fifty-four sonnets and a best-selling poem and other things – but were they useful? Of what use is art? Of what use is anything?

And then there was Anne – sexually extinct at fifty-five, having lived her sexless grass widow's existence uncomplaining for a quarter of a century. Now she had a husband again, retired at forty-seven, and after all those years of separation having to get re-acquainted with married life. I'd last known it in my early twenties. Can you picture it? Two old outlanders, strangers to one another, climbing into the matrimonial bed and lying side by side in the night, hearing each other's breathing through the soundless dark and waiting for each slow dawn to leak like a wound. Over wardrobes and walls. We were inches apart in the nordic drift of those sheets but the scale was an inch to infinity and if we rubbed shoulders or touched toes it was the unlikeliest of night-collisions for which apologies were not quite expected but sometimes offered. I wondered if she ever thought back to the eighteen-year-old lad she'd lain with in the fields. I did, frequently, to that same lad, star-struck in Shottery, and asked myself the same old question. Where does it go to, that ocean of love we swim in when we're young? The sea shifts in its chains but is always there. But love, my boy – what is it that lets it drain away till there is just nothing left of it? Not one drop. It goes, like the glory of youth that once glowed in us. Now there's a cracked and dry sea-bed, barren as the desert. And yet once she spoke so wittily and loved so briefly well. Why do people let the spark go out of them? Why do they let the child in them die? Time takes the blame, as we won't take it ourselves, and if the charge sticks and is just, then time has a lot to answer for.

Time was my worst enemy that first autumn, time that I'd played with, and that now played with me. My days were full of it and each day loaded more shackles onto the prisoner of retirement. Autumn ebbed into winter, and the white and black wave went over Warwickshire. Then the green wave of spring. And the golden wave of summer. And another autumn was on me again, like a cancer in the blood. Time to count the plums again. It was unbearable.

And I suppose old Hieronimo would have gone mad again, had it not been for the fact that relief suddenly offered itself like one of the plums of the past, the fruit I'd really been missing – the opportunity of a new play. It was forbidden fruit, of course, and I set out for London with a tight-lipped Anne fuming at the door.

'Off he goes again, the old fool, and with his sword on too! Wouldn't a crutch be better suited to his condition?'

Cold Lady Capulet. Not a complete figment of my imagination, Francis. Nothing was.

'And to London of all places! He'll not be satisfied till that stinking cesspit has killed him off like it's killed half of England!'

It killed Prince Henry in November. At least, the poor boy died – and why shouldn't London take the blame? It suited my wife's black book of looks to say so. Poor Jamie's only surviving daughter, the sixteen-year-old Elizabeth, was to be married to Frederick, Elector Palatine of the Rhine, prospective King of Bohemia. The wedding was to take place on St Valentine's Day 1613 and the king wanted a new play ready as part of the celebrations. His key King's Man of old was retired but not yet dead, so he had heard. Tell him to get his arse up here anon. It was always arses with Jamie. One last command. Very well, then, Will, every subject is a King's man, retired or not, his Majesty's wish etcetera, and the chink of cash was never unwelcome to my ears. But even more gratifying was the prospect of going up to London again after a year of spacious suffocation.

It was an even more changed place, theatrically, as if the rats had grown fatter for the absence of the Stratford cat. Ben was enjoying my retirement more than anyone. He was lording it over a stage on which a crowd of stars were showing their dim faces but seeming all the brighter for the lack of me – Chapman, Tourneur, Heywood. And black Webster – bright is hardly the word. Beaumont had given up the bachelor business and the stage business but Fletcher was still active, as I've said. And it was Fletcher and I that put our heads together and came up with an idea for a play suitable to celebrate the wedding of the king's daughter. What better subject in the circumstances than Henry the Eighth? My idea. To crown all those history plays and bring England as safely into the present as I dare, Elizabeth now being dead and rotten for a decade. It seemed a decent interval. Any sooner and those old bones of hers might have rattled in their fury, deep in their echoing vault. Memories of great ones never die. And even their corpses must be pacified.

So there it was. I ended up writing most of it, Fletcher not being an historical animal – and I lent a tired hand to his *Two Noble Kinsmen* and *Cardenio*, among other things. But the hand *was* tired, I noticed it one day, scuttering and scrabbling on the page like a palsied crab. What was happening to me? And by that time in any case I was producing decent passages only here and there, a speech or two that glowormed in the dark. I dabbed at patchy scenes. Even in the good speeches I was going round the ale-houses again, repeating myself, the master falling back on his laurels, feeding on stored fat. The old rough magic was no longer there. I had abjured it. I was tired. Yes, I was burnt out. *The Tempest* really had been my last big blaze, and though I'd groaned in retirement, there really was nothing left for me but to groan.

Henry could have been a bomb, about tyranny and religion, but I fashioned a damp squib. Henry Tudor? He cut down monks alive from the gallows, tore off their arms so that they couldn't cross themselves, then tore out their Catholic hearts too and rubbed them in their faces, because popery outside England was now piss in the conduits of religion, polluting his personal church – and he had a new breed of house-puppies to train. The man was a monster and I could have used the play to show the House of Stuart how far it had come. Instead I gave the king pretty much what he would have wanted for the occasion – a stiff pageant.

Or maybe he didn't really care that much – in spite of the fact that by an irony of history we put on the play in the very Blackfriars hall where eighty years earlier the ecclesiastical court had sat to hear Henry's divorce case against Katherine of Aragon, and the abyss opened up. What did that matter now to Jamie? The Henry play must have reminded him bitterly of his own Henry, who'd have been Henry the Ninth had he lived – but he'd never made it out of his teens and young Charles was not filling his empty shoes too well. God knows, I knew what it was to lose a son and to fear for the future. And I felt for the old dog when I saw those rheumy melancholy eyes cast bleakly on the King's Men at their work. Not that I was actually working myself, merely spectating. The days of treading the boards had also gone from my life.

'Yes, but the old businessman in you was still truffling about.'

Ah, the Gatehouse, you're right. It was when I was in London for the royal wedding that I saw a piece of property, the Gatehouse of the old Blackfriars monastery, not two hundred steps from the new theatre itself. It was a perfect location for a theatre man, heading the route down to Puddle Wharf where the wherries plied their trade taking play-goers to the Globe. Good for both theatres – you could be whisked between the two in no time. A man with a retired foot in Stratford and a working foot in London could look on it as ideal, after years of shuttling around among rented rooms, to have found his place of rest in the Gatehouse of a medieval priory. And an interesting place too – an infamously papist place, with many back doors and byways and vaults and dark corners and passages to the water. Notorious in its time as a foxhole for Jesuits, and priest-hunters kept an eye on it during the Topcliffe nineties. All good irony, if nothing more, though more to the point was that Burbage was quite close and so was the Mermaid. A possible bolthole, then, away from the uncounted plums and from cold Lady Capulet handing me the crutch. And those pointless dawns and slow angry sunsets of Stratford. And that stranger's face staring at me from the glass. Anyway, I argued it out, it was an investment, a place I could rent out.

Pathetic, isn't it? An ailing man's preparation for a future he knows is never going to happen. But I was so keen to push through the purchase I paid the owner a hundred and forty pounds for it, and mortgaged sixty pounds of the price, buying the property one day and leasing it back the next at the annual rent of a peppercorn – namely nothing. Heminges came along with John Jackson and William Johnson, host of the Mermaid, to join me in the indenture. Sold to Mr William Shakespeare, gent, of Stratford upon Avon, in the county of Warwick.

'10th March 1613, it says here in your notes.'

Anyway, I let it out to a friend, John Robinson, and came back here, mapping out in my mind plans for a return to the theatre. Like some poor old invalid, mumbling to himself about what he's going to do when he gets out of bed. His eyes glow with the brightness of his frail determination. But it's all a pretence. He knows he's never going to get out of that bed. And I knew I'd seen the last of London. The rest is all in the past.

And as if to symbolize the pastness of things, it was a performance of Henry Eight on 29th June that year that finally dissolved the great Globe.

'Ah, the fire.'

To mark Henry's arrival at Wolsey's house a cannon was fired. A single spark from the shot strayed into the thatch and started the blaze that brought down the theatre in flaming ruin. Thank God I was not there to see it. A lifetime's work sucked into the sky in seconds and settling to ashes in minutes. The Globe timbers had come from the original Theatre and had staged my first play. Now they'd gone up in flames during my last. There seemed to be something darkly fitting about that. Leave it, Will, leave it, a voice said.

The Puritans loved it. The hand of God – so they gloated – had given the filthy players a foretaste of the hell that awaited them. But hell is here and now. And that's how it felt at the time – the hell of all those costumes and properties and laboriously penned prompt books and scripts going up in flames, and along with them the livelihoods of all those who still depended on them. This had been their place of employment, this new world that we'd hailed with our swords in that winter dawn on the frozen Thames at the end of the previous century.

See the world's ruins...

So wrote Ben. But in under a year the tragedy was turned to apparent triumph when a new Globe stood in its place. It cost the shareholders a pretty penny. By that time I'd sold my own shares, cut my losses, and retired for good. That fire persuaded me the time had come, time to go home. And stay home. The theatre dream was over. After that day I never saw another play. And never will, except the last scene of this one.

'What one?'

Do you know a verse of Ralegh's, Francis? I don't suppose you do. It's another of those poems like Nashe's, that I wish I'd written. This is how it goes.

What is our life? a play of passion.
Our mirth the music of division.
Our mothers' wombs the tiring-houses be
Where we are drest for this short comedy.
Heaven the judicious sharp spectator is
That sits and marks still who doth act amiss.
Our graves that hide us from the searching sun
Are like drawn curtains when the play is done.
Thus march we playing to our latest rest.
Only, we die in earnest – that's no jest.

'There's more to life than playing, old man.'

Is there? It's a sombre and melancholy feeling and it opens up in you a deep emptiness and the ache of an impossible longing – I mean knowing for certain that those scenes and images that have constituted all of your working life and have been the body and soul of your existence, you are quite simply never going to see again: the Mermaid in Bread Street, the bookstalls round St Paul's, the spires and palaces catching the sun, the crowds flocking into the Globe, London Bridge, the Thames glittering on a May morning. And that stage – onto which I'd emptied my entire being, and which now stood emptied of me again.

Farewell to it all. Not for the life of the justice or the slippered pantaloon, the serious reader or the country gentleman. I slipped into a seventh age of my own, listening to a wife who didn't know who I was, talking to flowers, hearing old music in my head. And yes – counting the infernal plums.

It wasn't all boredom. Drayton visited from London. He had a friend in Clifford Chambers not far off, and brought news and gossip. Ben came down once or twice, even walked it once, waging furious but futile war on his belly. These were merry meetings, out of Anne's hearing, but they were few. Respectability had cast its sacred mantle over the player's hide and his house was seen as fit lodging for the visiting preacher giving the Whitsuntide sermon. Impeccably orthodox Will. Twenty pence subsidy from the Corporation for one quart of sack and one quart of claret wine to wet his throat and keep the good man in good voice for his address.

'Implacably retired at last.'

Retired? I started to retire a dozen years ago, when I wrote *Lear.* Retirement should be an ordinary everyday thing, a natural happy thing. Ah, but outside the castle gates is the bleak heath that awaits the retired man. Other things too await him there: loss of authority, loss of identity, loss of purpose, loss of reason. The antidote to this deep fear is work, work, and more work, more purchases too. The truth is I started to retire not twelve but twenty years ago, when Hamnet died. That's when the retreat from happiness began, when I started to retreat from any possibility of it after that, to prepare myself for something else, something other than happiness. I was declined into the vale of years, the sere and yellow leaf, long before my time, and considering my end. And yet I was still at the height of my powers. But what did my power consist of? Creating and destroying worlds, arousing passion in men and women, awaking the dead to make war on the living.

All that was over now. Now there were the little wars of the little world. There was a rowdy, loose-mouthed drunk called John Lane, who rumoured it abroad that Susanna had had intercourse with Rafe Smith, the haberdasher and hatter, and had contracted a dose of gonorrhoea. Susanna was about thirty years then.

'And *fidessima conjux* without a doubt.'

Without a doubt and with a child of five. But her husband John travelled a lot, so gossip about his wife left at home was to be expected to fester on vile tongues. Lane was a lout and his family was a blight on Stratford. He was also a rabid anti-Puritan and it infuriated him that even the anti-Puritans in the town respected John. So it suited his grubby little book to defame Dr Hall through his wife. Susanna prosecuted him for slander before the consistory court at Worcester Cathedral, 15th July 1613. Not surprisingly Lane failed to turn up and was excommunicated. Susanna's name was cleared and the nine days' wonder was over.

The following summer there was a fire in Stratford that devastated the land and damaged more than fifty houses. After that the enclosures dispute started up.

'Sheep do eat up men.'

That's what they said. But I couldn't have cared less about sheep. The next thing was that I had Judith to worry about.

'What is the Judith problem, Will? You said you'd tell all.'

All is a lot to tell. Pass me a drink and I'll make it last the glass.

69

Judith is thirty-two, Francis. Last month, desperate for a man, she married, as you know, a wretched apology for one, Thomas Quiney, twenty-seven. And why would a man in his twenties marry a woman in her thirties? I'd been there myself, remember? And I heard more than wedding bells ringing, when I first got wind of it. I knew the business.

A no-gooder, a no-user and a no-hoper, that's Quiney in a nutshell. He has so far reached the glorious heights of running a tavern of which he has only the lease. A glorified potman is my Judith's provider. Not good enough. And hardly a cause for celebration in itself – if that were only the whole story, which I regret to say it is not.

Quiney had been sniffing around Judith for years. He ran the Atwood tavern in the High Street at that time and ran it badly. I begged with her to wait and see how he turned out and she in turn pleaded her age. What could I say to that? Old Capulet said that one daughter is one too many. I made him a hard man for saying so but my daughter was well over twice the age of his, and waiting for Quiney to come good – it was a tedious prospect to say the least and one with small assurance of success. She went ahead, hard against my wishes.

February. Because of the Lenten time of year it was a wedding arranged in haste by special and irregular licence. Do you hear bells ringing again? I did. The licence was from the local vicar, John Rogers, who claimed his own right hereabouts to grant such licences. The Bishop of Worcester disputed this, however – more bells – advising that he alone could issue a proper licence in this case, and summoned the happy couple to appear before the consistory court at Worcester. Quiney ignored the summons, failed to turn up, and was immediately fined and excommunicated along with his wife, meaning that they'd be unable to baptise their first child if the ban remained in force. A fine start to the estate of holy matrimony, a pair of reprobates with a child in limbo, and although the pair of them were partly responsible for the unhappy state of affairs, not a penny leaves my estate to go to a church that has seen fit so to defame my daughter! Are you clear about that?

'Ah!'

Ah! Indeed. And that, Francis, was just the start of the unhappy chain of events that now unravelled.

After the ceremony in Holy Trinity I avoided the hypocritical handshakes, pleading that I was in pain and needed to take a turn or two. Bear with me, sirs, be not disturbed with my infirmity. I am vexed. My old brain is troubled... And I went off across the frozen February fields. The cold very quickly made me want to pee. An old ill man pees at a wretched pace. And as I stood and watched the pure white snow turning to a yellow puddle under the miserable dribble between my boots, I asked myself what sort of an end was this to thirty years of fatherhood? When a daughter that a dad has dandled on his knee leaves him at last to go to bed with another man, there's a sense in which he feels he's failed as a father, failed to keep her with him, even feels betrayed. Daft, isn't it? Nevertheless an age of innocence has passed away, and the pure bond has become ragged and stained, like that puddle of piss. Brrr! I shook myself and put away my poor old prick.

But when I did arrive indoors and took off my gloves I stared as dumb as any stone at my right hand. My gold signet ring was gone. It had slipped from my thin white finger when I'd taken off my gloves to pee. W.S. lay somewhere under the cold snow, as the man himself will soon enough. I'd lost my daughter, Hamnet's sister, and in the same hour I'd lost the emblem of myself: a double blow. An emptiness opened up in me, even though I knew that old Will's days were numbered anyway. But if I retraced my steps right now I'd find my ring, lying next to a tell-tale yellow hole in the snow. I went to the door and looked out. I was tired and breathing like a whale and darkness was gathering. And as I stood there, undecided, the first fresh flakes started to fall again. Within seconds I was wearing a shroud. I closed the door and sat down at the head of the empty table, shaking a little. Was I shivering or trembling? I couldn't be sure. I was sure of one thing, though – my daughter had married an arse.

Not long after the wedding he took his wife off to another tavern called appropriately The Cage. He should be locked inside it and the key thrown away. The ink was hardly dry on their apparently invalid marriage contract when worse trouble broke over our heads. The Margaret Wheelar affair. The Wheelars were the low-lives of Stratford, even lower than the Quineys and the Lanes – cursers and swearers and slanderers and lechers. And such was the company Quiney had been keeping while he was courting my daughter. Only a fortnight ago a member of this tribe, Margaret Wheelar, died in childbed and was buried along with her stillborn infant. Before she died she gasped out the name of the father of the wretched red shambles that had turned a childbed into a double deathbed and a bed of shame.

'Thomas Quiney?'

The very same, Francis. He's due to appear before the bawdy court tomorrow.

'And doubtless will be found *incontinentia cum quadam Margareta Wheelar?'*

And will doubtless confess openly to having had carnal copulation with the said female.

'*Fassus est se carnalem copulacionem habuisse cum dicta Wheelar.*'

Lawyer's Latin almost dignifies it. Yes, he occupied her. Let's put it less legalistically, Francis. He was fucking her while fucking Judith – unlawfully intimate with two women at once. He's married to one of them, if less than lawfully according to the Bishop of Worcester. But the other woman and the illicit fruit of Quiney's lust are now in the same grave, and that will be not so good in the moral glare of the court, though it's simply a legal footnote to his guilt. Tomorrow Quiney will have to face the church music.

'What a disgrace!'

Public penance: three successive Sunday appearances in church, wearing the white sheet, so that the preacher can shame him (and my poor Judith) in front of the whole parish – which will please some Puritans around here no end. Like father like daughter, to marry scum like that, and a filthy player gets no better than he deserves for a son-in-law, notwithstanding his grand New Place and his London airs. Vengeance is mine, saith the Lord. God is not mocked. Can't you hear them?

'Can't you do something? Pull some strings?'

I'm ahead of you, Francis. It has already cost me a deal of discussion with the vicar and a large cargo of claret to lubricate his larynx while he talked it through with me at length, including extra wine to take home with him for the better pondering a final judgement. I've been a busy man in this sick-bed and I think I've got Quiney off with a five shillings fine to be given to the poor of the parish, and a private penance to be performed elsewhere in front of another vicar and wearing his own everyday clothes. So he'll go in his street clothes to the chapelry at Bishopton which falls within Stratford parish but has no church of its own and is well out of the public eye. So at least we'll be spared the humiliation of his triple public exposure in white and the delighted whisperings that would have gone round Holy Trinity's walls.

'You *are* a genius, Will!'

Dismissus. Quiney will wriggle out of it – he'll escape the full wrath of the church, if not of the law.

But not mine, Francis, not mine.

'Well, we've seen to that, in good black legal ink.'

I never doubted from the start what it was that brought Quiney panting around a poor unmarried Shakespeare bitch and it was neither love nor lust, but naked expediency and greed. He had his financial problems, and marriage to my only unwedded child must have seemed like a dream to him as he sat among the old soaks of Stratford and drank small beer. Shakespeare's lass on the shelf would be worth more than a pound or two when the old man finally shuffled off, leaving all that London loot behind him. Quiney was easier to read than the hornbook. Then he got Margaret Wheelar pregnant and he panicked. He had to be married to Judith quickly, before the birth of his bastard which he knew to be imminent. Hence the haste – and the improper licence. That landed him in enough trouble, but he must have reckoned that if he didn't marry Judith in time he might be forced to marry Margaret, or that I'd refuse to accept him as a husband for Judith, which would mean a huge monetary loss to him in terms of the death he knew to be approaching and the terms of his future father-in-law's will. It has been no secret in Stratford that I am dying. And Quiney wanted to be in at the kill.

Well, he isn't. He's in all right, having made a good marriage, but there's to be no killing, not for him. I've done the killing myself.

'He's dead for a ducat, Will, no doubt about that!'

Steps had to be taken to punish him – Judith too, regrettably – and to keep his thieving whoring hands off my hard-earned money.

Meantime what more can I tell you? Things are as they are and there's no changing them. Susanna made a splendid marriage, Judith a miserable one, and it reflected their lives. Susanna a bright spark, Judith a foggy cloud, melancholy, brooding, the twin who'd lost a twin, always incomplete, always that reminder of a poor dead boy, poor girl, poor Perdita, lost girl, remembrancer of what had been rather than what still was and could yet be.

And yet she wanted love, you know, wanted marriage, had not lacked suitors. Oh, there was no lack of young men coming to this door with hope in their hearts – and always the same story. Someone turned them away, didn't he? The father who insisted on safeguarding his daughter from afar, from unsatisfactory suitors, the father who should have come from London to give his approval but either didn't come at all or came too late. He'd already lost one of that precious pair to the shadows and cared too much for the other to lose her to the shadow of a stranger. He cared too much about the possible dangers, the betrayal of innocence and beauty, about faithlessness in love, about which he knew more than most men. But in the end he cared so much he was himself her betrayer. Love like this doesn't always bring happiness from father to child, especially where another child gets in the way, alive or dead. She was too much in the sun. When the boy died I loved her not less but twice as much as before. Too much. The young men drifted away, married, grew older. Judith stayed unplucked till she was almost a matron. And then along came Quiney and supposedly took her by storm. It didn't take much. He was her last hope.

It didn't take much either to bring her father to his dying days. A man withdrawing slowly, day by day. When I knew she'd marry Quiney in spite of me, that's when I called on you, old friend, and we drafted out the January document. You wanted a signature at the time, remember? And I said no.

'You never said why.'

I was waiting... And I was right. There were muddied murmurings of a pregnancy. But it wasn't Judith's. Dr Hall thought I suffered a little stroke when the Margaret Wheelar affair broke open and let out the stink of Quiney's whoredom. A mild stroke, he said. Wrong, John, I said. I was cut to the brains. Beyond the power of my one good son-in-law to heal or succour. Hearing and sentence tomorrow, then. A foregone conclusion. This is Lady Day. Tomorrow everybody in Stratford will be saying that Judith Shakespeare is no lady – but Quiney's other whore.

70

Oh, my poor Judith.

'Quite serious. Let me just check through what we've done – for windows.'

There are none. Yet it kills my heart to punish her like this for an unwise marriage – the marriage will be its own punishment, God knows. But there's no other way if I'm to keep Quiney out of it.

'And he's out, by Jesus – not even named in the deed. *Such husband as she shall be married to.* Now I understand you, Will.'

And that's as close as I come to acknowledging his existence – with the hint, if they care to take it, that in three years' time she may be married to someone else. Or with even better luck the waster will be dead. He hasn't even come up with the hundred pounds in land that was to have been his share of the marriage settlement. So whatever that squalid little gold-digger hoped for by marrying into the Shakespeares has been rendered null and void. He gets not a penny.

'And out goes the word *son-in-law* from your January draft.'

God, yes, I can't even bear to refer to him in such terms, he's no son of mine and I've made that clear. And the rest is clear, Francis?

'As day. A hundred and fifty directly to Judith, the hundred for her dowry and the fifty only if she surrenders all claim to the Chapel Lane cottage.'

It hardly leaves her badly off. She'll get another hundred and fifty if Quiney settles the same sum on her, otherwise she'll get the interest and if they have children they'll inherit the capital when she dies.

'And that's Quiney well and truly shut out in the cold.'

It's as far as I can go without actually paupering my own flesh and blood. And the plate I left her in the January draft? Remind me, Francis?

'All that now goes to little Elizabeth and all Judith gets is the broad silver gilt bowl. And that's it.'

Dreadful, dreadful. But she married against my wishes and married a wretch. What more can I say? They've struck me to the heart.

What else now? There's one other matter. Brother-in-law Hart's dying, did you know, Francis? Hatter Hart. He fathered three sons – and a daughter dead before him. But in spite of the sons he's a failure. No matter. Joan's twelve pence a year will let her live in Henley Street until she dies. And also twenty pounds and all the clothes to Joan, did I say so already? And the money to the boys. William and Michael and – I still can't remember how they call him, the third one. I'm losing my grip. And the ten pounds to the poor.

'Two would have sufficed. Five would have been generous.'

Never mind that now. It speaks of a life well lived – and I was poor once too.

'It's always a last satisfaction to become poor in the end – back to nakedness, and giving your all away.'

To the right people, yes. Well, what have we still to see to, Francis? Forgive me my dull brain – it clouds over, though I'm still strong enough on dates. Did we do the rings for the fellows?

'All done.'

Add in there Will Reynolds, a good Catholic, and Anthony Nash, he farms my tithe-land, and to John Nash too, twenty-six shillings and eightpence each, and the same to Hamlet Sadler, – Hamlet, Hamnet, how many times did I write that word, speak that name! – and to my godson, William Walker – no, make that twenty shillings to him. And five pounds to Thomas Russell –

'Hold on.'

And not forgetting your good self, Francis.

'Now that won't be necessary – '

Quite apart from your fee, of course. For friendship, Francis, for friendship.

'Well – '

No, take it down, go on. *And to Francis Collins, of the borough of Warwick –*

'Which I hope to reach before dawn.'

In the county of Warwick, gent. – as you are, Francis –

'Yes?'

Thirteen pounds six shillings and eightpence –

'That's more than generous, old man.'

To be paid within one year after my decease. You can hurry it along if you like.

'No hurry, Will. And none for your decease either, I trust.'

And Susanna's safe – for certain?

'Will, she bears the palm away. This house and all the household goods, the two houses on Henley Street, the Gatehouse in Blackfriars, the lands outside Stratford and all your other lands and tenements, these to be entailed on her eldest son if she ever produces one, which pray God she will, down to the seventh, just as you said, and in default of her offspring surviving, on the heirs of Judith, unless she dies barren. We've seen to that, Will. You've done it all.'

Yes, the estate's intact, seven times over.

'Beyond even that, to her daughter's sons, your great-grandsons, and Judith's sons.'

Always assuming them to be lawful issue. These are the two things, remember, Francis, they should be lawful and they should be male. A true son must inherit.

'You won't let that boy go, will you?'

He won't let me go. There must be a son somewhere along the line, there must, there must.

'You've done all you can, Will.'

Have I? What have I done? What do we all do in our wills? We try to alter the past, to influence the future. We want to restore losses and end sorrows, and to store up riches in a world that's no longer ours. We should acknowledge and accept, of course, that the future does not concern the dead, that tomorrow does not belong to us. And the deathbed, above all places, ought to be the school in which we learn this final lesson. But we don't, do we? What is a will, after all? It's a dead man's hand rising from the grave and pointing the way. It's a last attempt to cheat death, to carry on living by affecting the lives of those we most love. Or don't. Down to the fact that nothing goes to the church that shamed my daughter, and that no Hathaway gets a penny.

Even, I suppose, down to the bed.

'What do you mean – the bed?'

Ah, I did forget. Take this down, Francis. *Item, I give unto my wife my second best bed with the furniture.*

'That's it?'

That's it.

'But what's the point?'

Well, what does it say to you?

'What will it say to anyone? What will it say to Anne? Beds don't talk.'

But this one will. It's a speaking bed. Does it speak of conjugal affection? of matrimonial bliss recalled? What would you think now, Francis?

'Well, I've known some men unwilling to leave beds to widows, thinking it unseemly to say the least to contemplate that she and some new man perhaps might make love in the same bed in which she'd loved the first.'

A second time I kill my husband dead when second husband kisses me in bed.

'But Anne is on the heels of sixty.'

Yes, and what would I really care? No, the bed meant little to me and means nothing much to her, I suppose, the bed in which we finally lay again together like two stilled fish. Take it as an apology, then, of sorts, for never having shared it with her for much of our marital time. An ironic kiss for the years of her widowhood. A hand extended to the long-suffering partner of a long-absent spouse. A nod to the three and a half decades of coldness and decline. Or take it as a dead man's hint that I found a better bed than hers elsewhere, a better woman, a deeper trust, a greater closeness, a purer love. *If only I had, Francis.* But maybe it will stop her short of wanting to share my final bed, my bed of dust. This isn't Jack Donne lying here, this is old me. And there'll be no bracelet of bright hair about the bone. It was her own bed in any case, the double bed she brought from Shottery. I'm giving her back her own, leaving her her own property – but also her widow's dower and her dowager's place in the house, with Susanna in absolute charge of these affairs. She will be well looked after by the Halls, needs nothing and will want for nothing. You needn't think me cruel.

'Not cruel.'

Only cold. Is that what you're thinking?

'It's not a question of coldness, it's a question of law. You've said she'll be looked after by the Halls. That's human matter. But on a point of law it could be construed that by specifying a single item – this bed – you the testator are in fact wishing to wipe out the widow's usual one third life interest, in a word to disinherit her. Now I have to ask you directly, is that your intention? Is that what lies behind your bequest?'

I never said so, Francis. And it's not what I asked you. I asked you if you thought me cold.

'Well, I've had some practice of this business, and I've heard other men speak from the grave in their wills of their wish to be buried beside their well-beloved wives – my dear Rebecca, my devoted Margaret, you know the sort of thing, my faithful and loving what's-her-name. What is her name, Will? You don't even mention it, do you, not once? You didn't even refer to her in the January draft. And this is your Testament. She's like Quiney, kept anonymous. Don't you want to rectify this? – the absence of emotion, the lack of warmth, not a memento, not the smallest keepsake, a ring, a loving word, nothing.'

But look, Francis, there's no feeling for *anyone* expressed here, at least not in words. The words are verbal signs, doing their legal business. This is my will, it's not *King Lear.* It doesn't mean there's no feeling behind it. On the contrary, Francis, there's plenty of sentiment there, tucked away between the lines, behind the scenes, the characters. We've spent a day and a night at it. There's emotion in every item, only I don't show it, not personally. You know me, Francis. A ring to Burbage, a bowl to a daughter, a bed to a wife, a widow – there's anger and joy and disappointment and fellowship and guilt – it's shot through with it, this document. You think it concedes little to flesh and blood – but no, Francis, it gives away much, just as much as I have given away. Which is everything.

'Well, it doesn't show it, that's all. You said something at the start about a will being unequivocal, didn't you? None of that rich ambiguity you get in plays. It seems to me you've pulled the same trick again, in spite of what you said.'

Maybe you're right, Francis, maybe there is a little drama in this document after all. Not what I've written but what I haven't written that speaks eloquently enough – about the hell of enforced wedlock. Plenty of that in the plays, if you look for it, missing wives, wives neglected, wives shut out, lovers mis-matched, married in haste, married too young, virgin knots untied too soon –

'You're getting off the point, and intentionally too. I know you, Will. As to the bed – '

As to the bed, if I'd left her the free fields of Shottery to walk in once more – but no, that would have spoken of a time when young Will Shakespeare was madly in love and Anne Hathaway his all in all. But we lived out most of our marriage apart, and we have renewed our acquaintance briefly and bleakly before death does us part, as he intends to do shortly. It's written on the walls. It's all around me. Thy days are numbered. I'm in the best bed now. Alone. With nothing left to add except my name.

'*In witness whereof I have hereunto put my hand and seal.* We'll have to strike out *seal* and leave in *hand*, as you've lost your ring. *And the day and year first above written, 25th March, year of our Lord 1616.*'

Oh! And my sword, I forgot my sword – one of the Combes left me money. Thomas Combe shall have my sword. It should have gone to Hamnet. My lovely boy. I had a son, Francis. And the shadows took him...

'You need to rest now.'

Afterwards. Hand me the deed, friend. Three sheets, is it? Each requiring to be validated. Very well. Two feeble efforts, forgive me, the last to be prefixed, *by me William Shakespeare*. There. There's a good William, as my mother used to say, written firm and fair. I've used all my strength – oh, now it fails me, and the name crumples into this wavering spidery scrawl.

71

No, I can't be dead, not yet. That's you Francis over there, for sure, the cup ever to your lips.

'That's right, old friend. One last cup – and one for the horse.'

How about one for me?

'Are you sure? You were falling asleep.'

I need reviving. There's one last thing I want you to do for me.

'Anything, old friend, but I hope it won't be the last.'

Last piece of writing, certainly.

'The will's sewn up, lad – signed if not sealed, had you forgotten?'

It's not the will, it's a little verse I made up just now, while I was asleep.

'That's a nice way to do it. Wish I could work like that.'

The mind works like a miner – does your dirty dangerous work for you, while you take your ease. Sometimes.

'Right then, what's this little verse about?'

Take it down, will you, Francis? I'm incapable of a pen.

'Pause a moment. Right, poised again.'

You thought my will rather dry, didn't you?

'Rather.'

But it wasn't quite my last will, Francis. This is.

'Now wait a minute – '

Don't worry, it's very short – it's a quatrain. The last one I'll write.

'What are you up to?'

Prepare to scribe.

'I'm ready.'

Good friend, for Jesus' sake forbear
To dig the dust enclosed here:
Blest be the man that spares these stones,
And curst be he that moves my bones.

'Well – it's your epitaph.'

Obviously.

'And what do you want me to do with it?'

Oh, for God's sake, Francis, what do you normally do with an epitaph! Cut it on my gravestone, of course.

'You could have wanted it published.'

I do. In stone. For all to see. Especially the sexton.

'Oh, you're back to him, are you?'

I was never away. And that's a little message for him, specially from me, something for him to think about. Not bad, is it, for doggerel?

'Sounds a bit like Ralegh, if you ask me.'

Or Hamlet penning verses to Ophelia. Or Prospero getting down to prayer. But 'tis mine own – just a word from Will to the local gravedigger, that farting old bastard.

'He's long dead.'

His line is still there. That's a line that never dies out. I want him to be kinder to me than his predecessor was to the occupants of the bone-house when I was a boy.

'*And curst be he that moves my bones*. It's a bit of a frightener, isn't it?'

He frightened me badly enough, now it's my turn. It's my final plea, my last will. For Jesus' sake. And for mine. I told you, Francis, as tithe-holder and lay rector I have the right to escape the earth and I'm choosing to exercise that right. I want to be buried at the east end of Holy Trinity and I don't want to be disturbed. It's not pride, it's fear, I don't mind admitting it, it's the old childhood terrors again, never far away, and always closer when the grave is near, the bones that frighten Juliet and horrify Hamlet, and that crude old Stratford spadesman, they all come crowding into the room, don't you see, to people my last hours, and they bring so many others along with them, all my creations...

'Sounds to me like you need a priest, my boy.'

Why Francis, you *are* my priest.

'I told you already, I'm not your priest, I'm your lawyer, pure and simple. Are you losing touch, old lad?'

Never more *with* you, I assure you. Why do you think you've been fed like a prize boar all day long? We could have scratched out that will in under an hour. You've been listening to my confession, old friend. Do you really think I'd confess to a priest? Or that if I did, I'd tell a priest everything I've told you? The problem is, Francis, this is the real thing at last, the ultimate thing, called death. You're standing on the verge of eternity, you mustn't dissimulate, you'd have to say in the first place what sort of a priest you wanted, and in so doing you'd be saying what you really believed, what you'd believed all your life. And so, Francis, if I were to name a priest for you to call, you'd know what I really thought, wouldn't you? And why should you – when I may not even know for sure myself? And if I did, that's between me and God – if there is one, and if he listens. I asked you at the start – would you have me die a papist? Or a Protestant? No, my friend, I'll tell you what, I'll die undiscovered, having confessed to fat Father Francis, a lawyer in disguise. Ultimately I'll die with an open mind – and that's my best advice to you – if I may advise my lawyer – or to anyone. Anyway Francis, I wanted somebody to talk to. There's nobody around here to talk to any more. John's very busy – he didn't even come up tonight. And Anne? You can see how it is. And Judith – well, well, well, no more of that.

'You *are* an old fox, Will. And don't think I didn't see the other object hidden away in that epitaph of yours.'

Really, Francis? What object was that, then?

'Oh, it's pretty obvious, isn't it? If your grave is never to be opened, then your widow will never share it with you, when her own time comes. You're excluding her to the last, shutting her out from your eternity.'

You're a wise old fox yourself, Francis. We were never really one flesh and we shall never be one dust. The divorce continues, even after death.

'A strange man you are, Will, underneath. And I'm feeling rather strange myself right now.'

Francis did look a little odd, I thought. Perhaps on account of the sheer amount he'd put away. But he finally clobbered off into the small hours. Trotting is not something a horse does with Francis on its back. And galloping with such a burden would be impossible, even for wingèd Pegasus.

72

But that was some time ago – wasn't it? Ralegh was released the week before and told to go for gold. A fool's errand. Henslowe died in January, they say. Easter came early this year – on the last day of March. The will was signed by then, as I remember. Brightness falls from the air. Will they quote Nashe when I go? And now it's April again. It was always April. There's talk of someone's birthday. This day I breathèd first; time is come round, and where I did begin, there shall I end – my life is run his compass. Old Cassius still.

Cassius? How ill this taper burns. Ha! Who comes here? I think it is the weakness of mine eyes that shapes this monstrous apparition. The light burns blue. Speak to me. What art thou?

Thy evil spirit, Brutus.

Why then, it's true. I'm dying. Let there be no noise, my gentle friends, unless some dull and favourable hand will whisper music to my weary soul. Music – bear with me, good my boy, I am much forgetful. This is a sleepy tune. O, murderous slumber! Lay'st thou thy leaden mace upon my boy that plays me music? Hamlet, O, Hamlet, what a falling off was there...

Why so, being gone, I am a man again. If I stand here I saw him, all of them. They were all here. Pardon me, sirs, these last larks of the brain...

But no, I'm clear again, and the crowded sheets and shutters free. I'm free to speak again. What would you hear? For they say the tongues of dying men enforce attention like deep harmony. Would you hear my confession? No, that's for priests and torturers, and Francis has it safe. Even the dead are not safe – from priests and politicians, and those terrible diggers of bones.

Death, I hope, is an end to misery, it's a sleep, dreamy or dreamless, it's worms and rottenness and stench, the charnel-house, the sexton's fart, the undiscovered country, cold obstruction, coral or clay or pearl. It's the everlasting mansion... the mason, shipwright, carpenter... the house that lasts till doomsday, it's the silence that has no end, it's the rest we only dream of, it's nothingness, it's what remains, it's the last enemy and the first real friend.

Oh, and the life to come. There is the bright day and there is the dark. No religion I know could ever fuse the two. When one is past you have to be ready for the other, whatever you think it is or isn't. I took my fill of love and life, laughter and pain. And I'm ready – not for heaven or hell, I trust, but for oblivion or adventure.

Yes, I'm dying now.

Brother Gilbert died four years back, was it? – an unmarried haberdasher in St Bride's. Like Edmund he followed me to London – a dangerous place for brothers. Dead at forty-five. We brought the body back to Stratford, as was his wish. Richard? Ah, Richard never left Stratford, died the next year. We were rehearsing, I remember, it was the royal wedding. He was thirty-eight, poor boy. And here am I, the only one of all those sons, and a single sister to push through the Shakespeare blood. And my two girls, alas, alas. Did I tell you Hatter Hart had died? And aunt Margaret, the last of my mother's sisters, the earth has her. But maybe that was last year. Or the year before. She was the last of the Snitterfield folk.

Dying, yes.

Is that the chapel bell I'm hearing just across the way, tolling for my passing soul? No longer mourn for me when I am dead, the muddy vesture of decay, slipping fast away, than you shall hear the surly sullen bell give warning to the world, and I lie here and wait, revolving many memories, that I am fled, the Snitterfield flames, Agnes and Henry, the shithouse and the stars, Harry's hand on my shoulder, Essex mounting the scaffold, the sunlight streaming through the windows of Whitehall, and Emilia at the virginals, dark and dangerous, Emilia coming on top, Emilia fading into Anne, young Anne, doing it in the fields near Shottery, first time for me, and the schoolroom, the shambles, the whores, the stink of sin, the crowds roaring for Harry at the Rose, the groundlings giving it all they've got at the Globe, death to the French! burn the Spaniards! open the bastard up! Hartley's heart torn from the stalk as the geese ebbed overhead, winging their way over England, England, winter's not gone yet if the wild geese fly that way, no, but I pray you sirs are those my daughters sitting by my bed? I am a very foolish fond old man, and not, I fear in my perfect...for if I am not much mistaken this is my son, my lovely boy, Mamillius, Hamlet, little Macduff, and my poor Perdita, my sad Marina, Miranda, my Imogen, my Alison, let me touch thy breasts, my little Alison, see, they've all come to say farewell, the walls are swarming with them, the furniture, the sheets, the shadows, take them from me, friends, they're all over me, they're weighing down my legs, yes, I know thee well enough, thy name is Gloucester, O, let me kiss that hand! The dyer's hand betrays, what if this hand, what hands are these, will all the perfumes, here's a spot still, a spot of mustard, no, let me wipe it first, it smells of mortality, as my mother would have said, yes, farewell dear mother, thy loving father, no, my mother, father and mother is man and wife, one flesh, and so my mother, my father, do you not come your tardy son to chide, that lapsed in time and passion...no, no, my father, he smote the sledded Polacks, axe in hand, methinks I see my father, alas, poor ghost, the bell then beating one, the bell invites me, silence, hear it not, silence that dreadful bell, the chapel bell still ringing, but ringing me not to school today, old Usher Higges, ushering me into eternity, all the way, Jesus, death is certain, Hamlet, the psalmist says, if it be not now, yet it will come, ripeness is all, for he was likely had he been put on to have proved most royally, he has my dying voice, absent thee from felicity awhile, speak loudly for him, and in this harsh world draw thy breath in pain, to tell my story, O thou, my lovely boy, go, go, bid the soldiers shoot, and flights of angels sing thee to thy rest, the best of rest is sleep, to die, to sleep, to sleep, to rest, the rest is silence, the rest is, the rest is, the rest –

Rest.

Rest, rest, perturbèd spirit.

Epilogue

It's not the fashion, I know, to have the Ghost speak the epilogue, but being now freed from all temporal restraints, I am well placed to do so. And what better voice than the unfettered soul of the subject of this story? No more muddy vesture of decay, my masters. I can speak directly to you all – whenever, wherever and whoever you may be.

First you will want to know more about my death. Everybody does – I don't know why. As I told Francis, there's only one way to get onto the great stage of fools but there are a thousand exits. And why should the manner matter? They all lead the same way. You go out bowing, laughing, cursing – to applause, indifference, or scorn. It matters not how a man dies – but how he has lived. I could have died of the venereal diseases, caught in my hell of time. Or with the weather suddenly warming up in that third week of March, could have been careless in that last fling with Drayton and Jonson – too much liquor, a chill and a fever, and a visit from the old man's friend to finish me off. Could have been a build-up of the London life: too much work, too little sleep, the solitary eating and drinking and scribbling, the midnight oil, the ill-dried lamps, fed with stinking tallow, the thick coarse folio parchment, the mind diseased, the shadows on the walls. No more the drinking and whoring about town with the roaring boys, to reel the streets at noon and stand the buffet with knaves that smelt of sweat – all that had long gone. But the respectable life took its toll too, the constant reading, writing, revising, acting, directing, managing, the touring circuit, head down amid the whirl. Or it could have been typhoid, or the palsy – or the plague come to get me in the end after so many miraculous near misses. But it wasn't. No, I did suffer something of a stroke after Judith's marriage and it was a slow downhill slide after that. But I was burnt out and tired by that time anyway – well through, as my mother used to say. In the end I died of being William Shakespeare. I died of forty plays, and a hundred and fifty-four sonnets, and some other things. If it hadn't been one thing it would have been another.

And the birthday talk I heard with foggy ears as the casement slowly grew a glimmering square? That was accurate enough. I died on the 23rd – April had struck again, true to form – and was buried on the 25th. Anne placed the pennies on my eyes, saw me off to church and under the ground, then got on with the business of being a widow – one in which she did not lack practice.

A man's last journey. There's something infinitely moving about it, isn't there? Death itself can be terrible, traumatic, tearful, tragic, or merely trite – a non-event. Which most philosophers would say it is in any case. But the cortège always strikes me as particularly touching, when the body is carried past those sights and scenes and through the streets the person knew so well. Mine was a simple enough passage: down Chapel Lane, past my old school – the bell then beating one, of course, the hated bell – and along by the willowy banks of the Avon, following the glittering river to Holy Trinity. They carried me among alders and limes, my ears deaf now to the lapping of the river-wave and the rustle of swans, and so in at the porch and up the nave to the resting place before the altar in the chancel, close to the north wall. And when all ceremonies were over, the sexton put me into the ground beneath the church full seventeen feet deep.

No explanations needed there. Deep six did for most folk in Stratford, but I'm glad to say I gave the gravedigger plenty of sweat at the time and something to chew on for the future. Yes, the epitaph, the famous quatrain, composed by myself. Francis took it down for me. And if anybody doesn't believe that – and I can understand why they'd doubt a ghost – I tell them to go and stand by my grave in Holy Trinity and look at the stone. What strikes you about it, you who are already in the know?

No name. That's what would strike me right away. Quite startling, considering it commemorates the greatest writer of all time – at last I can say it unboastfully – and with some surprise. Don't you think that if I'd left my survivors in charge of my interment they'd have chiselled me into immortality with many an outward flourish? My name, my fame, my works, my years, my gentlemanly condition, the famous coat of arms. *Not without right.* But the fact that I chose an anonymous exit into an earth already well speckled by famous names is a sure clue to you that I arranged everything myself, just as surely as I wrote that epitaph and Francis took it down.

It's a malediction and a ban – and one which has accomplished its purpose. My final revenge on a sexton who frightened a child. And on all such sextons. They'd come into churches, spade in hand, to remove the bones to the charnel-house, to terrify the Wills and Juliets of the future. My fears were justified too, when in due course even the bones of my daughter, Susanna, were turned out to make way for a tithe-holder. Imagine the indignity of it – to be knaved out of your grave and your skull become a drinking bowl, your bones turned into pipes through which these beer-swilling boors of pickaxe-men would smoke their black shag. Most horrible. That's why my last lines are doggerel by the way – I composed them crudely enough to appeal to the rude capacities of clerks and sextons.

And it worked. The Stratford sexton, hearkening to the curse (who wouldn't for safety's sake?) and fearing for his successors (possibly his own offspring), laid me deep seventeen. Never to be disturbed. So that when Anne Hathaway died seven years later, earnestly desiring to be laid in the same grave with me, her last wishes were not granted. And that's the way I wanted it. What I did not want was for my dust to mingle with the dust of the woman to whom marriage had been a lie. Would the companionship of bones for all eternity have compensated for a lifetime of separation? It would have been an eternal hypocrisy and a lie. But it was not to be. The curse prevailed. And the gravedigger, afraid to touch my stone, laid her alongside me nearby, as close as he dared, but in a separate grave, mine never to be opened to let Anne in, the two bodies kept apart, never the twain to meet, just as we had been during most of our lives, body and soul. The curse was more than a curse, it was an exile, imposed from eternity.

No cosy reunion, then, not even in death. The bed and the epitaph, a double snub – the last Act doesn't always end like a play, does it? And it didn't for Will and Anne. She's simply there at my side as she always was – at least she didn't desert me, as I had her. Unromantic but true. And as the river is only a few feet away and my dust has long since drained into its currents (that picked my bones in whispers) and trickled out to sea, everything of me that could die has long since gone from underneath that slab. No great sea-change either, no coral bones or eyes of pearl, and no punctilious sea-nymphs ringing my knell. That's as rich and strange as it gets. I no longer lie alone. I lie nowhere. Or everywhere. My atoms are yours, my molecules part of you. You breathe me in. And out. And perhaps that's richer and stranger than anything could be. Ben went on to call me a monument without a tomb. My Stratford resting place is a tomb without a body. But I'd best leave that subject before I'm led into making any grand comparisons. Let me just say that all writers are cursed – haunted by ghosts – but that all are blessed, as you are, who merely leave me in peace. I've told all there is to know. Any more – I don't even know myself. So my last word is a curse, yes. But it's also a benediction. For life is never simple.

Anne died on 6th August 1623 and was buried two days later, on my left. Her Latin epitaph, composed by Susanna with John Hall's help, memorialises the mother who gave breasts and milk and life and in return got only a gravestone. But one day an angel may come and move it away and the occupant emerge to seek heaven. Or so they liked to imagine in those good old glory days. Anyway, the stone is still there.

I was right to keep Quiney out of benefit. He went on from his dubious start – drinking, illegal drinking with his cronies out of hours, watering his wine at The Cage. He held some local offices but was never highly esteemed. In due course he tried to sell the lease of The Cage but the few responsible members of his family stepped in and prevented him, safeguarding the interests of Judith and the children. Finally the tavern was made over to Richard Quiney, who died bequeathing his feckless brother twelve pounds per annum to keep him out of the gutter and five pounds to get him decently into his grave. Impossible. No grave was vile enough to receive him.

The astonishing thing is that Judith saw out her life with this useless – well, I'd say arse, but ghosts don't swear and you'll notice I've stopped. All the same, what is it that makes some women nail themselves to shoddy crosses such as Quiney? She gave birth to three sons by him, all of them dead before her: one in infancy – that was Shakespeare Quiney, the year after me; Richard in 1639, aged 21, no issue; and Thomas also in 1639, aged 19, no issue. Each time the great bell of Holy Trinity tolled for them it was tolling the death-knell of all my hopes – no grandson to live on after me and carry on the line. Within a generation that line was doomed to extinction. In this family the women did better than the men. Judith was buried on the 9th February 1662. She had lived till 77, having had no more children and having survived her twin brother Hamnet by 66 years.

Susanna had no more children by John Hall, who died in 1635. Their only child, my grand-daughter Elizabeth, went to church on 22nd April 1626, aged 17, to marry thirty-three-year-old Thomas Nash of Lincoln's Inn. He died twenty-one years later – having given her no children. Two years later, when she was 41, Elizabeth remarried, becoming the wife of John Barnard of Abingdon, at Billesley, four miles west of Stratford. That was on 5th June 1649. Susanna died the following month. A year after Charles II was restored to the throne he made Barnard a baronet for his services during the Civil Wars, so that when Elizabeth died in 1670, aged 61, she died nobly. John Shakespeare would have liked that. But she also died childless. Baronet or no, John Barnard of Abingdon had failed to impregnate her. Hardly his fault. She'd had two marriages. Lady Elizabeth was as barren as a brick. Only Joan Hart's offspring carried the Shakespeare genes and in due course came into benefit. Joan herself died in 1646.

And so in spite of the will, that desperate attempt to keep together the material profits of my art, to keep on living in some sense, as it were, nature defeated art in the end, and that was the Shakespeare story. As to the material goods, the stocks and stones, when Susanna died Elizabeth inherited the estate, including Henley Street and New Place, but she and Barnard ended their days at Abingdon Manor. Her father had left his study of books to his son-in-law Nash, the first husband, to dispose of them as he saw fit, and among these books were my own. When old Barnard died he bequeathed to his family all the books along with the paintings, old goods, and lumber. And so my library was broken up like bread, and the crumbs scattered to the birds and the winds, just as all my property slipped away like water through the Harts, becoming no more mine than the dust, once mine, that filtered into the river and went with the Avon into the wider world and the atmosphere and beyond. Exit William Shakespeare. And all his line.

The main characters are still in the chancel of the church, inasmuch as we can be said to be there at all: myself; Anne on my left; Thomas Nash on my right, inhabiting the plot that had been reserved for Elizabeth, dead and buried at Abingdon; to Nash's right John Hall; and to the right of her husband Susanna, now only an epitaph commemorating the bones that were so rudely moved. A family gathering, of memories and dust, around us the walls of Holy Trinity, the silver-swanned river, the narrow streets and lanes of Stratford, Henley

Street, New Place, Snitterfield, Shottery, the old school, the bridge still leading to London, London itself and all the cities of the world from which they come to lay a flower and speak a line, see a play perhaps, before moving on to do Venice and Verona, knowing less and less as the world moves on, what to do with the real tissue, the heart of the matter – the poetry of soul, the soul of an age.

Anne had died just before the publication of the First Folio edition of my plays, brought out by my old fellows Heminges and Condell at the end of 1623. No great tragedy – I mean Anne's death at that particular time. She should have died hereafter. And missing the publication of the first collected edition of my dramatic works hardly mattered much to a woman unable to read. I'm relieved not to have been there to see it myself, as the title-page features a frightful portrait of your author, executed by the engraver Martin Droeshout, whose grandfather hailed from Brussels. He was young, inexperienced in his art, and so came cheap. Look on his work, ye mighty, and despair! I have two right eyes and wear a coat with two left sides. It won't take a painter or a Jewish tailor to spot those blunders. And the head on its ruff plate is monstrous, megacephalous. Even setting aside the hypertrophic horror of that head surmounting the dinky doublet, where did that fiddle-shaped face come from? It's the portrait of a fairground freak, and while it's recognisably me – the alert nose, the lips made for kissing and controlled courtesy, the large luminous eyes that took in life and reflected its glow, the balding domed skull, Will the egghead – I beg to inform you all that it's little more than an identikit – can I use that word now? – put together by an unpractised apprentice hand.

Of what manner of man is he, then, your Will? Why, of mankind. If you really want an image of me as I was, look in the mirror and there you'll see me, rather sadder and wiser than I'd have elected to be at my age, or you at yours. One of yourselves, that's all, one of the race of human beings, good enough for neither animals in their innocence nor gods in their wisdom. I was marked out not in appearance but in fortune – which buckled a talent on my back, a talent for words. I died in words and rose again like the phoenix, transformed. Words were the element I flew in, illogical images, strange impossible leaps, words dazzling and dubious and less dependable than good old loamy Stratford clay. But I wrote them down in the same way as a woman speaks and thinks, all in one, and in one sentence the next was born. It was a continuous coupling, the words made love to one another, and the eternal mystery was the birth of plays, my prolific talent. I carried it around all my life and used it to the full. Old Ben acknowledged this, not without irony, when he advised you on the adjoining flyleaf to the engraving, *Reader, look not on his picture but his book*. He was no Adonis himself. He then went on to praise my memory and my parts in a poem which Dryden considered an insolent, sparing, and invidious panegyric – and Dryden was not the only one to hear whispers of aspersion between the lines. But to be called a monument without a tomb, the sweet swan of Avon, the wonder of the stage and the soul of the Age, besides being hailed as not of an age but for all time – well, who am I to complain? Ben wrote his plays to be printed; I wrote mine to be played, and he knew that better than anybody. Old Ben brought himself to do me as proud as he was able, and by Ben's standards did me great honour. Of an old friend I couldn't have asked or expected more.

Heminges and Condell also laid on the tributes with a trowel. They said of their old friend and fellow that his mind and hand went together and that what he thought he uttered with such easiness that they had scarce received from him a blot in his papers. They didn't see the blots in my brain, of which there were as many thousands as even Ben could have wished when he elected to criticise me in conversation with William Drummond. But Ben was being Ben. You can forgive a man who will insult you in public and to your face while defending you in private when it counts. The First Folio counted. And I forgive my fellows, its editors, for all the boobs and botches in their work. These pale into nothingness compared with what they did. And Ben was right.

The Folio is a better monument than the effigy that was built into the north wall of the Holy Trinity chancel, just above my grave. It at least is better than what Droeshout did. I looked a little like Uncle Henry at the end of my life. It's a tough old countryman's face and it suits me. I could have been a butcher, not a bard. The tablet beneath is inscribed with praise indeed, and in Latin too.

Judicio Pylium, genio Socratem, arte Maronem:
Terra tegit, populus maeret, Olympus habet.

Nestor for wisdom, Socrates for genius, Virgil for poetry. The earth covers him, the people grieve for him, heaven has him. There are six claims here, five of them large ones. One of them is for certain. Do you think they are all true? Even if that's all you think about in the end, I'll not have wasted breath.

I won't have wasted ink either if you take my plays for what they are – *plays.* And nothing more. Lies and fancies, not statements of any sort to assist you in the running of your empires, institutions or your lives. They have no final point to make about illusion and reality, order and anarchy, self-knowledge, or about the darkness of man's heart, though they're full of all that, and more. They don't even aspire to the condition of life itself, though they reflect it, except that they unfold and ripen like people, and then they end, as people do. There's no necessary meaning. They're entertainments, that's all, sometimes dark ones. Sometimes there's simply a bare figure on a stage, maybe two or three companions in a storm. They keep each other alive by imagination, by sheer will power and inward obsessiveness, not by message or morality, they are simply there, on the world's stage, comforting one another with words, as do we all, comforting us who watch and listen to them. That's the meaning of my plays. That's the meaning of life. There's no eternal meaning – either in a life which is a living drama or in a drama which is an imagined life. All that matters is the vitality, the fact that you've drunk that life to the lees, or that the drama has done its work. Yes, there are times in life and art when you think you know the truth – but these too are illusions, epiphanies, angelic apprehensions, however you call them. We turn away from the magic of the theatre and go back to our sad sensible homes, where we turn from the mystery of living and face death – which is no mystery at all, in spite of everything that's been written about it. It's life itself that's the real mystery but there's no mystery in finally knowing death because the dead, as you know, know not anything.

Ah, but just one moment, sir! Hold hard! – I hear you arresting me. How can you say the dead know nothing when here you are, addressing us all from eternity? And your voice loud and clear and well informed?

But only the groundlings among you will have asked that question. The rest – sit back, and take your ease. You know the truth of it, that all this has been yet another play and nothing more. And it's ghost-written too, which adds to the lie. And so? Identity itself is play. Richard Gloucester says he plays many parts. Jacques says the same of man in general. Iago puts it even more challengingly. I am not what I am. Hamlet disagrees, and that leaves you with a question. Is there really an essential you, or are you nothing but the roles you play? Does truth exist in action or in thought? Hamlet or Iago, make your choice – they're both convincing. As for me, all I can say is that no one has ever been so many men. Or women, gods and monsters, so many souls under my skin, so many spirits, half a life of organised illusion. Then one morning I got up and suddenly faced the tedium and the terror of being so many suffering souls – leaders falling on swords, lovers expiring in tombs. And so I penned my farewell, sold up my shares and went home.

You know the rest. The son of a failed glover had become a gentleman – and not without right. I'd recovered the kingdom, triumphed over loss, the cause of human sadness, restored the king my father's loss. In a society afraid of vagrancy I'd turned vagrancy into a virtue, made acting an ascendancy, a noble accomplishment. But the recovery is never quite what it means or seems. Someone is always sad, for some reason, there is always doubt and discontent, the fear of illusion, delusion, and the shadow of that loss never leaves the stage. The wind and the rain are never far away.

Still, I kept up the pretence. I dabbled in lawsuits and lands and loans. Counted plums. It was intolerable, this so-called real life. I'd been seduced beyond infidelity, by and to the theatre. That's why I loved the theatre so much. It was the very essence for me of the play of life, short or long, the eternal pretence. You play the parts you have been given – by history, heredity, society, and you create others for yourself, your friends, family, foes. You weave plots, assign roles, invite the crowds, write scripts in your head, your life is your own, the future is yours. Or so you believe, or pretend. You fool everyone. Most of all you fool yourself. And you never forget that the sole purpose of words is to conceal thoughts. That's the game I played all my life.

I was an actor after all. The play's the thing. Is Gloucester really at the edge of Dover cliff? No. But he really is blind, because you saw his eyes gouged out. And that rustic really is his son because you heard him say so, heard him say that he was only pretending to be a peasant. But the eyes were put out on stage and that's where Edgar spoke his lines. They were sheep's eyes – and Edgar's lines were memorised, they were conned. You were conned. Both father and son are actors in a play. It's the same with Cassius, who with Caesar's blood ringing his fingers imagines the performances of posterity. How many ages hence shall this our lofty scene be acted o'er, in states unborn and accents yet unknown. But the man who says this is himself an actor, looking not only forwards but backwards too – to the original Caesar who was also an actor on the world's stage. Like all the men and women.

What is the purpose of drama? Escape – the liberating sense of being released into another world with its alternative sets of experiences. You quickly get used to that world and its characters, their imagined lives, and you yearn for them to experience a similar release. When it comes it's a double dramatic pleasure, sometimes to the purpose – the box-tree, the play-within-the-play. Sometimes it creates atmosphere, irony, like the crow making wing to the rooky wood, or the temple-haunting martlet sanctifying with its breeding habits Banquo's bird-watching soul and Macbeth's apparently innocent establishment.

At other moments it's freedom for freedom's sake – as when Edgar brings his father to the edge of that cliff. For what? For nothing, really. Except for this sudden surge of release and exhilaration. You are now outside the drama. The play has disappeared. In its place you have fresh air, fishermen, seabirds, samphire-gatherers, sailors, and the muted murmuring surge of waves on shingle coming up from the shore below. A height so vast that the sea can't even be heard, though you do hear it. In your mind.

You view this scene with nothing less than sheer joy because you have been liberated by the eye of the author, who shows you the work-aday world carrying on with its business, oblivious of the tragedy that surrounds it, just like the ploughman in the picture, patiently earning his bread, and the sailors turning the ship away, even as Icarus falls from the sky, men ploughing a straight furrow, charting a course alternative to destruction, heading for home again, in spite of tragedy.

Can I take this further? Yes, because the one truth binding life and art is that all of life is an escape from itself, and that even as you escape to art, the art itself must record that escape, the constant flight from what is there. But it's not a flight to fancy, it's a flight away from it, back to the sanities of the very thing you flee from. You are released from life into the world of the play, and you are caught up in that world. But only for a time. Soon, with blessed surges of relief, the real world comes breaking in again, like the importunate sea. You can sense it in Romeo's description of the apothecary's shop, where the atmosphere, though one of grinding poverty and wretchedness, is an antidote to destiny and loss of faith. The apothecary himself now has hope. Romeo has come and has made him rich, Romeo for whom riches are now so many ashes and nothing more. But not for the needy apothecary. His abysmal interior will soon be brightened, his life will be transformed. You suspend for the moment your contemplation of contemptible beggary.

You experience the same thing with Macbeth's dusky talk of rooky woods, yeasty waves, the multitudinous seas. Or in his hired killer's unexpectedly quieter perception of the lated traveller, trapped in the darkened hemisphere of the globe, spurring his horse on, anxious to arrive at the inn. You hear no details of his haven from horror, but you can picture its polished settles reflecting the firelight, the gleaming pewter and ranged crockery, the sand-strewn floor on which sheep-dogs take their ease, among the heavy unmoving boots of tired peasant farmers. Their lips too are unmoving – they're wearing moustaches of recent froth, white on the crinkled contentment of thirsty faces. The lawyer and doctor, who have not had such a demanding day, are engaged in animated talk. A brace of young bloods eyes up the barmaid, nudging and winking. You know that one of them – perhaps both – will lie with her tonight. And you can go on from there to the crack of doom, peopling the minds of the patrons with all their own memories, aspirations, intentions, all conceivable devices and desires – it's infinite, and it's all there in that one word 'inn', decorated only by the single transferred and impersonal epithet 'timely', with all its weight of relief from the murderous dark without, and all its possibilities for speculation on the part of the playgoer, if he is a true playgoer. Yet the truth is that there are no settles or sheepdogs or farmers or fire – there isn't even any inn. It's all a fancy by a fancied character, a fiction to liberate you from life and art together at a tense moment in the drama, and to keep you there, slightly perplexed, always enthralled, by men and women who step up onto the stage with no real outward motives other than that inward energy that thrusts them on and makes them act as they do without understanding what exactly it is that lies at the heart of them. And if they don't always understand, why should you, the shadow of a shadow?

These are the innocent glimpses that, more forcibly than all the rhetoric of darkness, disaster and despair, make you aware just how tragic is tragedy. Tragic figures are tragic because they have rejected this innocent normality of the fireside and the fields – the normality from which you yearn both to escape and yet to return to. You are always reaching out for such innocent perceptions, these brief sightings of how life could be. They are the narrow slits in the castle-walls of the known, and through them, as you ascend the spiral of the drama, you catch flashes of alternatives, an imagined happiness.

More. The playgoer inhabits the world you have created for him, and he makes it his, not just for the two hours' traffic of the stage, but, if it is a living world, for as long as he has life and memory, for his need is never done. Always he requires to be liberated from his liberation, to fly from rhetoric to life, just as he needed to escape from life to rhetoric. This is what it means to be human. And thus conscience does make angels of us all, soaring like seabirds across a sea of troubles, God's free messengers.

Freedom is the thing, and when it's denied you, you weep with them that weep – with Macbeth, cabined, cribbed, confined, with Hamlet in his prison of Denmark, his nutshell of bad dreams, with Othello, trapped like a toad in the cistern, seeking the Pontic sea, and with Lear, bound upon a wheel of fire, hands and feet bound to the universal compass points. You have gone to the theatre and been freed, only to see great princes lie in prison, and to suffocate and suffer with them every one, wanting the windows open again.

Opening the windows is the poet's work, thrusting the shutters aside at the darkest moments of the play. So Gertrude's gentle threnody when Ophelia dies opens up for us again all the innocences, rawnesses, and vulgarities of nature, far from the claustrophobic court, its sinister whisperings and dark fatal plots. In your frail fancy the passage frees you even as it puts fetters on the queen. Kate Hamlet dies again. But she goes back to the nature we all come from and return to, the crow-flowers, nettles, daisies, the long purples, and the willow-hung brook, the glassy stream, the Avon, the river that was never very far from my imagination. And for these two pathetic hours you sit in the playhouse and imagine that you are free.

You're not free, no more than was I, your entertainer. We all sit in an empty space with a need to fill it. I felt that need overwhelmingly. Maybe there was a sense of lack, in the end. Campion had a certainty, heaven was his. As for me, I had embraced that emptiness, the theatrical dream, the illusion, the nothingness, the pattern of lies. But the answering compensation for that end-of-life disenchantment is the embrace of the everyday.

It was the everyday, after all, that had always inspired me, the stuff of ordinary lives, the earthiness, the face of honest Harry Goldingham behind the mask of Arion, the touch of the real, the dabble of dew on the trembling hunted hare, and the realisation of just how extraordinary ordinariness could be. In my beginning was my end, and in my end my beginning: family, a daughter's love, a father's anxiety, concern, the faint prospect of a grandson in posterity, a line of princes replacing the lost one, the escape of Fleance from fate's clutches. That's what I came back to in the end, what I embraced – that and the banality of those plums, ripened, rotten, fallen, but all mine, along with the tithes, the plough tilling the ground I'd bought, the sheep nibbling the land I'd enclosed, the land I'd made mine, part of England. I'd come back to it finally, what I'd wanted away from when I was young and with a young foolish need, recognizing at last my kinship with earth, that old kinship we all admit to in the end, the one that goes all the way back to Adam.

Those who knew me often called me gentle – affable, amusing, urbane, a perfectly charming man. And such was my London self. It was a costume, which on this occasion I have chosen not to wear, though many have dressed me up in their own ignorance. You, my masters, are among the chosen few. You have seen something of Will, without the daily beauty wear. You've seen something of my feet of clay. I could tell you more. I was fastidious, over sensitive for my age – and Age – to many things. I loathed smoky lamps, greasy dishes, sickly foods, untidiness, sweaty armpits, bad breath, unwiped arses, dribbling dicks, lickspittles, lackeys, hypocrites, Hooray-Henrys, King Henrys, beadles and bullies, dogs obeyed in office, Puritans. I abhorred the abuser of power, the perverter of justice, the mob, instability. What else? A hatred of hunting, of violence, especially committed against all those who are weak and vulnerable – animals, children, the poor. Also a suspicion of change, a respect for the social order. Love may be an illusion, sex a cesspit, politics a bear-pit, religion a fairy-tale and chivalry a shadow and a dream. I had little time for such abstractions. But I never lost faith in the social nuts and bolts, in the lives of ordinary people, just living, just living.

As for the extraordinary ones, the movers and shakers, history for me was a rogues' gallery. The angel of history is the angel of death.

Idealists soon become tyrants and cheats, as power corrupts. Listen to them whine and bark. Their convictions divide the world and only an honest doubt can unite it again. But their minds are closed and moulded, they have none – no honest doubt – and that's what makes them dangerous. Certainty is lethal. Conviction kills. That's my credo. All I know is that I know nothing, and that truth is like January, Janus-faced, looking to a lost year and one to come. My father wore a Protestant face and my mother kept on her own face at home while her husband made his a vizor to his heart, so they were split, as man and wife often are, and he was fractured too, public and private, outward and real. And that split is the best key to the plays his son came to write. I saw that it was possible to be two people at once, to live a double life, and out of this came Hamlet, Iago, Hal, and many others, good and bad, including me, who mocked authority, aristocrats, land-grabbers, players, but strove for substance, standing, armorial bearings and theatrical assets, while regretting every inch that staged me to the public view and turned my art to profit.

And so the exterior me – discretion, moderation and reserve. How careful was I when I took my way, each trifle under truest bars to trust. I hid my beliefs in history, buried my voice in time and place, and like the Bay of Portugal had an unknown bottom. I was ever unquarrelsome – even abject, some would say, still begging each treacherous friend to spare me some crumb of love. Not one whose help you could clearly count on, because much of the time the man you thought you saw was never there. A playmaker who avoided the first person and in so doing became no person. A man who in writing about other men reprieved himself from the man he was. A man wanting a little self-confidence perhaps, except in plays. And outside the making of plays, a man even wanting in imagination, a compulsive acquirer, a land man, an Osric, burying his personal flaws in property, the safe palpabilities of earth and income, bricks and mortar, stocks and stones. A reversion, if you like, and a regression, back to the sucking dung that had clung to me and from which I'd longed to escape. The simple life. Yes, I could always smell the countryside through the squalor and the stench of London and the suffocating falsities of the court.

Yet, I longed for play, like any actor, and I longed for land, like any peasant. I loved beauty, especially woman's, and I paid for the pleasure, loved children and birds and plants for their simplicity and innocence, and all who kept boredom at bay and conquered the empire of dullness. Life itself I found far more interesting than anybody's opinions about it. I loved the surface of the earth and the whole process of human existence, which never ceased to fascinate me. I was enchanted by the maltworms and by the tapsters who served them. The human story was meat and drink to me. Osmotic, omnivorous, endlessly curious, that was me, that was your Will.

And the story of England?

I did create a myth of England, yes, but only a scurvy politician would believe it. Look at me. Look at my plays. Do you think Englishness stirred my soul? Abstractions like that were always anathema to me. And too much home is tedious. Give me the outsiders – Shylock, Othello, Mercutio, Thersites, Hamlet, the melancholy Jacques, and Caliban the Carib islander – not one of them English. I could be turned on by a handkerchief once my imagination had steeped it in other cultures and put magic in the web of it. Even in Scotland the rugged Russian bear appears, the armed rhinoceros and Hyrcan tiger, and all the perfumes of Arabia sweeten a home-grown hand. Even in the history plays you'll find more fascination in the men of other nations, the Welshman Glendower, the Irish MacMorris, the Scottish Douglas – and old Northumbrian Hotspur.

Except of course for old Jack Falstaff, the real hero of the Henry plays – of all my plays. This is my Englander, with whom I am at home, not your leader who wages his wars of aggression, who invites Jack and all his countrymen to fight a cause and die for a lie. Or pay the terrible cost. No, never wave your national flags over my bones, or shake your gory war-locks at me, as many of your Jacks-in-office have done, for my England was a place, not an institution, it was a system of circles surrounding the little points of home. My England was the soldier Bates, it was Shallow and Silence chattering about the past and about bullocks and beefs and Stamford Fair. It was Mistress Quickly sitting in her Dolphin chamber – remember? – at that round table by a sea-coal fire on that Wednesday in Whitsun Week, and still being conned by honest Jack. All that yes – and that home of his, with the hollyhocks high in the garden on a summer's night and the birds singing. That's what a man really wants. He doesn't want to be a hero and he has no time for abstractions or speeches filled with them, and even less time for those who make them, and that's why Falstaff's my man.

A man with his feet on English earth and his head in that green bible where all flesh is grass, and his dying memories are of green fields. He babbles about a green England that was far more enduring and moving than any imperialist images dreamed up by prating political pygmies that dropped their country in the gutter, lost their borders – and made my England bleed.

And so Elizabeth's mighty state, characterless, grated to dusty nothing, just like Troy. Not waterdrops, not wars or lechery could accomplish this, not even time itself could have taken the greenness out of the land and the character out of the people, the poetry out of scripture. But scurvy politicians could – and did. And honest Jack Falstaff is betrayed.

An angry ghost? Yes, and a sad one too, the soul of an Age talking to an Age without a soul. Is that too hard? Remember, the dead may speak only the truth, even when it discredits them, and as truth in itself is never discreditable, this dead man has no fear of anything he may have said. Which of you, after all, even knows himself? So pluck out the heart of your own mystery, and pity me not, but let me go. Let us be thankful for that which is, and with you leave disputes that are above our question. Let's go off and bear us like the time. And if I have offended you, gentles all, do not reprehend me. Remember I'm a shadow, nothing more. And think but this – that you have but slumbered here, while these visions did appear.

What do you say, clap hands and a bargain? I've bequeathed you my story and thrown away my mask. My charms are overthrown. Now gentle breath of yours my sails must fill, for my project was to please you, so let your indulgence set me free. Prospero's last request – and mine.

And so goodnight unto you all.

The words of Mercury are harsh after the songs of Apollo. You, that way: I, this.

Acknowledgements

Like Prospero's, my library was dukedom large enough. Off the shelves have come those old stagers, Bradley, Danby, Duthie, Granville-Barker, Wilson Knight, LC Knights, Dover Wilson, Harrison, Halliday, Hodges, Chambers, Rowse. I have also used more recent scholars such as Schoenbaum, Russell Fraser, Stanley Wells, Peter Levi, Peter Ackroyd, Frank Kermode, Park Honan, James Shapiro, Stephen Green-blatt and Jonathan Bate, as well as a host of writers on Marlowe, such as Charles Norman, Leslie Hotson, Michael Poirier, JB Steane, Harry Levin, AD Wraight, MJ Trow, Charles Nicholl. And hundreds more critics, biographers and Elizabethan historians. I could fill this entire book with the names of those I've read and who should be mentioned. My apologies to all those whose help has not been recorded, and I hope I have not leaned too heavily on any of those I've cited. They became an inseparable part of my thinking and writing over many years and I am grateful for the scholarship and wisdom they have imparted.

Writers and critics apart, I owe a huge debt to an exceptional English master, Alastair Leslie, who rescued me from ignorance and blessed me with his humanity, kindness, insight, intelligence and exceptional schoolmastering skills. As always I have enjoyed great support from my agent, John Beaton, my children, Catriona and Jonathan, and little Jenny in her own way; and massive tolerance and encouragement from my wife Anna, who typed out every word of this book from my longhand pencil scrawl and ink scrawl not once but many times in several versions over many years. In particular I want to thank my editor, Jonathan Wooding, for the enormous improvements he has made to the text, and Simon Petherick of Beautiful Books along with Jonathan for their incredible enthusiasm, confidence and faith, and their sheer speed and determination in getting this book off the ground.

Finally there is the man himself, the man Shakespeare. JK Rowling famously reported how Harry Potter simply strode into her head one day. Will Shakespeare did not stroll into mine – he burst through the door blowing my mind. I was in my early teens – and my life changed dramatically, sowing the seed for a book that has been growing underground for nearly fifty years and now sees the light of day. The Stratford man has given me a lifetime of enjoyment and understanding, and I can only hope I have passed on enough of it, and done justice both to the reader and to my wonderful subject, Will.

* * *